Praise for *The Vicious Deep*

"This mythical tale is a great read told on land and below the sea. These mermaids are not the lovely creatures you know—they may be beautiful but they are also deadly."

—*RT Book Reviews*

"An authentic 16-year-old male voice and viewpoint...the great title, killer jacket, and edgy portrayal of the mythical creatures should cast a wide readership net."

—*Booklist*

"*The Vicious Deep* is incredibly original and is plump full of funny, witty, charming, likeable characters."

—Night Owl Reviews

"A delicious debut that pulled me in and kept me entranced."

—Leanna Renee Hieber, author of *The Twisted Tragedy of Miss Natalie Stewart*

"Original sea creatures, fun side characters that heighten the adventure, and a deep, memorable romance that made me ache...This is a must read for every YA lover out there."

—YA Bound

"I'm warning you: this book's just like the whirlpool Tristan encounters in the beginning; it sucks you right in and refuses to let go."

—The Merblog

"*The Vicious Deep* is a daring innovative story that hooks the reader. Packing unexpected twists and turns…a story that you want to read over and over again!"

—Books with Bite

"Córdova has created a masterful, absolutely dazzling and refreshingly original mermaid world…sends a shiver down your spine."

—Bookish blog

BY ZORAIDA CÓRDOVA

Published by Sourcebooks Fire, an imprint of Sourcebooks, Inc.
P.O. Box 4410, Naperville, Illinois 60567-4410
(630) 961-3900
Fax: (630) 961-2168
teenfire.sourcebooks.com

Library of Congress Cataloging-in-Publication Data is on file with the publisher.

Printed and bound in the United States of America.
BG 10 9 8 7 6 5 4 3 2 1

To Liliana and Joe Vescuso, for everything.

Part I

Shut out from heaven it makes its moan,

It frets against the boundary shore;

All earth's full rivers cannot fill

The sea, that drinking thirsteth still.

—Christina Rossetti, from "By the Sea"

chapter ONE

For a merman, I've done very little deep-sea exploration.

I grew up in chlorine pools, racing from one end to the other until I became the fastest kid in all of Brooklyn. Those were fishbowls compared to the endlessness of the Atlantic Ocean.

I kick my legs harder and harder alongside the belly of the ship until I grab hold of the ladder.

I consider shifting into my tail, but then I remember these are my last pair of cargo shorts, and I've not yet mastered the half-shift combination of legs and scales to cover my goods. Instead, I let my gills develop, only freaking out a little that I, in fact, have gills. Then I give myself a pat on the back for being able to control them. Cold water trickles in and out, and I wonder if that's something I'll ever get used to.

With one hand, I secure my footing on the ladder and let the ship do the heavy lifting. With the other, I lean out to the ocean, combing my fingers through water. I want to shout out the thrill of the moment, of the powerful ship cleaving the ocean like a knife through the smooth skin of the sea. But I stop myself, realizing that shouting would give away my position to my opponent.

War games aren't supposed to be *fun*, not the way my guardian describes them. War games teach you skills—fighting, hunting, hiding. All meant to achieve one thing: survival.

I'm four days shy of turning seventeen, and though I was technically born with a blue fishtail, I've only been a merman for two whole weeks, ever since the Sea Court returned to Coney Island to hold a championship for the next king. That would be the Sea King (my grandfather) and me (one of four remaining champions). Yeah, me a king. I'm not in Coney anymore, Toto.

The clucking wail of a dolphin echoes from below. He swims up alongside me, and for a moment, I forget about Kurt lurking nearby. I reach out a hand and touch the dolphin's slick skin. I can't understand the sounds he's making, but I can sense the urgency. He dives downward and disappears into the blue shadows.

Then I see him.

Kurt's glowing violet eyes lock on me. He undulates like a serpent rising from smoke. His dark hair billows with every kick.

Kurt takes the dolphin's place beside me, like we're two cars racing on an empty road. He swerves to his left as if to knock me off my ladder, but I kick out and he swerves to the right. In our last skirmish, we managed to disarm each other. But I didn't account for the small knife strapped to his bicep.

Kurt holds the knife by the hilt. He raises it over his head, flicks his wrist back and forth. He wouldn't. As my guardian, he's in charge of making sure I don't meet an untimely death. He wouldn't.

But he does.

I dive to the left. My back hits the ship hard, and I let the current pull me away. His deep chuckle lingers in the rustle of water. He takes hold of my ladder and hoists himself back up onto the ship, which is getting farther away.

My muscles burn with every breaststroke, every kick. Then the dolphin returns, and I realize that being the grandson of the Sea King comes with some perks. His big black eye gleams at me, and I wonder why dolphins always look like they're smiling. I grab hold of his dorsal fin.

In seconds, we're caught up with the ship. I pat him on his back and grab hold of the ladder. Halfway up, I see Kurt's knife an inch deep into the wood. When I pull it out, there isn't much resistance. I break the surface and my gills shut against the wind. My body feels a hundred pounds lighter. The blisters on my soles pop and bleed with every step until I'm over the rail and planted on the deck. I strip off my T-shirt and toss it to the side.

I brush my wet hair from my eyes and spot Layla and Gwen leaning on the railing of the quarterdeck. All they need is a tub of popcorn, and it'd be just like being at the circus. Layla's biting her nails down to stubs. She runs her hands through the mess of her thick brown hair, which is growing bigger and bigger with the rising heat. Her hazel eyes flick between Kurt and me. He's holding his knees and breathing hard. He quickly adjusts the sheath at his hip. Great, he's got his sword back.

"Tristan," Layla says, "you guys are still just play-dueling, right?"

The Sunday morning sun is so hot that my chest is already dry. I pick up my sword off the deck.

"Best out of five," I remind her.

"You've lost twice," Gwen says, twirling a lock of white-blond hair around her finger until it coils on its own.

"He's also won twice," Layla counters.

"I don't know if that last one counts," Gwen says. "They went overboard, and the arena is supposed to be the ship. I say that last one didn't count."

I can't believe what I'm hearing. "It totally counts!"

"Uh—"

"Tristan?" Gwen points a finger behind me.

I hear the wet smack of Kurt's feet racing. Without a word, it's still game on. Kurt drags the tip of his sword along the floor. With his middle finger, he lightly taps the center of his forehead, something he does every time we fight. I never ask and he never explains what it means. It reminds me of going to church with Layla and her Catholic father. They do something similar—the father, the son, and the something spirit. I have no secret messages to tap like Morse code on my face like they do. I'm not exactly sure what I believe in anymore, now that I know monsters are real and good people die in the blink of an eye.

I raise my sword just in time to meet his and growl, "I wasn't ready."

"I'm a hungry merrow. I don't care if you're ready." He spins and strikes the opposite way.

I block, block, block, moving two steps backward with every blow. Sure, merrows don't care if you're ready or not. They come out of the shadows and attack, the way they attacked us in the football field of my school and at Ryan's house Friday night...

Too late, the thought of Ryan, my friend, dead on the ground, makes me miss a beat, and Kurt's sword comes a hair away from my face. I wipe sweat and seawater from my cheek, and a long stripe of red comes away with it.

"You cut me!"

"It's a *duel*, Tristan." Kurt rolls his eyes, a habit he's picked up from Layla. All of his movements, from the eye roll to the way he turns his dagger like the right angles of a clock, are uptight. "Of course I cut you."

But he doesn't let up. His face is ferocious, shoulders hunched like a predator. "When Adaro was your age, he slew white-bellied sharks for supper. Collected their teeth and dipped them in gold to decorate his armor."

Block.

The sun is in my eye and the rail of the ship digs into my lower back.

"Yeah, well," I say, "Adaro doesn't have the quartz scepter, does he?"

"There are still two pieces out there." Kurt turns, elbows me in the chest, and spins back around. "You only have the one."

Our swords are a mess of clinks and screeches. I'm running on pure adrenaline. It's a rush no swim meet has ever given me.

"One is better than nothing." I push him back with the ball of my palm, but that only makes him smile. It's got to be a record. When he was on land, he never smiled this much.

"Brendan might be young, but he can cut a man into ribbons with nothing but a spearhead."

Block.

I can't let him get to me. It's like when Coach Bellini swims alongside us during practice, shouting, *"You call that swimming? I met a turtle in Vietnam that was faster than you!"*

Sure, Adaro, champion of the Southern Seas, and Brendan, champion of the Western Seas, have been fighting longer than me. But my grandfather chose *me*. That's got to count for something.

Doesn't it?

"Dylan's so fast on his feet that you'd swear he was born sparring."

Right, Dylan, the golden boy, champion of the Northern Seas.

And then there's Kurt, King of the Show-Offs, who does some ballerina shit across the deck. I push hard, metal banging on metal. I hit his solar plexus and he braces, trying to regain his breath. He switches arms. Every five strikes, he switches arms to not tire one over the other. That creates the gap I need to strike.

I make my blow count, aiming where I know it will hurt Kurt the most. The swipe is painfully accurate, and a lock of his precious hair falls to the deck. His brow trembles, giving way to the first drip of sweat from his too-tight pores.

I'm about to say, "Don't worry, it'll grow back," but he raises his blade with a deep grunt and charges at me until I find myself stuck between Kurt and the edge of the ship once again.

Note: Don't mess with a merman's full head of hair.

It's the reaction I want—careless, reckless, thoughtless. Until we're stuck in a mirror image with my sword at his throat and his at mine.

"Draw?" Kurt suggests.

"I don't think so, bro." I shake my head, pressing the cold metal of his own knife to his abdomen. My heart is pounding, partly because I can't believe I did it. Partly because Kurt digs the edge of his sword into my throat some more.

"Easy," I say. Neither of us stands down. "If I show up to the oracle without a head, she's going to think I'm rude."

With a loud *harrumph*, he steps back, lowers his weapon, admits defeat by bowing. It takes all of me, and I mean years of discipline, to not shout, "Yeah, in your face!"

But this is not me beating my buddy Angelo at *Mortal Kombat*. This is how grown-up mermen fight. I bow back to him, accepting his defeat but keeping my eyes on him at all times. The clapping above us breaks our warrior trance. Kurt blinks into the blinding sun beating through the sails. I flip the small knife in the air, catch it on its blade, and hand it back to him. He grunts a short "Thanks."

"Well done, Master Tristan," says a baritone voice. Arion, the captain of our ship, hovers over us. He's a merman just like Kurt and me, but he's royally bound to the vessel. Enchanted black vines twine around his wrists and his tail. The black and silver fins lick at the empty air beneath him. The binding stretches all over the ship, allowing him to go as far as the topmast, but never into the sea. A punishment carried over from father to son.

I reach up and shake his hand. "Thanks, man."

"You're a fast learner," Kurt says, nodding. I can tell he doesn't say this easily. "A natural, really, if you adjusted your focus."

"You should have more faith in me," I say.

Kurt takes one step closer. Whatever he's going to say is interrupted by blue and purple blurs.

It's the urchin brothers, pulling sails and tying ropes to create a little bit of shade. When they stop running around, you can see their true shapes. Their almond-shaped eyes are big and black, like their gums, which freaked me out when Blue woke me up this morning. True to their name, the urchin brothers have spiky heads that are surprisingly soft to the touch.

Note: Don't mess with an urchin's head of hair, either.

The food they've spread out on silver platters, tarnished from being stored below deck, is decadent. Dried salmon skin, pink stuff that jiggles without touching it, and whole calamari jerky that looks like Buddha hands coming to get you. There's caviar in the brightest colors on top of crunchy dried seaweed. Steamed seaweed. Seaweed noodles. Seaweed chips. There's a great big seaweed party in my mouth.

Blue is studying my face. He's been trying so hard to make something that I'll like. "Special, for Lord Sea Tristan."

My smile is strained. I don't know if I'll ever get used to a mer diet. But he's trying so hard and I don't want to hurt his feelings. "Uh—thanks, little dude."

I make to sit down, but Kurt stands in my way. He flips his hair back, splashing me on the way. I knew he was a sore loser, but damn, let me live.

"What?" I ask irritably.

"Don't you think it's time, Tristan?"

"Time for what?"

"You said you'd tell us." He turns back to Layla, then to me. "About the other night. With the oracle."

Friday night. The night I claimed one of the three trident pieces from the oracle in Central Park. I've been putting off the details, but I've run out of reasons.

"It might help us with the next oracle," Layla urges.

"Perhaps later—" Gwen starts.

"Not later," Layla presses, sitting up on her knees. "I mean, you just *left*. Then you return with your giant metal toothpick and Princess Snowflake here, and you won't tell us what happened."

"Tristan doesn't have to tell you everything," Gwen says.

Layla ignores her and looks up right at me. "What did she do to you?"

I'm not sure if she means the oracle or if she means Gwenivere.

I hold my hands up in defense. "You guys. It's just—"

It's just what? They're my team. They're here for me. I hadn't considered that they might've thought I was dead. I didn't consider them at all. I sit down at our makeshift floor table and cross my legs meditation style. "Come. Let me start from the beginning."

chapter TWO

Ryan was dead.

"I heard his neck snap, but I didn't know who it was until he hit the ground. Everyone was screaming. Police sirens were getting closer. I was ready to give up.

"I figured, what the hell is the point? Maddy was screaming and drunk. She wouldn't give me the Venus pearl. Until the merrows came."

I pull down the zipper of one of my pockets and pull out a thin silver chain. A fat, smooth pink pearl hangs on a tiny hoop. "My mother stole it from Shelly, the oracle, a long time ago. I gave it to Maddy as a gift before I knew what it was. What *I* was.

"That's when Gwen found me. She figured out how to find the oracle."

"That I did." Gwen smirks. "So we stole—what was it?"

"A bicycle," I say. "We went to the train."

"How did you know where to go?" Kurt glances between me and Gwen.

"Scrying, my dear Kurtomathetis," Gwen answers sweetly.

"How do *you* know how to do that?" Kurt leans forward.

"I know many things." Gwen leans forward, too, just to show how unintimidated she is by him. "What would you have done? Threaten the pretty necklace with your sword until it answered you?"

"Easy," I say, putting hands between them. "Gwen held the necklace up to the map, and it hit right on Central Park like a magnet. Shelly was there, waiting for us near Turtle Pond."

"What did she look like?" Layla asks.

"Like a blobby fish," Gwen says, shivering. "Drooping and wrinkled. I had no idea oracles were so hideous."

"They aren't," Kurt says softly. "Not all of them."

"Shelly—don't laugh at her name, you guys. She's cool, okay? Said she was the youngest of the remaining five oracle sisters. That's why she's got the fewest powers. She was talking in this rhyme, all vague. Why are supernatural people so vague?"

"When you live forever," Kurt says, "you get bored. Riddles, games, quests. It's part of our life."

"O-kay." Layla's eyeing the Venus pearl spinning in my hand. "If you gave it back to her, why do you still have it?"

"She gifted it to me." I shrug. I wonder what would happen if I offered it to Layla. Would she throw it back in my face? I wish I'd never given it to someone else first. "Something about my bravery and good looks."

"I bet," she says drily.

Kurt nods to Gwen. "And what happened to your hands?"

As a reflex, Gwen balls them into tiny fists behind her back.

"Elias showed up," I say.

"Gwen's ex-fiancé Elias?" Layla asks. "Champion of the East whatever. I thought he disappeared."

"He was dead," I correct. Before they can interrupt me again, "I've never been around dead bodies, but I'll never forget the smell. Bits of his skin were falling off, but he was still strong. He spoke in Nieve's voice."

They're silent. *Nieve*, the silver witch of my nightmares.

"I recognized the voice from my dreams." I push my plate of food away. "I'd swear on anything that Nieve was the one pulling the strings. Can she do that?"

"I wasn't alive when Nieve was at court," Kurt says. "The king banished her after she killed the queen and led the rebellion against the throne. They say she was able to make you see things—cruel things, nightmares. Until your mind was weak enough to control."

His eyes fall back on Gwen. "How did you get rid of Elias?"

Gwen lifts up her chin defiantly. She holds out her palms to show us the black scabs of burn marks. "I took Triton's dagger and drove it into him."

He shrinks back, surprised. "Oh…"

We're quiet for a moment. Gwen gets up and walks away from us. She leans on the side of the ship and watches the mountains of clouds left behind in our wake.

Layla rests her hand on my knee. "That wasn't so hard, was it?"

I place my hand on top of hers but don't answer.

Kurt is staring at Gwen. "Is there anything else?"

Gwen with her smoke-bending magic fingers. In the Sea Court, the merfolk who still have traces of magic have to register with the court and king. The merfolk fear magic the way humans fear lunatics with guns. They think it's unpredictable and unreliable. Gwen is by no means registered. After everything she's done for me, I can't betray her secret.

"Hey, Arion," I call out. "Where in the world are we?"

Arion uses the black ropes to pull himself over the deck. The strong winds ripple against the sails so he tightens them. "Steady on the Southern Channel. We'll have to wait for Lady Thalia to return with an approximation of time."

"She's been gone since sunrise," Layla says.

Arion tugs on his black beard. "It won't be long now, Master Tristan. The trick to the Vanishing Cove is making sure we don't *miss* it."

"You're not saying it literally vanishes?" Layla asks, wonder-struck.

"I don't like this." Gwen pounds her fists on the wood. "I don't like being stuck on a boat."

Casting a long shadow over Gwen, Kurt points an authoritative finger in her face. "None of us are stuck here, Lady Gwenivere. You're more than welcome to return to Toliss Island and resume your duties at court."

Under the shade of the mainsail, we stand in a broken circle. Now I know why Thalia volunteered to swim off and scout the remaining distance to the cove.

"Ah, right you are, Kurtomathetis of the Sea Guard." Gwen crosses her slender arms over her chest, emphasizing the cleavage her bikini barely covers. "The only one *stuck* here is our captain. As is this foot-fin over here." She waves at Layla dismissively.

Layla seethes, "Don't call me that."

Gwen smiles through it. She sees the argument forming on my lips and looks away, but doesn't apologize. "What I mean is, we've been on this ship for nearly two days."

"Congratulations on your accelerated ability to count," Layla says.

Gwen throws her hands in the air and makes very un-princess-like exclamations. "What I mean is there are other ways of getting to the Vanishing Cove. We are Sea People. We swim."

Unbidden, the attack of the merrows returns to the forefront of my mind. "We're stronger together."

"The championship ends in six days and seven nights," she reminds me. "Then the champions return to Toliss for the final duel. Need I remind you that, without a trident, there is no king, and without a king—"

"We know what happens," Kurt says roughly. "Without a king, we will be left with destruction and chaos. That is why the champions travel on ships armed to the masts with soldiers. When the throne is weakened, not even the sea is kind to us."

Gwen's cheeks are sucked in like she's holding back the venom on her tongue. I can see the rage in her with nowhere to go. She throws it at the most vulnerable person she can find.

"Oh, is that it? Here I thought we were staying dry because the foot-fin can't swim."

Layla, one the fastest swimmers I know, freezes. She takes a step toward Gwen, but Kurt gets between them first. On any other day, I wouldn't mind watching a girl fight. Especially when it's pretty much about me. But the thing Layla doesn't know, the thing even Kurt doesn't know, is that if it weren't for Gwen, Layla wouldn't be alive.

"*Layla…*" I warn. When she turns to me, I've forgotten what I wanted to say. Under the scent of washed wood and the salt of the ocean, I get a whiff of her—lavender and honey and *light.* Her nose is sunburnt and peeling. It makes me want to stand in the way and let the sun set me on fire instead.

"Fine," Layla says, steadying her breath. She turns around and climbs the steps to the ship's wheel. "Take her side. I'll be over here doing whatever *foot-fins* do."

"*It's not about sides*!" I yell.

Gwen pushes past Kurt and me, growling, "You know that I'm right."

With Layla and Gwen at different corners of the deck, Kurt and I are left standing at the mainmast. "We have to fix this," I say.

"Lord Sea—" Kurt says.

I put my hand on his chest and press him against the mast. "Don't. Call. Me. Lord. Sea."

He looks down at my hand and smirks.

"Tristan," he lowers his voice, "come with me. Your sword needs sharpening."

Kurt and I duck past the barrels of sea mead and the trunk of weapons. Two cannons are lined with seaweed so soft that it feels like velvet.

"I think I found where the urchin bros sleep," I say.

"Definitely more comfortable than the deck was last night." Kurt unloads his weapons on a table slab.

I unbuckle my sheath. I add my beat-up sword and Triton's dagger to the mix. Unlike the dull broadsword I've been training with, Triton's dagger is pristine. Handed down from the man himself, it can only be held by his descendants. I'm imagining the other mermen who used this weapon when Kurt snaps me out of my trance.

"It was kind of you to give your chambers to Thalia." Kurt sits on a crate level with the table and examines my sword.

"No worries. They're technically Arion's. He's captain of the ship."

"He's *bound* to the ship, Tristan. He'll never be more than the one who ferries it."

"Arion's more than that. He's been my friend and I will free him."

Kurt shakes his head, sighing. "Don't make easy promises."

"Isn't that the point of having a new king?" I cross my arms over my chest. "Just because we're supernatural beings doesn't mean we have to live in the Middle Ages, slaying dragons and having squires and shit."

Kurt sharpens the sword with a black stone, sending sparks flying with each strike. "I've killed my share of dragons."

"Is that why you wanted to come down here?" I sit facing him on a barrel of sea mead. "Because this isn't a two-man job, and Triton's dagger doesn't need sharpening."

He stops. Sets his weapons down carefully. "I didn't want to say this in front of Gwenivere—"

"Because you don't like her?"

He rolls his eyes. "That isn't what I said."

"But you don't deny it?"

"Does it matter to you?" he asks defiantly.

Truthfully, I don't know anything about their relationship before they joined up with me. Maybe they dated and it didn't work out. That might explain all the venom.

"Why don't you like her?" I ask. Other than her general air of entitlement and her finger-snapping attitude.

"What has she done to make you two so close?"

"*That* was subtle." I instantly think of Gwen's eyes turning black for a flash, her magic. "It's not like that."

Even in the shadows, I can see him flush. "Forget it."

"Oh, come on. Learn to take a joke. You should know me by now. What did you want to say that you couldn't say in front of Gwen?"

"Thalia has been gone too long," he says. "I trained her myself. I know she can take care of herself. But with the boy's—Ryan's—death…She was rather attached. I don't know if she'd be reckless."

Thalia's the only mermaid I've met, other than my mom, who loves being on land. When she left this morning to scout the distance to the cove, I figured it'd be good for her to be alone. But that was hours ago.

"Maybe we should go now," I say. "Make sure she's safe, then just you and me keep on going."

"I've been to the oracle here before. I told you. And while strategically it's safer to enter through land, there are also the tunnels beneath. I'm willing to take the chance. If you are."

That's a challenge. I match the smirk on his face. "Of course I'm willing. Though, the girls are not going to like us leaving them behind."

He seems startled. "Haven't you ever said 'no' to a girl before?"

"Plenty of times. Doesn't mean I like to do it. Then they get all sad and it's my fault and I'm the one who's the jerk."

"We could have the urchins whip up a calming brew."

I punch him in the chest. "Are you crazy? We don't drug our friends to stop an argument! What's wrong with you?"

"Then you'll have to be the one to tell them. They listen to you."

"Since when? Between the four of us, our stubbornness could fill a black hole."

Kurt bursts out in a rare laugh. "Let's get our weapons ready. I'll meet you on deck in fifteen minutes. Which one of these do you prefer?"

"I don't need a sword." I duck back the way we came from and start climbing up the ladder. "I've got something even better."

chapter THREE

The captain's chambers are small and unused.

There's a long, stiff bed and a table with some old maps, a magnifying glass, and a rusty water pitcher. The gas lamp swings precariously above my head. In the three hours of sleep I was able to get last night, I woke up sweating because I dreamt the quartz scepter was gone. Even now, removing the long rectangular box from the trick compartment under the bed, I'm afraid of opening it.

But that's stupid, because it only opens to my touch.

Then her voice makes me jump, and when I stand, I hit my head on the gas lamp.

"Weren't you just talking about how we don't want to swim down there?" It's Layla. She's jittery, like the minutes before a meet. She lets all of the nervousness wash over her. Then when she stands on the ledge, she uncrosses her arms and lets it all go.

"What else do you want me to do? Sit here and duel with Kurt?" I set the box on the bed, trace my finger from top to bottom. The effect is instant. Symbols etched carefully in golden leaves, circles, and flurries hum beneath my finger. I think, *this* has to be what magic feels like. Buzzing, kinetic, electric. It purrs under my skin, shooting pinpricks of energy until something unhinges and the box sighs open.

I let go of the breath I've been holding.

The scepter is still there.

I grip the dusty golden hilt and pull it out. The quartz piece comes to a sharp point. A soft glow emanates from inside the crystal. It comes and goes like the fluorescent tubes in my old classrooms. Kurt says it could be because the three pieces are meant to work together, and when they're apart, they're erratic.

Layla hooks her thumbs on the back of her shorts. "Is it heavy?"

"Not really." I hold it horizontally and press on its weight, like a too-thick branch I can't snap. "It's solid, though."

"Can I touch it?"

"*No.*" I hold it over my head and away from her. "Did you see what my dagger did to Gwen's hands?"

"Fine, I'll get my rock candy on a stick."

I make like I'm going to throw it at her, a fake basketball pass, and she flinches. "See? You don't really want it. You just want it because I have it. Like when you stole my G.I. Joes."

"Only because *you* stole my Barbies. Which makes so much sense now."

"I took better care of your Barbies than you, *Ecuadorian scissor hands.*"

"They looked better with short hair!"

I strap on the leather harness Blue made for me. I can sheath my dagger at the center of my chest, and my scepter between my shoulder blades. I use Layla as my mirror. Her eyes flick from my feet to my weapons and settle on my face. She reaches out to my cheek where Kurt nicked me.

Layla's never been delicate. She'd rather punch you than kiss you. But right now in the captain's cabin, with her sun-kissed hair and her chin tilted up in that stubbornly cute way, I wonder—

I close the space between us one step at a time. She can step back if she wants to. She knows that.

But she doesn't.

Her hands unhook from her shorts and fall on my hip bones. The pads of her fingertips press firmly on my sticky, sweaty skin.

I tuck a strand behind her ear, trace the length of her neck. "I think you only like me when you think I might die."

"I think I like you better when you aren't talking."

We exhale at the same time. The heat of it is like the hum of the quartz piece in my hand, and because she's frozen still, I know I have to be the one to banish the gap between us and I lower my lips to hers.

But then the heat is gone.

"You said fifteen minutes." A very naked Kurt stands at the door, which I forgot was open.

I put a hand over Layla's eyes. "Why are you naked?"

"Those are my last trousers," he says. "I didn't want to ruin them. This is why we have armor on the Sea Guard. Too bad—"

Layla's batting my hands away. "Really Tristan, It's not anything I haven't seen before."

"*What*?" Kurt and I shout in sync.

"I don't mean Kurt. I'm one of three girls on the swim team. The guys aren't exactly shy. Neither are you." She pinches my abs and walks right past Kurt, like it's just another Sunday morning.

I put my hands on his chest and shoo him out of the way. "Come on, let's go."

There isn't a plank on the ship, so we just have to jump off the starboard rail. I drop my shorts, ignoring the tittering from Layla and Gwen, and try to take on a serious voice. Like a commander. A captain. Someone they can't laugh at for having his ass out. "Arion, whatever happens, get to the Vanishing Cove."

"Aye, sire."

"Dive on my count," I tell Kurt.

He nods once, securing the leather sheath around his hips.

"Three. Two. One."

chapter FOUR

I shift midair.

The numb prickle starts at my spine and trails all the way down. Seconds before I hit the water, I catch sight of the turquoise blue of my scales, and my adrenaline races. Then I break the surface.

My gills flare and my chest expands. Out of habit, I have the urge to kick as if I'm in the pool. The movement jerks me forward and turns into a flick. I spin in a circle at first, just to get used to the fins. It's constricting, being one movement instead of two, but the speed is addicting. I press my arms at my sides and get into the undulating rhythm of the current. When I turn around, the shadow of our ship is long gone.

Kurt swims ahead of me by a foot, keeping closer to the surface for now. His long tail is a flash of violet, barreling into a swarm of fish. They scatter, then reform their circular pattern. We swim side by side until we're the only ones as far as I can see.

Then Kurt stops abruptly.

I double back to where he's floating and staring into the far-off darkness.

"What?" I ask.

"Listen."

But I don't hear anything aside from the swish of our tails and the slow current. I kick out to swim again, but Kurt grabs my wrist and anchors me. He shakes his head and shuts his eyes. "You have to sense it."

His gills open and close with the deep gulp he takes. I try to do the same. Above water, this hypersensitive sense allows us to smell emotions. It's annoying—and nauseating when I'm surrounded by tons of hormonal classmates. But down here, it's different. I can taste fear, like melting copper on my tongue, and it's coming right at us in a cloud of white.

I nudge Kurt. His eyes snap open.

Leading the pack is Thalia, her deep green hair pulled back against the current. Her powerful tail is a good chomp away from the mouth of a great white shark, his jaws wide open in a perpetual bloody grin. As they come closer, the white cloud comes into focus, shark by shark by shark.

Thalia wails again, glancing behind. I think I hear her shout, "Stop," but I can't be sure.

Kurt raises his sword over his shoulder like a lance.

Something is wrong.

The coppery fear I sense isn't coming from Thalia; it's coming from the sharks. I haven't met many sharks, but I know one saved me. I've seen him in my dreams. Always the same massive one who comes and saves me from the silver mermaid's grip. He had metal chains around him, like a shark muzzle with handles at the sides for a rider.

These sharks are not part of the guard, but I know they're swimming away from something big enough to scare twenty sharks.

Thalia's scream gets closer, and this time she's waving her arms in the air. She doesn't want us to attack.

But Kurt's ready to strike.

I lunge and tackle him around his waist.

He pushes against me, wrestling out of my grip. "What are you doing?"

They're feet away from us now. Thalia reaches her arms out for us to hold. She's moving so fast she can't stop. We grab hold of her tightly and the sharks, all of them, zoom right over our heads as if we're not even on their radar.

Thalia presses a hand over her heart. I can hear the thud of it, the ragged strain in her breath. There's a long gash of blood down her arm.

"No time." She takes our hands and tries to pull but there's no strength behind it. "No time."

"What is it?" I ask, looking back at where she came from. "Merrows?"

"Worse." Her eyes are brilliantly green and panicked.

Kurt shakes her, but there's no need. In the murky darkness, something slithers. It weaves into the cracked sea floor and back out again. Kurt's face goes slack. He grips both of our wrists and pulls us up and onto the surface.

"What the hell is that?" I cough out the water in my throat as my gills clamp shut against the air.

"Makara demon," Kurt says. "The king buried them centuries ago."

"The cove is three channels south," Thalia says. "That's where the demon rose, eating everything in sight."

"It's happening," Kurt says. "Now that the trident is broken, the king's seal is loosening. That's how the demon must've broken free."

"How do we fight it?" I ask.

"With six of my best guards and lots of luck."

"Thalia, go back to the ship. Tell them to keep going to the cove," I say.

She nods and swims away.

"We can't lead the beast back to the others," Kurt says.

He looks torn between following his sister and staying here with me. But his duty wins, and he follows me back down.

The thing—the makara—is undulating in wide arcs, eating. It shakes its head back and forth with a twelve-foot-long shark in its mandible.

"I think I just peed myself," I say. "How can you tell down here?"

Kurt shakes his head, gripping his sword even tighter. "If we live through this, I'll point it out to you."

As it swallows the shark like it's munching on an Oreo, the makara is unaware of us watching. It's curled up on a jagged black rock. Its head could belong to a crocodile—the long snout, the raised bumps that start on its nose and continue all the way down to the sharp tip of the tail. Crooked claws grip the bits of shark meat that fall from its mouth. It reminds me of a T. rex, arms short and close to the mouth. Chomp by chomp, the great white shark disappears inside the makara. There's a dorsal fin off to the side, but nothing else.

Then the demon's head snaps up. Maybe it can smell us. Maybe it caught the glint off our weapons. Whatever it was, two yellow eyes lock on us.

"No matter what," Kurt tells me, "I will get you to the cove."

"Don't talk that way now," I say, wracking my mind for something—anything. The makara is twice as long as our ship. Its body retracts, watching us carefully before it lurches forward. "You go left. I go right. On my go."

"What?"

"Just do it!"

The demon drops the rest of its meal, blood billowing around it. The makara snaps its mouth once, twice. The sound of the crunch is so hard that the shock vibrates all the way to us.

"Now!" I dive to the right, up, and arc around.

But the demon isn't following me.

It's following Kurt.

I swim right behind them, trying my best to avoid the pointed tail. If there were ever a time for the scepter to work, it would be now. Why didn't my grandfather give me a clue? Anything. Maybe he didn't think I'd actually be able to get a piece of the trident. No,

I can't think that way. I was chosen for a reason. The hum of the scepter is dull, but I know its power is down there, like a prickle beneath the skin. I have to make it surface.

"Tristan!"

With every chomp, the makara gets closer and closer to Kurt's fins. In a desperate move, I swing my scepter like a bat.

The demon's skin is so thick that I'm not sure it actually feels the hit. The pointed end of its tail flaps around, trying to skewer me. I need to get closer to reach it with my dagger, so I swim underneath it and swipe. Blood flows from the cut.

The makara writhes, swimming past Kurt and up and up until it breaks the surface. Its cry is terrible, like a million snarling crocs. A thin line of blood trails from Kurt's fin. We swim away, but not fast enough. It dives back down, barreling into me with one of the ridges on its face, pushing and pushing until I crash against the ocean floor. Something inside me crunches, hard. My vision is cloudy and every breath is a fire in my chest. I can feel the abyss of its open mouth over me, lips peeled back to expose the rows of massive teeth.

I search the ground around me until I find the cold gold of my scepter, screaming as I thrust it out. A blast of white light shines from the crystal.

The makara growls.

It shivers from snout to bleeding tail. Mouth open, eyes wide, it doesn't move from the light. Slowly, I inch the crystal to the left.

It follows.

To the right.

It follows.

Kurt hovers above us. He holds his sword by the hilt, raises it high over his head. We look at each other for a second, nodding for reassurance. Kurt drives the sword between the makara's eyes, piercing straight through the mouth until the hilt won't go down any farther. The creature wails, a terrible sound that must carry on for miles. Blood pools in dark clouds around us as Kurt pulls the sword out and stabs it again.

I try to get out of the way, but I can't move fast enough. The creature goes slack and falls right on my tail. Kurt's so bewildered by the creature that he floats there and stares.

"A little help," I groan.

"Yes, yes, of course. Can you move?"

"If I could move, I wouldn't be asking."

"Right." His chest is heaving. He swims around and clutches the makara by the jaw. He lifts and pulls, and I push. My scream is a violent echo, scaring away the creatures that were just starting to peek their gills back into the clearing.

My breathing is short and painful. I shake my head against the blurriness clouding my eyes. "What are you doing?"

Kurt has propped the great jaws open. The smell coming out of the creature's mouth is enough to keep me awake. I turn over, and everything I've eaten today comes right out. Every heave worsens the pain in my ribs.

With the careful precision of a dentist, Kurt uses his sword to carve out three of the makara's teeth.

I spot my dagger and crawl to reach it. I put it safely back in its sheath. Kurt throws a tooth at me, which I barely catch.

"How come you get two?"

"One is for Arion." He takes my arm and drapes it around his shoulder.

"That's nice of you."

"I can be nice." He wonders at the makara, then turns to me with a cocky grin. "Saved your mer ass, didn't I?"

I hold on to my side. "Don't make me laugh—it hurts."

"Should I take you back to the ship?"

The angry bones in my body protest, but I shake my head. "Let's keep going."

We swim south for two miles along the jagged black floor of the sea. There is no life down here, except for patches of seaweed. I have to lean against Kurt for most of it.

Then there it is again. The growl of a makara.

Kurt and I exchange worried glances and float back to back. I can't see anything other than green water and miles of black rock.

"It's coming from beneath," Kurt realizes.

I inch for a few yards along the ground to where it stops at a precipice. Steam rises and I back away from the heat. My heart sinks when I see them deep below against a stream of red rock. Makara, slithering among themselves, feasting on the creatures down there.

I shake my head at Kurt. "It's a nest."

"That must've been the mother."

"What do we do?"

"That's the entrance, Tristan." Kurt looks up at the surface, then back at me. "That's the entrance to the oracle's caves."

"We can't just leave these things out here in the open." I swim up and float over the steaming head of the fissure with my scepter in hand.

"Are you sure?" Kurt says.

I shut out his words. Concentrate on the sound of the makara feasting below. My grandfather put them away once. I can do it again.

The scepter comes to life in my hand, energy winding from right inside me. When I shut my eyes, I have a faint memory. It isn't mine. It can't be. It's the king, raising his hand and aiming it at the ground. When I open my eyes again, I let the power flow from me, through the scepter, and back again, like we're feeding off each other.

The light shoots straight out, blasting the ground. Stones and boulders rain onto the trembling ocean floor. The fissure collapses on either side, closing the gap until all that's left is the vibration of the makara demons' screams.

Kurt shouts into the mess I've made. I hold my scepter at arm's length, soaking up the images that flood from it.

The thing I'm not ready for is the blowback of energy. I can feel it recoiling back into the scepter. The light is blinding, and I know this is going to hurt.

chapter FIVE

Blue hands me a cup full of a tea that smells like my gym locker that one time I didn't clean it out between sophomore and junior year.

"Your own scepter did that to you?" Gwen asks.

They're gathered around me in the captain's cabin. The winds have returned and Arion's steering us as fast as he can. Soft rays trickle through mountains of clouds into the square windows. Kurt's polishing the makara teeth with a black cloth. He stares at them with a happiness I've never seen in him.

Note: The way to make Kurt happy is to pit him against ancient sea monsters.

"It was the recoil." Layla says. "Like when you shoot a gun."

"I don't think merpeople use guns." I set the tea aside, but Blue picks it back up and holds it up to my mouth.

His blue face is scrunched up, lips trembling. "No, Master Tristan. Must drink it all."

Trying not to gag, I take another gulp. Then another. A sense of calm spreads through my body. The pain from my ribs dulls, replaced by a strange grinding sound, as though my insides are shifting.

"Urchin secret," Blue says. "Cures all."

"Pound it." I hold out my fist to him. And he does, pressing his tiny knuckles against mine in a fist bump.

Layla, who's been pacing the length of the room muttering to herself, shoots me a nasty glare.

"Say it to the whole class, Santos," I tell her.

She stops mid-step and turns to me with furious watery eyes. "You're a big, dumb idiot."

Gwen laughs, patting my knee. "I've been saying this since I met him. But you've got to admit, he must be doing something right. Since he's still alive."

I test the state of my ribs by sitting up. I stretch my arms up toward the ceiling, across my chest, and behind my back. "Oh, that feels so good."

"I've never seen a makara eel before," Kurt says. "It's smaller than I thought."

"Small?" I choke on the last drag of tea. "You call that thing small?"

"Only in comparison to the stories." He gives his tooth one last polishing stroke and smiles down at it. "Blue, do you think I can make a spear out of this?"

Happy that he's being addressed, Blue nods. "Oh yes, Master Kurtomathetis. Straight away." He takes the giant tooth in his hands and rushes away with it.

Layla stops pacing. She sits to the left of me on the bed, giving me her back. "I don't get how something like that can exist without anyone knowing about it."

"Think about what you just said." I take a lock of her hair and run my fingers along it. She bats me away. "No one sees the giant, floating Toliss Island that contains the whole Sea Court, either."

"That's different," Kurt says. "There's a spell around the island so it appears to be a storm at sea. To keep humans away. The makara and others like it were put away years ago. They caused so much destruction that the king buried them deep in the earth, hoping they would die. That explains their size. They've adapted to the constraints of the cave."

I twist my torso to stretch the soreness out of my rib cage. "So why did one just happen to show up and start snacking on great whites?"

"It's the king's power." Kurt motions at my quartz scepter and Triton's dagger on the table. "It's ebbing. The trident *is* the king's power. He creates with it. He destroys with it. Now that it's broken in three pieces, everything will come undone."

"I don't get it," Layla says. "Haven't there been other kings? Why is this happening now?"

"The line has been unbroken for thousands of years. Our kind is bound to the power of the throne. Which is why, if at the end of the fortnight, the trident is not pieced back together, everything—from the creatures banished in caves beneath the sea, to those banished from court—would be able to return. Even our kind would be able to go on land."

"We don't always behave very well among humans," Thalia says darkly.

"Speak for yourself, guppy," Gwen says. She's got her arms crossed like she owns the world. Then the ship heaves. Gwen falls into Kurt, who holds her by her shoulders at arm's length. Layla falls back against me and I take this moment to put my arms around her. The pitcher of water on the table wobbles but doesn't tip over.

Thalia throws her hair back, just missing Gwen's face. "I think I'll check on the progress. We should be there shortly." She presses her hand on my shoulder before leaving.

Kurt looks from Layla to me to Gwen, and as though he'd rather face another Macarena eel thing than stay with us, he says, "I'll join you."

Gwen tries to pick up my makara tooth, but doesn't realize how sharp it is, and cuts her finger on its edge. She sucks on the wound.

"Time for an edible seaweed Band-Aid," Layla says, mock-sweetly.

Gwen shoots a terrible glare at her. I'm expecting her eyes to glow white and sparks to fly from her fingers, but she just stalks out.

Which leaves just Layla and me.

I get off the bed and pour myself a cup of water. It's cool, slightly salty, and perfect. I drink it eagerly as it trickles over the cup and down my chest.

"Thirsty?" Layla asks.

I set the cup down. "Just a bit."

I grip the dusty golden hilt of the scepter, trying to remember the power I felt when I was facing the makara.

"How do you make it glow?"

"I don't. Not really. Even when I was down there, I could tell it wasn't me doing it."

"What do you mean?"

I hesitate, trying to find just the right words. "It's like it has its own power. Separate from me. Somehow, we feed off each other."

She cocks her head to the side. All of her hair is pulled over her shoulder. Footsteps scatter on deck. I sit on the bed beside her. "You must be bummed you broke the entrance to the oracle lady, huh?" she says.

I take her hand in mine and cross our fingers together. "I'm looking forward to seeing the Vanishing Cove. This is the farthest away I've ever been from home."

"Me too."

"You've been to Athens. You've been to the equator. That's way farther."

"It's not the same." She shakes her head, not letting go of my stare. Not for a moment. "Promise you'll be careful from now on."

I smile. "And miss out on seaweed bandages?"

She doesn't laugh, the way I intended it. It's even better. She takes my face with her hand and brings it closer to—

"Many pardons, Lord Sea," Vi says.

I throw myself backward on the bed. "What is it?"

Layla pours herself some water.

The purple urchin shifts from side to side, wringing his little fingers until I fear he'll pull them right off the knuckles. "We're nearing the coast."

"We'll be right out."

He bows so low to the ground that his long, pointy nose nearly touches the wood, then leaves in a purple blur.

I take my scepter, nestle it into the back of the harness, and sheath my dagger on the front.

"Really, Tristan." Layla stands back to look at me from the doorway. "I think you need more weapons."

Behind her I can see the others loading up as well. I take a skinny blade with a bronze handle and hand it to her. She doesn't hesitate when she takes it, but her hands are shaky.

"The way things are going," I say, "we're going to need them."

chapter SIX

Leaning against the side of the ship, we're still surrounded on all sides by nothing but water. "I thought you said we were nearly there."

Arion lowers himself on his black ropes. "Take a moment, Master Tristan. Close your eyes."

It sounds hokey, but I do it.

"Envision your destination."

"But, I've never been there before. How will I know what I'm envisioning?"

"It's a feeling, Master Tristan. Knowing you have arrived."

I peek from my left eye. The others are standing with their eyes shut facing the water. Arion nods encouragingly at me.

I know I should be picturing a strip of land. Maybe a white sandy beach. Or a port? A small town where the oracle will be living. The truth is, I have no idea what I should be picturing. I keep thinking of the Coney Island skyline—the pier, the dark water pulling in with the tide, the silhouettes of the Wonder Wheel and the Parachute Jump. It warms my insides because I know when I see that, I've come home.

When I open my eyes, I have to rub them shut again. A coastal town flickers in the distance.

"Whoa." Layla points at it. "Vanishing Cove. They weren't just being funny when they named it."

"Yes, Miss Layla," Arion says. "Humans, even some of our kind, will sail past without knowing it's there. If you know what you're looking for, sometimes it's easier to find."

As we get closer, I can make out the ascending line of crooked homes along the jagged coast. Ships bigger than ours are docked farther out, letting down rowboats full of passengers. From a tiny strip of beach on the far side of the island, I can see a recently extinguished fire still smoking.

Arion moves his hands skillfully, molding the air. The masts and sails bend in turn to his movements, adjusting to catch the wind from a different angle until we're nestled in the port between a weather-beaten ship called the *Golden Rose* and a nameless narrow black ship with a dragon carved into the bow.

The port market smells like the time my friend Angelo's mom made us go down to Biddy Early's pub to tell his dad he had to come home. Beer, men, and burning meat. Merchants argue in loud languages I don't recognize, but the hand gestures suggest the speakers are not exactly loving each other.

"Those guys look friendly." I set foot on the dock. A wobbly sensation washes over me, as if the sky and the ground have switched places. I know my feet are firmly planted on the ramp, but somehow it's like I'm floating.

"Jelly legs," Thalia laughs, hopping beside us and extending her arms out in hang-ten position.

Kurt and Gwen seem unaffected.

I head toward the bow where Arion is making his presence known. He's hovering midair off the ship on his black ropes, arms crossed over his chest. The usually kind smile is replaced by the same face my mom wears when she's trying to haggle with a guy at the farmers' market—all "Five dollars for an apple? I don't care if it's organic!"

"Are you going to be okay here?" I ask, not getting a particularly warm feeling from the men unloading other ships. In clothes yellowed by the sea air and with scarred faces, they mutter and point fingers at us.

Arion nods once. "We need supplies. Rope, sails, fresh water. The hull needs a scrubbing. I can find everything we need. Sea mead goes a long way in places like this." Arion motions back to our ship where Blue and Vi are stacking barrels on deck. "We are the only creatures who manufacture and supply it."

"Liquid currency," Layla says. "Seems fitting."

I hold my arm out to Arion. He taught me a sweet new handshake, the way the guys at the Sea Guard do it. Gripping the forearm, like you're feeling the other person's strength. When Arion grips my forearm, I think he might be the strongest person I've ever met. "I don't know how long we'll be."

"Do not worry, Master Tristan," he says. "We will not leave without you."

And with that, my team—consisting of a commander of the Sea Guard and his sister, a magical mermaid princess, and my best friend and almost girlfriend—head up the dock until it becomes a cobblestone market square. The tents form a loose semi-circle around the church. At the center is a massive cathedral with a bunch of kids kicking a ball around. The gong of a bell sends fat scarlet birds scattering into the sky. The clock marks 5 p.m. The sun is sinking, but the sky is still a gradient of blues.

Layla points at the church. "Doesn't it remind you of something?"

Tall winding turrets, tiny winged gargoyles and cherubs, high arched windows—yeah. It looks just like our high school. "Thorne Hill."

We pass an Indian woman standing at a booth, her hair braided to the ground. Her eyes are big as an owl's with a fringe of white feathers for eyelashes. She weighs beans in her hand and yells at the man trying to sell them to her. When they see us, they stop and fire away with poisonous scowls. The owl woman hoots at me.

"What did I do?" I ask.

"Just keep walking," Kurt says.

A horse-drawn carriage passes us, stopping in front of the church. The driver hops off to let out a couple. The man takes her arm, and she lifts layers and layers of puffy skirts so they don't trail on the ground. They walk past us, nodding in our direction but not *really* looking at us.

"Uhh—" Layla's eyes follow the couple as they weave through the shops. "Is that carriage a time machine? They look like they just hopped out of 1869. That corset *cannot* be comfortable."

Kurt shrugs. "You'll find many extraordinary people in places like these."

"What exactly is this place?" I ask Kurt.

"A world away to you two, I suppose." Kurt picks up an apple from the fruit vendor beside us. He reaches into his pocket and hands the beefy man a shiny copper coin. I'm guessing they don't take American down here. Kurt gives the apple to Thalia, who gobbles it in quick bites.

The kids playing ball kick it to my feet. I raise my leg to kick it back to them, but one of them runs over in a heartbeat. He has long, pointy ears and sharp green eyes. He sticks out a tongue that's forked like a snake's, cackling when I jump back from the shock of it.

"A world away," Kurt repeats. "There are many more, all over the world. As human numbers grew and pushed anything remotely *unnatural* farther and farther into the fringes, villages like this were created. Others left with the fey court on floating islands, similar to our Toliss. Then there are those who leave the sanctuary of places like this for the anonymity of cities, like your Coney Island."

Layla still watches the couple from 1869. "You mean everyone in this town is supernatural?"

"Not at all. There are humans who are more—" His eyes fall on Layla. "…enlightened, that have found themselves here one way or another."

The marketplace is starting to feel cramped. I'm picking up something in the air. It's hidden beneath the mounds of smoke and spices. I decide it's the perfume tent and the throngs of people we pass. "How do we find the way to the oracle?"

Kurt, who's rarely at a loss for words, stands with his mouth open. "Uh—"

"Look at these!" Layla runs over to a stand with pots and tubes full of colorful smoke called Fazya's Wish Come True.

Kurt calls out after her—all "Stay together"—but the woman has Layla hooked. The vendor is tall with a wild mane of curls. Her eyes are rimmed black against rich coffee skin.

"Come, my darling," she says. Her voice is as soft as the smoke in one of those jars. "Come to Fazya."

I pick one up and give it a shake. The smoke spins in a coil of blood red.

"Tut, tut." The vendor pries it from my hands. "Mustn't touch."

"What in the seas are these?" Kurt demands, not hiding his disgust.

"They're wishes, of course. What your heart desires." She sweeps her long, elegant hands over her display—every color of the rainbow and jars in all shapes and sizes. "True love granted. Hair longer than Rapunzel herself. Sight in the darkness. Flight to the heavens. Power in the palm of your hands. Loved ones returned from the dead—"

Thalia's hand reaches out toward the jar, the vendor's eyes becoming dark saucers as she does so. She has a hunger that reminds me of Nieve—taunting, searching, waiting.

I take Thalia's hand and jerk it back, breaking whatever trance was beginning. The jar topples over and cracks with a steam-engine hiss. Fazya's eyes become red as embers. When she opens her full mouth to hiss at me, a black tongue slithers out, while her hips sashay from side to side. Her sultry voice is replaced by a very flat Brooklyn accent. "Ya break it. Ya *bought* it."

Gwen claps. "Good show, Tristan."

Kurt throws Fazya a gold coin and leads us farther into the market. He gives me a look that screams, "You should know better." The thing is, I don't. I've never been in a place like this. I might as well be at my dad's office being reminded not to touch anything.

"We shouldn't engage with those people. Our goal is to get underground," Kurt says.

Gwen stops walking. The traffic of people weaves around her. Her head is cocked to the side, waiting for an explanation. "*Those* people?"

Kurt huffs and puffs. "Dark magic. Sorcery. You know very well what I mean, Lady Gwenivere. It's dangerous. It consumes the soul, the magic. That's what happened to the silver witch. Her power grew bigger than herself. That woman," he points a finger at a still fuming Fazya, "uses false wishes to take advantage of others. Those are the people I mean."

"How would you know any of it?" Gwen asks. "Read it in a book? When you get to be my age, you'll learn to tell the difference, Kurtomathetis of the *Guard*."

"And just how old are you?" Kurt crosses his arms, puffing out his chest until he towers over her. “Other than being promised to the former herald of the East, we knew so very little about you at court.”

Gwen raises her hands slowly. Maybe she’ll try to choke him. Maybe she’ll blast him with her magic fingers. As much as I’d love to watch, I know I can’t.

“Guys, come on. That’s enough.” I step directly between them, facing Gwen. I take her slender wrists in my hands and she brings down her guard. I can feel Kurt’s hot breath on my back so I turn to face him. “Are you forgetting that you’re on the same side?”

Deep in my heart, I know that’s not true. Gwen made it clear to me the night we were on our way to Shelly. She considers herself to be her own team, like a lone wolf. The way Kurt’s been treating her, I can see why. They step away from each other, and Gwen takes a step behind me to be shielded from them.

“I apologize,” he says dismissively. “Let’s resume our search.”

“Not that I’m doubting you, Kurt,” Layla says, “but do we even know what we’re looking for? A magic cupboard? Enchanted armoire? Fancy-looking glass?”

“Whatever would we do with that?” He looks down at the ground and the smooth cobblestone steps beneath his feet. “We have to get beneath. The underwater entrance is sealed. There has to be a passage somewhere here.”

“Is there a sewer?” Layla suggests. “Maybe if we find a manhole.”

“As much as I love the idea of wading through muck—” My attention snaps to a man closing down his tent. His sign reads

Felix's Oölogy Emporium. Crates are piled with eggs in different sizes and colors. One egg looks more like a football with its ribbed brown shell and white stripes. A set of small furry hands creep up from beneath the table. They belong to a young boy. He's shirtless, skinny as a wire. He smiles with the wet nose of a fox and tiny teeth to match, closing his hands firmly on a golden egg.

"Leave it alone, Tristan," Kurt warns.

But then I look at the squat, fat vendor, sweating to reach the back awning of his shop. His face is red and oblivious, and I know that I just can't leave it alone.

Fox Boy sees me approaching and starts, losing his grip on the egg. It falls back into the crate with a *thud*. The vendor whips around and, realizing what's happening, trips off his stool and onto his knees. Fox Face flips over, scrambling to his feet, but not before turning around to spit at me. I grab him, but he whines and sinks his teeth into my arm. I cry out and let Fox Boy go.

I clamp a hand down on the bloody beads sprouting from the round marks of his teeth.

"That's what you get for sticking your nose in the foxhole, dude," Layla says.

I shake my arm, as if that'll get rid of the pain. I don't make a face, though, because I know I was right.

The vendor comes around, fussing over me with a glass bottle and a rag. He's gracious, but he can't seem to form a proper sentence because his face is so red. I'm about to tell him, "No worries. It's no big deal," when he tilts the bottle right over my wound.

I don't recognize the scream coming from me. The liquid burns. It freezes. It numbs. I want to pull my hand away, but my brain isn't connecting to my limbs. I can't move.

"You must burn away the saliva," he says. "It's paralyzing."

For a moment, I feel as if I've just stepped off the ship again. My legs want to give out and my head spins. Then he holds the rancid, clear liquid over my nose and the dizziness goes away. I bite down on my other hand as the vendor wraps the cloth around my forearm and pulls it tight.

"Better?" he asks.

"Much." I don't realize I've started to fall down until I notice Kurt's arms holding me up.

"Come," the vendor says. "Come and sit. The venom takes a few minutes to wear off."

Felix, the vendor, ushers us into his tent. Stacks of crates marked BEWARE and FRAGILE form a wall between the front of the tent and a closet-sized living room. They sit me on the lone chair while the others sit on the bales of hay.

When I look up, Felix is gone and my friends are staring at me with incredulous faces.

Layla places her hand on my bandage. The bite mark throbs under the pressure of her hand, but I don't pull away. "You couldn't leave it alone, could you?"

"Really, Tristan," Gwen whispers. "You've got enough problems to deal with."

"Leave him alone," Thalia hisses.

As promised by the vendor, I feel much better. I give my arm a good stretch. Considering I've spent all day abusing my body, I'm no worse than a full day of swim practice. Whoever said high school prepares you for real life might've actually been on to something.

"Here we have it," Felix shouts merrily, emerging from the front of the tent with a fancy-looking teapot and tiny cups like the kind my neighbor Mrs. Horbachevsky brings out when she has my dad fixing her computer.

"It is my lucky day," he pops a squat on a large crate and starts pouring, "when such a brave youth graces my doorstep. You've done me a great kindness. The fox boys have been nicking my stand all summer. Think they're getting close to a dragon egg." He leans in close, brandishing a secretive smile. "They don't know where I keep the real stuff!"

The tea is a burst of cold licorice on my tongue. I decide I like it.

Gwen sets her teacup down without drinking from it. "You mean to say our friend got poisoned for nothing?"

"*Gwen,*" I warn.

"Of course not!" The vendor's cheeks flood red. "In fact, I am rather moved. Now those boys will know others are watching. Someone has to do the right thing. Though what the right thing is around these parts is hard to tell. I apologize for your trouble—?"

"Tristan," I say, standing. "It's cool. Really. I feel great. Thanks for the tea, Mr. Felix."

"It's simply Felix." He shakes my hand. "Now, now. Sit. Please don't think I don't appreciate your kindness. A reward?"

"That's not necessary. I wasn't trying to—" Then I realize that this is exactly what I need. Someone who knows their way around here. Everyone else seems to shoo us away. I sit back down, confusing my friends who are between standing and sitting. "But perhaps you could do something for me."

Suddenly his eyes squint at me. I'm afraid I've said the wrong thing. Then a daunting smile widens his face. He slaps his knee and booms with laughter. Something about him reminds me of Coach Bellini, and that alone makes me like Felix.

"Treasure hunters, are you? Searching for the Infinite Abyss? I did my share of traveling in my day. That's how I ended up here." His eyes fall on a rigid Kurt, staring in that intent way of his that makes you want to run for the hills. Felix's face blooms with curiosity. "What an interesting sword. May I?"

Surprisingly, Kurt hands it over. Felix turns it in his hands, bounces the weight on his open palms, even brings his nose right against the blade and inhales deeply. "Haven't seen this kind of craftsmanship in many years. I should've realized. Sea folk, are you?"

We all nod, even Layla. I can't help but think of what a beautiful mermaid she would make.

"Seems funny," Felix says, returning Kurt's sword. "I'd seen one mermaid in my whole life during my days fishing up in Maine.

Now, you're everywhere! Drinking merrily about town. Saving my own shop from thieves. I tell you, crime rate's been going up since I moved here twenty years ago. Mayor Alvarez and his wife have been having a hard time keeping things in order the last few weeks."

"This place has a mayor?" Layla asks.

Felix smiles at her. "Certainly. You might've seen them. Been here since the 1600s, I hear. Haven't changed a bit neither, like the cove itself."

"Why has your crime rate been going up?" I ask.

He shrugs his meaty shoulders. "Things are changing, as they must. 'Sides, tourism's gone down an awful lot since the oracle closed her doors to us. That's why people come here in the first place."

Kurt nearly drops his teacup. "She's closed her doors? What do you mean?"

"Folk search far and wide for this oracle. Say she can talk to the gods and predict the future. I'm not one for that stuff, despite all the things I've seen. I wouldn't want to know, would you?" Then the realization comes to him. "That's why you're here, is it?"

"Yes," I say. "Is there an entrance?"

"Like I told the other sea boy," Felix says. "The ladies of the oracle came above ground. Creepy little girls they are. They took away the entrance right in the church. Nothing but rocks in that tunnel now."

We shift in our seats. I'm sweating against the leather chair. The walls of the tent seem to be getting smaller. "Wait, what sea boy?"

"Like I says," Felix drains his cup and refills it. "Last two days

I've seen more sea folk than in my whole life. Just last night, a second ship's crew came in. Stumbling down the dock bold as you please, drunk as worms in a pirate's belly."

"Are they still here?" I stand abruptly.

"Was he wearing anything?" Kurt pats his chest. "Any symbols?"

"Aye, the serious one came first, three nights ago. Left as angry as he'd arrived. He had a medallion with a sort of octopus. They're long gone."

"That's Adaro," Gwen says. "That's his family's crest."

"The others, they were here this morning, naked on the beach all of them! Talked about a championship of sorts. Came around to my shop asking for the town pub, though I dare say after last night, they don't need it."

It's like I'm in a boxing ring getting the snot beat out of me. *Bam!* There's an oracle. *Bam!* You can't get to her. *Bam!* Others just like you got here first. *Bam!*

"Will you show us where this pub is?" I reach into my pocket and pull out some gold coins.

Kurt adjusts the sheath around his hip. "What are you thinking?"

"If it's another champion," I say, "I want to know their progress. Don't you?"

He seems hesitant but says, "I suppose."

"Your gold's no good to me, Tristan." Felix pushes my hand away. "It is I who owe you a gift. I have just the thing!"

He stands from the crate he's sitting on and shifts objects around until he finds a box about six inches wide. Like a good salesman, he opens the lid with a flourish of his hand and waits for our reaction.

My initial thought is: what am I supposed to do with a bunch of tennis-ball-sized pearls?

Then Thalia cries out. "Are those sea-horse eggs?"

"Very good," Felix says. "Though, without the father, about as useful as a paperweight. Pretty, nonetheless."

The only time I saw a sea horse, it wasn't the tiny curled things that fit in a fish tank. He was huge, greedy, and slick with a long snout and fins for ears. He had great forelegs with talons and a great tail that curled back into his spine as my grandfather, the Sea King, fed him. His name is Atticus, supposedly the last of his kind, and he belongs to Thalia.

I hand her the box, and the sheer happiness on her face makes the fox bite worth it.

"So…" I stand, holding out my hand for Felix to take. "Will you take us?"

Felix chuckles giddily. Suddenly I can picture him running around a ship searching for his Infinite Abyss. He makes sure his crates are locked and waves to us over his shoulder.

Wind blows through the tent flaps, carrying with it the chatter of the market and the sudden blare of instruments. Felix leads us out of the tent into the red glow of the sunset and the chime of the cathedral bells.

chapter SEVEN

"I wonder who it is," Kurt says, matching my pace beside me. "And how the champion could reach her if the two entrances are blocked."

"That's the end-of-the-world question."

We weave through the market crowd fairly unnoticed. A woman in a bright dress tries to pull me into the dancing in front of the church, but I pull away and keep my eyes on the road.

Felix walks with Thalia up ahead, probably discussing sea-horse eggs, behind a silent Layla and Gwen who take turns glancing over their shoulders at me.

Past the church, up the hill we go. I remember the jagged coast as we docked. Up close, the houses lean against each other for support. Everyone, it seems, is leaving their homes and heading to a celebration in the square. Couples holding hands. Families with their children. It all turns my stomach into knots. What if I'm too late?

"Why won't you tell us about her?" I ask abruptly. Despite Kurt being my ally, he's still such a mystery. I know that when their parents died, Kurt left Thalia at court. His journey brought him to this oracle who led him into slaying dragons to avenge his parents' deaths. Thalia said he's tight-lipped about it. Then he returned and resumed his life at court and in the guard until my grandfather charged him with my protection.

Kurt keeps his eyes on the road. "I told you what to gift her, didn't I?"

My hand goes to the bag of glittering rough-cut jewels in my pocket. "I mean, like what to expect."

"That I can't do."

"Why?"

"Because no two experiences are the same."

He goes quiet again. The more we climb the hill, the better view we have of the sunset, the ships waiting in the shadows of the dock, the white surf crashing against jagged rock.

"Here we are." Felix stops in front of beat-up double doors that belong to a saloon right out of a Western. "I ought to warn you. Do not offer nothing you won't want to part with, and that includes your personal limbs. Do *not* gamble with fishermen, unless you're seasoned, like yours truly. Most importantly, tip Reggie the barkeep. He's part troll and can have quite a temper on him."

"Are you not coming in?" Thalia asks.

Felix shakes his head. "Me wife's making meatballs."

I hold my hand out to him again. "I can't thank you enough."

Felix pats my hand, ready to go back to his regular life, to his wife, to a supper to come home to. I wonder if their conversation will start: "How was your day, dear?" Then I'll become a memory, the guy who saved him a few bucks on his inventory. That's what all of these things are, memories.

"Fair seas to you, my boy," he tells me.

My thoughts are all in knots going into the dimly lit Kraken's Tooth.

The walls are all brick, stacked together with black cement that oozes between the red. On the ceiling is a taxidermied beast. I wonder if it's the kraken the bar is named after. It's arresting, with giant tentacles frozen in great curls like it's crawling across the ceiling. The fury still captured in the creature's eye gives me the creeps, like it will unfreeze here and now and swallow us whole.

If I were him, I'd start on whoever is making that tinkering noise. I wouldn't exactly call it music. In the corner, a slender woman in a lace dress plays a makeshift piano. The keys are flat stones pulling on exposed rusty cords.

As we all file into the tavern, there's a shift in temperature. The coolness of the sunset is replaced by the humidity of bodies crammed into one place. Their emotions are raging, which adds to the queasiness in my gut. I prefer the super senses underwater, thanks.

Between the smells of beer sloshing in puddles on the creaky wooden floor, the sea salt and sweat that permeate these sailors' skins, lily-weed and bubbly sea mead, there's something else. I can't single it out and I start doing what no self-respecting New Yorker ever does—I stare.

I'm staring too long at the fishermen playing cards while drinking amber liquid from dirty, chipped glasses. They could use a bath or a shave or eyedrops because their eyes are so red. One with graying hair and skinny scars around his eye, like the points of a compass, stares back at me. He licks his ringed fingers, looks down to shuffle his cards, looks back up at me.

Gwen pulls me closer to the bar. "Get over here."

I pat my dagger for the familiarity of it.

Kurt walks the length of the room, searching for the same thing I am—great, big, glaring mermen with their entourages. So far, there are plenty of fishermen and wimpy young pirates trying to make out with some fairy girls, but no champions. He takes a barstool beside me. "They aren't here."

"Really?" I mutter. "I hadn't noticed."

A tiny part of me is glad. The knot tying my insides starts to loosen. What would I have even said to someone like Dylan if I saw him again? *Hey, good to see you? Say, I know we're both searching for the same trident pieces, but let's compare notes. Your family probably has* tons *of resources, while I have a group of friends who might kill each other before the night is over.*

"There *has* to be another way down," I say.

"You heard Felix," Layla counters. "The oracle police closed whatever entryway there was, and you blew up the other. Kurt, what do you think? You're the only one who's ever seen her."

Kurt contemplates this for a while. In our conspicuous cluster of barstools, he pinches his chin thoughtfully. "I-I don't know."

And there it is.

Kurt, my greatest source of *knowing*, says he, in fact, doesn't know.

Before I have time to wallow in my premature defeat, Gwen literally smacks me. "You're all looking at this wrong."

I rub the sting on my cheek. "Enlighten us, princess."

"So other champions are gallivanting around this goddess-forsaken cove of creatures that have nowhere to go? That doesn't mean they've found her. They don't seem to be trying very hard if they're seducing locals and showing up in this shabby hole."

"What are you suggesting we do?" Kurt's seething through his teeth. "*Sit* here awhile and make friends with the locals some more?"

Her smile is stunning, bright as the sun yet somehow still cold. "That's precisely what I mean. Your problem is that you've got a giant spear up your—"

"Gwen—"

"What I mean is, your approach to everything is to stab it. Tristan doesn't need that. His actions brought him to Felix, which brought us here. All the creatures on this cove are linked, the way we are on Toliss and at the Glass Castle. Let's see, *for a moment*, if there is anything worth finding out before we storm the city, shall we?"

"She's right," Thalia says quietly, sitting on the side where she's turning an opal egg between her hands.

That smell is driving me crazy. I thought I sensed it in the market, but I disregarded it as incense and smoke from the tents. I smack my hands on the bar top. "You guys can't tell me you don't smell that?"

"What's wrong?" Layla asks, pulling on my pinky the way she did when we were little. All, "Come on, Tristan, keep up."

"There's a certain scent—" I look to Kurt and Thalia. They should smell it too.

"I think it's the liquid freezing the kraken," Thalia says.

I close my eyes. Concentrate on singling it out. There's dew in the wood arches of the ceiling. It must have rained just before we got here. I find the smell of the chemicals in the beast above, but no, that's not it. There's the sweet burn of molasses from the greedy fishermen and lusting pirates. That's not it either. Maybe I'm imagining it.

"Never mind." I open my eyes again, wishing they wouldn't look at me as if I were seconds away from getting committed.

The tavern vibrates as Reggie, the half-man, half-troll barkeep, stomps from the far end of the bar to us. My head reaches his nipples, which are barely covered by a thick leather vest. And here I thought trolls were supposed to be little and hairy. I used to have tons, with their pointy tufts of multicolored hair and tiny jewels in their bellies. Actually, they were Layla's. Yeah, Layla's.

"You gonna order or sit there looking pretty for us?" says the troll man.

"Order," I say.

Reggie lines up glasses in front of us, doesn't ask what we want but starts pouring the familiar green bubbly. Except for Layla. He gives her something that smells like roses. Kurt takes some coins out of his pocket and lets them cluster on the table. Reggie scoops them up like jacks and weighs them in his sausage-y palm. Satisfied, he leaves us to our drinks.

"What the hell is this?" Layla asks. She sniffs the glass but doesn't take a sip. "Perfume?"

Thalia takes the flute glass from Layla's fingers. "It won't kill you."

"Milk of the rose," Gwen says, pursing her lips at our ignorance. "All the princesses like to drink it, of course. Better than the disgusting burping you get from sea mead." She arcs her back and snaps her fingers at the trollish bartender.

"What are you doing?" Layla whispers.

All we need is for Reggie to snap at us and we'll never get any information.

Gwen smirks with her pretty pink mouth. Reggie takes her in for a moment, and whatever he sees in her eyes, he seems to decide he doesn't want to argue with her. The movement, the command, the way he switches her drink without ever asking why. It's all impressive. It's so very Gwen.

I lean into her ear and whisper, "What did you do, bewitch him?"

She elbows me jokingly and says to us, "Sometimes you have to show your claws a bit. Try it."

"I don't have any claws," I say.

She glances back at the gambling fishermen, then back at me. "Grow some."

"Are you quite finished?" Kurt asks.

Gwen touches his nose with her fingertip. "You're no fun, Kurtomathetis."

"You're not helpful, Princess Gwenivere."

"Oh, many pardons, Kurtomathetis," she says, taking a dainty sip from the flute. "Best make myself helpful."

I don't even want to ask what she's doing. Gwen takes on a charm she hasn't shown any of us the past two days. Or ever.

"Reggie!" her voice is as delicate as crystal, rid of the dry edge she uses on Kurt.

I don't know anything about trolls, but now I know that when they blush,, they look like they're farting. His face is scrunched up, sinking into his shoulders. If he were a turtle, his neck would've popped back into his shell. He comes back to our side of the bar. "M-me?"

Layla rolls her eyes as Gwen reaches out a slender hand to lightly graze Reggie's hairy arm.

"Of course, you," Gwen says. "We were just looking for our friends. They might look like these strapping young men—" she nods to Kurt and me "—probably lascivious and followed by many, *many*, beautiful girls."

Okay, I get it. All the other champions have a bunch of princesses following them around, and I have Layla, Thalia, and Gwen. But I like it that way. I do.

Whatever she's said has broken the spell. Reggie stands up straight again. His face is stony, defensive, and pissed off. It's the same realization Felix had in his tent when he figured out we were merpeople without tails. Only, Reggie isn't quite as excited. It's the look of the owl-faced woman who shooed us away. Fazya's scorn.

"Yeah, they was here. Pain-in-my-asses."

Thalia snorts. "Plural?"

I stand in front of her and hold my arm out. "Were they really that bad?"

He thumbs at the beast of the ceiling. "Tried to take down Daisy up there."

Layla giggles. "You named your giant octopus Daisy?"

"She's a kraken! There's a difference, dontcha know? Was a right fine golden color when we caught her. Pity what the years is done to her." Then as if remembering why he was angry at us for being merpeople, he frowns again. "Thought it'd be *funny* to set it back in the wilds of the sea! Don't care for sea folk, I don't. Wreaking havoc all over the cove with their ships and tricksy *devil girls.*"

Gwen scoffs and Layla sniggers at the implication.

But Reggie's not done with the mer hate. I'm starting not to care for it, either. He looks down at my drink, which is untouched, then back at me. It's not *my* fault all the other merpeople didn't exactly behave.

I'm like, "Yes?"

He picks up my drink and sets it back down. "Not good enough for you?"

I can't handle my drink. Not even one, so I try not to do it. But I'm not about to tell Reggie the troll man that. "Just watching my carbs, dude."

He wants to smile but he doesn't. "Which one is you, then?"

"What do you mean?" I say, imitating polite Kurt as well as I can.

"Did I stutter? The champions. Which. One. Is. You?"

"What makes you think I'm one of the champions?" Though I can't help but puff out my chest and straighten my back. You better believe I'm a champion.

Now Reggie lets himself laugh. "Your ass reeks of your glittery mermaid shit." He spits on the floor.

Layla lets out a booming laugh, which no mermaid or merdude present wholly appreciates.

"I'm all mer*man*, Reggie." I start to point at him but think better of it. I think I'll need the use of my fingers in the future.

"How many?" Thalia asks sweetly at the same time Kurt briskly asks, "Do you know where they've gone?"

The troll man smiles with surprisingly perfect teeth. He shakes his head and busies himself drying chipped glassware. "You're all the same, you know. Mum always said the sea folk are responsible for their own downfall. Said your concern is about your secrets. That's what's important to you. In the end, the secrets are what's going to do you in."

My temperature rises. I haven't been a merman for very long, but no one dogs on my people. "Do you always listen to what your mom says?"

"It's why I'm still alive," he says proudly.

Just then we all start thinking of our mothers, or something, because we get real quiet. What did my mom say to me? She said she wasn't going to stop me from choosing this. She didn't exactly plead for me to stay home. Did she think I didn't have a choice? Maybe I remind her too much of the life she was trying to get away from. I think of her kind eyes. Her lullabies that sang me to sleep until I was too cool for it, and suddenly I don't mind this music so much.

Reggie scoffs at me and starts walking away, and I realize if my mom were here, she wouldn't be a dick to him. She'd be his friend. Like Gwen is doing now. Minus the flirting. I hope.

"Wait. I'm sorry." I reach over the bar to touch his hand.

Note: Trolls don't want their hands touched.

I retract it immediately.

"What is it, then?"

I push the drink away. "If I drink this, I'll pass out. Got any orange juice?"

That sends him rolling back with laughter. It booms above the hushed conversations, the makeshift piano, and the chorus of dogs barking outside. Reggie digs in a bin of ice and pours me a pulpy glass, which I chug thirstily. I wipe my sticky mouth with the back of my hand and set the glass on the bar top.

"So you're the mutt, then," Reggie says. "Shoulda guessed it. Human spirits dehydrate the sea folk. And sea spirits make humans hallucinate. I predict a life of weak beer ahead of you, Mermutt."

I shrug, not denying it. "I guess I am a mutt."

"So am I." He shoves a fat thumb into his chest, all *you bet I am.* "Got a special place in all three of me hearts for our kind."

Kurt's eyebrow cocks all the way up to his hairline. "Our kind?"

"Mutts. Halfsies. Neither here nor there, but everywhere. Call us what you will."

Kurt puts his hand on my shoulder, friendly. "He's not like the other champions, that's for sure."

"Cheers to that," Reggie says, raising a glass of brackish liquid. "The other, the serious one, he practically had a scavenger hunt with forty men looking like some lost army of conquistadors. Didn't realize you can't find her, the oracle."

"Because all the paths are sealed?" Thalia asks.

Reggie takes a big gulp of his weak beer. "'Cause she ain't wanting to be found. She has to find you."

Just then, something startles him. The smell I've been trying to figure surrounds us. All merfolk turn their faces up to the air as if we can suck it all in. The scent is lonely and thin and winding its way inside.

"Tears," Kurt whispers.

Reggie's large body shivers. He knocks on the bar top. Backs away slowly and tells me, "Fair seas to you."

The bit of white at the corner of my eye sends my heart jumping. At the door it's just a girl. She's so translucent that, for a heartbeat, I wonder if this is my first time seeing a ghost. There's a rawness at the corners of her eyes and under her nose, like all she does is cry. I've never felt this way before, like she's rubbing her sadness all over my skin. Kurt's right: she smells like tears. Something inside me is twisting, changing slowly. There's a wonky bit of glass across from me. It's cloudy and speckled, but I can see myself in there somewhere and that in itself is a relief.

Like Reggie, the patrons that glance at her busy themselves with pretending she's not there. Others tap crosses over themselves. One man covers his ears and leans his forehead on the table.

She's staring at Kurt.

I nudge him. "Friend of yours?"

"Not at all."

When the girl in white turns around, she exposes the white ripple of her vertebrae, the blue spiderweb of veins. She looks back over her shoulder once.

"Think she wants us to follow her?" I say.

"She will lead us to the oracle," Kurt says, taking one foot toward the door.

"Or, with our luck, to a dark pit of despair."

He's trying to compose himself, leveling violet eyes at my blue ones. "You heard the barkeep. She will come for you. I will be by your side."

"Right. Time to grow some claws." I draw out my dagger. Then I remember the girls. "I don't think we should leave them alone here."

Gwen pounces off her chair. "Hardly. We can take care of ourselves." She holds my face in her hands so I can feel a tiny electric hum that threatens to fry my face off.

"Okay, I get it." I take a step back.

"We must go *now*," Kurt says.

Beside me I can feel Layla's heartbeat racing, the panic in the way she balls her fists. Kurt grabs my shoulder and pulls me to the door. This is why I'm here. This is what we've been waiting for.

"We'll meet back here," I say to everyone, but I'm looking at Layla.

Hers is the face I take with me as I follow the faint smell of tears and this girl dressed in white around another dark corner.

chapter EIGHT

For a girl her size, she runs fast.

Kurt and I are head to head, eyes straight up the narrow hill as if we're climbing to the heavens.

"What does she look like?"

"I suppose she looks like a ghost," Kurt says.

"The oracle, smart-ass!"

He glances at me but doesn't say a word. Why would he think he had to hide a girl from me? If there's a guy you want giving advice on girls, it's me. Or…it used to be me. I've gotten girlfriends for all my friends at one time or another. So why can't I keep my own?

The sky is clouding over in fat, black and gray tufts. The row of slanted buildings is an echo of slammed doors and shutters. The girl makes a quick left into a skinny unlit alleyway.

I stop running.

"Why are you stopping?" Kurt bumps into me. "We'll lose her!"

"I don't know, man." I bend down and squeeze my thigh muscles. "What if she's, you know, evil?"

"She's not evil. She's one of the oracle's handmaidens."

"You said you didn't know her."

His violet eyes are like beams against the shadow cast by the slanted alley walls.

He says, "When you found the oracle in Central Park, she had women with her, yes?"

"Fairies. But—"

"All the oracles do. They're protected by other women."

"Fine. But if she tries to eat your head off, I'll let her."

We shuffle sideways into the narrow path. The stones are cold and slick with moss, the cobblestones like walking on crooked teeth. When we reach the end of the path, the high walls form a circle around a well. The girl in white hops up on the edge.

"Oh, *hell* no." My first reaction is to take a step back. Really, truly, the bravest thing I've ever done. "Don't you people have clean and sunny passageways? Something with palm trees and girls who don't look like Jack Skellington? It's the goddamn rabbit down the goddamn well."

She looks down the well, then back up at us. Her white dress hangs on her bony shoulders like on a coat hanger. Her lips are blue. If this is how the oracle keeps her, then the oracle is not someone I'm dying to meet.

"Why won't you speak?" I ask.

She taps her stick-skinny fingers on her throat. She gives me a smile that makes me cold all over before taking one step forward and vanishing down the black hole. I move to follow her.

Kurt smacks a hand on my chest. "I'll go first."

"No, your part is done. Go back to the others." When I say it, the path behind us shifts. The brick walls close in on themselves. When I look up, the sky is a dark speck at the end of a narrow tunnel. "Or not."

For the first time since I've met him, Kurt seems unsure of himself. It's in the way he presses against the walls closing in on us. "If this is a trick, I should go first."

I wave my weapon in the air. "Hi, supernatural dagger here? We don't know how deep this goes. How will you signal me? I'm the king's champion. I should be the one to go first."

He grumbles and tightens the leather strap around his waist. "And the king named me your guardian. Let me dive first. If only to preserve the customs you are so haphazardly breaking."

I gesture at the well. "Lead me to my premature death."

And he does.

Down the well.

The blackness swallows him in a second. I look up to the bit of sky above, the hovering clouds. I tap my forehead the way Kurt does, just in case. I take a step and let the mouth of the well swallow me whole.

This one time, the team got the inspiration to go skinny-dipping on Valentine's Day. It was freshman year and pretty much the coldest winter I can remember. Your nose would turn red and runny the second you stepped out into the street.

I wasn't sure the guys would go for it. The cold doesn't exactly do the most flattering thing to us, but I reminded them that the girls would want to huddle up when they got cold. They called me crazy but did it anyway. Before I jumped, I didn't feel cold. Even standing on the pier in my boxers, peeling off my socks, I wasn't shaking like the others. The shock of the dive took my breath away for a second. I think I even liked it because I lasted the longest and the guys were pissed at me for showing off.

They wouldn't call me a show-off now.

Here in the well, the freezing water wraps around me even before I hit the water. I tense my body as narrowly as I can, just like passing through a tube at a water park, switching the slippery plastic for brick. I am colder than cold. Colder than getting locked in the school's refrigerator as a prank. So cold my gills won't open and I choke when I inhale.

When I shut my eyes, I see a woman's face. The memory pushes its way so deep inside me that it feels real. She's golden against the sun. I'm a child in her arms. She brushes my hair away from my face and stares with violet eyes. I can feel her warm breath, smell sea and lilacs, and even though I *know* this memory isn't mine, it shakes the cold away. I can breathe and see again.

The rough brick passage is gone, replaced by thousands of soft and slick tiny tentacles. They tickle my face, grab at my hair. Their suction cups suck hard on my skin, leaving slimy white circles. I'm breathing hard.

Then the foreign memory of the woman is back. Not like the last vision. This one comes from a different mind. Her hair is pulled to the side and this time she's under me. I love her. The kind of love that makes the heart clench like a fist, that makes you want to part seas, stay above clouds. I bring my whole body down against her, and then she's gone, replaced by a flood of others.

The tentacles suck harder on my skin, and I realize this is where those memories are coming from. I see a girl in a white robe running from an army. A man diving off a cliff. The sorrow of thousands. The joys of few. The feelings permeate my body until all I can do is scratch my skin raw.

I'm about to scream, but the well spits us out into the shallow stream of a cave. I tumble onto Kurt who covers his face with his hands. I wonder if we saw the same things. Felt the same things.

I choke. "What was that?"

"I don't know. I—"

My muscles feel like rubber. The first time I try to push myself up, I fall back down, so I just roll over and crawl onto the cool rock. Something steel and sharp pokes my arm. "Kurt?"

In the darkness of the cave, we don't hear them waiting for us. Their steps are soundless as they circle us. Fire sizzles from a torch held by the mute girl in white who led us here. At least, it could be. The girl now jabbing a spear at my ribs looks just like her and the rest—pale, skinny, blue at the mouth, and with big gaping eyes as if all the lights in the house are on but no one is home.

Kurt and I stand back to back. He whispers, "I'm sorry."

"Remember when I said I'd let them eat your head off?"

The girl with the torch, the one who led us here, takes a step forward from their circle, right up to my face.

I try to smile. "Hey, we're the good guys, remember?"

She cocks her head, confused.

"I'm Tristan Hart. My grandfather is the Sea King."

"*Was* the Sea King." Her voice fills the cave, but her lips don't move. "You are here because you want to take his place."

"And who the hell are you? You didn't mind us so much when you came to get me at the tavern."

Her pale eyebrow arcs. "You have a foolish tongue."

"At least I have a tongue."

The spear digs into my skin a little bit more.

"You are the laria, aren't you?" Kurt says quickly. "We are here for the oracle."

The voice laughs. "He is. But why are you here, Kurtomathetis?"

"How did you know his name? What the hell is a laria?"

In unison their harmony fills my head. "We are the laria, maidens of the oracle, protectors of the Well of Memories."

"I've been here before," Kurt says, "and I didn't see any of you."

"She did not want us to be seen," the girl says.

"Okay, then. You came to get me. So why won't you let me pass?"

Their laughter is a chorus. The girl with the torch steps closer to me. Unmoving, endless black eyes. "I wasn't there to find you. I was fetching our supper."

My fingers itch for my dagger. If I'm fast enough, I can pull the spear poking me and knock her back with a hit in the chest. If I'm not fast enough, I'll be a sashimi kabob.

"Prove to me you are the king's heir," she says.

"Call off your girls and I'll show you."

They step back in their lithe ballet movements. I reach behind my shoulder and draw the quartz scepter. Now would be a really good time for it to spark or light up or do *anything*. And it does. Its soft glow is too bright for some of their eyes and they look away. Except the girl with the torch. She isn't afraid of me. I think she wants to eat me.

In a swift movement, she draws out a tiny blade and takes a swipe at my belt. The bag of jewels falls to the ground and into the stream where they wink as they get carried downstream. Some of the girls cluster to pick them up, smiling at the precious things in their palms. The girl with the torch stares at the other girls with distaste, but she lets them.

Kurt scratches his head. He picks up a ruby from the stream and squeezes it in his palm.

I ask the question I read on his scrunched-up merman face. "Why'd you do that?"

"You won't be needing them." She points her torch south into the blackest part of the cave, and we follow her deeper and deeper into the dark.

chapter NINE

The cave is smooth rose stone. Round pools light the entire ground. Down here, the energy crackles in and around me. Traces of others who've passed through here linger in the air. But the emotion is a fraction of what I felt coming down the well. Kurt whispers, "According to legend, the laria feed on the memories of men." I wonder which of my memories are mingled in with the others.

"Mind the floors," Kurt says. "The pools are chambers of eternal sleep. Only the oracle can release you once you've plunged in."

In one of the occupied pools, a girl's hair floats up to the surface like weeds. I wonder why she's down there. What is she running from that would make her want to do this? I tell myself that I want to remember all of my life, no matter what happens.

At the end of the cave is a great basin made of polished moonstone. A tiny waterfall fills it, and the runoff trickles into skinny rivers that line the grounds. "Pretty sweet Jacuzzi."

Kurt elbows me in the ribs. "*Shh.*"

I want to tell him to chill out, though my insides are as uneasy as the tremble in my legs. I miss Shelly's pond in Central Park. The bright Thumbelina-sized fairy maidens that blew me kisses. Even Shelly's kind, wrinkly face.

Then, she emerges.

Her movements are slow and delicate, like a doll coming to life. Wondrous and strange, from the belly up she's so *pink*. Her eyes are like the blush of new roses. Her smooth, naked torso is obscured by powder-pink hair tumbling down to the water. At her hips, she disappears into a giant, golden nautilus shell. I wonder how she bends her legs to fit. Maybe she doesn't have any legs.

"Surely you've seen creatures more wondrous than me on your travels, Tristan Hart." Her voice… Her voice is achingly lovely. Every word fills me with a peace I haven't felt in so long. I want to put a smile on her sad face.

"No, ma'am." I know I sound dreamy, but I feel very, very good.

She turns a fraction, setting pink jeweled eyes on Kurt, and I suddenly hate it. I want her to keep looking at me. "Surprised to see me, Kurtomathetis?"

"You're not Lucine." His words are steeped in disappointment and hurt, but when I wait for him to turn to me and explain, all he can do is stare at the nautilus maid.

"Come forward," she tells him.

And he does it. Kurt, the most logical guy I've ever met, goes to her without even thinking. It happens slowly, the brush of his feet on the ground, then all at once, into a memory pool with a heavy splash. The space is narrow but he manages to lift one hand to punch against the force containing him until he stops moving and finally sleeps.

"Why'd you do that?"

"Because I don't *need* him, that's why."

Somewhere in my mind I know she's wrong. But here I am, agreeing with everything she says.

"Your girl," I say. My tongue is like wet cotton in my mouth. "I had something for you and she took it."

"I've no use for trinkets."

"But I have nothing else." I sound whiny. I don't want to sound whiny, but I do. It's like I'm complaining to my mom. I miss my mom. My bed. My friends. I want to sleep like Kurt. Then the cave whispers, and I snap awake.

Her voice is like a trail, and I follow it around the danger of the sleeping chambers and right up to her basin where she finger-combs her hair. "I know something you can give me."

The cave dims. We're alone. She dips her fingers in the water around her. There's that smile, brilliant as dawn. When she looks back up at me, her eyes glow with eager newness. I wonder what happened to her legs, then I study her face—the slope of her nose, the bow of her mouth—she's the most beautiful thing I've ever seen.

Second. *Second most beautiful—but I can't remember who the first is.*

"Why was he surprised to see you?" I ask.

"You mean why am I here?" Her smile is strained. I can tell

she doesn't do that very often. "You mean how could I possibly be stuck in this cave on an island full of degenerates? I don't belong here. I belong in Eternity. Eternity is my home. But my sisters and I, we are all shifting, moving, breaking, like the plates beneath us. We're moving like we're intended to. I must be here and now for you. In the Well of Memories."

I rub my face. *Wake up, Tristan.* "I saw things that weren't mine to remember."

"When you go down the well, you leave traces of yourself behind. Don't make that face. You aren't losing anything. Only now I know your mind as well. From kings and heroes to lost boys and girls, they all leave their memories here. The water is impregnated with the past. The oracle is the keeper of the well."

"What do they get in return?"

"Unburdening of the soul. Reflection. If they're lucky, perhaps insight to the future."

"And what do you want from me?"

She sets her delicate hands on the smooth gold shell. Moves her hair all to one side, exposing herself to me. "I want you to come closer."

"So you can stick me in a memory hole?"

"So I can look into your eyes."

There's pressure at the base of my neck, a force that pushes me right to her until we're eye to eye. It's like wading through hip-high water while wearing ankle weights. Her rose irises are as hard as jewels. I can see flashes of lightning, the ground tearing like an open wound, seas whirling, beasts rising from the depths. I shut my eyes against it, but that's no help. It's in me—the uproar, the turmoil. The sky rips apart.

Then it's quiet again. I keep my eyes shut and I'm surrounded by the sea. Behind me is Coney Island. I'm undressing and Layla is laughing, holding her hands to her closed eyes. It's the first time I let her see me shift into my tail. I let her climb on my back and suddenly I flip her over. She wraps her legs around me and we fall back into the water, kissing.

I'm not prepared for the ragged chuckle that wakes me.

"What's so funny?" I ask the oracle. Closer like this, I can finally see that the deformity of her legs starts at the hip. The skin has rough grooves as if the skin were burned.

"Even after everything you've seen, everything you are, your most powerful memory comes from a girl?"

The pressure around me is released some. I scratch at my scalp where my skin tingles. It's like she was digging her fingers into me without actually touching me. "Damn, you people are creepy."

"I'm not people, Tristan. I am eternal. I am the sky that blankets you. The sea that is your home. I am the ether between your dreams. So call me anything you'd like, but don't call me 'people.' I am better than that."

"Your top half is pretty people-looking."

"This is just a body. We are modeled by our makers. As you can see, my maker didn't want me going far." She pats the smooth shell that holds her.

"Well, if you don't want anything material, then what can I give you? I'm kind of in a time crunch. Championship and all."

The smile that plays on her lips sends a tingle down my spine all the way to my toenails. Think of anything else. Think of Kurt stuck in that tube with nowhere to go. Man, he's going to be pissed when I get him out of there.

"I will give you a choice. You can give me a memory or make me a promise."

"What do you mean *a memory*?"

"The one of you and the girl. It's been so long since I've experienced that kind of happiness from any memory."

My heart is racing. My first real kiss with Layla. "Like, you borrow it?"

"No, stupid boy. It'll be my memory. Mine to keep. Mine to cherish. It doesn't do you any good. Human love doesn't last. All you'll have left are hazy images. You hoard them in the corners of your mind and they stop you from living. No, it'll better be kept with me."

My ears are hot. She doesn't know the half of it. With the way things are between us, it's the only thing I have of Layla. Memories. If I have to leave her—no. I won't think that way. But something snakes its way into my thoughts telling me I will have to leave her; I will have to go. Even though I know I don't want to, I have to blurt out: "*Promise.* I choose the promise."

She frowns, the frown of longing. Maybe I've chosen the wrong thing. But she recovers and calls out, "Mina!"

The laria who led us here emerges from a dark corner. I make note that she never really left. Mina carries a conch shell. It's the size of a basketball with golden patterns. Then I feel the sting of a knife slashing my arm.

"What the—"

"Words are so willingly spewed, like water from the mouth of a gorge. Blood, when taken, means so much more."

Mina hands the conch with my droplets of blood to the nautilus maid, who accepts it, cradling it against her belly. She brings it to her lips and drinks from it.

"You will swear to me that the next time we meet, you will kill me." Her voice is so alive, grazing my skin, nuzzling a warmth against my neck. I haven't felt this way in so long, and I don't want it to stop.

I can't do that, says a whisper in the blackness of my mind. But it's like shutting the door of a dream, and the whisper is gone.

"Swear," the oracle repeats.

"I swear."

Mina brings the conch to my lips and tilts it back. The copper drops coat my tongue. They roll down my throat, burning all the way down.

The nautilus maid sighs, filling the cave with a new breeze. A cloud is lifting over me. The pressure completely dissipates from my muscles. It's like waking up from a long sleep.

"You can't do that." I spit on the ground. The burning taste lingers. "I can't kill you!"

"Haven't you ever killed anyone before?"

The memory of Ryan landing splat on the ground, dead, rushes into my mind. "Stop it! Stop doing that! I didn't kill Ryan." There. I've said it.

"Will it make it easier if you remember that I'm not a person?"

"You're immortal."

"I'm eternal. There's a difference. The gods are immortal. They can't be harmed. But this? I'm only skin and bones. If no one touched me, I could live forever. "

No matter what she says about not being a person, all I can see is the blush of her skin, the sadness in her eyes. People have emotions. I shake my head. "I won't do it."

"Say no all you want. The promise is sealed with our blood. If you don't do it, you will be the one to die."

I want to scream. I unsheathe my dagger and stab it in the ground. Sparks fly as it cuts a shallow wound into the stone.

"Believe me, Tristan, it will be for the best."

"If you want to die so badly, why don't you just kill yourself? Have one of your laria do it."

"It has to be you."

My whole body is shaking. I turn my back on her. "Give me Kurt and give me the trident piece and pray, just pray that we never meet again."

Her smile is sad but pleased, as if she's the cleverest thing in the world. It feels like she's set me on fire when she says, "My darling Tristan Hart, I do not have any piece of the trident. But you may take your companion, for soon the day will come when you will no longer call him that."

The blood in my mouth makes me want to retch.

The pool holding Kurt splashes like a geyser. Kurt chokes on some water. His hands grope at the ground until he grabs my hands and I pull him out. He holds on to my neck for support, reclaiming the use of his legs.

"Mina will show you the way out." The nautilus maid turns to look at me once more before retreating behind her waterfall. "And don't forget, Tristan. Don't forget me."

chapter TEN

The moon hangs low over the Vanishing Cove, the sky speckled with stars I've never been able to see in Coney Island. The church bells ring in the distance. The drumbeats and singing and laughter are replaced by the rush of wind and the creak of old houses.

I don't know how we got back here. We took a tunnel that led out onto the main road, back downhill the way we came. When we turned around, Mina was long gone, along with any signs of the door that slammed shut behind us.

I punch open the doors to the Kraken's Tooth. It settles a silence over the remaining patrons, who shrink from me.

Layla's the first one to ask, "What happened?"

The girls have moved from the bar and are sitting at their own card game.

"It didn't go very well." I pull up a chair.

I try to give her a look that says, Not now. Not here. But right now the only expression I can manage is anger. How can I tell my friends that I got manipulated by the oracle? Did the nautilus maid think I was weak? Too weak to give up a simple memory of a kiss?

Thalia places a hand on my knee and offers me a smile.

I point at the card game and the mess of things collected at the center—gold coins, a pack of cigarettes, rusted gold rings, a jar of pickled frogs, and a small barrel labeled "Wind." I pick up the barrel, and Thalia warns, "Don't let it out! We need that to get back home."

I set it back on the table. "Is this all your winnings?"

Gwen, who's been studying my face, thumbs at Layla. "This one here took the pirates for everything they were worth."

Layla reluctantly smiles at Gwen. "Tristan taught me."

I dip my head in a little bow. "This place really cleared out. What time is it?"

"Nine," Thalia says. "Reggie says there's a curfew. Says too many strangers have been appearing. Not just the champions. Ships seeking refuge from terrible monsters out at sea."

Reggie rings a shrill bell. I cover my ears to stop my head from pounding. "Go on, you festering sores. Last call."

The remaining stragglers get up and stumble out into the night. Reggie gives the girls a black sack to throw all their loot in. Kurt shoulders it and I want to ask if merpeople have a Santa Claus, but the words just won't come out.

I get up and lean against the bar. "Bit early, even for a curfew."

"Mayor's orders. Nine p.m., we start closing up shops." Reggie takes a sip from his mug. "Ten p.m., everyone in their beds until further notice. For everyone's safety. Last week, we had an attack.

Came in the dead of night. The night men that keep watch couldn't get a good look at them. They were searching for something. When they couldn't find it, they tore apart whatever they could. Tried to get into the cathedral as well, but we've got our own protection for that."

"The entrance to the oracle was through there," I say. "Wasn't it?"

Reggie nods once but doesn't elaborate. Gwen pushes the double doors open, letting in the cold.

"Best if you get back to your ship." The troll man salutes me. "Fair seas to you, Mermutt."

The farther we get down the hill, the darker the town gets. The yellow glow of the street lamps casts long shadows. I see faces where there aren't any and hear whispers that shouldn't be there. I wonder if it's the lingering effect of the well memories. I concentrate on the cobblestones beneath my feet. The coolness of the stone. The daylight hours away. Hands, warm small hands, grab onto mine and squeeze. She leans her head against my arm, and for a terrible moment, I realize I'll keep my promise to the nautilus maid just for this.

"Is that fire?" Thalia breaks into a jog.

Layla and I drop hands and sprint ahead. We follow the light of the moon on the water and the crosshatch of lit apartments until the pier comes into view. Our ship is bobbing in the wind alone. A blue flame crackles in the crow's next.

"Where are the other ships?"

"Where's Arion?" Thalia yells.

It's too dark to see where his ropes lead, but Arion is missing from the masthead. Our footsteps are a stampede down the pier and onto the ramp. The deck is empty. "Blue?" I unsheathe my dagger and it hums frantically in my hand. "Arion?"

"There's no one here," Gwen says.

"That's not possible." Kurt throws the black bag over his shoulder and onto the deck. "Arion can't leave the ship."

In the wind I pick up the smell of the oil feeding the small lantern flame atop the mast. The ramp connecting us to the dock splashes into the water. The sails billow like clouds against the wind and I fall back, nearly toppling overboard.

Red claws snap at me. A merrow is climbing up the side. Its face is all teeth and red gums chomping at the air. It levels up to me and takes a snap at my face. I swing my dagger out, cleaving its head right off. Black blood oozes all over me, and before the merrow can decompose, I push it overboard.

We form a circle at the center of the deck. The Vanishing Cove is a dark mound in the distance.

With the dying wind, I can smell them perfectly. Dirt and decay and death and the stink of rotting fish. They're climbing over the sides of the ship, waiting along the ledges, merrows and mermen alike.

Kurt's shoulders are right against mine. "Twelve, I think."

I shake my head. A figure steps forward from the shadows. "Make that thirteen."

Number 13 towers over all of them. If not for the fin-like ears, I'd say he was a merman. But with the scars that cover his bare chest and shoulders in rough patches, the tan of his scaly skin, and the dorsal-like ridges that form a Mohawk down his bald head, he's a merrow—and he's holding Arion with a jagged knife at his throat.

Arion's face is red with fury. His fists are white and, more importantly, powerless in helping him defend himself. My dagger hums with frantic energy matching the rush of adrenaline that makes my knees shake. I take a step forward but the giant merrow holds out a careful finger at me.

"Now, now," Number 13 says. They've never spoken before. It's always been sharp teeth and flying fists. "Would you believe me if I told you I mean you no harm?"

"Would you believe me if I said 'no'?"

"Mother told me you were funny." His high cheekbones are pronounced when he smiles. "The only difference is that I mean you no harm tonight, in this moment. I was seeking another ship. But when I recognized this prisoner here," he gives Arion's neck a squeeze, "I couldn't resist meeting you in person."

"Let my captain go and come meet me." My heart is booming in my chest. Kurt catches my eye. I know he doesn't want me to throw the first punch. We're severely outnumbered and the merrows are getting smarter. At least, this one is.

"As you like," Number 13 says. "He isn't going anywhere any time soon."

He throws Arion overboard, and the captain grasps at the air as if his ropes are failing him. A loud *thud* echoes when he hits the side of the ship, then hangs slack.

"Who the *hell* are you?" I ask.

"So small. So feisty." Before I can counter with another insult, he continues, "My mother calls me Archer. I am the voice of my brothers. Our condition makes it so most of us can't communicate the way *normal* sea folk can. Then again, we are not normal sea folk. We are stronger. Better. Our mother nurtured us, took care of us when your kingdom threw us away like driftwood."

Kurt spits on the floor. "You're a fool. You can no more trust the silver witch than the eye of a storm."

Archer cocks his head to the side. His men encircling us are getting restless, but with one hand motion from him, they stop shuffling. "I've heard of you, Kurtomathetis. Such beauty, wasted in the end."

At the threat, Thalia tries to step forward but Gwen holds her back.

"Not that this isn't fun for all of us," I say. "I mean, I love meeting new people. But we have places to go. I'll thank you to get off my ship."

"I thought you were the civilized one, being human *and* merkin. I knew the rumors of your greatness were exaggerated. Believe me, I will feel your spine crumble in my fist."

I smirk. "I thought you were here to be my friend."

Archer takes another step toward me. He's a good foot taller. His fists are calloused, and his teeth are rows of perfect canines.

"No," he says. "I don't want to be your friend. My mother says we are not to hurt you."

"Why?" Nieve, the silver mermaid, the *itch* in my veins I can't scratch.

"Because we are to be brothers." Archer holds his blade forward, pointing it at Kurt. "I can't say the same for your shipmates." His eyes fall on Layla. Her breath catches in her throat as she takes a shaky step back against me. He breathes her in. "She smells divine. Mother would like her."

Then he reaches out a hand for her, keeping his eyes on me the whole time, and I do exactly what he's been waiting for.

I throw the first punch.

chapter ELEVEN

Forget Nieve.

Forget the throne.

Forget the oracle that tricked me into a promise I don't want to keep. Forget Kurt shouting my name to stand back.

When I throw the first punch at Archer, I lose myself. Hell, it doesn't even hurt him. Not the way it hurts me. It's like hitting cement, and even though the pain hasn't hit me yet, sticky blood drips from my knuckles.

The shouting starts instantly, along with swords clashing, wood splintering, and bodies splashing.

Archer said he doesn't want to hurt me. Though I have a hard time believing him exactly, all he does is grin. He breathes in the rage, the adrenaline.

I'm not ready for the blow he reciprocates with. I fly across the deck. Right smack against the side of the ship. My head spins, and my shoulder makes a loud crunch. I scramble for my dagger with a trembling hand, and despite the black spots floating in my vision, I get back up.

To my right, Thalia attacks a red merrow with a shark fin on the back of his head. She fakes to his left and jumps on his back, straddling like a horse. She's this wild thing, bringing down her daggers into his back until the hilts won't let them go any deeper. Planting one foot on his spine, she kicks. He slides off like butter, breaking down the way they do into oozy black blood and sinew.

She holds out her hand, and despite how small she is, she pulls me right up. "Where's Archer?"

He's gone from the deck but I know he's still there somewhere. One of them lunges at Thalia, but I block his arm and drive my dagger deep into his solar plexus. I hold my breath from the retch snaking its way up my throat.

"Brother!" Thalia shouts, but she's blocked again. "I've got this, Tristan. Help him!"

Kurt is wrestling with a merman and a merrow. The merrow, like Archer, is more human looking than the others I've encountered, except for his shark-like face. The merman is covered in tattoos. A trident is tattooed on his chest, and a nasty scar runs from his clavicle to his belly button, as if he was gutted and then put back together. He's fast. Faster than even Kurt, the way he uses the edge of his hands to deliver crosshatch hits until he's got Kurt in a master lock while Shark Face sucker-punches him in the gut.

I tap Shark Face on the shoulder, and when he turns around, I bash the hilt of the dagger in his eye. He makes a terrible sound, cupping the nasty black blood pouring down his face. Something the nautilus maid said bugs me. *Would it make it easier if you didn't think of me as people?* Bad time to feel her freaky vibes in my head, but Shark Face doesn't even come after me. He's going back after Kurt.

My hands are shaking. I don't like killing anything. Not merrows, not mermen. I hated it in elementary school when Angelo used his BB gun to kill squirrels. But if I don't do it, my friends are going to keep dying. I grab Shark Face around the throat in a nelson, and from behind me, Layla screams, pushing her sword into his chest. It takes her two tries to get it through to the back.

I can feel the tip of her blade as the merrow breaks down all over me, a hand still grabbing onto my wrist. "That was too close," I say.

She smiles, wiping the black ooze from her cheeks.

I pull the merrow's hand off my wrist and throw it at the merman fighting Kurt. He turns around, eyes glowing like headlights. "You're lucky, prince."

"And why's that?"

"Because no one is to lay a finger on you."

That's enough of a distraction for Kurt to kick the breath out of him. Kurt lifts his sword over the merman's head. Kurt's breath catches and he hesitates, just for a moment but I can see it. He drives the sword right through the merman's back, and the merman turns to a slopping pile of foam.

Behind Kurt, Archer shows himself again. He's crouching on the edge of the ship, one hand under his chin. He's studying us, smiling the whole time.

There's a bang on the other end of the deck, and its force knocks me forward into Kurt. Fishy chunks of merrow spray everywhere. We scramble to Gwen, who is fending off the last merman in Archer's troupe. He's so tatted up that there isn't any bare flesh except for his face. He's holding his knife right over her, execution style.

I reach out with my dagger, but Archer's hand clamps down on the merman's neck with a powerful squeeze. The merman strangles, eyes peeled back and body shaking until Archer's fist is full of surf and air.

An arrow falls to the floor, and I realize Archer's grip wasn't what killed him. Someone shot him.

"You've fought well tonight." Archer runs to the ledge of the ship. "But soon our numbers will span the entire sea, and you, brother, will join our cause."

"We shouldn't let him get away," Thalia says, craning over the ledge. "We can swim to him."

I hold my hand out. "If that's what he wants, he'll have a whole lot more of these guys waiting for us."

Kurt picks up the foreign arrow and examines it. "Cedarwood. Gold leaf. Golden spearhead. *Ouch*. It's very sharp."

"You didn't shoot?" I look to Thalia.

"I couldn't reach my bow in time." She holds up her daggers in her hands.

"Then where the hell did it come from?"

The unanswered question settles over us. We reform our circle, careful of the shifting shadows along our ship. There's the rustle of water, the flapping of loose sails, the creaking of the old wood swelling against the sea, and the extra loud thumping of Layla's purely human heart.

"We know you're there," I warn.

"Easy now," he says, stepping forward.

His hands are raised, holding up his bow. Even in the dark, I recognize him instantly. Brendan, champion of the West. Starlight gives a coppery sheen to his bright red hair. His clothes look like he had a fight with a big pair of scissors.

Though the only time I met him was for a brief hello at Toliss Island during the presentation of the champions, Brendan runs down the steps and pulls me into a strangling man-hug. "It's good to see you too, Cousin Tristan."

chapter TWELVE

Brendan and I huddle around Arion on the quarterdeck.

We insist on dressing the cut on his shoulder with the muddy gunk Blue used on my knuckles. It stings like hell, but Arion doesn't twitch.

"How's that?" I say, slathering it on with a patch of seaweed.

"Don't worry about me, Master Tristan," Arion says. "I've been through worse."

"That's not the point." I wipe my hands on a dirty rag. "You should have been able to defend yourself properly."

"A hundred years ago," Arion says, tugging slightly on the ropes at his hands, "I would've gutted that Archer like the beast he is."

I spit out a nasty chunk of meat stuck in my teeth.

"I don't want to think about what you might have swallowed during that battle," Brendan says. "If I told my father of this, he wouldn't believe me."

From a leather pouch slung on his belt, Brendan pulls out a long, hand-rolled cigarette. When he lights it, I recognize the smell as lily flower. Even when his father was presenting him in front of the court, hands in the air, Brendan didn't strike me as the serious type. Not like Elias. Not like Adaro.

"How bad is the damage to the ship?" I ask.

Arion points to the sails. "The main sail's been cut and some of the ropes burned. Nothing the urchins and I can't fix."

"There's also this," I say, digging through the bag of loot we managed to salvage. "The girls won this at the tavern. From the look on your face, I can tell you know what this is."

Arion takes the barrel in his calloused hands. He beats his knuckle on the wood. "Aye."

"Great," I say. "What is it?"

Brendan laughs. "It's potted wind, cousin. Young demigods make a trade of their gifts. Sell a bit of rain to a city with drought. That sort of thing."

"With this," Arion says, "we could return to Coney Island waters by morning. It will suck the air right out of the skies, leaving other ships stranded."

Arion excuses himself to adjust the sails, taking the barrel with him.

"Wish I'd gotten here sooner," Brendan says between puffs. "My crew was too far away when I saw the commotion. Arion here noticed me and pulled me up just in time."

"And you came alone?"

Brendan pats himself on his chest like *No big deal.* "Don't be fooled. I'm a lot more ruthless than I'd like to admit. Besides, your mermaids here have bigger cockleshells than half the boys of my court. You wouldn't *believe* the guppies I ended up with."

I think of the last two days. The snide comments, the sword fighting, the death threats. And still, I wouldn't trade them for a ship full of heavily armed mermen. "Yeah, my crew's *all right*."

Brendan hoists himself on the ledge with one leg up. With his cigarette hand, he points down to where my friends are gathered on the clean deck around a toasty fire. I've never had a cousin before. It makes me feel cool. This is my cousin Brendan with the killer bow and arrows. He smokes lily flower. Awesome hair runs in the family.

"Is that the girl that swam against Elias?" he holds onto his stomach, laughing. "You must truly have Grandfather's charm to get those two following you. Layla, was that her name? Exquisite. Those eyes, like melting amber. But surely I don't have to tell you that."

As if she knows we're talking about her, Layla sends her death-beam stare at me.

"Yeah. Too bad she can't decide if she wants to punch me or kiss me."

"Lucky bastard." Brendan punches my shoulder. "Those are the best kind. Keeps it fresh. Don't you find the princesses boring? After a while it's like, I don't care how many shipwrecks you've single-handedly created this year."

"Gwen's okay, I guess."

He gives me a funny smile, all "Are you serious?" "You mean you haven't been with the other princesses that showed up to your court?"

"Dude, I don't have a court. I have a high-school infestation."

"I have no idea what that means." He flicks the butt into the sea and lights the next one. "As we speak, I have twenty princesses on my ship."

"Twenty?"

"It's a big ship." He smirks. "How do you think I knew to come here?"

I'm not keeping up. "One of the princesses told you there was an oracle here?"

"Not exactly. I was after something else. My own personal quest." He presses his finger to his lips. "Don't tell the others."

"Sure, sure. But how exactly do the princesses help you?"

He's studying me as if I'm a totally new species, which I suppose, in the end, I am.

"It's part of the championship. Beautiful gems from the most powerful families. Some, completely clueless. Others, with surprising skills, like star charting. Did Kurtomathetis not tell you? They can get out of hand when ignored. You know mermaids."

Honestly, I don't know mermaids. I don't know anything. So I'm like, "Totally. Out of hand."

"Anyway, I should congratulate you on your success. The quartz scepter was always my favorite part of the trident. When I was little, I'd like to dare my squires to go up and touch the crystal. Wouldn't hurt them or anything, just give them a good jolt." He blows the sweet smoke in a cloud puff and laughs through it. "Did you find that oracle back in the cove?"

"Did you?"

He holds his hands up and flips them back and forth. "Didn't really look, to tell you the truth. Charming little town, the cove. Though a bit prudish for my taste."

"I *did* hear something about extremely naked Sea People walking about."

Brendan shrugs, happily tugging on his cigarette. "You're Grandfather's champion, not me."

I turn to the calm, black sea. "I didn't ask to be."

"No one does. It might have been me, but he didn't like that my mom ran away to be with my dad."

"My mom ran away to be with my dad too."

"Grandfather's a funny one." Brendan flicks the stub of his cigarette overboard. "They call him the best king our people ever had because there are fewer executions."

"Isn't that a good thing?"

"Not when the alternative is to have more prisoners. He's more lenient than the kings of the past. Some see that as a weakness, but my father says he's smart. He wants to keep our people alive when so few of us are left. Slow aging and wars. If only we could make more of ourselves like vampires. I'll tell you one thing. I wouldn't want to follow after him."

I remember what Reggie said at the bar. *The sea folk are responsible for their own downfall.*

"I'm confused," I say. "Then why are you even *championing*, or whatever it's called?"

Suddenly he reminds me of Angelo and the way he shrugs when

I ask him if he wants sausage on his pepperoni pizza. The entire sea kingdom is at stake, not to mention the safety of my Coney, and it all comes down to a shrug.

"It's expected of me. My father wants me to change things for our kind. Told me I could have a ship and gold, and if I don't become king, he'll fund an expedition for me. But he *knows* me, and me? I like being alive. Every time I see one of us reduced to surf, it shakes me to my core. One moment we're whole, then the next moment we're gone. *Poof.*"

The lily flower must be kicking in because he's grinning so hard. "*Poof,*" he repeats.

"Hey, champions," Layla shouts from the deck. She raises a string of dried octopus like a ruler. "When you're done with all your warrior chat, come join the rest of the class, won't you?"

Brendan jumps off the ledge and runs down to the deck, nestling himself between Gwen and Kurt. The only one he hasn't met formally is Layla. He takes her hand and kisses it a little too long.

I don't have the stomach to eat, but the urchins felt guilty over allowing the ship to be captured. The others scarf down the plates of food. Thalia uses Brendan's arrow as a shish-kabob stick, which is incredibly gross, considering the arrow was just stuck in someone's chest.

Layla takes a bite of the tentacle in her hand. "Is it just me, or is anyone else freaked out that merrows can talk now?"

"Not all of them," Kurt says. "Just the leader, Archer."

"For now," Thalia says. "Can you imagine a thousand Archers?"

I remember flashes of the silver mermaid slithering in my dreams. "She's not strong enough for that."

"Didn't want to fight, for such a shit talker," Layla says.

"He was scouting us." I crunch down on a handful of seaweed chips. "Now he can go back and tell Nieve. They'll come back stronger, and we have to be prepared for their next move."

"Especially since both of you came back empty-handed from your visits to the oracle," Gwen says. "Sorry. I didn't mean it that way."

"Charming as always, Lady Gwenivere," Brendan says. He offers her a lily-weed cigarette, and suddenly he's her new favorite person.

"No, it's fine." I take the cup Blue leaves for me. It's his own brew of tea because he notices I rarely touch the sea mead. The bittersweet liquid warms my insides. "She didn't have a piece of the trident anyway."

Kurt's shoulders sag sheepishly. "That's my fault. I was so sure—"

"We can't go back and change it. The thing is, we're alive and from here on, we work our way to the next game plan."

"You sound like Coach Bellini." Layla leans her shoulder closer to mine. "Minus the swearing."

"Listen," Brendan says, throwing the latest butt into the crackling fire. The tiny thing is so potent that it floods us with its scent instantly. "You are more than welcome to tag along with my ship. We're heading down and south. Galapagos. Lovely place. Lots of strange things hidden."

Layla smiles. "My dad is from there."

"See? All the more reason to come with me. My ship is full of *boring* people, and you have proven to be quite fun."

For a moment, I wonder if I could do it. Stop right now and take my scepter on an adventure with my new cousin. We could discover new worlds or just party on his boat. Would Nieve keep searching for me? What would my mom think? What would become of the court? Only for a moment.

"Brendan," Kurt says in his awkward cordial way. "If I may ask, if you don't search for the oracles, what *do* you seek to find?'

Brendan's blue eyes shine with excitement. "One of the princesses claims she knows the location of the City of Clouds, full of winged people. I needed a map from the cathedral at the cove."

"Aren't you worried about what happens to our people?" Thalia asks.

Her words remind me of the nautilus maid. Our blood promise lingers on my tongue.

"You mistake me for a leader, lovely Thalia." Brendan's charm is contagious. I think I have a dude crush on him. He reminds me of me before the storm. "Now Adaro, there's your challenge. He's got more men on his ship than me, you, and Dylan combined. The princesses, that's your own personal map to the next oracle."

"What do you mean?" Kurt asks.

"Alone, Tristan has nothing. He can swim all the seas and still not find anything. The princesses are resources, like a map of the seas laid out for you. You simply have to *coax* information out of them."

I cough loudly into my fist. "There has been zero *coaxing* here."

But I have to admit, without Gwen there to help me find Shelly, I'd still be in Coney Island waters chasing my tail.

"Also," Brendan smirks, "if you don't pay attention to them, they're likely to decimate your village and drown all the men."

"What?" I choke on my tea.

"No king." My cousin shrugs. "No rules."

"He's right," Gwen says. "I can think of three, maybe four of them with powerful families."

"Good thing Gwen's here," Layla says. "You have your own personal matchmaker."

I chew on my food extra long so as not to go near that statement. When I swallow, my throat is dry. "All roads lead back to Coney Island."

"Are you sure?" Brendan holds his hands out to the fire and rubs them. "My offer stands."

I stare at my friends for a moment. Would it be easier on all of them if I quit? Would I still have to kill the nautilus maid? Can I go back home and try to pick up my life the way it used to be?

"Or you could come with us." I don't know why I say it, but once it's out I'm hoping he'll say yes. "It would be nice to have family around."

Brendan smiles. I can see the indecision in his hesitation. South, he can explore his dreams. North, with me, he would face more of this, more of Archer, and I'm bummed when he says, "Maybe next time."

After Brendan says his good-byes to the others, he pulls me into another man-hug. He balances on the ledge and bows properly. "May the seas bend to your journey."

Then he dives, shifting in the air, a metallic blue ripple sliding into the wave that is taking us back home.

Part II

A mermaid found a swimming lad,

Picked him for her own,

Pressed her body to his body,

Laughed; and plunging down

Forgot in cruel happiness

That even lovers drown.

—W.B. Yeats, from "A Man Young and Old"

chapter THIRTEEN

Coming home isn't what I thought it'd be like.

It's not a parade of balloons and trumpets and flash photographers documenting my success. Because, right now, I'm empty-handed, and Coney Island is just as it was when we left. Luna Park is even lit up with thousands of flashing lights while the rest of the boardwalk sleeps.

The digital clock on the Cyclone stadium billboard reads 3:33 a.m. Still Monday before sunrise. The barrel of wind propelled us north with so much force that at one point the ship was flying over the surface of the water.

After saying our good-byes to Arion and the urchins, I take a moment to breathe in the hot summer night. No matter what gum, dirt, or dog piss is lingering from the day's tread marks, I press my forehead on the ground.

"That's disgusting," Gwen says. "No one will ever kiss you with those lips."

Layla snorts, still waving at Arion's retreating ship. "His lips have been worse places."

"As much as I've enjoyed time with you..." Gwen tugs on the same clothes she's been wearing for *three* whole days and grimaces. "I'm going to sleep somewhere decent that doesn't smell of mead and urchin."

"Come on, Gwen," I urge. "You don't want to go on the carousel?"

"The wooden horses with the manic eyes and open mouths as if they're frozen in terror? Thank you, but I'd much rather take a ride on our Shark Guard." She waves halfheartedly. "I will find you when the sun comes up."

I wonder out loud, "Where does she go?"

"The princesses have their own land-stay," Kurt says. "It's irritatingly pink."

"How would *you* know?" I ask.

He frowns. "I've delivered messages there. That's why."

"Sure, sure."

"Enough, you two," Thalia says. She points at the lit-up rides of Luna Park. "Is that normal?"

"What's normal?" Layla shrugs.

"The rides?" I point. "Maybe it's a new summer thing they're trying. Usually they're shut down at ten p.m."

"What are you talking about?" Layla stares down at the boardwalk. "I just see creaky old rides."

A group of kids brown-bagging bottles walk toward us. I wave them down. "Hey, yo. What's going on at the park tonight?"

One of them, with a Mets baseball cap and an angry scowl,

turns to where I'm pointing. Then back to me. He laughs. "You're tripping, man. I want whatever you're on."

They collapse in tipsy laughter and brush past us.

"Come on." I take Layla's hand, stomping down the boardwalk. It's strange being here in the dead of night when all of my days here have been full of sun. The moon is a fat ball in the sky, swollen like the bruise on my cheek.

"This is how all the *Scooby Doo* episodes go wrong," Layla says, giving my hand a squeeze.

The usual entrance to Luna Park is crowded by a line of large ravens. They caw and walk along the fence like precarious guards. I take Layla's hand and pull her in through the entrance. The instant she's in, she gasps, "Oh!"

Spinning rides light the boardwalk. The Wonder Wheel spins, and from down here, I can see girls with glittering wings waving.

"Fairies can fly," Thalia says. "Why do they even bother?"

"It's part of the Coney Island experience," I argue.

"Figures." Layla stands in front of the carousel. "The only ride I like isn't even on."

We pass a food stand manned by a young guy with powdery pink skin and gold hair. His smile is so bright that I have to look away.

"Can I interest you in some sweets?" He waves at a selection of candied popcorn, pretzels, sanguine chocolates, and golden apples.

"What is sanguine chocolate?" I ask.

Suddenly I feel a wind chill at my side. It settles on my shoulder with mild gloom. My heart jumps to my throat when I realize it's a person. Sort of.

Frederik, the only vampire I've ever met who rocks long black hair and Hawaiian shirts, is standing right beside me. "Ian, I don't believe the Sea Prince likes blood chocolate."

I put the blood-chocolate box back on the cart and decide I'm not hungry, leaving Ian selling the same box to a pale girl no taller than my hip.

"Damn, Frederik," I shout. "That's creepy as hell."

Frederik shoves his hands in his long shorts pockets. He shrugs. "Wasn't my intention to startle you, little merman. Just saying hi."

Layla points at the swinging pirate-ship ride. "Are those Vikings?"

"Demigods," Frederik corrects. "Just called them in. After the incident this Friday, the Thorne Hill Alliance feels we need extra protection details until the Sea People are done with their championship."

I don't like where this is going. "Wish I had better news for you, dude."

"Then I suppose we'll all enjoy the summer solstice festivities in the meantime," he says, turning to the girls. "Did I hear you say you wanted to go on the carousel?"

"Uhh—"

"Really, it's no bother."

Without being asked, the conductor comes out of a nearby ticket booth. His gait is forced, like he's trying to be calm when the energy around him is more wound up than Principal Quinn after the girls' soccer team went on a no-sports-bra strike until they got the same funding as the boys.

"Everyone," Frederik says, "this is Patrick."

"Heywhatsup?" Patrick says in one breath. He's tall and lanky, borderline anorexic, with hair down to his hips and an unkempt beard. He can't be more than twenty and definitely human and definitely shit-scared of Frederik by the way he never quite looks the vampire in the eyes.

"Do you think you could hook my friends up by turning on the carousel?"

The question is a formality. I can sense the tension in the command. Patrick goes to the ride, sticks in a key, and pulls a lever. He waits for Layla and Thalia to hop on. Even Kurt joins them, but I have a feeling that's more because of his disdain for vampires than his curiosity about carnival rides. The lights come alive, along with the twinkling song I've heard all my life. The white hides of the horses are dirty and some of the bulbs are burned out, but the carousel still has the same cool effect.

"Thanks, dude," I say, about to pat Frederik on the back, but then I think better of it. "Did you just Dracula Patrick into submission?"

"He's a friend. Of sorts."

"Meaning?"

"His sister got…turned this winter. In front of him. I've been trying to help them acclimate."

Oh. Suddenly I can't get that image out of my head. "That's decent of you."

"Believe me, it's not easy watching your sister turn into this," he says. When I wait for him to elaborate, he doesn't, and we keep leaning against the railing in front of the carousel. I breathe in the Coney Island air, the lingering cigarette smoke, virgin piña coladas spilled on the ground, the spun sugar of cotton candy.

"Where's your other half?" I ask.

"If you're referring to Marty McKay," Frederik says, "that shape-shifter and I aren't on speaking terms for the next hour and a half. He spilled my O-Neg slushie and is trying to find me another. You try getting that in the middle of the night when everyone is out partying."

"That's tough."

"It's tragic, actually. I'm still hungry." Frederik turns his dark eyes to me. Then he smiles. "Don't look like that. I wouldn't bite the future Sea King. I'm the High Vampire of New York. It'd be bad politics."

I laugh. "I'm glad you have so much faith in me."

"I take it things didn't go so well on your journey?" He nods at a pale, brooding couple walking past. The guy is carrying an oversized blue monkey as a carnival prize. Everyone who walks past Frederik stops for the briefest moment to acknowledge him. It's what I used to feel in the hallways at school.

"Things could've gone better," I say.

"Do you ever think everything happens just as it should?"

"Like that 'meant to be' crap? Hell no. If that were true, I'd be sitting around waiting for someone to put a fork in my hand and a crown on my head."

"Good man." He pats a cold hand on my back. "Where do you go from here?"

"Well, there are a few things I could do to advance my standing as champion." All these lights are making me sweat. "I'm not sure how to go about it just yet."

"I've been researching your people since you arrived unannounced."

"Listen, bro," I press my hands on my chest defensively. "I've been here since I was born."

"Very well, since the *court* arrived. All I know of your kind are the landlocked and the old man under the bridge. Not to mention those terrible creatures that attacked your school and the Sea Breeze community. I'm sorry for your loss, by the way."

"Those creatures," I say, "are called merrows. They're getting stronger. Just a heads-up."

"We've got more of us patrolling the city. But those creatures are not the only thing you should worry about."

My stomach plummets five flights when he says that. "What do you mean?"

"The landlocked of your court worry me. They've always been quiet, but Marty's noticed them meeting more often."

"Meeting? Like, together?"

"Yes." He sighs. "Together is usually how people meet."

I bite the inside of my cheek. "Why is that bad?"

"It is my understanding that the landlocked have never had a voice at the Sea Court before. It is not my place to tell you what to do. But you may want to investigate."

Over on the carousel, the music gets louder. The girls shout, switching horses and holding their hands up. Frederik sniffs the air like he smells something foreign he can't place, then ignores it.

"Each of the landlocked is different," I say. "Some, like my mother, were stripped of their tails and left to live on land. Others were banished as a punishment. They pay tithes every time Toliss Island coasts to a new shore in exchange for protection from creatures here, but they're second-class citizens of the mer world."

"I was a duke once," Frederik says matter-of-factly. Something about the way he speaks and holds his posture makes me totally able to picture that. "When the forgotten rise up, it is never good for the crown."

"Not that I mind," I say, "but why are you so helpful?"

"You remind me of someone I used to know." He turns his attention behind me, toward the boardwalk. "I have a soft spot for lost causes."

"Thanks. I think."

"Just think on what I've told you. We don't ask for these burdens. It's just the price."

"Price for what?"

"Being better men."

The carousel slows to a stop. A new wave of thrilled screams and giggles chime along with the bright lights and trilling music.

In the distance, sirens blare and cars honk. That good ol' Brooklyn lullaby. After two nights at sea, I'd started to miss the noise.

"Ahh," Frederik says with the first genuine smile I've seen from him. His teeth are slightly yellowed, but even so, I feel strangely pulled into the angular lines of his face. He brushes his thick, black hair away. "I thought I smelled sunshine."

For the first time, I notice the familiar set of faces walk past us. Unintentionally, I turn around.

"Friends of yours?" Frederik grins at the mermaid princesses.

I try to compose my face, get rid of the gore and exhaustion of the last couple of days. I want to channel my cousin Brendan or a little of the guy I used to be. When I turn around, Princess Sarabell and her girls have made a beeline for us.

"Remember that *thing* I can do to further myself?"

"Mm-hmm."

"Here they come."

His stoic features are a mess of shock, then sheer amusement.

"Hello, ladies." The High Vampire of the Hawaiian Shirt bows low. I don't know much about genuflection and shit like that, but that looks pretty legit, even for a guy who was a duke a couple hundred years ago.

Sarabell holds out a hand, and without missing a beat, Fred McCool Guy kisses it. Her face is orgasmic, all giggles and sighs. Then she realizes I'm standing *right here* and she composes herself.

"How did you fare, Lord Sea?" Sarabell says to me. Her amber eyes glow under the theme-park lights. Brown ringlets of her hair look soft and silky, and the breeze blows them everywhere, carrying her sweet scent of brown sugar.

"Uh—"

"I'd love to hear of your journeys."

I wish Frederik would smack me upside the head. At the same time, I thank the gods that Brendan isn't here to watch me make a fool of myself. I am Tristan Hart. Never have I ever had a girl reject me, and on a scale of one to ten, Sarabell is an eleven. But she's not my eleven.

Then Brendan's voice is in my ear saying, "Her cousin is a champion. Pump her for information."

Not literally.

Then, as Sarabell glances awkwardly from me to Fred to her entourage to fill the void of Tristan Hart's ultimate choke moment, I tell myself this is for the greater good.

"Why don't we go out?" Smooth. "I'll tell you about it. Later. When we're out."

I have the sudden urge to seppuku myself and spare us all the indignity.

"Tomorrow afternoon?" Her mouth is so sweet. "We can go for a swim?"

"Sure," I go. "Sounds good."

Sarabell shakes off the confusion and takes my fumble for sheer adoration. She dips in a girly bow and takes my hand, looking up at me with her amber eyes. "You won't regret it."

At once, they're gone, and I throw myself against the fence behind us.

Frederik is staring at me. "I was under the impression that you were skilled with the fairer sex."

"Were," I say, "is the key word. I don't know what's wrong with me."

Layla, Thalia, and Kurt hop off their white steeds, and as they walk back to us, Frederik glances from me to Layla and says, "I think I know."

Layla is holding Kurt and Thalia's hands. "Aww, look. Tristan got himself a date."

"She's Adaro's cousin, you know," Kurt says. "Perhaps you can find out if he saw the oracle at the cove."

I grit my teeth. "*I know.*"

Layla's face is beet red. "Are you guys going to an underwater drive-in? Park on the back of a shark-drawn chariot?"

Frederik takes one step closer to her and smells her. Layla leans back but not without blushing at his dumb vampire perfection. "Jealousy suits you," he says. "Your blood is boiling."

Kurt crosses his arms over his chest. "We don't have chariots."

Then Frederik turns to the boardwalk, nose up in the air. "Ahh. Early sunrise. My least favorite part of the summer. I'm sure we'll see each other soon."

I reach out to take his hand. He stares at me as if I'm holding a wooden stake and a hammer.

"Don't forget what I've told you tonight," he says.

As he stalks away through the flickering red archway, the first ravens take flight.

chapter FOURTEEN

My sleep is restless.

Full of sharp teeth and claws and screaming. Frederik standing under the Brooklyn Bridge saying, "Hurry." He faces away and then I'm back on Arion's ship. Archer calls to me and I drive my dagger through his heart. He melts away and Nieve rises from inside him.

When I open my eyes, my whole face is swollen. Morning-after pain is always the worst. In the shower, my muscles unknot, and bruises bloom all over my skin where the tentacles sucked on me going down the well. After I get dressed, I take out a bag of frozen peas and hold it over my right knuckles.

Kurt comes in and grabs a stool beside me. "You have to use both hands."

"I'll just add 'become ambidextrous' to my to-do list." I wince when I stretch out my fingers. "Get any sleep?"

"Hardly." He stares at me for a bit, starts to say something, but changes his mind.

I hate when people do that. "Just spit it out. What?"

"You were talking in your sleep."

I chuckle. "What did I say?"

"Brother." Kurt takes the frozen peas from me and presses the bag to his cheek where a merrow got a really good hit. "You kept saying, 'Brother.'"

"Yeah, well. Archer's not easy to forget."

I get up and stand in front of our Command Central wall. While we were gone, my parents added a calendar, crossing off the days to the championship. It's Monday morning. I can hear my dad in the shower getting ready for work. My mom gets up just after he does and makes breakfast. On a regular day, I'd swing by Layla's house and we'd take the train, picking up the rest of our team on the way.

The marker bleeds through the white paper and I think of the merrow blood dripping. "Why hasn't she killed me?"

Kurt returns the soggy peas to the freezer. "I would think you'd be glad she hasn't."

I laugh, straining against the pinch in my abs. "I just—I hate that I can feel her. That for some reason she wants me. Her magic…it's like this *force*. Like the nautilus maid. Like she could turn me into a puppet with just her will, but she'd rather toy with me instead."

"It wouldn't be the first time," Kurt says darkly. "That was part of her seduction. She made you feel what she wanted you to."

"Sounds like a party."

"I don't have an answer for you." He runs his hands through his hair. "She's before my time. All I know are stories."

"Then guess."

He sits for a moment. Rays of sunlight break through a patch of clouds and illuminate the kitchen. "Power. The throne. It's what she wanted the first time. You are so very different from the other mermen competing. Perhaps she wants you on her side. You are the only champion with a third of the trident, and you're of her family."

I scratch the inside of my elbows, suddenly feeling like she's in my veins. "Or she's just after all the champions, and she's going to take us out one by one."

"That too."

Suddenly my mom walks into the kitchen and pulls us into bone-crushing hugs. Her red hair gets all over my face, and I breathe her scents in deeply—powder and roses and somehow always something of the sea, like she never left.

"Bruises." I groan. "They hurt."

"We've been so worried." Her bright turquoise eyes search my face like I just fell off the monkey bars and make me feel self-conscious in front of Kurt.

For a long time we don't say anything else.

She turns on the TV in the kitchen. The morning news is reporting a dead boy on the beach this morning. The footage is dark and grainy. They interview a homeless woman who used the pay phone when she saw the kids screaming on the beach. The reporter comes back on. Despite her neat lady suit, the reporter has hair that's messed up like she got a call and rolled out of bed. She's standing on the Manhattan side of a bridge.

It reminds me of something Frederik said. The news lady glances back at the remnants of a second crime scene. Another boy was found in the Hudson by the South Street Seaport yesterday. The wounds are consistent with shark bites, and local fishermen are trying to catch the rogue shark blamed for the attacks.

"Rogue shark?" My mother sucks her teeth. "It's muddy Hudson water, not Cape Cod."

Then the weather girl comes on and announces bright and sunny skies for the rest of the week until a storm on Thursday. My stomach heaves. Another storm?

I hit the mute button.

"There've been more of them," Mom says. "Always boys. Your dad's been using red tacks for where bodies have turned up. The blue tacks are for you."

I look at the map of the world and the smaller one of just New York. Clusters of red along the Coney Island coast. Ryan's house in Sea Breeze. Even up by the Bronx. I add another red and then a blue to the Key West part of Florida where I estimate the Vanishing Cove might be. The news shifts back to the bridge and I think of my dream. Frederik standing under it.

"Mom, do you know the other landlocked that live in the city?"

"I'm not landlocked, Tristan." She frowns. "I chose this life."

"Okay, but you got stripped of your tail. Even if it was your choice, you still can't go back to court. Isn't that what the land-locked are?"

"Why are you asking me this?"

Kurt says, "What Tristan means is, has there been a time when you've come across the banished?"

That's *not* what Tristan means, but Kurt and my mom seem to have a "court" bond that I'll never understand.

"It's just something my friend Frederik said this morning." I don't know why she's getting so mad. "He said all he knew of our *people* were the landlocked and the old man under the bridge. Does that mean anything to you?"

"I don't like the idea of you befriending vampires." She starts making breakfast. Cracking eggs open and tossing out the shells. She clucks her tongue when she misses the garbage.

I clean it up for her. "Ma, Frederik's a cool vampire."

"Doesn't change that they like to drink mermaids dry. Either way, I wonder if he means Gregorious."

"The historian?" Kurt asks. "I thought he was dead."

Mom pinches her chin thoughtfully. "If he's alive, he must be six hundred by now."

I raise my hand, regretting the pain that shoots up my arm. "Share with the class?"

"The last time Toliss came to the shore," Mom says, grinding tons of sea salt into the pan, "not the time that I stayed, but around the '40s, one of our historians stayed on land. He wanted to record our histories here. I tried to find him when I was pregnant with you. I wanted to ask him if there were records of other human-merfolk children, but the house looked deserted.

"I went back a second time and still nothing, so I stopped trying.

I figured he either died or went back to court." She shakes the salt ten times into the pan. "Though if he is alive, I'm rather offended he wouldn't see me. He was our teacher once. My sisters and me."

"The *vampire* must have mentioned it for a reason," Kurt says, drawing out "vampire" the way I say "homework."

"Where is the house?" he asks.

"Under the bridge, obviously." I smirk.

They ignore my sarcasm.

"It's a brownstone under the Brooklyn Bridge. Water Street. I remember because I thought it was ironic. Number 33. There aren't many houses on that street. Mostly factories." She jots something down on a scrap of paper and gives it to me. "I'll pack up some food. Landlocked or no, our people hate it when strangers show up without gifts."

"What about your…other engagement?" Kurt says.

I down my breakfast like it's my last meal and ignore my mother's prying eyes. "That's not 'til later. Let's go see the merman under the bridge."

chapter FIFTEEN

"Thanks for the ride, Dad."

"Don't mention it, kiddo." He adjusts his mirror and pulls the top down. "Probably the only useful thing I can do for you."

I know he's joking, but when I look at him, I notice the dark circles under his glasses, the slightly green tint to his face. He turns up the volume when his favorite song comes on, something about a girl who's a sweet little thing and his pride and joy. Then pats my shoulder reassuringly.

On any other day, my dad would start singing at the top of his lungs while giving me and my friends a ride, and I'd roll my eyes and groan. But today with the top down, music blaring, and my dad tapping his finger to the beat of the song on his steering wheel, I just smile at him and promise to always remember him this way.

Dad drops us off in front of a dilapidated brownstone. He hesitates as he drives away. The vintage surf-green Mustang is out of place on a street that's seen better days.

This isn't much of a neighborhood. Across the street is a parking lot with only three cars. One is missing all its tires and a bumper. Someone's written "WASH ME" on all of the windshields.

Farther down is the river, murky and still. I shiver in the heat of the day when I see something sleek and shimmering undulate just above the surface. My first instinct is to go to it, but Kurt points at a wreath hanging on the door to #33. The wreath is a wide coil made of twigs, broken bits of coral, and seaweed.

"*Spirula spirula*," Kurt says. "The symbol of the king."

The front yard is dry, packed earth with weedy shoots lying at slanted angles, like a bad comb-over. Ivy has overrun the sides of the building. Underneath, the brick is broken where two other brownstones used to flank this one.

I press on the bell, but the sound is muted. My neighbor does that so when Halloween rolls around, he has no reason to come to the door. "Maybe Frederik's wrong."

Kurt hops off the front steps. "Perhaps there's a way in through the back."

"That's trespassing. I'm impressed." I knock a few times while Kurt goes around the back. The windows have a thick layer of dust that nearly hides very yellow blinds. I can't tell if the shadow I see is a man or a lot of dirt.

I give up on the front door and follow the path of decaying leaves to a small backyard buried in withering branches and dry leaves, as if spring never happened here.

In the last couple of days I've learned to trust my gut more than ever, and right now I get a familiar coil, like when we went down the well. I pay attention to every twig we snap, the traffic nearby, the unsettling quiet from the house.

Kurt stands on a crate with his hands cupped against a window. It gives out under his weight, and he's left kicking it off his foot.

There's a marble water fountain in the center of the backyard beneath a big, fat tree. Fresh green leaves float in the basin that fills up with the spit of the chubby merbaby. His tail coils behind him, and he's wrestling an equally fat fish with sharp teeth. "Talk about ugly babies."

Then there's a loud snap.

The ground is rising around me.

My foot is caught in something beneath the leaves. Kurt tries to knock me out of the way, but we don't make it and we're hoisted into the air in a thick, itchy net.

"A *fish*net?" I shout. "Really?"

This is a lot closer to Kurt that I've ever been before.

"I think it's safe to say the historian is alive."

"Watch the hands!"

"I don't have anywhere else to put them, do I?"

A door slams open and someone shuffles out. Every breath he takes comes back out in a heavy wheeze. The net spins with our weight so all I can see is a mane of white hair and a cane.

"By King Karanos," Kurt says, "you will let us down this instant!"

"Yo, stop *poking* me."

The old man laughs. He holds out his hand to stop us from spinning. Muddy green eyes squint at us. "You're in no position to be making threats."

"We're looking for someone," I say. Then add, "And we have presents."

"What kind of presents?" He gets close up to my face and looks into my eyes. His eyebrows are like fuzzy white caterpillars crawling in opposite directions. He gasps like I'm the ghost instead of him. "You're the son of the king."

"No. I'm his grandson. Are you Gregorious?"

He shakes his head. "No one calls me that anymore."

"What do they call you?"

He shakes his head, tsk-tsk-tsking away. Hand pushing hair back, cane tapping dry dirt. He makes to turn away, then hunches down to our faces once again. "Nope. No court politics. Not on my doorstep."

"Please," I say. "You're a historian, right? Aren't you supposed to, like, keep track of important things? You must know of the championship to the throne. I have the quartz scepter."

"And, Lady Maia made you *breakfast*." Kurt says "breakfast" like it's the eighth wonder of the world, which in our house it pretty much is.

The old man taps his finger on his thin lips thoughtfully. "Very well. But you'll have to cut yourselves down. I'll put on the kettle."

"Is he serious?" I whisper.

Kurt is trying his best to sit up, but his foot slips and his weight crushes my sensitive areas. "Your hand is closer to my dagger."

"Can't. Breathe."

"Swear by the seas you will not utter a word of this to anyone."

"My pleasure." I manage to pull out his dagger and start cutting our way out until the net rips open enough and we fall on the dried branches on the ground.

The back door is open. Stringy broken cobwebs hang from the door like a curtain.

"Come on." Kurt pulls me up. "Before he changes his mind."

chapter SIXTEEN

The back door leads to a kitchen that smells like bath salts and moldy library books.

Flowery wallpaper fades in splotches. Naked bulbs hang from nests of red and blue wires. Every step we take seems to rattle the foundation. The table is a plastic patio set complete with an open umbrella. Stacks and stacks of brittle paper cover every surface, even the floors leading to the living room. I thumb through a stack right in front of me, and the old man smacks my hand away.

"Sit." No-One-Calls-Me-That-Anymore-Gregorious sets down three chipped china cups, a tiny blue flower bulb at the bottom of each.

I point to the umbrella. "That's bad luck, you know."

"What does an old man like me need luck for, anyway?" When he pours in the steaming water, the flower blooms. Blue bleeds from the petals into the water and releases a whiff of mint.

"Where did you find blue poseidonia?"

The old man gets up close to Kurt's face until Kurt is so

uncomfortable that he leans back. "I have my ways. Now, where is my gift?"

I take out the plastic containers, one full of a stack of pancakes and another with bacon. His white eyebrows wiggle as he opens the container and dives right in with his twiggy fingers.

As soon as I take a sip of the tea, I gag. "This tastes like feet."

Gregorious smacks the back of my head. "*Bah.* It's the best tea for healthy, slick scales. Drink up."

I do, just to keep him quiet. "So, if your name isn't Gregorious, then what is it?"

"It's Greg. I've assimilated to this shore. Now. Tell me why you've come here. I've paid my tithes, if you're here collecting."

I burn my tongue on a big sip. "You weren't on Arion's ship last week with the others."

"Because this visit isn't real." He jabs my chest with his bony finger.

"Uh—there's a pretty real island floating off the coast of Coney Island."

His fist comes down on the table. "I paid my tithe sixteen years ago when Toliss made its scheduled stop. *Championship.*" He says the last word like a curse. "Never in my days."

"I take it you don't agree with the king's decision." Kurt licks his lips and helps himself to more water.

"It's why he released me from my position as Head Keeper in our Hall of Records. Among other things."

Kurt and I exchange skeptical glances. "You mean to say that the king planned for this championship even before Tristan was born?"

Gregorious-Greg scratches his head. His hands are jittery as he crosses and uncrosses his fingers. I follow his stare to a row of clear bottles lined up on the cabinet. He licks his lips with a very blue tongue. "The line of kings has been unbroken since your ancestor Trianos united the trident pieces, therefore unifying our realm."

Sweet. Go, ancestor Trianos. "If my grandfather just *gives* me the throne, wouldn't it cause a civil war?"

His eyes go to the bottles in the cabinet, then to me. "Show me the scepter."

I take it out of my backpack, still nestled in my sternum harness. When I hold it, it glows bright, then goes dead.

"Good," he says. "Very good."

I don't get it. "What's very good?"

"The other two are still out there? That's why you're here."

"Yes."

Greg stands. Goes to the window. The hinges of the cabinet squeak as he opens them. He takes one of the bottles and tips the clear liquid into his teacup. He doesn't offer it to us. Then he drinks.

I look to Kurt who shrugs and proceeds to eat the smelly blue flowers in our cups.

When I look at Greg again, the change in him is so subtle that anyone else might miss it. The muddy green of his eyes becomes brighter, more emerald. His skin less yellow. Even his hands have stopped trembling.

"What is that?" I ask.

Kurt elbows me.

Greg bats a hand in the air. "Medicine. This body isn't what it used to be."

"O-kay," I say. "Well, now that you know who I am and what I'm doing, I was hoping you could share anything that would help us find an oracle."

"Sorry to disappoint you, child. I have nothing to do with oracles."

"But you know of our past, don't you?" Kurt asks. "You know everything that's led us here. We're giving you the opportunity to help shape our future when no one else could do the same, and you would turn us away?"

Greg stares at Kurt for a long time. A grandfather clock dings on the hour from somewhere inside the house. It's not even noon yet, but the house already feels like a sauna. "I was there when you were born, you know."

Kurt sits back so hard that the plastic chair nearly topples backward. "Me?"

I'm starting to think Greg's too senile to help. The way he's shaking again reminds me of the patients at the old folks' home where the swim team volunteers during Christmas. Sometimes they just need someone to let them talk.

Greg nods once but doesn't elaborate. "You have to understand that I watch history. I write it down. I don't shape it."

"But you do teach, don't you?"

"That I did. I taught all the king's daughters, for what good it did them. Or me, for that matter. A simple disagreement with the king and I'm left to die in this house."

I reach for the empty teacup to keep my hands busy.

Kurt asks, "You mean you want to go back to court?"

Greg crosses his arms over his chest. "I used to. A few days ago, I went to one of those landlocked meetings. A mistake, yes. I am not disgraced as they were. I am not a traitor to the crown. The king and I had a disagreement. In turn, I was allowed to walk away. But I don't want to see the crown broken to suit my needs the way they do."

"They said that?"

I think of my friends who are landlocked. Penny and her kid. They seemed cool—on my side.

Greg's wide eyes nod. "Aye. Though not in those words. I'd keep away from them."

"That's sage advice," Kurt says. Easy for him to say. He hates them.

I take my chances, reaching out to put a hand on Greg's shoulder. I can feel the bone jutting out. "The way I see it, you don't want the line of kings broken. If you help me, we both win."

"The Council of Keepers was meant to hold our secrets." The old man takes his time studying Kurt and then me. "But this—the king's choice—will bring those secrets to the surface." His lips tremble. He twitches like he senses something else in the room. It makes me jittery. I wonder if it's too late to bolt out the door.

"If the crown breaks, that will be the end of us." He waves a finger from me to Kurt. "Both of you, do you understand me?"

I don't. I have no idea what he's saying but I nod. *Yes. Yes. I'll take anything you can give me.*

Maybe he likes what he sees. Maybe he just wants us to get the hell out of his house and leave him alone. Whatever it is, he says, "Very well. I have something for you. Don't touch anything while I'm gone."

He disappears down the hall into his living room. From the kitchen, we can hear books toppling over and an angry cat hissing. I inch to the cabinet with the clear bottle he drank from.

"Tristan!" Kurt says, gritting his teeth. "Stop it. He'll see you."

The cabinet door is slightly open. I stick my hand in and grab a bottle by the neck. The hinges creek ever so slightly. Kurt fiddles with his teacup to mask the noise. I pull the cork.

I've never smelled anything like it—like my mother's hair, summers on the beach, riding with my dad's car top down, the coolness of his aftershave, honey and lavender. "Whoa."

Kurt whispers my name as a warning, but I can't stop. I tilt it back and drink, longer than I intended.

I wipe my mouth with my hand. "That doesn't taste like anything."

When I hear the rustle of the old man coming back, I put the cork back on and set it down. I pretend to look at the stack of paper in front of me and hold a sheet up to the light. It's an etching of a tree, the branches reaching up to the heavens and a stream dividing the trunk. There's another stack of mermaid drawings. They're all incredibly voluptuous with pouting red lips and thick, winky eyelashes.

"Give me that!" Greg says, snatching the paper from me. He covers up the mermaid pin-ups and turns red.

"Come on. I was just curious. You must remember being my age."

"Here." Greg fights a smirk. He holds out a stack of ancient crumbling paper. "I hope you're smarter than you look."

"Thanks?"

"Don't thank me just yet." Greg sets a finger on the top of the stack. "Now let me return to my peace and quiet. No more court will come to my doorstep. I've given you my last secret."

He shoos us out into the backyard, and the whole house shakes when he slams the door shut.

"Drunk old pervert," I mutter down the street. We walk until we find a train station. "Let's head down to the boardwalk. I have to meet Sarabell soon. We can eat and go through these papers before they crumble any more than they already have."

"That was…different," Kurt says. "Why did he remember my birth? I wonder what was in those bottles."

"Do I look different, the way he did?" I stand on the sidewalk and try to take on my best superhero pose.

Kurt tugs on his chin. "No."

"Buzz kill." But when I look at my hand, my knuckles are healed. There's the faint trace of a scar. Even my hickey bruises are fading. "Look."

Kurt rubs the back of his neck, more worried than impressed. "I've never seen that before. We don't heal that quickly."

"I wonder. Maybe that's why he's got the traps in his backyard. For someone who's supposed to be long gone, he seems really protective of his stuff."

In the subway, a fat rat scampers across the platform. Its eyes glow, reflecting the light of the arriving train. Kurt steps into the opening double doors. "With all the things crawling around this shore, we should figure out traps of our own."

chapter SEVENTEEN

Kurt and I sit on the Coney Island boardwalk against the metal railing. I lean my head back and tilt my face up to the sun. Despite the police tape and warnings to stay out of the water, the beach is packed with people. I dig into my hot dog, ketchup and mustard dripping down my chin. I wipe with the back of my hand and wash it down with root beer.

I'm not enjoying it as much as usual.

Honestly, I kind of miss the seaweed chips Blue makes.

The noise of the boardwalk makes me jumpy. The snap of the toy guns in Luna Park, the pop of cars backfiring. Every girl with curly brown hair giggling past me makes my heart jolt in an I'm-going-to-regret-this-later way.

"You should read some of this too." Kurt arcs an eyebrow. "It's mostly about the kings and their accomplishments. King Karanos built the first great prison for the merrows."

"Too bad all it did was provide a massive nursing room for the sister he couldn't kill."

A fat man, covered in baby oil and reading a beat-up paperback, glances over at us from his bench like we're making too much noise. He ignores me and keeps reading, just like Kurt.

"Plus, my hands are dirty with oil. It could damage the paper." I dip the last bit of my hot dog in mustard. When I bite down, bits of sand are mixed into the sauce but I swallow it anyway. I dust my hands and hold them out to my guardian. "All right, I'll take over. Your dogs are getting cold."

I set the papers in my lap, but I can't concentrate. I wonder where Sarabell is. What if she stands me up and I never get to find out anything about Adaro? Sitting down here, I can watch the crowds without being noticed. Tons of young hipsters with top hats and clothes that don't match on purpose. A mother tries to keep all six of her kids from killing each other over a volleyball. Some photographer directs a model to pout as she contours herself across a hand-painted garbage can. An old man power-walks in nothing but neon-green spandex shorts.

Then there are the things not everyone can see. I rub my eyes and squint against the sun. There's a girl with tattooed wings on her back. At just the right angle, I can see that the wings are real, white feathery things retracted against her snowy white shoulders. She holds her ice cream cone to her boyfriend's lips, the vanilla rolling down his brown skin.

I rub my eyes again and see what he really is, with skin like copper blood. His lips smile and take a giant bite of her ice cream with sharp teeth. Two small horns poke out of his forehead. Something passes over his angular face, and he finds what's troubling him—me. He can *feel* me staring. To my surprise, he doesn't flip me off. Instead he nods once, as if to just acknowledge me, then slings his arm around his angel girl, grazing the down feathers as he leads her farther down the boardwalk.

"Are you paying attention?" Kurt asks.

"You see that?"

He follows my stare to the heavenly hellish couple and shrugs. I guess he's too cool and has seen everything under the sun.

A familiar boy runs down the boardwalk. When I point out, "Hey, is that Timmy?" a new horde of beachgoers barrels past us, obscuring our view.

"Timmy!" I call out, but my voice is drowned out by a boom box strapped to the back of a bike zooming by. Timmy runs into his mom's arms. His mother, Penny, scoops him up and rubs the hard shell of his back. From here, he seems to be a kid with a weird backpack. When I met them on Arion's ship, I discovered it's a part of him. Penny, on the other hand, has arms that shift into tentacles. They're the landlocked. Here in Coney Island, they don't seem so out of place.

Penny shields the sun from her eyes, scanning the crowd for someone. I shout her name, but she doesn't see me.

Kurt buries his nose back in the papers. He's not exactly a lover of the landlocked. But Penny clued us in on what the merrows were after they attacked my school. Penny and Timmy embrace a green-haired girl. "What's Thalia doing here?"

When I mention her name, Kurt snaps to attention.

"What? Where?" He gets up for a better view of them, but in the shifting crowd, I've already lost them.

Suddenly a man gets in my face. He's stick skinny with skin like used charcoal. He nods at the food on my tray. "You gonna finish that?"

Kurt rolls the parchment papers into a tube and tries to catch up to Thalia, but he's going against the current of beachgoers.

Then the man looks at me. I mean, *really* looks at me, and backpedals. "I'm—I'm sorry, my lord. I didn't mean—"

There are scabs around his neck and ribs. They could be scars or dried acne or, in his case, leprosy, but I know better. They're what remain of his gills. His eyes are sharp sapphires framed by a face that is gaunt and poreless. His 'fro is untamed. His pants are filthy and ripped, and right at the center of his chest is a keloid in the shape of a trident. Just like my mom's scar. Just like the tattoo between my shoulder blades.

"I'm sorry," he repeats louder, still eyeing my food.

I hand my tray to the old man in a hurry. "Take it."

"I couldn't." His voice is hoarse and dry like paper.

"Please, take it. I'm not hungry." It's not exactly what I want to say. I want to say, "I'm sorry that this happened to you. I wish I could fix it." I should sound nicer, soothing.

The man takes the food, ripping bread and meat and shoving it into his mouth. Between swallows he manages, "Thank you, sire. Thank you."

Kurt has stopped in the middle of a crowd, shielding his eyes from the sun. People shove him out of the way, but he keeps standing his ground. The boom-box bicycle speeds back the other way. More children are crying. The photographer is snapping away. I stuff my garbage in a plastic bag.

"I lost them," Kurt says.

The fat, oily man on the bench beside me taps my shoulder.

"What?" I don't mean to sound so exasperated, but that's how it comes out.

"You shouldn't do that, you know."

"Relax, I'm not littering," I say, showing him my bag of garbage. But he grabs my hand. If people keep grabbing me, I'm bound to start chopping off hands—like a real king.

"I meant feed them. You shouldn't do that. They're like pigeons."

I pull out of his hold and start walking to where Kurt is waiting with a worried look on his face. The fat, oily man keeps shouting after me. "You give them a little, and they just keep coming back for more."

Kurt pulls me away, farther into the crowd. "I don't want Thalia with those people. I have to find her."

I hate the way he says this, like somehow we're better. I keep a steady pace beside him, weaving through the throngs.

Suddenly I flinch. A hand comes out of my blind spot and smacks me across the face. I stumble into a group of angry dudes who push me back. I fall at her feet. I follow the slender ankles, the bare legs beneath a sheer dress. Her hair billows wildly in the breeze, framing radiating amber eyes.

When I stand, I'm a foot taller than her, but somehow she makes me feel small.

Her full lips part slowly and growl, "You're late."

chapter EIGHTEEN

"How am I late?" I press my hand to the hot sting on my cheek. "We said afternoon."

She points at the sky. People are starting to look. I grab her as lightly as possible by the shoulders and walk her toward the railing separating the boardwalk and the sand.

"It was high noon two hours ago!" She crosses her arms over her chest. "I've been here surrounded by the beastliest of creatures. I'm hungry. My *legs* hurt. Do you know what that feels like?"

"Sara—"

"Do you even care?" She presses a slender hand over her chest.

"Oh boy." I look to Kurt who can't do anything more than scratch his head.

"Well?"

This girl, this incredibly beautiful girl, is seething in my face. Her shoulders are hot under my hands.

"Of course," I say. "Of course I care."

Her eyes soften. "You do?"

"I was just looking for you." I run my hands through my hair. "There are so many people, you know?" I try my most charming smile, the kind that's gotten me in (and out of) trouble in the past. I pretend I'm smiling at Layla and it becomes easy. Sure, there's a nasty knot in my gut, but I have to push through. Since leaving the Vanishing Cove, I've felt like I have a bunch of broken pieces in my hands. If Sarabell can point me in the right direction, I'm going for it.

"Come." I take her hand. She crosses her fingers with mine, and I resist the urge to pull away. "Let's swim."

This is the girl who's supposed to get me closer to Adaro and the next oracle?

They might as well lock me in a cage with a hungry tiger. Sarabell is all smiles now, raising a proud chin to the sky and turning her mischievous eyes to me. "You appear nervous, Lord Sea."

"I'm not nervous," I lie. The sand is boiling hot under my calloused feet. Sweat seeps through my T-shirt against my backpack. I've never seen the beach so deserted on such a perfect day to cool off.

"Don't worry," she says, and in that moment, I'm lulled into a calm I haven't felt in days. Somewhere I know this is the effect of her voice, but the dulcet melody reminds me of the guy I used to be. That Tristan didn't get sweaty palms. That Tristan didn't think twice before leading a girl under the pier. Somehow, it's easier to be him…

Sarabell pulls her dress over her head and throws it on the wet beach. Her long brown hair tumbles to her hips in waves. She smells like the sea, not Coney Island water but like salt and rain and the turquoise, warm waters of Vanishing Cove.

"You're not afraid of being seen," I say.

"Didn't Gwenivere tell you?"

"Tell me what?"

She twists her hands in the air like a belly dancer. "I'm an expert at glamours."

When the water reaches her shoulders, she turns around and blows me a kiss playfully. She pinches her nose and sinks under. A second later, her hand shoots up and waves me in. Her feet kick and she swims away.

I stuff my clothes in my backpack and dive in before I change my mind. At first I can't find her. The water is muddy and cloudy, and I have to swim for a mile before it clears up. My heart is pumping in my chest, nervous, excited, and dreadful all at once. Then I see her. Her hair darkens and smooths out with the pull of the water. Her gold scales blossom and the iridescent glimmers of her tailfins flick my chin.

My entire body sighs when I shift. It's like a great release, like breathing new air. We swim for what feels like miles. I marvel at the way the water bends to her. Even underwater, the sweet hum of her voice is entrancing. She gets up close to me, teasing with her lips inches away from mine. She nudges me with her nose. I think I've seen dolphins do this at the aquarium. I place one hand on her lower back where her skin becomes soft golden scales. Without meaning to, a part of me rises…

Then she smiles and I flatline. I swim out of her hold with the flick of my tail. Her canines, too sharp, remind me of Nieve—her pale face, her frail silver body—and Archer, the merrows, Layla dying in my arms. My thoughts are a train wreck I can't stop.

Sarabell can't understand why I've pushed her away. I swim up to the surface. We're far from Coney, all the way to maybe Long Island, maybe Queens. My sense of direction is discombobulated. There's a nasty taste in my mouth. I want to puke up my breakfast.

She surfaces beside me, smoothing out the water around us. "Did I offend you, my lord?"

Sure, she's all formal and stiff now. A second ago she practically had her hands all over my—

"I'm sorry if I'm too forward. It's just…you're so terribly lovely. Everyone says so. And I've never been with a half human-half merman."

I head for a mound of boulders and grit my teeth against the rip of the shift back to legs that stops mid-thigh. The half shift. I can't help but feel like I'm wearing glittery boxer briefs.

"I've got a cramp," I lie.

"Then we can just sit."

"Hey, Sara," I say, "why are you here with me? The day you

arrived, you guys wouldn't even look my way. Why aren't you at Adaro's court?"

She's flustered. She stands in her half shift, wet hair getting carried by the wind. There aren't people on this shore. The beach is stony and uncomfortable, and the water is full of seaweed and broken shells.

I catch her hesitation. "You are so much more interesting."

I hold her hand so she doesn't slip on the mossy boulder, and she sits next to me. I lick the salty water running over my lips. "You don't have to pretend. I'm not good at this court stuff." Then I swallow hard. My heart jolts, anticipating my deceit. "Wherever Adaro is, it has to be better than here."

She scoots over so our thighs touch. "Don't you see? You're so very new. All of court says you have the king's face as he was in his youth. The blue eyes of Triton—" Her hand hovers over my face. I inch back instinctively, but she follows.

"Adaro is my cousin. While I wish I could see our bloodline return to the throne, I also wish I could be queen. I've already been presented to the other champions, before the championship started. Elias chose Gwenivere, for all the good it did him. Brendan would make a terrible husband. Dylan would not take a queen but a Sethos, a minor king that is. Then the ones beneath my station are afraid of my magic."

"So everyone knows about you…?"

She nods sadly. "It's required."

Looking at her now, I can see something broken inside her, beneath the wicked smile, like the biggest parts of herself are hiding.

"Do you have much contact with Adaro now?"

As soon as I say it, I wish I hadn't. Her guard is up, but her eyes sparkle in the sun. She leans over and rests her head on my shoulder. "He says if he were king, he would welcome magic into the court once again. Would you do the same?"

I tense against her fingers tracing my chest. "I—"

Then she sits back up and takes my hands in hers. "If I tell you everything I know of Adaro, everything *he* knows, would you take me as yours?"

"Mine?"

She smiles. Not the wicked way she does on the boardwalk or among her entourage. It's her real smile. Insecure. Nervous. "As your queen. We could do many great things together."

"I wasn't exactly expecting a marriage proposal," I say, slipping off the rock. I have two options, say no to her and return to square one. Or I could pretend. I could tell her that I love her, that I want her to be my queen of the sea. I could look into her eyes and make her feel she's the only one in the world to me. Take what I want from her. Ask her to betray her family. Then I could take it all back, like I've done many times before.

I want to shower.

Suddenly a guy walks down the beach hand in hand with a girl. Oblivious to us, they start making out. He pulls on the strings of her bikini top and she runs her hands all over his chest, his hair, his face. I feel a pull in my stomach. A pull to be somewhere else with my own girl. I realize the feeling is coming from Sarabell. The wordless melody of her voice fills my head. It floats in the air like smoke, wrapping around me, the couple on the beach. The girl stops kissing the boy and turns to us. Her eyes are glazed over and dazed.

"We should go back," I say.

She bares her pearly teeth encouragingly. "Don't you see? This is a perfect chance to experience life together. Then, we could continue as one—"

The couple is hypnotized by her voice. She calls the couple forward with her fingertips, leading them back into the water.

"Sarabell, no. What are you doing?"

Sarabell bares her teeth and walks backward into surf. The couple follows.

"What are you doing?" I whisper. But the warmth of Sarabell's voice is like light filling my chest.

"It's a present to you. A show of good faith to join our lines."

I roll out the tension in my shoulders, the pressure of her voice weighing me down. I think of everything that's happened in the past couple of days. Everything I've lost and everything I can lose. I silently curse Brendan and Kurt and Gwen. All of them. I've got a mermaid who wants to be queen so badly she'll give me everything I want to know about Adaro on a silver platter. The couple is knee-deep in the water, Sarabell winding them in with her song. A show of good faith, my ass.

Her spell breaks around me.

I take the couple by the arms and pull them back on the shore. They're confused, but they're fine.

"What did you do that for?" Sarabell screams.

She's wading back to the couple, but I wrap my arms around her and pull her against the tide. I dive backward, yanking her with me. My fins push against the water for both of us. She shifts, too, and her weight is powerful for such a small thing. She wails like a banshee. It ripples and scatters anything in sight.

She struggles against my hold, but I have to take us deeper and deeper where she won't be able to swim back to the shore so quickly. She sinks her teeth into my forearm and I scream as I let her go. She spits and swims up to the surface, crying and sobbing and wiping the water from her eyes with wet hands.

"What kind of merman are you?" She hiccups. "Any merman would've loved the look on their faces underwater. They were beautiful."

I rub the angry spot on my arm where the salt burns and licks the wound. I'm too stunned to even make coherent noises. "You can't just go around *drowning* people. That is not an okay present!"

I can't understand what she says between sobs. Her eyes cloud over, her hair black and stringy all around her.

"Don't do that again," I warn.

Then her wicked eyes return. "I've given you a chance, champion. Now, you will be powerless against Adaro's triumph."

"What do you mean?"

"You'll see." She turns and swims away, smacking me across the face with her fins for good measure.

chapter NINETEEN

I shift out of my tail about a mile out. I let my frustration with Sarabell fuel my arms, cutting powerfully through water. Ever since I became what I am, I've stopped using my arms as much, preferring the powerful kick of my tail. Now I welcome the pain, castigating myself for being such a *dick*.

My friends and I have one rule: we never, never, ever set each other up on blind dates. Why did I think a championship would somehow make it better?

It never ends up well.

I cut through Long Island Sound until I feel I'm back at Coney Island. There's a miniscule change in the taste, though I don't want to linger on what's in Coney water since I've peed in this ocean more times than I can count. The kick of my legs feels foreign and numb, and I try to massage feeling back into my legs as I trip my way under the shadow of the pier.

But there's already someone there, and when we see each other naked, we scream.

"What are you doing here?" Gwen is just out of her shift and stepping into a red dress.

"Just fresh off my first date." I pull my damp clothes from my backpack and throw them on. "Thanks to you."

She throws her head back and cackles until she's out of breath.

"It's not funny," I shout.

Gwen tries to take my hand but I pull away. "Was Sarabell not everything you expected?"

"She wanted me to make her my *queen* in exchange for telling me what she knows about Adaro. Is that what they're all going to ask for? Because I can't make the same promise to each girl."

Gwen settles her gray eyes on me. "Why not?"

I have sand on my tongue and I spit it out. "Because it wouldn't be true."

"Do you plan on making Layla your queen?" She leans against the dark, wet pillar of the pier. "Our people would never accept a human queen. Just as a fair warning."

"I didn't—I'm not—" I take a deep breath. "I'm sixteen. I'm *not* getting married. Anyway, I couldn't get any useful information out of the mermaid sociopath of the year." Though Sarabell's words are digging into the back of my head where I'm accumulating all the things I'd rather not be thinking about. Nieve. Archer. Leaving Layla.

Gwen purses her lips and tugs on one of my wet curls. "We're not all bad, Tristan."

"Are any of them normal?" I laugh. Gwen has that effect on me.

I can't not smile at her. "Say, not thinking drowning humans is a good engagement present?"

"Normal? Is that what you want?" She spots Sarabell's dress getting pulled by the tide. "Would you believe me if I told you she's not even the worst of them? Seas, I hate the way she dresses."

"So *I'm* the punishment? Know what? Forget it. What are you even doing here?"

"Don't be angry with me because Sarabell didn't work out." She points her finger in my face. "This just means you have to move on until we can find something that will lead you to the next oracle."

"I'm sorry, okay?" I force my mouth into a comical smile. "Why aren't you doing important mermaid things like weaving pearls and shells in your hair?"

She squints angrily but doesn't deny it. "I couldn't stand Layla and the angry pout she's got smeared all over her face. Then there's Thalia who simply vanished, leaving Kurtomathetis running about the boardwalk looking for her. Doesn't he understand? If a mermaid doesn't want to be found, she won't be."

A dull blast sounds in the distance, like someone pressing down on the horn. Then I realize Gwen is bleeding. "Your arm."

I reach out but she pulls away.

"Did something attack you?"

"No, no. There's a shark in the waters. Small, but hungry."

I think about the animal accidents on the news this morning. We were all so sure they had to be merrows. "Are you sure?"

"I know what a shark looks like, guppy prince." Under the

shadow of the pier, she swipes at the dark trail of blood with Sarabell's dress. I can feel the pull of Gwen's magic. It comes from within her, and that pulls from the sea itself. The bleeding stops and the beginning of a scab starts to form. Gwen says magic isn't instantaneous. It's gradual.

"Let me see." I take a step that's followed by a gooey crunch. "*Ugh.*"

A medium wave crashes and retreats, leaving behind a line of mangled fish. I pick up the one I stepped on. Its head is still intact, but the body is all bone. The glossy eye is iridescent under the sun, mouth open in a final gasp.

"The sea will only keep getting disturbed." Gwen traces a finger along the pewter scales. "This is a freshwater fish."

A lifeguard's whistle blows. He waves his hands in our direction in warning, but when he realizes it's me, he turns it into a friendly wave. I signal back that we're leaving and he shakes his head, smiling.

I throw the fish carcass back into the waves. Then I say something I never thought I'd say. "Let's get the hell off this beach."

chapter TWENTY

We trade the hot, noisy boardwalk for the quiet of Command Central. The other champions may have seers and prophets and ships, but I've got a microwave and Hot Pockets.

When Gwen and I arrive, Kurt's sitting at the counter reading through the papers from Greg. Gwen is equally fascinated with them, touching them with the utmost care. I tell her all about Greg and his booby traps.

"You don't think the old fart was messing with us?" I ask.

Kurt shakes his head. "I believe Greg wants to see you rise to the throne. There is something in these papers, I tell you. As a scholar, he respects knowledge." Then he mutters, "Unlike some of us."

I take the parchment from him. "I totally respect knowledge!"

"I wasn't referring to you." He takes it back.

Gwen sing-songs, "Yes you *we-re*."

"Gregorious, or whatever he wants to be called," I say, "was shady. What's the point of giving us drawings? It doesn't tell us anything about the next oracle. Neither did Sarabell, by the way."

Kurt shuffles the papers like a card deck until he finds the ones he's looking for. "You're looking for easy answers, and the search for the truth is never easy."

"Did some *psychic* tell you that?"

"No," he says, "my father taught me that."

"Oh." My foot tastes rather nasty.

"Forget it. Look at this," he says. He's so happy with these papers that he's finally stopped wondering where Thalia is. "The trident is one object. It's been *thousands* of years since they were three separate pieces and our kingdoms were three corresponding factions. Each king wielded a different part of the trident. The quartz scepter, the center staff, and the trident fork. It says here that our people were at war so often that one of the oracle sisters proposed a final championship to unite all three kingdoms as one."

"Are these them?"

"Yes. These are the original kings."

"These dudes are no joke. What's with the animals?"

"My teacher told me of this," Gwen says. "Back then, the kings believed their strengths were linked to animal spirits. The sleeping giants, they called them. It was long ago, but if I remember correctly, this was Kleos, the eldest king. He wielded the quartz scepter you have now."

Kurt seems impressed but lingers on her for too long. "Who was he, your teacher?"

"*She*," Gwen says, "was of my court. We've always had more

mermaids as elders than the mermen of the court. She rather liked Kleos here." She taps a finger on his gold-leafed face.

Kleos is drawn with a mane of brown hair, blue eyes, and the slightest hint of a smile. He's sitting on a sea horse whose long snout is in the middle of neighing. Do sea horses neigh? There's a kingly quality in the way Kleos holds the scepter over his head, conjuring a wave and a stroke of lightning.

"This is Ellanos," Kurt says, pointing to another dude. "He was the one who used the blood and ink of the cephalopods to give us legs. He believed he'd conquered the gods who wanted to keep us in the ocean. It made him powerful, despite having the center staff, which alone is the weakest part. But without it, there would be no trident."

Ellanos's hair and eyes are filled in with the blackest ink. His skin is red and his jewels are etched in gold. At his feet is a giant octopus, one tentacle wrapped around Ellanos's ankle.

"Is that thing still alive?"

"Yes. It lives in the king's private chambers in the Glass Castle."

I point at Ellanos. It's like looking at the Greek exhibit at the Met with all the broken vases and plates. "Doesn't he look like Adaro to you guys?"

"That's because Adaro's family are direct descendants," Kurt says. "As you are of this king, Trianos, who wielded the forked tip of the trident."

Trianos looks much like my grandfather. The big white mane of hair. I wonder if it was ever another color. The skin is like gold. His eyes are carefully inked in a deep violet. He stands firmly on the back of a turtle. The turtle isn't one of the cute slow things at the aquarium. This turtle's shell has hard ridges. There's anger in its eyes, power in its limbs. I like this turtle.

There's another paper that's so thin and black that it breaks apart at the edges where I pull it. "I think someone tried to burn this one."

This one shows the trident put back together. I trace the outline of the familiar shape of the quartz scepter. There's text all over it, but it's in a different language.

"I'm not familiar with these symbols. It shows the way the three are meant to be one. The three-pronged tip and the quartz fit in either end of the staff, which is a catalyst for the two."

"How did one oracle decide there shouldn't be three kings anymore? I thought they just *see* stuff." I know quite well they do more than see. The memory of the nautilus maid makes me shiver.

"There is no mention of *how* that decision came to pass. There is only a mention that it happened."

I tug on my chin, surprised at the fresh stubble. "Remind me to thank Greg for giving us an old piece of paper with hieroglyphics. Gwen?"

She's surprised when I say her name, like snapping out of a trance. "By the seas, I don't know where to begin. I believe—" Her eyes flick to Kurt as she hesitates. "I believe this is the language of the oracles."

"They get their own language?"

"It's not *their* language," Gwen says smirking. "It's the language of the gods. Their purpose is to translate it. Send some poor soul to war and another to murder his children. That's why humans have always sought them."

"I wonder if my mom would know. Greg did teach her once. Maybe he knew she'd look at it." The kitchen clock marks just past five. My dad would usually be home by now, and my mom would be yelling at me for tracking sand all over the rugs after finishing my lifeguard shift.

"Good," Gwen says. "Why don't you summon her?"

"You don't *summon* your parents."

"When you're king, you can," Kurt says, pointing at the drawing of Kleos grasping the quartz scepter. If he could wield it as one piece, then maybe so can I.

"Why does your face look like that?" Gwen says.

"Ah," Kurt says smartly. "I believe Tristan is *thinking*."

I pull the quartz scepter from the leather harness. The gold is cold. Orange sunset light fills the crystal and kaleidoscopes against the kitchen walls. "Let's see what I can learn from King Kleos."

chapter TWENTY-ONE

"Are you sure this is a good idea?" Gwen asks, lounging on a rickety old chair.

From the rooftop of my building, you can see for miles. Behind us there's Brooklyn—brownstones and the handball court, Carvel ice cream, and even the church by Layla's house. Before us are the Wonder Wheel and the beach and farther out the horizon where my grandfather is waiting for me to show up with this thing that I'm holding. The quartz scepter.

"This may be the best idea he's had since I met him," Kurt says.

The dusty gold is cool in my hands. I'm holding it over my head like a sword, the pointy quartz part up in the air.

"Trust me." And even if they don't trust me, I'm sure they're not going anywhere. "I need to learn to use it."

"It says here that Kleos was the light that shook the earth." Kurt reads off some crap about channeling some powers within. The strength of *blah, blah, blah* self.

His voice actually helps, because I can concentrate on blocking it out.

All I want to feel is my heart pounding and the current—ancient and strong—sizzling its way all over my body. It's what I imagine the third rail in the subway would feel like if I touched it, minus the electrocution part. I shut my eyes and imagine lightning crashing across the horizon the day of the first storm. I remember the strength of the wave clamping down on me with the full force of the sea. The crackle of thunder. The whip of the wind.

It's all inside me.

Kurt's scream follows a sharp blast. Above us is a single black cloud. It cracks open with a spurt of lightning, crashing directly into the cluster of satellite dishes on the roof. The cloud vanishes like smoke against the sunset sky.

"That was killer, man." My hands are buzzing.

"Just don't kill *me*," Kurt says.

"You have to get yourself one of these."

"I can't. It's one of a kind."

Unlike the other times, the light of the quartz is still blazing. I feel a thrill go through me, and it must be linked to the scepter because it sputters another burst of lightning. This time the ledge where the satellites are hooked up catches fire, right where Gwen sits.

"How do you turn this off?"

"You control it!" She yells, dusting herself off the ground.

Kurt is running around the roof looking for a source of water. "Stop getting excited."

"Yeah, I have that problem." I give my scepter a shake, but it's not a remote control with nearly dead batteries. I close my eyes.

The crackle of flame whips in the wind. I breathe and imagine, like Arion had me do when coasting into the cove. I can feel the current retreating, containing itself.

Gwen shouts my name.

The flames are six feet tall and getting taller with every gust of wind. Kurt is entranced by it. He crouches down, pressing his hands against his temples.

"You okay, man?" But of course he's not okay.

I set the scepter on the ground before I set anything else on fire and run back inside the building where the fire extinguisher is. I take my shirt off and wrap it around my knuckles to break the glass. I run back upstairs to where the flames are twice as tall as Kurt.

"Stupid child lock!" I cut myself on the plastic but it doesn't matter. I've set my building on fire. I point the nozzle at the flames and the cold pressure blows all over the place.

I kneel beside Kurt. "It's okay. It's out."

Even Gwen rubs his back and shoulders.

"I hate fire." He's breathless and shook and rambling, so all I can make out is: "My parents" and "dragons" and "fire."

"Come, let's go back inside," I say once I make sure the fire is completely out. "Even if no one's called the fire department, I'm pretty sure they called their satellite providers."

First, Gwen and I take a shaking Kurt under our arms and leave him on the couch.

He repeats the same words, "fire, mother, father, dragons," like a mantra.

Then we race back to the rooftop for the fire extinguisher. I set it on the Command Central floor and my scepter on the table.

"I don't know what to do," I whisper to Gwen.

She stretches her arm around my back and rests her chin on my shoulder. "He's in shock. It'll pass in a bit."

"I know he said something about hating fire." I run a hand through my hair. "I had no idea it was like *that*."

"Many of our warriors were like this. When they came home from battle." She presses her forehead against my cheek. Her breath is warm on my neck. "Those who made it home."

I stand, tugging gently away from her grip. "We call it PTSD. Post-traumatic stress disorder. My friend Jerry, his brother's a Marine. It's our version of warriors. When he made it home, he shut down completely."

"He wasn't fighting dragons or fey, was he?" She asks so innocently that I can't laugh at her.

"No," I say.

Gwen nods, studying the pins on the Command Central maps. "Seems silly, doesn't it?"

"What does?"

She traces the length of the map. North to south. West to east. One big invisible cross. "We're all fighting for a bit of home, and even if we get it, we're not satisfied because it isn't really home, is it? It's still just an ocean. A bit of land." She turns back to me, and I can feel the shift in her body.

"Where is your home, Gwen?"

Startled by the question, she stutters, then laughs. "I suppose court. With Elias gone, I don't have anywhere to go."

"I'll always have a sleeping bag for you," I say.

"I'm not certain if I should thank you or not." She reaches out to touch my face. But I go to the fridge and get cold water. Despite the AC, I'm sweating.

"I'd better go," she says.

"Where do you go off to?"

She takes my water and drinks from it. "I know things didn't work out with Sarabell, but perhaps I could learn a few things they'd never say with you there."

"You mean *spy* on then?" I take my water back. "You'd do that for me?"

Sometimes I think Gwen's eyes are going to burn a hole right through me. It's like staring into the stormiest sky and not knowing if you want to run from the rain or stand there and let it fall all over you.

"For you." She presses her lips on my jaw, just under my mouth. "And for the kingdom."

chapter TWENTY-TWO

One look at our freshly scrubbed guilty mugs, not to mention the glaringly empty fire extinguisher on the kitchen floor, and Dad asks, "What happened?"

Mom has a bag of ice cream in her hand. "We passed Gwenivere in the lobby, and she smelled like smoke."

Kurt joins us in Command Central. We exchange one look of solidarity as he sits beside me. It's not like we stole the car and went for a joy ride, which, if this wasn't all happening now, would be pretty sweet to do in this weather.

So I give my parents the SparkNotes version of visiting Greg, the papers, the landlocked on the boardwalk, and the fire. I leave out the parts with Sarabell and the moment on the roof when I felt *awesome* blowing stuff up. "I've seen *CSI* and my fingerprints are all over the fire extinguisher."

Dad cleans his square glasses on his untucked work shirt. "The super is downstairs fighting off an angry mom because their cable isn't working."

"Technically," I point out, "I only burned down the satellites on the roof. Including ours."

"What were you thinking?" Mom yells. "There are cameras up there!"

"Actually, last year Janie said the landlord was too cheap to install a real system," I point out. "Only the elevator and lobby ones work."

"Janie? The super's daughter?" Dad asks, trying to keep the grin off his face in front of Mom.

"Dad—"

"What matters is that no one is hurt." Dad points to me, giving off the guilty smells of dirt and the excited burn of fireworks. Underneath all of that is Mom's melting strawberry ice cream. "Just, no more fires in the house."

I hold my hand up. "Merman's honor."

Dad rubs his hands together, like twiddling an invisible stick to make invisible fire we're not supposed to have in the house. "We're actually glad you're here. We have something to tell you."

"We do as well." Kurt clears his throat, the familiar stoicism returning to his posture. "We were waiting for Lady Maia."

Mom brushes his hair back tenderly. "Kurt, please. I'm not a lady of the court anymore."

"You'll always be a lady to me," he says, softening under the gesture. "My mother would've wanted me to address you as such."

"I'll just stick with 'Mom.' Hey, *Mom.* Greg says he was your teacher how many years ago?"

She flushes like she's going to whack me on the head with her spoon. Dad throws his hands in the air and chooses the safer option of the sofa instead. "You're on your own, kid. I'm not going near that one."

"Come on, guys," I say. "Just trying to lighten the mood. Greg gave us all this riddle stuff and we need your help."

Kurt spreads out Greg's parchment papers.

"I can't believe Greg is alive." Mom wipes her hands on a towel. "The old crab. I could've used his knowledge when I was pregnant with you."

"He wasn't exactly happy to see us," I say. "What with ol' Grandpa firing him and all that."

Mom shakes her head. "That's not what Father told us."

"One of them is lying," I say. "He wouldn't leave a cushy gig on Toliss for a house that's falling apart, would he?"

Side by side, Kurt and my mother are mirror images, each with one hand examining the face of a long-gone sea king and the other tugging on the tip of their chin. They even say, "I suppose," at the same time.

"He said he taught the king's daughters." I wave my hands in the air to get their attention back. "So you're one of the king's daughters and Kurt doesn't know how to read these symbols."

"It's not that I don't know *how* to read them. It's that I never learned."

"Mmm. Hmm. Which means you *don't know how* to read them."

"Enough!" Mom puts her hands up between us. "Kurt, you wouldn't know how to read this. This is the language of the gods.

Only the oracles can translate it. Greg wanted us to learn, but after a few years Father changed his mind and forbade it."

"The king forbids his kids to get all bilingual and has a disagreement with Gregorious, who ends up fired. Sounds like Grandpa was hiding something."

"Don't say that," Mom whispers.

"Sorry. It sounds shady, that's all."

Kurt takes the paper once again, trying hard to see words in the symbols, but it's like all those times I tried to fake my way through Spanish. "Mom?" She looks unsteady and I reach a hand to hold her.

"I think this word is 'death.' Yes, I remember because we were trying to translate the prophecy of the hero Milanos, destined to die at the hands of a sea prince during the age of the Greeks. I wonder—"

"Death never sounds good," I mutter.

I flip the crumbling paper over and smooth it out. "What's this bit right here? 1907?"

Mom looks to Kurt. "You were born that year. I remember because I was in the room with the midwife, and my sister Avelia kept saying there was a rainbow over the human island in the distance and it was a good omen for you."

"That's all awesome and kind of weird, but how do we find someone who would know about this?" I feel like I'm chasing my own tail again.

Mom places a hand over the face of King Ellanos. She gasps, pain spreading all over her face. Her hands fly to her stomach.

She's going to be sick. I can see it in the green flush of her face. She breathes deep and long.

I get up. "Are you okay?"

"Lady Maia, perhaps you should sit."

"I haven't felt this terrible since—" Her big blue eyes scan my face, and before she can finish, she runs to her bathroom. We can hear the puking all the way out here.

Dad stands at the kitchen entrance.

"Should I go to the pharmacy?" I start to run to the bathroom and stop. "Should I bring her water?" I run back to the kitchen and fumble trying to get a glass and the pitcher of purified water from the fridge.

Sure, when it comes to fires and evil merpeople, I can be concentration guy, but put me in front of a girl crying or puking, and I don't know the difference between my ass and my elbow.

Dad shakes his head. He's part worried, part nervous, and the combination smells acrid. And that's coming from a guy who showers three times a day in the summer. "There's no easy way to say this, so here goes."

"Dad? Spit it out. You're freaking me—"

He fist-pumps the air. "Your mom's pregnant."

chapter TWENTY-THREE

I get a broom for the broken glass on the floor. When Kurt tries to help me, I shoo him away and he sits next to my dad at the kitchen counter, watching.

"I didn't mean to tell you this way," Dad says. "We were going to wait. Maybe 'til after this championship stuff. We didn't want you to worry."

"Why? Why would I be worried, I mean."

The acrid smell of nervousness is replaced by the smoky sweetness of excitement. It's what I felt when I set fire to the roof. I tie the garbage bag in a knot and pass a mop over the floor. This is the most I've ever cleaned. Look at me being a grown-up.

"I believe congratulations are in order?" Captain Awkward says.

"And much merriment," Dad says in a mock-Kurt voice. Dad goes to the fridge and gets three light beers. "I know these go right to your head because of your bodily water ratio, but hell."

Together, the three of us pop the lids of our beer cans.

Dad and Kurt start talking about names and hoping it's a girl because Maia wants a girl, and I just sit here giving him a thumbs-up while still trying to drink this thing.

Not only is it incredibly gross to picture my parents still doing it, but I'm sixteen. Most people who want to have more kids usually pop them out all at once, right? Angelo's one of seven, and that's not counting the kids his dad has from his first marriage. Come to think of it, Layla's one of the few friends I have who's an only child.

If I'm Sea King, how am I supposed to be someone's older brother? I'd want to teach him how to swim, how to play ball. Tell him about the first time I shifted. Wait, Mom wants a girl, so I'd have to be around and chase guys away from her. I'd have to make sure she'd always be protected. Wait a minute. What if the baby isn't half merkin after all? What if they get to have a no-complications, fully human life?

I'm on autopilot, getting more beers from the fridge. Kurt just says yes to being the unborn baby's godfather. We're not even Catholic. How come *I* don't have godparents?

"When my boy here becomes Sea King, we'll use his college money as a down payment on a house."

"Wait, *we're moving*?"

I hate that I've put such a hurt look on my dad's face. He says, "Too much too soon? I knew we shouldn't have said anything. We weren't planning it, if that's what you're wondering."

"Ew, Dad. You don't need my permission. I mean, you guys should get the chance to raise a normal kid and a normal family that doesn't involve a freak son and his new life under the sea."

My own hurt is twisting into my chest like screws. I can't believe how selfish I sound. Here is my dad really happy, and I'm taking it away from him. So I put on my best smile and give another thumbs-up, even though this is somehow worse than Archer kicking me in the gut.

Dad slings his arm around my shoulder. "There is nothing more wonderful than having you as a son. We didn't even think we *could* have another baby until it happened."

"No, totally." My face hurts from smiling. "This is awesome."

"This isn't about getting another shot," he says. "You have to know that."

"I do. Don't worry about me."

At some point, the sun starts setting, and Dad goes and checks on Mom. I clink Kurt's beer and Thalia walks in. Her hair is damp and she smells strangely of pizza.

"Where have you been?" Kurt's voice is a boom, but it has to do with the beer and not anger. He scoops her up in a bone-crushing hug.

Thalia is too stunned to even push him away. "I was hungry."

But her cattish green eyes find mine and I know she's lying. I shake my head once, wishing I could tell her we saw her on the boardwalk.

"You were with those people," Kurt says. "I saw you."

Thalia's eyes go wide. She takes the drink from her brother and sets it on the table. "Is this a celebration? Did things go well with Sarabell?"

I hold up my hand to show her teeth marks but my heart jumps. The teeth marks are gone except for the pearly shadow of her canines to match the bite on my other arm from fox boy. I didn't expect that trying to do the right thing would lead to becoming a human chew-toy. What the hell was in that vial I drank at Greg's?

"Uh—she wanted to be my queen and then bit me when I stopped her from drowning happy beachgoers."

Thalia cringes. "I'm afraid to ask who's next."

"Next?" I choke on my beer. "No way. I'll find the oracle another way. I have a lead. Only, none of us can translate it because it's the language of the oracles."

Kurt giggles to himself. He sounds out the word: "*Ohhhhh-racles.*"

Thalia smacks my arm. "I can't believe you let him drink this!"

"I'm fine." Kurt shakes his head and clears his throat. "Oh-racles. Ha-ha! They like to play mind games. It's all a game of the mind. And here." He takes my hand and places it over his heart. "Mermen like you and me, we play games of the heart." He presses his forehead against mine as if we're in on some new magical secret. I should slap myself for letting Kurt have so many beers. "That's why she wasn't there."

"Who?" Thalia asks. "Who wasn't there?"

"The Oh-racle, my lovely sister!" Kurt gets up and makes a beeline for the bathroom, mumbling about how *this part is so much easier in the sea*. I'm not sure if he's talking about princesses or peeing.

"Tristan, fix him!"

"I can't." I take the beer cans and dump them in the sink. "He just has to pee it out."

Thalia grunts. "Then why *are* you celebrating?"

I tell her about my parents and their new brat, and she says, "Be happy for them. They'll be losing you. This may make it easier."

But I don't like that idea, either.

Then I hear Kurt flush. "We have to tell your brother."

"I can't. Not until I know it can truly happen. That you can truly make me human." She takes my hand softly. There's a strange noise in the living room. Someone falling down.

"Uh-oh."

Kurt's on the floor, sprawled across our fuzzy white rug.

"Is he okay?" Thalia goes to him and tries to lift him up, but he's dead weight.

Kurt gathers his hands and folds them under his face like a pillow. He makes deep, guttural snoring noises.

"I think he's—smiling," I say. "Probably the first good night's sleep he's had in a while."

I dig my hands in my pockets and feel the coolness of the Venus pearl I forgot was there. I bring it out and cup it in my palm. I really wish I could have given it to Layla.

"Tristan!" Thalia hisses, snatching it from me.

"Careful!"

"Don't you see?" She dangles it in my face.

"Yes, I see a sweet present I can't give to—" And I realize. "Shelly! Shelly can translate the oracle speak."

I take Thalia's head and kiss her forehead loudly. "Only problem is, what can I gift her? I'm thinking we've run out of precious gems, and the pearl won't work twice."

"Get your backpack." Her smile is cunning. "I have just the thing."

"It's like a great metal makara," Thalia says, hopping on the train.

We take the F all the way to Manhattan. This late on a Monday night, the subway platform is full of the strangest people only New York breeds. Couples full of PDA, a man with a dress made of balloon animals and plastic bottles. People coming and going, and those with nowhere to go at all.

Thalia clutches the wooden box Felix gave her, and I pull on the straps of my backpack for the security of my weapons. I can't decide if I want to sit forward or lean back. Uncertainty is the worst feeling in the world. Worse than rejection and worse than failure, because at least then the action has been completed. Uncertainly is emotional limbo.

Deep in my heart, I know I have all the pieces and now I have to make them fit.

"What were you really doing with Penny?"

"I wanted to see them." She stares at the speeding blackness out the window, the graffiti rolling by like a flip book of colors and shapes that never stop changing.

"You should call Layla."

"I know," I admit. I don't want to tell her about Sarabell. She'll hate me. Even if I didn't do anything wrong, I still hate me for going. "Did you see her today?"

"At Thorne Hill. In the field with the others."

"The schoolyard?"

"That one. There was a huge commotion because your friend—" She snaps her finger. "The one with the tall hair."

"Angelo."

"Yes. He was running with Princess Menana on his shoulders. All the adults were furious. They were naked right down to those little trousers for your foot-fins."

"Socks?"

"Not that the adults are better. They're all mad. You remember what it was like when the rest of the princesses arrived. They're making all the boys happy as seals in mating season. Layla's been put in the ground by her parents so she had to leave immediately."

"You mean grounded?"

"That's what I said."

I place my face in my hands. "Should I do something?"

"Become king. Restore order."

The train barrels into the station. I take her hand and lead her up and out through the Manhattan streets. I realize Thalia's never been in the city. She stares at the checkered lights of the buildings and I explain that's where people live. She laughs and pets a fire hydrant because she likes the shape. When we're in Central Park, I try to remember the direction Gwen and I took Friday night. But the winding paths are dark, and the shadowed trees all look the same. Thalia picks up a baby mouse at her feet and cradles it.

"Ugh—cut it out, Snow White. Those things are gross."

She places it back on the grass and pinches me. "All life is precious, Tristan."

"Come." I lead her through the urban woods and up a hill, until the castle comes into view.

"Oh my," she gasps. "I didn't know you had royalty here."

I laugh as we head straight up toward Turtle Pond. "We don't. It's for kids to play in."

But before I can take another step into the shadows of the castle walls, a tall woman emerges. Her black leather clothes glisten in the moonlight. Her hair is a shock of bloody red cascading over one shoulder.

"Tristan—" Thalia takes a step back, crushing a twig that seems to echo all over the park.

The woman bends her face over the crossbow in her arms.

I raise a hand, about to say, "Don't shoot!" but I hear it. The crunch of leaves beneath her feet. The spring release of her bow. The way the air is split by the arrow, silver and sharp and headed right at my face.

chapter TWENTY-FOUR

The arrow shoots right through the center of my palm.

Thalia screams my name.

A familiar voice barks, "Rachel! No!"

Frederik is a shadow in the park, zooming toward the redhead with the bow. I can hear the bow fall against a rock.

I grunt through the pain, fighting the reaction to ball my hand into a fist.

"Nice friends you've got, *vampire*," Thalia says.

She examines my hand. The shaft went right through. There's so much blood. On the ground. In my palm. When Thalia wipes her forehead, a red streak comes away like a brushstroke.

"They were trespassing, Fred."

Another set of feet rush through the trees. It's Marty the shape-shifter. He pushes past the redhead, swivels his black baseball cap backward, and kneels down by me. "They're friends."

I grind my teeth as he takes my hand.

"I have to break the shaft," he says, "and pull it straight through. Okay?"

"Just get it out." I let myself scream once, then hold my breath.

Fuzzy numbness starts to crawl along my entire arm. I have the vague feeling that's what an army of ants crawling on your skin would feel like.

"Want me to turn into someone more appealing?" Marty's pale face turns into a blond I'm pretty sure I've seen on the cover of one of Angelo's *Maxim* magazines. Then my stomach heaves when Marty turns into Layla. The hazel eyes smile down at me. But the thing about supernatural creatures is that they don't smell like anything, and I turn my face to the side.

"I don't think now's the time," Frederik says.

Then Marty is Marty again, messy brown hair beneath his baseball cap. "On three." His mouth twitches. "This is gonna hurt."

I clench my jaw, bracing for the snap.

"One."

But he doesn't make it to three, and the next thing I feel is the arrow sliding through my open palm, leaving a bloody hole.

"Knew you were going to do that." I nurse my hurt hand on top of the good one. The blood isn't pooling anymore, but my whole hand is numb and swollen.

Rachel, the Red Menace, stands with all her weight on one leg.

"Why are you pissed when you just tried to shoot me in the head?"

She flips her hair over one shoulder and turns away from us. "I'll tell Shelly not to worry."

"I'm going to find something to dress the wound with," Thalia says.

Frederik stares at my hand with a possessed look. I retract my hand, realizing blood plus vampires aren't a good combination. His hand clamps down on Thalia's shoulder. He says, "There's no need."

"No *need*?" I'm so confused. Unless he means he's going to lick the blood off.

"Look."

And when I look, my hand is changing.

The gouged hole is closing, the skin mending. I stretch my fingers and flip my hand front to back. It's like there was never a hole to begin with. My hand looks like I dipped it in a jar of blood.

"That's new," Marty says.

From behind them, a short somebody wrapped in green fabric waddles over with the help of a walking stick. She gets to eye level, and I can see the folds of her white-gray face. Her tar black eyes are *not* happy to see me. Instead of a welcoming hug, Shelly, the oracle of Central Park, pokes me in the chest with her cane. "You have much explaining to do, Tristan Hart."

The poker table is a slab of polished stone.

A mishmash of things is piled high in the center: jars of live bugs, a golden dagger, black apples, and stacks of regular, old American cash.

"*This*..." I point a finger in Rachel's disgustingly perfect face. "This is why you shot me?"

She sits on one of the massive toadstools growing in a circle around the table. She takes her cards, glares at them, and throws them down. "I had a good hand. I should shoot you again."

"Now, now," Shelly says, taking her seat. "There is no killing in my neck of the woods. Frederik?"

The vampire looks up to the sky and sighs. "I didn't know she had the bow. She's a demigoddess. She can conjure lightning and puppies from thin air if she wants to."

Shelly sucks her teeth. "Well, conjure up some manners while you're at it, dear. This is the future Sea King, and he's got some answering to do."

"Me?"

Shelly sets her eyes on me. Her palm-sized fairy maidens flit about, tugging on my hair and blowing kisses from the trees. Thalia bats them away, taking a seat beside Marty.

"The last time I saw you," Shelly says, "You couldn't regrow your body parts."

"I can," Marty says. "Sort of."

"Look, I'll get to that later. Right now I need your help," I say.

"Gah! Always help." Shelly throws her hands in the air. "Not just popping by to say hello?"

"No," I stutter. "I mean, I wanted to visit you also, but the championship and all."

Rachel and Frederik share a smirk at my expense.

"I saw your sister," I tell Shelly. "The one in the shell that can't move. I like you way better, just so you know. And those laria are lame compared to your fairy girls." This makes the fairies sigh and giggle in twinkling chimes.

Shelly *tut-tut-tuts* and offers me a seat on one of the toadstools. "What is it you need help with?"

I glance at Marty and Fred and Rachel—

"Come now, Tristan. You've already achieved a great thing. You have the scepter. You do still have it, don't you?"

I tap my backpack. "I do."

"Then?" Shelly gives a no-nonsense headshake.

"Don't worry about Rachel," Frederik says. "She's impulsive and new to our fair city and the Thorne Hill Alliance, but she knows to keep quiet." Then he sends a look that I'm not sure is meant to scare her or turn her on. "Or else."

"Uhm. Okay." I unzip my backpack and bring out the paper I need translated.

As soon as she sees it, Shelly mutters in a strange language. I'm pretty sure it's all curses. "That bloodied barnacle."

"So you know each other?"

Shelly purses her lips. It makes the folds of her face pucker.

"Gregorious," she says his name like an ex-boyfriend. "Always searching and searching. Can't just write things down without raising too many questions."

"What is this?" I hold it up. She tries to take it but I pull it away. "I know this is your language. You're swearing in it right now."

"The king wanted no record of that prophecy."

"Why? What does it say?"

"Give it here, son," she says, trying to take a motherly tone.

"No." I yank it away. "Not until you promise to tell me what it says."

She crosses her arms and looks away. "My services don't come for free."

"We brought something," Thalia says, offering an apologetic smile.

Shelly's ears, wherever they are, perk up. "Let me see."

Thalia takes out the small box of sea-horse eggs and opens it. I know how much she loves the eggs. I can't thank her enough. They gleam in the moonlight.

"Gah, I've no use for eggs that won't hatch!"

Thalia closes the box, shielding the eggs protectively.

"I have an idea." Frederik's voice is like a purr. His eyes glance down at the deck of cards and then at me. "Tristan, can you play?"

I scratch my throat. "Sort of."

"How about we let Tristan play this hand?" Frederik offers. "Him against all of us. Winner takes all. If Tristan wins, Shelly has to translate his text. Then he will leave and continue his quest."

"What if Shelly wins?" Thalia asks.

Shelly clears her throat and glances at Marty. He chokes on a fit of laughter and says, "I think Tristan should put up seven minutes in heaven."

"What if any of us win?" Rachel looks as if she could spit on my shoes. "He's a bit short for my taste."

"We're all playing for Shelly," Frederick says. "Tristan versus the table."

"That's not fair," I say.

This makes them all smile, even Rachel, who says, "Sounds like you haven't many options."

Whatever Greg has in that parchment has to be important. I stretch the fingers of my miracle hand. I set the parchment in the pot, where it shrinks and turns into a glowing neon poker chip along with everything else.

"Temporary charm," Marty says. "Space saver when a game is in session."

I smile and cozy into the cushion of my toadstool. Cicadas and fairies whisper their sounds into the night.

And I say, "Deal."

chapter TWENTY-FIVE

My buddy Angelo's dad plays poker.

He has his own table in their basement, along with a full bar and a pool table, a jukebox and a collection of NY Jets memorabilia that, if sold on eBay, could probably buy a Third World country.

Here, under the moonlight, they watch me. Rachel, the newest demigoddess of crazy to arrive in New York, Marty the shape-shifter, Frederick the High Vampire of New York, and Shelly, the youngest of the sea oracles. I take a deep breath and remove any traces of a smile. People playing poker never seem to smile.

Thalia watches with the utmost curiosity, flicking fairies like marbles every time they try to sit on her shoulders.

Marty shuffles the deck of cards. He holds them out to Thalia, who blows on them. Each person's hand is dealt. I'm fighting the urge to look at everyone right away. I want to read their faces. The problem is that I can't sniff out their emotions like regular humans. Frederik, as always, is steel-faced and apathetic. Rachel has a very pretty red smile going on, and the folds of Shelly's face are distracting.

I finally peek at mine, and my mind flashes to the arrow driving through my palm so I wince. Ace and king of spades. My hand feels better than ever.

I realize Frederik can probably hear my heartbeat, so I try to get it down.

Shelly waves her fingers and a golden chip appears, representing her promise to me and calling my bet.

For the most part, I keep my eyes on the cards and the glowing chips on the table. When Angelo's dad bluffs, he shrugs his shoulders and sighs a whole lot. Even though his friends play with him all the time, they always fall for it.

Rachel calls it by throwing in a tiny knife the size of my index finger, and the knife shrinks into a chip as red as her hair. Fred throws in a tiny jar containing a small flower. It becomes a pink chip.

Marty reveals the flop. Jack of spades, ten of hearts, and three of diamonds.

Fred groans and throws his cards into the muck pile, folding.

Another burned card. Then the turn—ten of spades.

Burn. Then the river, right in the middle. The queen of spades.

I can't show them how freaked out I am, so I reach in my pocket and bring out the Venus pearl. "Raise."

This is the first time I've ever heard Frederik gasp. I didn't peg him for a jewelry kind of guy. He gets up and stomps around in circles.

"Call," Rachel smirks. She pulls a ring with a sparkling black diamond from thin air. It flips into a silver chip and gets added to the pot.

Shelly holds her palm out and produces a red stone. She weighs it in her hand and hesitates, like she's not willing to part with it. But she has to call or fold.

She throws the stone in the pot, pursing her lips ever so slightly.

The silence of the forest is incredibly loud—every chirping bird, rustling squirrel, and all the other creatures that must be lurking are soundless.

Rachel growls from deep in her throat, like a roll of thunder. She reveals a straight—Q-J-10-9-8.

Then Shelly, jiggling on her toadstool. Her smile is as wide as a slice of the moon. "After you've lived a few decades, you learn your way around the table."

The smack of her cards is a loud snap. For an ancient being, she's a worse winner than the boys of the Thorne Hill football team. "Get your ChapStick out, champion. *Full* house."

When I see her tens full of jacks, I realize I've been holding my breath.

Shelly reaches her hands into the pot, but I place my hand on top of hers. "Hang on, hang on."

I flip my cards over and there they are, white under the belly of the sky. A royal straight flush. "Beginner's luck."

"You hustled me," Shelly growls. "You said you couldn't play."

"You guys *assumed* I couldn't play," I shrug.

Marty nearly falls on the ground laughing. I take the chips and scoop them up to my side. The items revert back to their normal shapes. I drop my winnings into my backpack, except the crumbling sheet of paper.

In my hands, a few more pieces crumble. Shelly's shoulders relax, giving in. Maybe even happily. She smiles and says, "Give it here, champion. I knew you had it in you."

"Where is she?" I pace around a toadstool. "It's been, like, ten minutes."

Shelly vanished into some trees and hasn't come back yet.

Frederik isn't paying attention to me. He's staring at Rachel, who's using the poker table as a sofa. They share a secret smile with each other.

Marty's giving Thalia a lesson in basic card games. "Relax, dude," he says. "She's probably counting her corny shells. I made a joke about pawning them off to a psychic friend. Go fish."

Thalia pulls a card from their stack.

"Have you been to see the landlocked yet?" Frederik asks.

"Not yet."

"You should."

"I've been a little busy," I say drily.

I know in my bones I'm on to something.

Frederik's going to speak again, but the chime of fairies returns through the bushes. They form a curtain around Shelly in a fluttering march. She's changed her green sari dress into a red robe.

"Didn't figure you for the never-wear-the-same-thing-every-hour type, Shell Bear," Marty laughs.

Shelly *harrumphs* and says, "Don't make me get my stick."

"No, ma'am." Marty takes off his baseball cap and bows to her.

Shelly turns her cheek to him and says, "Also, I was just kidding. The Yankees are going to lose. Hope you haven't made that bet yet."

"*Any*way." I wave at her.

"This is the oracle's procession," Shelly snaps. "Just because I moved to the big city doesn't mean I've turned my back on the old ways. Once, I would've sat under a pyre and waited for the words to strike. Now, the gods have retreated. They've left us alone. But I still wear the robes of the gods."

"Takes you half an hour to change a dress?" Frederik asks from the table.

Shelly looks over my shoulder at him and yells, "I had to relieve myself. Some of us eat more than *blood*."

She takes the paper from my hand and holds it at eye level. Her hands are pruned, wrinkled, white. They glide over the paper. Wax on. Wax off.

I can feel her pulling on something, but it's not on my wavelength, whatever her magic is.

The writing flows, the letters scramble. Her face goes slack, hypnotized and facing me but not *looking* at me at all. In the black of her eyes, the symbols scroll like Internet code.

When it stops, she blinks the daze away. Suddenly she appears to be drooping. I realize it's the way she slouches.

"Shelly, what is it?" I take her chin with my fingers. The skin is cold and soft as leather.

"Are you certain you want to know this?"

"Yes." I don't hesitate.

Shelly considers my answer. "Our secrets are rising to the surface. This is the prophecy of the Star of the Sea. My ancestor."

"Which means?" I turn back, wondering if the others are still there because they're so quiet. Covered in shadow, they watch.

Shelly stares right into my eyes as she recites:

"When known is the last son of kings,
Only the sea will remain.
The sky will shatter
And the king will rip the earth once more.
Beneath, the heart of the sea awakens.
When Death sets fire to Eternity,
The daughter of the sea weeps darkness,
In darkness we will remain."

"Are there any happy prophecies?" Marty asks. "Like, born will be the last son of kings and he's going to shit rainbows."

"That sounds terribly uncomfortable." Thalia groans.

"What does 'Death sets fire to Eternity' mean?" Fred asks.

"What does *any* of it mean?" I ask.

Thalia drops her cards and walks over to Shelly and me. "It's got to be about Tristan. He's the last son of kings. The Sea King broke the sea, technically, when he split the trident apart."

I'm nodding, staring at Shelly for anything. She's cold as stone when she says, "Our kind is shifting, moving like the plates beneath the earth."

That's the second time I've heard that. Eternity. Shifting.

Kurt said *his* oracle was supposed to be at the Vanishing Cove, in the Well of Memories, and she wasn't there. Eternity. Shifting. If the oracles are physically *shifting*...

"Shelly," I say, "Is Eternity a place?"

She nods once.

"So the nautilus maid's home was in Eternity?" I say slowly. "And then she switched with the oracle that belongs in the Vanishing Cove?"

Shelly stares at me curiously. "Yes. Chrysilla's true home was Eternity."

I swallow the dryness on my tongue. "Can you tell me where it is?"

"I can't."

I'm about to argue, offer anything. And I mean *anything*. But she holds up a finger to my lips and traces it along my face in a motherly gesture. "I was never allowed. My sisters and I, we were given our destinies and our homes. I have not seen them in ages. My magics, they are naught but a sigh in the breath of the world."

I take her hands in mine. "Thank you, Shelly."

She holds up her hand. "This does not mean you do not have the *means* of getting there."

"How—"

"This championship is orchestrated. I do not pull the strings. Those around you have the answers."

I rub my face. I'm tired of riddles.

"Though," she stands, taking my hand, the one with the palm gouged out an hour ago. "If I didn't know any better, I would think you've already been to Eternity and back."

chapter TWENTY-SIX

In the train, my legs are shaking.

Racing from Central Park, on the 6 train, all the way down to the Brooklyn Bridge.

"Old drunk pervert," I mumble. "I knew he was hiding something."

Thalia pats my arm to placate me. "It's not our way to give up our secrets. That isn't who we are."

"His shelf was lined with it. Water from Eternity. No wonder I feel so stupid! I drank it and that's the reason for my super healing ability." I wave my hand in her face.

"It's a good thing you did drink it," Thalia says. "Or your fighting hand would be useless."

"Greg knows where Eternity is," I say. "Find Eternity, find the next oracle."

"I wonder…" Thalia says. "Why is Greg here? Why is he not at court? Before tonight, I've never heard of such a place as Eternity."

The doors ding open and we get out. Manhattan twinkles on the other side of the bridge. Despite it being past midnight, dozens and dozens of cars speed hungrily to their destinations. We take the same turns as before on the Brooklyn streets. The same cars on the same empty parking lot. The same silence on this dead-end road.

I march up the steps to Greg's withering house. I knock, and it feels as if the whole structure will shatter like glass under my fist.

On the sidewalk, Thalia is frozen. Nose turned up to sniff the air.

I want to ask her, "What is it?"

But I hear the shuffle of feet crunching over the dried leaves in the backyard. Thalia's face is suddenly lit by a blue flame. The force that pushes us is like a powerful gust of unstoppable wind. Glass shatters and falls like rain. Brick crumbles to ash. Greg's house erupts into blue fire. I land on the sidewalk, ears ringing. Hands try to pull me up from the ground. My head is shaking, split in two. I hear Thalia's voice, muted and far away.

Debris pelts all around.

There's Thalia again, tugging on me, but the blue fire is mesmerizing and consuming. It's alive, like hands reaching out to me.

"Tristan!"

My ears pop. Thalia is screaming at me. I get up and take her hand. We race back up the street in the direction we came from. I can hear the booming wail of the fire truck in the distance.

We stop after a few blocks to check our bodies for missing parts. We're intact, although covered in dirt and sweat. Then we keep running, and when I look over my shoulder, I can still hear the crackle of flames, as if they're following me all the way home.

When I dream, I dream of the silver mermaid.

I hate saying her name, even in my mind. Nieve. *Nee-ehv.* In my dream, Layla is sitting on a white beach. It's snowing. She's speaking to me in Spanish, and I can't figure out what she's saying because even in my dreams I can't understand it. In my dream, Layla is a mermaid. She has a golden tail that matches her eyes. She shifts in the water and I'm chasing after her until the musky Coney Island water turns navy blue and cold. There's a whale eating silvery fish by the ton, and I swim beside it until I reach the surface.

Above us, the sky is a clean white. It hurts to look at so much snow, and everything is so pristine that I don't even notice *her* sitting on a block of ice until blood trickles from the head of a silver fish. It dots the snow like a constellation and spills into the clear sea in muddy clouds. When she sees me, she smiles. The lovely angles of her face are marred by a nasty set of razor sharp teeth.

"You've found me…" Nieve's voice is a tired breeze.

She loses interest in her meal and dives in for me. Her voice is thin and weak, like her body. I know I can swim faster than she can, but when I turn around, she's still swimming right at my tail. Her jagged nails touch the tip of my fins. I can hear her all around me, like an echo.

"You're mine, Tristan. You're going to be mine."

chapter TWENTY-SEVEN

When I wake up, I'm in a tight embrace with someone.

I hug the warmness to me and rest my forehead on the warm back—

When I open my eyes, I notice the broad shoulders. Soft, wavy brown hair, just like mine. At the same moment, he turns around and we roll over. I fall out of my bed and curse at pain from my toes to my temples.

But I manage to laugh and say, "You pervert."

Kurt groans. There's a sickly green pallor on his face. I'm afraid he's going to throw up on me so I get up and throw some clothes on.

"Good morning, Sleeping Beauty."

"Why are you shouting?" He picks up the closest shirt on the floor and puts it on.

I bat my hand over his face. "Sweet baby Zeus, I can still smell the beer in your pores."

My laugh is cut short when I remember yesterday. My craptastic date with Sarabell. My parents and their new baby. The arrow piercing my hand. Midnight poker. The prophecy. Eternity. Gregorious. Blue fire.

Kurt rubs his eyes slowly. I throw a pillow at his head. "Come on, Captain Lightweight. You slept through all the good stuff."

"Why do humans do this to themselves?"

Kurt holds on to the kitchen counter for dear life.

My mom comes in and makes tea. She holds it up to Kurt's face and he drinks it slowly.

I take the black marker and draw a big X on Monday. Dad's already at work and it's Tuesday morning. I feel about a hundred years old. Then I flip on the news. A great blue fire ought to have gotten someone's attention.

Eighty-five degrees and partly sunny with a storm warning for Thursday is followed by the morning news. Behind a frazzled newscaster is the great blazing fire, and farther behind that, the Brooklyn Bridge is backed up with traffic. Firemen blast the house with water but the flames are violent, living things like hands reaching up, climbing up the tree and fanning out against the open space on either side of the crumbling brownstone.

"That's our combat flame," Kurt says. "How in the world did it get here?"

My mom gapes at the same time I drop my spoon on the floor. Layla says that when silverware falls on the ground, it means unexpected visitors. I really hope that's just a bunch of superstitious bullshit, but my merman senses are tingling.

"We were there last night. At Greg's house." I stand in front of the television so they look at me instead. I tell them about Shelly and the translation and running to Greg's house. "What gets me is that he has the protection stuff. The wreath that the court gave him."

"It's a symbol, Tristan." My mom rests one hand on her belly, even though she isn't showing yet, and places the other on my shoulder. "Just like the one on our door. The king is only king right now as a formality to crown the new one. But without the trident, his power ebbs. Whoever did this knows that."

"My behavior is unacceptable." Kurt broods. "I should've been there."

My mom takes my hand and examines the smoothness. "She shot you?"

"She's new," I say. "Frederik's been calling in reinforcements because of the rise in dead bodies."

"And they were all there," Kurt asks. "The vampire and the shape-shifter? They heard everything Shelly told them?"

I don't like what he's implying. "They're our allies, man. Anyway, I figured something out."

I take five index cards and flip them over to the unlined side. I tape them in a row on the Command Central wall. "We've found Shelly in Central Park, but that's been her home for a long time. She hasn't moved anywhere. Unlike the others. Kurt, what do you know of the oracle from the Vanishing Cove? The one you were expecting to see?"

"Her name is Lucine," he says.

If Shelly is the youngest, I'm afraid to see what the oldest one of the oracles looks like. But when I start to write her name down, Kurt hops off his seat and takes the marker from me. He draws the outline of a mermaid with a split tail.

"She's the Starbucks mermaid?"

Kurt ignores me and labels her name and location.

"Then, there's Chrysilla, the nautilus maid." I draw a spiral and label her as well, leaving us with two blank cards. "If Chrysilla came from Eternity, that means one of her sisters took her place." I put the cap back on the marker, expecting them to start shouting out compliments for my brilliance. "Greg was my only chance because that's where he got this water. That's why I was healing so quickly. Only now he's gotten blown up."

Mom and Kurt exchange skeptical glances.

"What?"

"It's just—" Mom says, like the time she confessed there was no Santa. "There *is* no place called Eternity. It's a state of mind."

I shake my head. "How do you explain my hand? Kurt, you were there. You saw Greg change after he drank that stuff."

"Perhaps it was something else," Kurt says. "Lady Maia is right. I've never heard of such a place."

I can't believe what I'm hearing.

"Darling, you don't understand. What Kurt is trying to say is perhaps Shelly's throwing you off. You can't trust them all."

I throw my hands in the air, exasperated. "Who am I supposed to trust? Kurt? You? I have nothing else to go on except for riddles, because that's what you people are good at, right? Riddles and prophecies. I have Nieve trying to take over the seas. Merrows killing on my own shore. Oracles swapping places. And I'm the one who has to fix it. Because of you, Mom. Because *you* never told me what I was. Don't you see? I am what I am because of you, and if I fail I have nowhere, *nowhere* else to go."

As soon as I say it, I wish I could take it back. My mom's face is crushed.

Kurt shifts in his seat uncomfortably.

"I *never*," Mom says, "*never* wanted you to get hurt."

I laugh. In the last couple of days, I've been injured more than during the last twelve years of school sports combined. "I'm on the right track. I know I am. If you guys don't want to help, there are plenty of other mermaids who will."

"Like Gwenivere," Kurt says.

I'm about to argue, but someone knocks on the door and I run to answer it. I need to calm down. Never in my whole life have I yelled at my mother that way. I can't even look at her.

Even before I reach for the doorknob, I know it's her. Her greeting is muffled as I pull Layla into a hug. She resists at first, putting her arms up, but then she relaxes and wraps her arms around me.

"What's wrong?" she whispers.

"Thalia says you were put in the ground." I change the subject.

"Yep. Six feet deep." She looks over my shoulder and, as if

sensing I don't want to go back into that kitchen, pulls me out into the hallway.

"What are you doing here?" I ask.

"I came to get you. Coach called an emergency meeting." She traces her finger on the pearly scar of Sarabell's teeth marks. "And it's Ryan's memorial."

"I have to find—"

"I know." She rests her hand on my chest and I shut up. "I know you have the championship and it ends in four days. But when it's over, you'll hate yourself for not—"

"For not what?"

"Not saying good-bye to your old life."

chapter TWENTY-EIGHT

Even before we climb the steep steps leading to the gothic building that is Thorne Hill High School, I can smell it.

Dirt, covering my body like I'm digging into wet earth with bare hands.

At the school entrance, beneath the archway statues of two clashing angels, is a massive flower wreath with Ryan's graduation photo at the center. Thick white candles drip on the floor like waxy tears.

I realize that the dirty smell of guilt is coming from me.

If I'd told him my secret, maybe he'd still be alive. He would've known to run, to hide. I pull out an action figure I've had since fifth grade—Captain America with his tiny toy shield. The year he transferred from Nowhere, North Carolina, with his side-swept blond hair and big gray eyes and honest face—well, it was pretty annoying. So we called him that until it stopped being a joke and just became part of his shtick. Ryan was better than the rest of us. Better than me.

All around and along the wreath are tiny things left by the rest of the school. Amid all the roses and daisies are a cluster of forget-me-nots from Mrs. Santos' garden and an Italian horn Angelo had always promised to give him but just couldn't part with.

Kurt shifts uncomfortably. "I didn't know to bring something."

"It's okay," I say.

He shakes his head, frustrated. "It isn't."

I thought I'd feel weird coming back, but despite the silence in the halls, I think I still fit right in. The tension is familiar, clinging with loss, excitement, hormones, and anxiety. Yep, still the average high school.

Ryan didn't have a funeral in Brooklyn. As soon as his parents got his body back from the morgue, they moved back to North Carolina, convinced of the dangers of the big city.

Flanked by Layla and Kurt, we file into the auditorium, which is full to the brim with kids.

"Are you okay?" Layla asks, crossing her fingers with mine.

"No." I hate the way the swim team is looking at me. The day I left for the Vanishing Cove, we had our final meet. We wouldn't have swum, not without Ryan, but I'm their captain. Was their captain. "I shouldn't be here."

"Yes, you should."

For a second, Angelo stares at me with that way he has, like he can't decide if he's going to deck you in the face or shake your hand. Then again, Angelo doesn't shake hands. Everything about him—his messy button-down, the gelled hair that feels like a helmet to the touch—is comforting. No matter what, he'll never change who he is to the core. Then he grins and pulls me into a man-hug.

"Can you believe Principal Quinn asked me to give a speech?" Angelo holds out his fist and I bump it.

Principal Quinn finishes setting up the microphone. Angelo puts on his game face. The real concentrated kind he reserves for meets or when he's on lifeguard duty. People can say a lot about Angelo: he's a player; he probably stole your lunch money at least once in first grade; he chews with his mouth open; and he doesn't stop to think about what he wants to say. But when it comes to being your friend, he's your friend for life.

"Uhh, I don't really need an introduction," he says into the mic as he loosens his tie from the knot his mother probably redid three times. "We're here to talk about Ryan Morehouse. I met Ryan freshman year. He was this dorky little thing. I-I made him buy me lunch sometimes because I knew he was so happy to have a friend, you know? One time, I went out with this girl he liked. I sort of knew he liked her, but he still didn't turn on me like Tristan."

I sink down in my seat. "I'm pretty sure it was the other way around."

"Don't worry you're still my boy, T." He pounds his fist on his chest, then points to me so that *everyone* turns to snigger.

Angelo's voice trembles and I realize he needs to make fun of something; otherwise he won't get through it. "Anyway. Ryan still helped me with my homework because he knew I wasn't so good. All week I've tried to replay that night in my head. I try to put myself in a different location. Maybe if I wasn't so busy trying to protect a stranger, I could've had his back. Maybe—who knows, right? All I know is we were a team, and Ryan was always on our side.

"We used to call him Wonder Ryan, 'cause you know, he was so vanilla. All nice and proper and stuff. But now, we should still call him that because he risked his life, like a superhero.

"I make a promise to my friend, right here and now. I never knew what I wanted to do with my life. Now I know. Maybe I'll be a cop like my brothers, maybe those cool FBI guys. I just know I'll make sure that what happened to Ryan doesn't happen to anyone else."

The auditorium cheers. One after another, they go up there and talk about him. How awesome he was. How cool. How nice. How cute. I refuse to go up because I know I'd get up there and say one thing: "I'm sorry."

Coach Bellini gets up and accepts the Triborough trophy. The other team forfeited before we could. Four boys from their team went missing, and only one washed up on the New Jersey side of the river. The other three are still out there. Coach reminds us to be safe this summer and to come back stronger next year.

Layla squeezes my knee. "I can't go up, either."

"Can you believe it?" I say. "Angelo with a gun."

"Hey, everyone has a calling." She turns to me and kisses my cheek.

Angelo hops right off the stage and lands in front of us. He flicks an accusing finger between our faces. "Layla, did you hit your head or something?"

I get up and pull him into a fake headlock, our way of greeting each other every swim practice. The gathering is breaking up. School is over but open to those returning books and studying for state tests. Not me, though, because, in my heart, I know I can't come back here.

"I got a surprise." Angelo pulls off his tie and hooks it around my neck. "Quinn's leaving for some board meeting. Bellini gave me the keys to the field. As long as we don't do anything crazy."

"Define 'crazy,'" I counter.

"All I'm saying is, it wouldn't be a proper good-bye without some fireworks."

chapter TWENTY-NINE

The sun is a white disk behind the gray overcast sky.

Angelo sets off a line of firecrackers right in the middle of the football field.

I sit in a circle closer to the track with Layla, Kurt, and some of the boys from the team. Some of the guys remember Kurt's speed during a practice session a few days ago and grill him on how he does it.

I down a water bottle in a second and take a moment to enjoy this. Layla sitting between my legs with her head against my chest. My hand is over hers, fingers crossing. I lean forward and kiss the back of her head.

And then she asks, "How was your date with Sarabell?"

I stutter.

"Did she take you *down to where all the fish is happy*?"

"No. How can you even—" I may as well be choking on my tongue. "You know that I'm not—I wouldn't—"

Jerry runs past us, screaming at the top of his lungs. He and

Angelo have matching red welts all over their arms from throwing snap pops at each other.

"She didn't tell me anything. Then I tried to stop her from eating a couple, and she bit me." I hold out my arm for her to see.

"That's from the fox boy!"

I hold my arms side by side. "I *told* you about the juiced-up water."

"You're right." She pats my knee and gets up. "I have to go to the bathroom."

I get up to follow her, but Kurt grabs my wrist. "About what you said this morning. You were right."

"I was?" I should ask for that in writing.

"We've had different lives, you and I." He glances around the field at the chaos my friends are bringing to the summer day. "Perhaps that's why it's easier for you to see the things I cannot."

"I *think* that you're trying to say you agree with me about Eternity being a location."

"In your manner of speaking, yes."

"Good." I pat him on the back.

"We'll need Princess Gwenivere for the next part."

Then Bertie plops down beside us. "Yo, T, where've you been?"

Angelo and Jerry stop running and join us.

"Family stuff," I say, trying my best to act cool, but I think I've forgotten how.

Angelo smacks my back extra hard. "What I want to know is how the hell did you get Layla to go out with you?"

"You're the man, Tristan," Jerry says. "Total upgrade."

Bertie goes, "Yeah, T, you're so cool now."

"Too bad it's a downgrade for her," Angelo presses his hand to his chest, and the guys bust out laughing. Even Kurt McTraitor.

They look at me like puppies wagging their tails. "Well?"

I dump the rest of my water bottle on them. "I'm not talking about that."

"*Ohhhhhhh.*"

"*Not even PG details?*"

"*I think he's serious this time..*"

"Don't listen to them." Angelo pats my shoulder, even though he's the one who wants at least PG details. "I don't blame you. That's a serious girl. If you hurt her, I will *mess* you up with a capital MESS."

"Word," they chime in.

I hold my hands up defensively. "Aren't you the one who bought a 'Bros Before Hoes' T-shirt for my birthday last year?"

"That was just a joke!" Angelo takes out his lighter and starts flicking it. He's already itching to light those fireworks and then run for the hills.

Surprisingly, Kurt adds, "I'm sure Layla and Tristan are well aware of what they're doing."

"Hold up. What's *your* deal, man?" Angelo leans forward, staring intently at Kurt. "You look like the kind of guy that should have a different girl on each appendage."

It's my turn to sound incredulous. "You don't even know what appendage means!"

And I duck for his punch on my arm.

"I do so. Half the girls in school who aren't faithful to me—no offense, T—are fiending after Kurt, but every time I see him, he's like, *alone*. If it's not your thing, I get it."

Kurt shakes his head. There's something about being with my friends that makes him more open. I don't exactly see him pouring his heart out to the other stoic members of the Sea Guard. It might be his secret, but he likes humans more than he'll ever admit. "There was someone, once."

"He? She?" The guys press.

"She." He picks up the empty beer can and plays with the tab until it breaks. "She was more than—she was everything. Then we were separated."

Truth, I'm a little jealous Kurt tells my friends this. Where was all of this when we were on Arion's ship together, duking it out? For the first time, I wonder if Kurt sees me as a friend at all.

"I guess it happens when you move around so much," Bertie says.

"You don't know shit," Angelo says. "Don't worry, Bertie, we'll find you a girlfriend. Tristan's cousins are still in town. That Sarabell was giving me the eye the other day."

"She's—don't go there, dude. I'm so serious. She's bad news." And I've got her denture marks to prove it.

"Like juvie bad news?" Jerry's eyes peel back. "Like she'll steal my wallet or something?"

Kurt and I exchange smirks. "Let's just say you wouldn't be able to bring her home to mom and dad."

"Ohhh," Angelo nods. "You mean she's not a Catholic. Yeah, my mom would be pissed. Still—I'm an open-minded guy."

I'm not feeding my friend to Sarabell for dessert. "So, Kurt is always alone? Let's talk about that."

"Was she hot?" Jerry asks. "I bet she was hot."

Jerry has had one kiss in his entire life, and that's because we paid a freshman to do it. He was pretty mad when he found out, but then he got over it when he realized it was better than having no kiss at all.

A flush creeps across Kurt's face. "Her hair was long, like rich copper running down her back. Skin white, soft. She made me feel as if I was the only person in the world for her, like I was important. Special." Then he sits up straight. His wall of reserve is starting to come back and the spell of the day is dissipating. Fat gray clouds are covering the afternoon sun. "Then I had to go. I had to leave her."

"Why don't you go back for her?" Bertie asks.

"I don't know where she is," Kurt says.

"That sucks," all of the guys admit.

Kurt tries to put on his best smile, and that's when I realize Layla's been in the bathroom for a long time.

"I'll be right back," I say.

I run down the stairs to the basement. It's deserted except for a few stragglers petting each other in the dark corners of the stair-well. The closest bathroom is in the girls' locker room. I can smell the pine-scented floor cleaner, the stale residue from the dirty gray mops. Beneath that I pick up Layla's scent, all frazzled energy, burning sugar. It coats my tongue and I swallow against that pull I feel in the pit of my stomach.

When I push the door open, she's standing at the sinks, staring at herself in the mirror. She jumps, hand flying to her chest. "You scared me."

"What's going on?" I stand behind her. Place my hands on either side of the sink to stop her from running away. I lower my face into her hair and inhale deeply.

She closes her eyes and I can feel her heart hammering right against my chest. Her hair is soft against my skin. I can feel the tension leaving her body. She lets herself fall into me.

"This is so screwed up," she sighs.

I bring my lips right over her ear, kissing the tender skin of her lobe. "What is?"

She turns around, slowly, so I feel every inch of her graze against me.

She grabs my face.

I don't have time to catch my breath before her mouth finds mine and I lose my balance, falling backward and backward until I hit the lockers. The doors rattle, louder than the surprised gasps that come from both of us.

She bites on my bottom lip lightly, then pulls back and keeps kissing me harder and harder. She's overpowering me, stronger than me somehow, and I let her. I've forgotten what to do with my hands because all I can think is how much I need her, all of her. I kiss her neck, the length of her collarbone to the dip of her clavicles and down. Warm fingers trace up and down my chest. She undoes my top button and my knees go weak. I press my hands on the hard metal of the locker for support.

Laughter fills the locker room.

We spring away from each other.

"What the hell, Angelo?"

"I didn't realize the room was taken," says the freshman girl clinging to Angelo's arm.

I turn on the cold water and let it fill my hands. I splash it on my face.

"You need an ice bath, bro," Angelo says.

Layla doesn't say anything. She walks around them and runs up the steps. I call her name, but when I get back out to the football field, she's gone.

Instead, Kurt's standing there waiting for me and I know we have to go. Jerry and Bertie set off a blast of fireworks. The sky is still so light that the bursts are barely visible, and yet everyone cheers just the same. I turn toward the street, away from the field, and Kurt follows silently behind me. Even when we reach the train station, I can still hear them—laughter and life and fireworks.

chapter THIRTY

The street leading to Betwixt, the underground supernatural nightclub, is teeming with people. Everywhere except the metal door with a red star at the top. An invisible cloak makes people cross the street so they don't have to walk in front of it, keeping unsuspecting humans away.

This is what cold feet feel like.

"Are you sure Princess Violet and Princess Kai are down there?" I ask.

Out of all the mermaids running around Coney Island, Gwen singled out these two. Kai's father is Keeper of Records and Violet's father is one of seven council members.

The last couple of days, I've trusted my gut instincts. And my gut is telling me that Violet is going to try to eat me like Sarabell. Then again, everyone says your gut, your heart, and your mind have different agendas. My heart says, "Go find Layla and finish that kiss," because never in my expert years of kissing has a girl kissed *me* that way. My mind, which sounds too much like Coach

Bellini, says, "Get it done, boy. You're on the right track. Just get it done."

"They love it down there," Gwen says, knocking once on the door. "When Toliss comes to shore, it's the only time we get to see other creatures. Mermen get so *boring* after a while."

Kurt and I exchange glances.

"Not you two, of course." There's the knock-back and she steps right through the portal.

Kurt and I follow, shivering through the cold door. The girl at the front podium is different from the last time. She's blond and very human. She smells like candied apples and copper. Her fake wings are doused in glitter and she takes my money. A red-haired giant of a dude lets us in through the second entrance.

Twinkling balls of light cling to the ceiling. Some of them stray away and over to around the long strip of bar. The music is loud and robotic, like the bald guy at the DJ podium is playing a video game instead of music. But everyone shakes their wings, pumps their claws, and sways according to the *untz-untz-untz* of it all.

I try to look for Marty and Frederik. Hell, I'd even take Rachel and her trigger-happy crossbow just to see a familiar face.

"She's in the VIP lounge," Gwen shouts in my ear. "I'll go bring us some drinks."

When I turn around, Gwen and Kurt are gone. I'm sandwiched between two elf-looking dudes with glittering skin, who are twirling light sticks between their fingers. I squeeze past and bump into a vampire chick whose deep black eyes make me cold inside despite the inviting perfection of her face. Deep down, I know it's a trick. That's she's dead and her yellow fangs would rip out my throat in a heartbeat. I push past her harder than I mean to until I break through into the less-crowded VIP section.

I spot the princesses draped around guys in black leather with tattoos and long hair that smells like grass and dirt and fur. Princess Kai is the easiest to spot with her shimmering long blond hair. She squeezes into the corner of a plush, scarlet couch, trying to push a guy's hand off her thigh. I step toward them to help, but she gets up and goes down a dark hallway.

I realize I'm standing right beside Princess Violet. Her smile is forced, almost pained, when she sees me, like I'm holding her at gunpoint.

"Hey." I can't even hear myself say it. The electronic song vibrates over everything.

She looks over my shoulder at the crowd, scanning and scanning. I can practically feel the breath she's holding.

"So…" I start.

"Where's Kurtomathetis?"

I don't think I've heard her right, so I lean in across the table and shout. "*What?*"

"Your guardian!" She scratches her head nervously. "I thought I saw him enter with you and Gwenivere!"

I'm not exactly hurt, but maybe yeah. I think I'm hurt. It's like the time Angelo went out with this girl just so he could hook up with her hot sister. I feel like *that* girl and Kurt is her hot sister.

It's the lowest low. So I smile and turn around. I don't need this. When Kurt and Gwen come back, they can deal with Violet and her purple hair, which isn't even as amazing as everyone says it is. I weave through the undulating crowd as if I'm getting carried by a wave. Someone bumps into me from behind, a real hard shove. I turn around, ready to fight.

But it's Princess Kai. Her powder blue eyes are wide as saucers, a hand over her mouth in an extremely familiar way.

"Wait—no—"

She hiccups and lurches forward, vomiting all over my feet.

The crowd splits around us, forming a neat path to the exit.

"Lord Sea." She keeps hands over her mouth.

"Come," I take her by the hand and lead the way. Kai hesitates before pushing out the silver door. "Shhh. Don't worry."

And we reappear on the Coney Island street.

chapter THIRTY-ONE

We clean ourselves at the shower stations on the beach.

Out in the distance, the grayness cloaks the sky. Unwillingly, I flash back to the day the storm appeared. The sky changed. The wave came. And then I was inside out.

"I'm so humiliated." Kai drops onto the sand. Her clothes are wet and her face is red from scrubbing. "I hate it here."

"What are you talking about?" I hand her a piece of gum that was squished in the bottom of my backpack. At least it's minty. "This is the best place on earth…when you're not getting messed up at a supernatural bar and barfing on people."

Her voice is high pitched but she laughs all the same. "You clearly haven't been to many places."

"That's true, but no matter what, Coney is still my favorite place."

Her face is skeptical so I ask, "What's your favorite place, then?"

"The Hall of Records." She licks her lips. "My father's an elder of the court. A historian. I'm supposed to be his apprentice, but he wants me to be *here* and—"

She doesn't let herself finish the sentence. I've never been around so many girls who find me this repulsive. I'm almost humbled, except I'm pretty sure they're the crazy ones.

"Your dad wants you to court a champion?" I say it as suggestively as I can because I like the way she blushes, from the tip of her chin to her big blue eyes. My gut, my heart, and my mind seem to be cooperating. I wonder if it's not having the pressure of Gwen and Kurt breathing down my neck. Then again, when I was captain of the swim team, I ate pressure for breakfast.

She gets up and dusts sand off her butt. "I didn't think it'd be so exhausting."

"What? Talking to me?"

She smiles. "No. Being with those girls. I've seen better behaved piranha. I told them I don't like that fizzy stuff but they get nasty so I drank it and it made me sick—on you. I was trying to find a basin to wash my hands. Everything in that place was covered in slime. And when I opened a door, I saw Menana doing something—let's just say that her father, King of the Rockies, would find a way to kill that demigod. So I turned and ran right out. Why are you laughing at me?"

"It's not you." I take my empty soda bottle and dunk it in the closest garbage can. "It's all of this. Everyone is acting crazy and they use this championship as an excuse, you know?"

"I suppose so."

"Come on. I'm going to prove to you that this is the best place on earth." I hold out my hand to her, and to both of our surprise, she takes it.

I get two tickets to the Wonder Wheel. The thing makes all kinds of creaky noises that let the fear of falling linger in the back of your head. But once you're up, you can see the whole park, the black line of the horizon, and the winking Brooklyn streets.

Kai twirls her hair and glances at me every now and then, like she's never been alone with a guy before. Her powder blue eyes remind me of those Precious Moments figurines you get at communion parties. When Layla had hers, Mrs. Santos bought about a hundred of them, all depicting a little girl in a white dress with doe eyes staring up to heaven. Layla drew a mustache and little devil horns on half of them, which got us both in trouble even though I didn't do anything. Even now, as our car climbs the Brooklyn sky, my thoughts come back to Layla. Kissing against the locker. Her hands—

"I'm not used to heights," Kai says, scooting closer to me on the cold metal seat. "My father said if the gods had intended us to fly, they would have given us wings instead of tails."

I put on my best reassuring smile. "This thing looks old, but I've seen two guys the size of boulders get on it without falling."

She takes in the new sights and sounds as we get higher and higher. I wish I'd bought her cotton candy or some strawberry-sugared popcorn. The thing about me is that I love making girls happy. There are just so many of them that I never know where to start. Plus, Kai is sweet and isn't trying to eat me.

"You said your dad's a historian?"

Her eyes brighten. "He's quite famous actually. He's the eldest of the elder historians, which sounds funny but it's a great accomplishment to have served under two sea kings. Three, once the championship is over. I've grown up cataloging and organizing scrolls my whole life. He's forced me to come here. Thinks now that Brendan's champion, I have to do it for the family."

"Yeah, there's a lot of that going around." I hook my finger on the side of the car and lean my head back. Below us, some girls in the swinging car shriek at the top of their lungs. Kai looks horrified, and I'm glad I opted for the stationary seats. "How are you related to Brendan?"

"I'm his aunt."

Just that sentence makes me retract the arm that I've slung around her shoulder. "I don't think I'll get used to this age thing. You look sixteen."

She seems relieved that I've put a little space between us. "My brother is the herald of the North. I'm the youngest at forty."

"I guess you and I are related by marriage, then? Brendan's mother is my aunt. Never met her, though."

"I've read all about your mother, Lady Maia!" She laughs giddily. "Bit scandalous when it happened. Even more than Lady Maristella eloping with my brother, a lowly scroll keeper. My brother wasn't herald of the North yet when that happened. He had to fight for that title."

"So you're a lady of court who really wants to be a scroll keeper? Are there rules against that?"

She doesn't laugh at my ignorance, which is nice. "Our people are changing slowly. A thousand years ago, merfolk with magic couldn't marry into the court families. They were sent away. Our stations have changed, but slowly as does everything we do."

"No wonder Sarabell's having such a hard time finding a husband." I almost feel bad for her.

The breeze around us picks up, and a thin fog comes in with the sunset. There's a strange horn blasting in the distance. I wonder if that means more accidents.

"It seems to me that merpeople aren't that different from people-people. Everyone just wants to be on top of any kind of pyramid."

"I don't think you'd be that kind of king."

"I'm not even sure what kind of *anything* I am lately."

She offers me a smile. "Had I…done that"—she can't bring herself to say *vomit*—"to Adaro, I'd be missing a head right about now. No, you'll make a just king."

She sounds so sure when she says it that now I feel sheepish. If Kai believes in me, then maybe she can help us figure out how to get to Eternity.

"I mean, I feel like I'm at a disadvantage in all of this. I wasn't raised on the island, and up until a few days ago, all I did was swim and hang out with my friends. Now, all of a sudden, I have a piece of the trident and I'm carrying around a dagger in my backpack that would get me locked up—sorry. I shouldn't be dumping this all on you. I mean, if you're going to help anyone, it's going to be Brendan."

"Really, Tristan?" A surprising laugh comes from deep in her belly. She dabs at a tear falling from her long, fringy eyelashes. I can tell she digs me even if it's just in a friendship kind of way. "First of all, if you've met Brendan, you know he isn't taking the championship seriously. He's always had the heart of an adventurer—not a king. My father blames it on the fact that he's read too many of our scrolls depicting pirates and ladies in towers and islands full of treasures. Even among our kind, we take pleasure in new worlds. It's why we travel on Toliss."

"He can't blame the books," I say. "You've probably read the same ones and aren't off looking for the pot of gold at the end of a rainbow."

"I've also read enough that makes me want to stay hidden away in my family's caves." Her smile falters. "There's a lot more in the sea to be wary of than on land. Don't you feel you'd be safer if you kept to your human life? I don't mean to put doubt in your mind. I really, really do believe you're brave. You've got the heart of the heroes I've only read about."

"You're going to make me blush." And I do. I feel the heat and confidence flooding back to me.

"I'm going to tell you this." Her eyes flit from side to side like she's feeding me answers of our history final. "From the last tournament I read about, the champions didn't *hunt* the oracles. The sisters are secretive, even for our kind. It's almost cruel the things they can do. Don't make them any promises. It always backfires. I read about one champion who was asked for his heart in exchange for the Trident of the Skies. He agreed and then she *ripped* out his heart."

My own heart clenches when she says this. I rub my chest. "That's pretty harsh."

"The oracles are harsh. Their duty was supposed to be to interpret the word of the gods. Now, I don't know. They've always been a mystery. I know the king only calls on them when important war decisions have to be made. I've never met one. You've met at least one."

"Shelly's cool. She hasn't got any voodoo or whatever." I don't want to talk about the nautilus maid or the terrible thing I promised to do.

"She must be the youngest." Kai bites her lip. I can tell the oracles are as much a mystery to her as they are to me.

"You called it the Trident of the Skies?"

She shakes her head and takes on a new air—the confidence that comes with everything she knows. "Our people aren't exactly spending their eternity reading, which is a shame. Once the trident was pieced together, no one seemed to care what the separate pieces were called since its power is strongest as a whole.

"The quartz piece is called the Scepter of the Earth. Quartz is the most common mineral in the world, but this kind is ancient, from the deepest depths of the earth. Poseidon was called 'earth-shaker,' and one legend says he shook the earth so hard that a great mine of quartz opened up for us to use in making weapons.

"The staff is the Staff of Endlessness. The symbols etched on it were burned with the blood of the oracles that forged it. Even if you're a regular witch, it magnifies your powers. But for most, it's really best to give someone a beating with. The trident tip is simply Trident of the Skies. It pulls on all the elements to create thunder and lightning and whirlpools. When I was little, it was always my favorite part of the whole trident."

"Scepter of the Earth." I enunciate it in different voices—voice-over hero, evil villain, even a badass Russian accent. It all sounds kind of silly but I like the sound of it, strong and powerful and, most importantly, mine.

Bonus points: I make serious, bookish Kai laugh. It's a lovely sound until it's followed by a scream.

We're halfway back down to the ground when something bangs into our car and we fly back against the hard metal door. There is nothing like getting crushed by your own backpack full of weapons to end a date. Kai grabs on to me, and even though I want to make her feel safe, I need to see what the hell is happening. The bang leaves a shapeless dent where our door should be. I try to pull it open but the metal is warped and the lock is stuck.

"Come on!" I rattle it with my hands. "One time I saw a guy climb out of these things when it was stuck."

"I thought you said this was safe!"

"I said it could hold our weight! I never said anything about safety."

Kai gives me a good shove, which I guess I deserve. Then again, I can't control external forces, now can I?

Down below, the crowds are mob-like, running out of the park. The other cars on the Wonder Wheel are in full panic, their occupants screaming and trying to punch their way out. The shaky technicians let out the people closer to the ground.

A screech echoes through the park. It fills the air in a *swoosh*. I unzip my backpack with sure fingers.

"Did you see it?" I ask her.

The ride jolts, like the lever is hitting stop and go at random. There's one guy left manning the station, because the others are running the hell away.

Kai isn't freaking, though. Why isn't she freaking out? Instead, when she sees my dagger in hand, her eyes go wide and she smiles. "Triton's dagger! I've never seen it so close. I have a profound affinity for ancient swords."

"It's always the quiet ones," I say. My dagger makes a terrible scratchy noise as I try to cut our way out. There's another *bang!* The Wonder Wheel strains against the pressure, and for a heartbeat, we fall. A shadow flies over us. Our car swings. We're not supposed to swing. I paid for the stationary seats. But our car swings back and creaks and screeches, and I know we're breaking away from the rest of the rise.

I shut my eyes hard. "Please tell me I'm not seeing what I'm seeing."

Kai gasps, elated. "Oh my goddess!"

"Don't. Move."

She takes a step forward toward the shadow perching at the center of the Wonder Wheel and ready to pounce on us. "It's a sea dragon."

"Okay, so that wasn't going to be my first guess. I was going to go with flying dinosaur of unusually small size."

"I've never seen one before." Her eyes are like mirror balls, spinning at the creature.

In the catalog of my childhood storytelling, I always pictured dragons to be the size of Godzilla. This thing is iridescent blue and green, hard and slick at the same time. It huffs into the air and takes off again, undulating through the sky. A row of ridges starts at the dragon's neck, like a Mohawk, and gets smaller and smaller toward the tip of its tail. The head is what surprises me the most. The sea dragon's face is soft with eyes that shine golden and glossy, even in the diminishing lights of the park. Until the creature opens its mouth to growl.

"Well, it doesn't seem to like us, so I say we get out of here." I stab the door. The blade slides through the metal with some resistance, but there's good give and I shout, "Stand back!" The lock on the door opens with my second strike. I kick hard, and the door falls and slams into the cement ground, just missing a group of kids running away.

It's probably not a good time to tell Kai that I'm not a fan of heights either. I stare at the open space below. It's not that far, but landing without a cushion will hurt.

"You're not saying we jump?"

"Unless you've got a magic portal to get us out of here, the only way is down."

For a moment, the sea dragon vanishes into a patch of thick fog before making a circle toward us. This close, I can see the barnacles growing around the pink slits of his gills. Of course. All the princesses and pirates and evil sea witches want a piece of me. Why wouldn't some nearly extinct dinosaur want in on it? I ready my dagger to stab at it, but Kai pushes my hand away.

"Don't hurt it!"

"It's trying to eat us!"

The sea dragon bangs into our car once again. We tumble back in. The metal hinges creak and finally break apart. Kai falls into me and holds on. I hold on to her with one hand and my dagger with the other, but we never hit the ground. Talons break through the ceiling to clutch the car, and the dragon starts to fly away with us.

"I think we're too heavy!" I shout, not at Kai but at the dragon.

It struggles to fly while holding us. We're barely skimming above the ground, and if he dips below a foot or two, we're going to ram straight into the carousel. I let go of Kai and ready my dagger to take another stab at the sea dragon.

"No!" Kai yells, pulling me away. "Tristan, please!"

"Kai! I don't care. I'm trying to protect us."

The beast screams. I didn't touch it but it screams and releases us. I get that familiar tickle in my stomach as we fall like a rock straight into the large seat of the teacup ride. We lurch forward as the car hits the ground. Kai is injured. The dagger's cut her arm. The skin is singed where the blade touched her.

Blaring sirens wake me up. When I move, my shoulder is burning up. I'm nauseated and dizzy, and there's a pulsing in my head.

"Hurry," a strange voice tells me. He's poking me with a stick. Holds out his hand. My first thought should be to smack his hand away with his own stick. Instead I wonder: *Why is Salvador Dali wearing a pink tie?* That's the thing with concussions. But he's real and he says, "Hurry now!"

I shield my eyes against the light that creates a halo around him and take his hand.

Then voices around me tell me not to move and that help is coming soon. They wonder if it's a terrorist attack. They scream about the apocalypse. They say it's the thing killing all those boys. Sirens are whooping nearby.

Salvador Dali catches me as I wobble forward and says, "Quickly, before the paramedics want to get their hands on you."

That sobers me right up, and I fight through the pain in my shoulder. I find my dagger, sling on my backpack, and take my princess by the hand. "Kai, are you okay?"

She nods, holding her arm where the skin is burnt and bleeding. Her first step is a limp that nearly sends her to the ground.

"Carry on, young prince," Salvador Dali says.

I sling Kai around my shoulder. We push past the throng of people that encircled us after the fall. We run down the ramp and cut through a passageway I've never seen before. We come out on the side of the sideshow by the seashore entrance. And there, as we enter through a red curtain into a dark corridor, Princess Kai sighs and faints in my arms.

chapter THIRTY-TWO

The room is draped from floor to ceiling in plush, scarlet velvet. Taper candles flank the edge of the table in front of me. A neon PSYCHIC sign hangs above the day bed that I lay Kai on. Her hair spills over the side like a waterfall and her hand hangs off the couch like she's reaching out to the ghost of a prince who sure as hell isn't me.

I try to roll my shoulder out but the pain is like a hot poker digging into me. So I sit as still as I can until the pain becomes numb.

In front of me is a deck of tarot cards. The borders are brown with age, but the scenes the cards depict are as bright as if printed hours ago. Three cards are laid out facing me. A heart with three swords driven through it, ten coins hovering around a couple in a garden, and then there's the Devil with a naked man and woman chained on either side of his throne.

The Devil card is singed at the edges. I wonder, why do people always picture the devil as being red? Mrs. Santos says hell would be a cold place. Somewhere where life and breath and everything that makes you happy gets sucked right out. When I think of hell, I think of colds and blues. I think of Nieve and her cold lips. I'm about to pick it up when the skinny, mustached man returns and says, "I wouldn't touch those if I were you."

I retract my hand instantly. The last thing I need is to stick my hand in a pot of psychic fire or whatever. "Why?"

"Because they aren't yours to touch." He sits across from me wearing a jewel-tone blue suit that's tailored to his every angle. I've always wondered what wearing those things would be like. Granted, I wouldn't top it off with a pink tie and a matching hanky, but still. I'd clean up well. "Who are you?"

"Comit," he says, unbuttoning his blazer to reveal a super-crisp shirt and black suspenders. Do people even wear suspenders anymore? "Charlie Comit. I *live* here."

Despite the suit and facial hair that make him look older, a twinkle in his blue eyes reveals something that is young and full of life. When he touches the tip of his mustache, I notice an elaborate red garnet ring.

"Why did you help me?" I ask.

"Would you believe me if I said I was a good Samaritan?"

"You can be good and still do bad things."

"I suspect you speak from experience." He leans back in his chair and crosses his legs on the table, careful not to touch the cards with his polished, black leather shoes.

"Hey guy, you're the one that helped me out of the car. You could've waited for the ambulance people to do it. Are you like a wizard? Because out of everything I've seen the past few days, that's one I haven't gotten around to."

Comit smiles, holding up his cane for me to see. The staff is dark cherry wood. Tiny wings, leaves, and intertwining branches are carved carefully all along it. It ends with a golden arrowhead, which makes a sharp *click* sound when he slams it on the floor.

"When I was told to be careful of the Sea People trolling about on the boardwalk, I had no idea they meant *you*."

"What the hell's that supposed to mean?" I get up, knocking my chair back. "Know what? I don't even know you, man."

"Tristan, please." Comit stands and places a hand on my arm. "I only meant that I've seen you on the boardwalk. Even in the throngs of people, you stood out, and now I understand why."

"That's not creepy at all." I pick up my chair and settle back down.

"I can identify with being different. That's why I chose to make a home here in Coney Island."

"Different? You look pretty normal to me." Then I add, "normal*ish*."

Comit laughs and rests his staff across his lap. "I was one of nine kids. Father was a ranch hand in Wyoming, and I was so little that no one paid attention to me.

"Then one day, my dad realized there was something different about me. The farm animals listened to me and did as I asked. From the stallions to the barn mice. He tried to beat it out of me a few times. Said, 'God would never make something so unnatural.'" At the last bit, he takes on a drawl. I wonder how many times he's said it to himself.

"But in the end," he continues, "my daddy was smart. Knew how to stay alive. Decided God don't make imperfections. Made a few bucks off me."

I break the intensity of his eyes by checking on Kai. She makes a whimpering noise from the couch and curls up even tighter, like she's in a cocoon.

"Lucky for me, the circus rolled in. I ran off. Started as a lion tamer. Ain't *no one* in any state had a lion tamer so young. I made my own way through this." He holds his hands out and balls them into fists, as if everything he *is* can be contained in the center of his palms. "And soon enough, a man found me and took me hunting in the Amazon, finding beasts that time has forgotten and creatures only ever seen on rotting pyramid walls. It was like peeling back my own skin and finding a new version of myself. Have you seen any monsters, Sea Prince?"

My mind flashes to the makara. The merrows. Nieve's face. "Yes."

"I mean like *beasts.* I mean creatures that roam in the shadows of our world while we try to make it so—livable. After the Amazon, he brought me here to run things. Downstairs is filled with the most exquisite beings on this plane and others."

The taper candles are long and bright; their flickering flames seem to have a sway of their own. Outside is the faint sound of sirens and commotion. Then there's the echo of laughter coming from somewhere downstairs. "So you're a beast tamer?"

"I'm a beast *master.*"

"And you know what that thing that attacked me was?"

"It was a sea dragon." He smacks his knee and practically shakes with excitement. "I've never seen one before, and boy, it was beautiful. You know, a lot of people think the Loch Ness monster is a dinosaur? But it's not. It's related to the family of sea dragons. Did you know that sea dragons are the only branch of the dragon family that can't breathe fire?"

"I had no clue," I say, trying to hold back a laugh.

"Not many people do. Nasty venom in the saliva. They're supposed to be extinct. The few that are left are controlled by beings more powerful than you or me. I can tell you one thing. Whoever sent that creature after you is not your friend. It took all of my concentration to get him to let you go."

Even as he says that, I know who it might be. Someone who wants to rattle me. Someone who's trying to get under my skin. "I think I have a clue."

"Would you like to see more of these creatures?"

Kai twitches in her sleep. I know I have to go home and keep pushing. But part of me is curious and I want to see for myself what he's talking about. "I really have to get going."

"Tell you what." He cocks his head to the side. His hair never moves. It's a perfect swish to the side. "We have a special show, not open to the public. I'll give you these to take." He holds his closed fist over the table. There are thin scars all over his hand. I wonder if they are from his father or one of the beasts he claims to be in charge of. He presses two gold coins into my hand. They're stamped with the Roman numeral II.

"Tokens," he says, "for the show. You don't want to miss it."

"Thank you." I pocket them quickly. "And thank you for the save."

"Don't get too sentimental. As cute as you are, I did it for the dragon. A thing like that, goddess knows what would have happened to it if it had been captured." He dips in a proper bow, then retreats behind the curtain.

chapter THIRTY-THREE

Because Kai is still passed out, I do the one thing I've been trying to stop myself from doing, and that's get my parents involved. But I can't exactly carry a girl with a bloody gash on her arm in the subway, and just holding her makes the pain in my shoulder flare.

So I called my dad, who must've broken all the speed limits, because it only took him five minutes to get here. I can smell the crackling nervousness around him, like burning cables.

"Saw it on the news."

"Was there footage?"

He shakes his head. "Some blurry camerawork on cell phones. It's gray and foggy. No real eyewitnesses except some kids."

That's the thing, right? No one believes children. "Mom?"

He doesn't have to answer that one. "It's amazing the things people will say. The official story they ran on the news was a failed Air Force experiment from the base out on Long Island."

"Yeah, because all jets have scales and teeth."

"You'd be surprised, son. Sometimes the mind can't process things, so it creates its own reality."

I stare at the dashboard.

"Your mother said you were fine." I can feel him look over at me, then at the traffic. "But I know better. I felt the same way when your aunt was born."

Now I turn to him.

"The baby is not going to replace you," he says.

"Dad—"

"Hear me out." He turns the volume down on the radio. "When your grandfather came for your birth, he said he'd bind your powers or whatever they do. I never truly trusted it. And when you started swimming, loving it the way you do, I was afraid to let you do it. Maybe if one day you went out, you might never come back."

"What made you change your mind?"

"I didn't." We run our hands through our hair at the same time. "I was right. In the end. It's like you're going off to college. Maybe, just maybe, if I think of it that way, it might be better."

"Is it better?"

"No. But you're meant for big things. I always said so." He reaches out and grips my shoulder. "Even without your mermaid tail."

"Merman."

"That's what I said."

I raise the volume on the radio. The song carries through the thick summer air. The strain in my shoulders loosens just a bit and I lean back into the passenger's seat.

"What was it, anyway?" Dad asks.

I consider lying, but I've never lied to my dad. "Sea dragon." Then typical Dad, he busts out laughing. "What's so funny?"

"And here I was wondering what to get you for Christmas."

I'm ready for my mom to go into hysterics when we come through the door. I'm ready for the news report, but thankfully, the camera crew arrived way too late to get any footage of the beast. There are only fuzzy videos and low-resolution photographs. What I'm not ready for is Kurt and Gwen sitting at Command Central looking pale and green.

Gwen rushes to me and punches me on the shoulder I banged up during the dragon attack, throwing all of her weight into it.

"Gwen!" Kurt shouts.

My face must be blue from holding my breath. "Why are you hitting me?"

"You left us!" She sees Dad carrying sleeping Kai into the living room and takes a second to process the information. "Then we couldn't find you and saw the wreckage."

I cradle the aching side of my body until I nearly double over. "I was making a love connection after Violet said she wanted to have Kurt's babies. With his eyes and her hair they'll be the biggest purple—oh my god, this hurts—"

Kurt tries to grab me but I recoil from him. My reflexes are slow and his thumb is digging into my shoulder. "It's dislocated."

"No. It's not." I walk backward around the kitchen table and he follows me. "It's just a bruise."

"Let me see you roll it, then."

I bite on my lip, and my eyes water when I try.

"Come here."

"No."

"Trust me."

"No, no. It'll just heal on its own. I mean it—" And then he grabs hold of me, and I swear the *pop* can be heard all over my building.

"Better?"

I squeak out a "Thank you" and lie spread out on the cool tile of the floor. Dad walks over me to get something out of the fridge for my mom. On his way back, he holds out his hand and pulls me up. "What's with Sleeping Beauty?"

I grab the stool beside Kurt.

"Kai tried to stop me from stabbing the dragon. She was all *Oh don't kill it—it's going extinct.*"

"Hippies," Dad jokes.

"She's right." Mom takes the bag of popcorn Dad is still holding. "I had one once. It wasn't meant to be mine. Pretty little thing. She had this funny tail, like a rainbow fish—"

"Uh—and lots of venomous spit? If I want an evil pet, I'll get a cat."

Mom shoots me her "You be quiet" glare and points to the living room. "Get me an aloe leaf, will you?"

"Fine." The leaf crunches when I rip it off and leaves a sticky trail.

Mom cuts it down the center. She likes to drink the liquid, which is disgustingly bitter. Growing up, I had so many cuts, rashes, and scrapes that an aloe plant in the house came in handy. I still make an *ick* sound when she scoops up the jelly and eats it. The second scoop she takes to Kai and rubs on her wound. Dad throws away the bloody paper towels.

"Remind me again, why were you out with this girl today? I just thought—"

"*Dad.*" I don't want my love life to be a topic of discussion, ever. But especially not right now. "The princesses are like a resource. My cousin Brendan has a boatload, literally. We picked out the ones who might lead us closer to the next oracle."

My parents exchange skeptical looks.

"It's true," Kurt says.

"It doesn't matter, because all three of my dates have Bombed. Capital B. One tried to chew my arm off. The next one was using *me* to get to Kurt. Yeah, I'm talking to you. And Kai got pissed off because I was trying to slay the dragon that was going to eat her. What does it take?" I take the bag of frozen peas my mom hands me and let the cold numb my shoulder. "I used to be good at this."

"Wow," Dad says. "You really are a bad date."

"Thanks. That's comforting."

"How did you manage to escape its grasp?" Kurt asks.

"This guy from the freak show. He's got this cool staff thing and he's a beast master." I tell them all about Charlie Comit and his welcome save.

"I don't like this," Mom says. For the first time, I smell her fear. It's real fear, like sand coating my tongue.

"I'm fine, Mom. Look." I raise my hands in the air but hold my breath at the angry stiffness in my muscles. She's all pregnant with her shiny new baby, and I have to show her that I can be fine, that I can take care of myself. I go to her because I've been the worst son ever and hug her. I whisper, "I'm sorry," and she rubs my back. She has that face Kurt's so good at—focused and all business.

"Focus on your next target," Mom says.

Gwen points at the living room. "Kai is the answer. Her father has the most archives. There has to be something about the location or existence of Eternity in his records."

"She's really passed out, Gwen," I say. "In the meantime, we should figure out a way to disaster-proof this apartment. That sea dragon knew just where to find me."

"This apartment is still under the king's protection." Kurt stands and closes the blinds. "For four more days, anyway. And then the championship will be over."

"So was Greg's house," I say, "and look at what happened."

Kurt paces around the kitchen counter. "What if Kai—"

"What if Kai what?" Kai says, walking from the living room into the kitchen/Command Central.

"Kai, these are my parents. And you probably know Kurt and Gwen."

Still with a dazed look, she takes the stool my dad gives up for her. Then she takes in the room, the framed family pictures, the rooster magnet collection on the fridge. She smiles at the maps on the wall. Then she gets to my mom and freezes.

"Lady Maia!" She gets up so fast that she fumbles with the blanket around her shoulders. "I forgot myself."

Princess Kai takes my mother's hand and bows. Even though she reminds Kai that she's not royalty anymore, Mom isn't exactly shooing her away. Maybe it's hard to forget everything about being the daughter of the king.

"It's okay, sweetheart. You're safe here."

I fill Kai in on what happened after she passed out. Assuring her a hundred times that "Yes, the dragon is fine." Even though I don't know that for sure. "Remember what we were talking about before the dragon came? About the trident?"

"Yes," she says, embarrassed. "Forgive me for not being more grateful for saving my life."

"No sweat." I give Kai my full attention. It makes her uncomfortable, as if no one ever looks at her. "Do you think you could look at something for me?"

She rests her hand on the bandage around her arm, thumbing the unfamiliarity of it. "What is it?"

I grab the parchment drawings from the kitchen and rest them on her lap. "This is—"

"The Star of the Sea."

"Come again?" I say.

"It's the symbol, right here. This star? It's the symbol of an ancient oracle. She was called the Star of the Sea because she was so beautiful. Her magics made mortals believe she was a goddess. Though there was no way she could be. Her power made her lose her mind, stuck between her sight, the future, past, and present."

"Crazy oracles," I say. "That doesn't surprise me."

I catch Kurt's scowl when I say this.

"But Tristan." Kai goes to get a better look at the maps on the wall. "How did you come by these parchments? They're not supposed to leave the Hall of Records."

I tell her about Gregorious. The manic look in his eyes. The way he changed after drinking the water. The way I did, for a little bit. I roll my shoulder and remind myself that I'm clearly no longer impervious.

"He's dead?" She sits back down, clutching her heart. "He was friends with my father. I remember the last time he came to visit us. They argued and my father sent me away to collect items from a shipwreck for study."

I can practically feel her mind racing. She gets up and traces a hand over my crappy drawings of the oracles. "You didn't say you found another oracle. The nautilus maid?"

"Nothing to say. She didn't have a piece of the trident." I say it so quickly that I can hear the guilt in my voice. *But I agreed to kill her, or die myself.*

"I don't understand," Kai says. "What makes you think I can help?"

I read the prophecy aloud.

"When known is the last son of kings,
Only the sea will remain.
The sky will shatter
And the king will rip the earth once more.
Beneath, the heart of the sea awakens.
When Death sets fire to Eternity,
The daughter of the sea weeps darkness,
In darkness we will remain."

I study her face as I say it. She's more wonder-struck than frightened. Then a tiny smile plays on her lips, and I know she's thinking what I'm thinking. "Can I ask what your theory is?"

Theory? I wouldn't go that far. I don't have theories. I have accidental enlightenments.

"Greg was in possession of powerfully healing water." I pace back and forth in front of my parents, Gwen, Kai, and Kurt. "I drink it and for a little while, I heal like I'm in one of those fast-forward sessions on the Discovery Channel. This makes Shelly suggest I've already *been* to Eternity.

"Now I know it has to be a place because her sister Chrysilla, the nautilus maid, said that's where she *belongs*. But oh no, my mom and Sir Doubts-alot over here think I'm wrong because it doesn't fit in their old mer-textbooks." Then I add, "Sorry, Mom."

At once, they start talking over each other.

Mom's all, "It's not that I doubt you—"

Kurt's all, "I decided to go forth with your plan, did I not? It was my idea to search for Violet—"

Kai's all, "Really, you went to Violet first?"

Gwen's all, "Just because Tristan figured something out, finally, I believe Kurtomathetis to be jealous."

I lean back. "Me too."

Dad, the only sane person among us, holds his hand up. "I have to say, as the only original human biped here, I'm completely shocked at how incredibly close-minded you all sound."

They start to argue again, but I take out my scepter. It glows in my hand, and a thin whistle settles over the room, like it's the sound of the light inside the scepter. It's enough to make them quiet and listen to my dad.

"You're *merpeople*," he says. "By all laws of nature, you don't exist in this reality. Yet here you are, fighting for your futures."

"My dad's right. Kai, is there a physical place called Eternity?"

The shift in Kai's posture is drastic. When she's around the princesses, she's like a crab digging herself back into the sand. Now, she's beautiful and confident.

"Yes," she says. I cross my arms attentively, but it's to fight the urge to wag my finger in front of Kurt's face. "In fact, all the protective charms that come from the king have been bathed in water from the Springs of Aurora, or Eternity."

"My grandfather gave Layla a necklace. She was poisoned by merrows and it saved her."

"But the necklace was the symbol of the king's family," Kurt says. "*Spirula spirula*. That's what grants protection."

"Haven't you been listening?" Kai counters. "It's a symbol, Kurtomathetis. Which, as there is no king, no longer matters."

Kurt gets huffy. "We've always been told it is the protection of the king."

Kai leans forward, a deep red blush creeping over her face. "What you *haven't* been told is what it was blessed *with*."

"Why would it be kept from us?" he shouts.

"Tristan, where is your dagger?" Kai turns around to me like a whip.

"I don't think violence—"

"Get it, please!" And the pleading look in her eyes reminds me that she's trying to prove a point. So I unsheathe Triton's dagger. She takes a marker and draws the *Spirula* coil on a piece of paper. She gives it to Kurt to hold.

"There. Tristan, stab him."

"What?" Kurt takes a step back.

"Go ahead," Gwen says. "Take a stab at Kurtomathetis."

Kurt's mouth is hanging open, maybe partly because he's wondering if I actually would. "Very well, Lady Kai. You've proved your point."

Kai smiles victoriously. "This is a symbol. The king is power. And his symbol has power, but it needs something else. Water from the Springs of Aurora."

Kurt raises his hands. "Don't stab me, but if this place is real, wouldn't we all be drinking from it, Lady Kai?"

"Don't forget," Gwen says. "We were immortal once."

"So the Springs of Aurora and Eternity are the same place?" I ask.

Kai's smile is wicked but brilliant, as if she knows all the secrets we aren't privy to. "One and the same. It was said that the water from the springs was the source of our immortality. It was the original home of the Sea People. Its waters have the most regenerative properties on Earth."

Kurt shakes his head. "No, we were immortal because Poseidon made it so. Then he took the gift away and left us in the human world with nothing but the ability to age slowly and live for hundreds of years."

"That's one of many theories of where we come from," my mom says.

I raise my hand like I'm in class. "I thought we came from Triton and those Greek dudes."

Kai nods thoughtfully. "Yes and no."

"What do you mean no?" Kurt's hands are flailing in the air. "Our origin is irrefutable."

Now it's Kai's turn to laugh. "You may be the king's most prized warrior, but I've got half the Hall of Records memorized. Our kind wasn't born to age this way at first. We had a short lifespan, like humans. Then Triton wanted immortality. The gods denied him, but he was Poseidon's favorite child. Cutting open his wrists, Poseidon bled and from his blood formed the Springs of Aurora for Triton and his kind to live in."

"Gross," I say.

Kurt makes to speak again, but Kai cuts him off and keeps talking. "The Sea People lived there, deep, deep down in the earth, away from the rest of the world. Until we got a visitor. One of the winged fey. He had magics we didn't. After all, we were only half fish. And so with his queen and our king, we agreed to trade. Magic for eternal life. Years went by and soon the fey wanted more and more. They bred quickly and in multitudes, unlike us. When the king put a stop to them coming to the springs, we went to war. It devastated our numbers, but we pushed them out and barred the entrance. Only the King of the Sea can unseal it."

"That's a great story, Lady Kai," Kurt says stubbornly.

I laugh. "Will you two listen to yourselves? Let's say Kai is right. That still doesn't mean you're wrong, Kurt. We're still Sea People with massive life spans."

And then I want to throw up. The realization creeps up like bile in my throat. "Since the king's powers are weakening—"

"Then the seal is broken," Kurt catches on. "Open for anyone."

"In my dreams, Nieve is weak and fragile," I say. "Imagine how strong she'll be if she drinks from the springs. If anyone can bring *death* to Eternity, Nieve can." I repeat the line of the prophecy, "*And the daughter of the sea weeps darkness*. That's Nieve right there."

"That could explain where Gregorious got the water," Mom says. "You said he knew of the championship before it happened. He could've realized what it would do to the seas and seized the opportunity to restore himself."

"But how would Nieve find out about Greg?" I stand in front of the kitchen window. Between the twinkling buildings, there is a patch of darkness where, for the first time this summer, Coney Island is completely turned off.

"I'm sure the sea witch would find a way," Kurt says. "Though I wonder—only the guard has access to combat fire."

"Kai," Gwen presses. "Is there a *map* to the Springs of Aurora?"

I snap my fingers, trying to pull a memory from my exhausted mess of thoughts. "Oh. Oh. I'm having a thought."

"Speaking of myths," Kurt mumbles.

"Shut up. I have thoughts." I shove him and he shoves me back. Gwen stands between us, and I turn around and walk to the other end of the table. "There was a map of a tree. It had stars and a river. It was in Greg's giant stack of mermaid porn."

"My father could be in danger, Tristan." Kai rubs the chill off her arms. "If Greg was a target, any of the elders could be next. My father's collection is extensive. I think we should go to the Hall of Records. It's ten leagues south of this shore."

I take Kai by her shoulders. "Does he have a map?"

She clenches her hand over her heart and nods. "We have to go now."

I point to Kurt. "I need you to stay here."

"You need me," Kurt says.

"Someone has to stay here and make sure everyone is safe." Then I add, "I trust you."

"Take Gwenivere, at least," Kurt says painfully.

Gwen is almost as startled as I am. She reaches out a hand and strokes his bicep. "I knew we'd start getting along sooner or later."

Kurt shakes his head, fighting a smile. "That has nothing to do with it. Just get Tristan there and back."

I load up my weapons and Kai takes one of Thalia's swords. Kurt grips my forearm and squeezes. "May the seas bend to your journey."

chapter THIRTY-FOUR

Kai and Gwen slink into the baby waves.

I turn around once to look at the dark boardwalk, the yellow tape around the closed park, and I promise myself I'm going to make this right.

The slits of my scales itch when water hits them. I pull tight on the straps of my backpack and the holster around my hip. When the water is up to my waist, I dive.

The water is dark, hard to see through. Sand gets kicked up. My neck tickles where the cold water rushes in and out. My breathing feels tight as my lungs expand in anticipation of my shift. The numbness starts at my hips and races down to my ankles. If I had toes right now, I'd be wiggling them. Ahead of me, the girls have already shifted and I follow the gleam of their sparkling tails.

For miles, there is nothing. No fish, no stones, no boulders. No shadows of ships drifting above us. For miles, it's just swimming.

Kai leads the way. Her scales are a powdery green. The tips of her tail look like bursts of chiffon trailing along. Everything about her is grand and slender. Like watching a flower dance underwater.

Gwen, on the other hand, is a strong and fast swimmer. Her scales are white with splotches of black. Her hair is like a white cloud melting into water. Where Kai is delicate, graceful, Gwen swims with a confidence I recognize in myself. She even sings a wordless melody that fills the whole sea.

Kai stops and swims circles around us. She points to a dull, rippling current that cuts through the ocean like a pipe. She dives in, and the next moment, she's zooming away. The suction pulls me down, so fast I have to shut my eyes. My mouth pulls back, and I have to spit out tiny fish that are getting stuck in my teeth. I lose count of the minutes, enjoying the numbness of the current until Kai yells "Here!" and makes a sharp right out of the current.

Unlike the pair of them, my exit isn't graceful. It's like trying to stand up on the anti-gravity ride at Luna Park. When I do, I hit a boulder and hold on to my head to stop it from shaking.

Kai points to where the ground widens beneath us. Branches claw out of cracks in boulders the size of trucks. My eyes adjust to the darkness. I graze the hilt of my dagger for reassurance. It's a really sharp security blanket.

When we swim into an underpass, I shiver down to my fins. Here the stones are blue, iridescent where they've been chipped away, revealing the gem underneath. Fish the size of footballs gather around us in neon colors. Their teeth are sharp, their faces like arrows leading the way.

Along the walls are etchings depicting different scenes like a time line: the circle of the earth, the separation of the heavens and seas and volcanoes. The three separate pieces of the trident, wars, and the trident whole again. Then there are things I don't recognize: beasts cut out of whole animal parts and symbols I have no name for. Clouds, stars, and moon phases.

The current draws us deeper into the tunnel until we reach an opening. We swim up again toward the clear light near the surface. When I'm above ground, it takes a second to readjust. The cave is massive, lit with torches.

"Where are we?" I trace the cool, blue stone.

Kai is in a half shift. The scales stop at the top of her thigh and wash away everywhere else. Her feet smack wet on the ground. "The entrance to the Hall of Records."

I grab one of the torches on the wall and bring it with us.

"Father?" Kai calls out.

At first it's enthusiastic, like she's just waiting for him to come out of the dark room and hug her.

We inch deeper into the hall. The room is lined with books, shelves made by cutting away at stone walls. There are papers all over a long rock slab of a table, ripped and crumbled. Pots of incense, candles, powders, and roots are smashed to bits.

"Father?" Kai repeats.

I stick my hand out to stop Gwen from taking another step into the den. "Be careful, there's glass."

"What a mess," she says.

I pick up a bit of parchment, singed at the edges and soaked at the center, ink running down the pages. When I try to lift it, it becomes dust in my hands.

I reach out to grab Kai's hand but she's so quick, running over the glass and into an opening to the right. We follow her into a darkly lit room. At first I don't know what I'm looking at. Then Kai's scream fills every nook and cranny of the cave. Atop a gleaming onyx table is an old man with armored scales along his arms and legs. There's a knife stuck in his chest, just below his heart. His fingers rest around it, keeping the pressure. His breath is a shallow rise and fall. Eyes, the same crystal blue of his daughter, peel open. When he blinks a few times, the color drains. It's like I'm underwater again, numb and wading at the bottom of the sea wearing ankle weights.

In the darkness, his eyes find mine. The sound from his throat is a gargle. His hand, soft and brittle, reaches out to mine. "B—"

"Shhh," Kai whispers. Her chest is filled with ragged breath, hitched and frantic. She grabs on to his robes. "Don't talk, don't talk."

She turns around, looking at the jars along the walls. She pops open all the corks and sniffs. Not finding the thing she's looking for, she sweeps her arms across all of them, sending them shattering on the floor. Her hands are bloody and glittering with glass shards.

I reach out to her, but she pulls away and stands over her father. He releases the hand from his chest and reaches out to her face. Then he takes my hand in a bone-crushing grip. The blue of his eyes returns. His breath is a gust rattling inside: "Don't let it burn."

His mouth opens wide, releasing his last breath. The hold on my hand goes slack, and my heart seizes.

I've never seen a merman die this way. He's looking at her. Convulsing. Shaking. Shivering. His skin melts away, leaving behind the powdery whiteness of coral and bone.

chapter THIRTY-FIVE

There's someone else in the room with us.

Gwen takes a step back and grabs Kai's arm to keep her in place. Kai's whole body trembles as she cries. I hold my finger over my lips and flick my eyes down. Along with the hiccups Kai is trying to hold back, the whisper of her tears running down her face, I hear an extra heartbeat and a sob that shouldn't be there.

Gwen hears it too, and I follow her cloudy gray eyes down. For the first time, I see the set of toes under the table. I unsheathe my dagger slowly. I reach under and grab hold of a handful of hair.

"Please!" His arms go right to his face as a shield. He's whimpering. "Please. I couldn't stop them."

"Let him go, Tristan," Kai's voice is raw as gravel. "That's Delios, my father's apprentice."

He looks about fourteen, arms like twigs. "I'm sorry, I'm sorry," he repeats. "They came and I hid. Master said to hide so I did and then—oh goddess, the screams—they broke things and—"

"What were they?" I ask, though in my heart I already know.

He shakes in Kai's arms, letting loose the hiccups he was holding back. He turns sadly to the coral bones on the table and he hugs himself. With his long fingers, he taps his forehead three times, the way Kurt does in his Morse-code way. "Merrows. I've never seen them so large before. One of them could talk."

"Archer," I say.

"What did they want, Del?" Kai asks, rubbing his hair back for comfort.

"The old map. Master wouldn't cooperate. They tortured him. With the blade. You have to know just where to cut, you see, to not kill our kind so quickly. To make it last…"

"As if she knew we were coming," I say.

The silence returns.

"Where is the map?" Gwen asks.

Del can't take his eyes off Gwen. From the pearly scales covering her breasts to the damp mess of blond hair. He licks his lips nervously and brushes his hair back in a bad attempt at cleaning up. We follow his eyes to the wall behind us where an onyx circle tablet as wide as my spread arms is embedded into the wall. There's a crack at the center of the tree. I touch the grooves that must be from Archer's fist. Despite that, the tree on the tablet is grand with branches reaching up to the sky. Right at the roots, a tiny waterfall spills into a spring.

"If this is the map, then what does it mean? It's just clouds and stars and stuff."

"Actually," Del holds his finger up to the deep silver crannies marking stars, "these are constellations. Cancer over here." Del gets a geeky smile on his face. It turns my stomach into knots. Ryan used to get that look on his face when I'd ask him to help me with my biology homework. They even have the same naïve glimmer in their eyes. Hopeful—

"But where is it in the sea?" Gwen presses. "On this earth and not the heavens?"

Del rummages through the things on a shelf, looking back to smile at Gwen, and pulls out a roll of parchment. It's an old map of the world.

"This is from eighty years ago," I point out. "Alaska is America now. Also, the Soviet Union is dismantled or something."

"In one way, yes. The surface of the earth is different than below it. There are more tunnels and caves down here than you humans would ever dream of. It's a labyrinth, hiding everything the world has forgotten. Some are prisons. Some are palaces. I've been studying it for fourscore years, but even I still need to reference manuals. Human maps only show the surface of the world. We need dozens of maps to show our layers beneath the earth."

Kai stands closer to me. I put a hand on her shoulder but she doesn't move.

"No wonder my ears won't un-pop."

"Get on with it," Gwen urges.

Del draws a line with charcoal from the middle of the Atlantic Ocean to the Mediterranean Sea. "This pass right here is where you want to go. The Cross-Atlantic Channel should take you there. The caves are protected by the ancient magics. But as long as the trident is broken, the magic won't hold."

"And to think," Gwen says darkly, "a young merman like you knows what the heralds of our kingdom do not."

It sounds like a compliment to Del, but there's acid to her tone. She shakes it off immediately and forcibly avoids eye contact.

"I can take us there," Kai says.

"Kai—you've been through a lot," I say. "I can't thank you enough. But maybe you should take Del to Toliss."

"*No*!" she barks. "My father led a long life. Don't feel sorry for me. It is not the way of our kind. This was his secret to bear and I will make sure it is kept. I'm going with you."

I squeeze her hand and nod. There aren't enough words for me to thank her.

"When I was younger, my father used to take me to collect samples there. There are shipwrecks for miles down there. I knew it was sacred land. The king forbade traveling there."

"What about me?" Del squeaks.

"Go to Toliss," I say. "Tell no one but the king." I look through my backpack for anything I can find. I have a sealed packet of gummy bears. "Give him this. He likes candy."

Kai runs into the back room and returns wielding a short metal sword. "Take this."

"What's th-that for?" Del's voice cracks. Man, I'm glad I hit puberty before becoming a merman.

I press my finger on the tip. It's slightly dull, but it'll do the trick. "Just in case anything tries to eat you, bro."

"Yes, sir. Lord Sea. I mean, thank you, Lord Sea."

I pat his back, trying to remember the fear that comes with driving a sword into something—anyone, no matter how terrible. We follow the cold stone path back to the channels and I tell him, "Just call me Tristan."

chapter THIRTY-SIX

Eels scatter as we race between boulders and down ridges with nothing to light the way except the Scepter of Earth.

The graceful movement of Kai's fins has become quick, flicking like a whip. Along the way, she cries out in a song. I can feel it snaking in and out of my heart, filling all the empty places. Longing, sadness—it's all there sifting out of me into the water.

We swim hard and fast until I think my tail will fall off. Nearly an hour passes before we can locate the channel. It's not like highways with big green signs ticking off miles.

No matter how hard I try, the current is so hard that my face might as well be the grill of my dad's car catching lots of little sea bugs. The water gets warmer and bluer as we go along.

Kai is the first to pull out of the channel. This time, Gwen makes a face and holds on to her stomach like she's seasick, which makes me laugh until I realize puking underwater is probably worse than on the surface.

The ground is speckled with geysers. When they blow, we're

surrounded by warm bubbles. Here there's a shipwreck, the bones of the ship covered in coral and seaweed and shadow.

Kai hovers around a thick yellow patch of weeds. She parts the grass in half, then, unsatisfied, moves along to the next.

"What are you looking for?" My voice comes out in a clear vibration.

"The entrance."

"What does it look like?"

"I'll know when I see it."

We sift through a soccer field of weeds and still there's nothing but sand and rock and the hollow skeletons of shipwrecks. An entire fleet must've sunk here. Golden trinkets are strewn about, along with soggy rags and undisturbed human bones.

"Over here!" Gwen shouts.

Past the ships, away from the geysers where stiff green trees sway in a semi-circle, there is a speck of gold beneath the sand. The ground has been turned over and littered with gravel. The three of us dig with our hands until we uncover the round door. It's solid gold with the image of the tree etched in it, like a manhole steaming in the middle of Times Square.

"Be careful," I say. "They might still be down there." I head down first with the light of my scepter. The tunnel is gray stone, glistening where light hits. Maybe it's the plummeting darkness. Maybe it's the pressure of being down here. Maybe it's just my nerves, the idea that Nieve and Archer are on the other end of this tunnel. But there's an acrid taste on my tongue.

Something hits my shoulder. Then more and more, fish swimming against our current. Only, they're not swimming. They're dead. Pale and gray, fleshy mouths wide open. There's a faint taste of sulfur and minerals in the water.

And with one forceful push, the current turns, like someone pulled the drain stopper out of the sink, and we've got nowhere to go but down.

I spit out the water in my mouth. It tastes like rocks. Not that I've licked a lot of rocks. My head throbs right where I've landed on long, wet grass. My tail licks at the air, and I lie back and grip the ground, concentrating on the half shift and bracing for the tear of my legs.

I roll out my ankles. Crack my knees. When I stand, my legs give out. "Holy leg cramp."

On my knees, I look up. I don't see the tunnel we came out of. It's like the air just opened up and dumped us here. But at least there is sky. Lots of it. Stars move like a mobile against a dark blue night that fades to the sun hanging low. It doesn't seem to be moving, just hovering and tainting the horizon with pinks and yellow.

"How are we under the sky?" I hold out a hand to help the girls stand.

"It's Eternity." Kai dusts ash from her elbow. "It is its own world."

Gwen bends back, cracking her bones. "I can't believe I'm here."

We're surrounded by a bright green field. The grass blows in a breeze that is refreshing on our wet skins. I take a step forward, disturbing the grass. Fat butterflies with glowing wings scatter. The change inside me is instant. The pain in my ribs vanishes. I close my eyes and inhale the happiness of sun on slick tanning oil, blue skies and cool sand, the warmth of a kiss. "Wow. Do you smell that?"

"I don't smell anything," Gwen says. "Except for wilting grass."

Kai leans her face to the sky, which feels like it's moved closer to us. "I smell parchment. And squid ink. I used to get it all over my hands. And the sweet crab cakes my mom used to make."

"Look." In the distance, there's a great big tree with gnarly branches atop a hill.

A bird with a white beak and red feathers flies past us. He lands on a stone smack in the middle of a dried stream. He pecks at the water and tiny glowing things that float like pollen.

"The stream leads to the tree," Kai says.

"Is it supposed to be this…dry?" I pull a blade of grass and it turns to ash in my palm.

Gwen bends back down to the earth. The patch where we fell is losing color, yellowing under cracked dirt. The ashen earth breaks away in her fingertips. "There is a pulse here. It's faint."

"Hurry," I say, pointing forward with my scepter. We follow the stream toward the tree. The dribble of a stream washes over mossy stones. The animals here are tiny. I can't imagine it would be able to support anything else. I try to picture the stream full to the brim, the grass bright and blue, and mermaids swimming and lying on the banks. I try to imagine living here forever.

When we reach the tree, the sun is still in the same place over the horizon. The tree is as tall as the sky, branches yawning and shuddering back into place. Leaves fall all around us, on the grass, in the spring nestled at the roots of the tree.

"I'm pretty sure I can make a fort under here." I pat the fat arched roots of the tree. A piece of bark comes away like a scab. I try to put it back into place, but then I just let it drop into the water.

Tiny animals emerge from the insides of the tree. They're all glowing from the inside out. Ladybugs and dragonflies. Tiny translucent frogs hop from roots to toadstools. One frog shoots out a neon green tongue and catches a dragonfly twice its size. The bug seizes inside the frog and lights up its belly.

"Why aren't there any big animals?" I ask.

Kai shrugs, stumped for the first time. Her sad eyes scan everything—the sky, the parched trunk of the tree, the tall grass, and leaves the size of my head. "I suppose they left when we left."

"What's wrong?" I put my hand on her shoulder.

"I think I landed wrong on my ankle." She sticks out her leg.

"Let's try something." I go to the tree where a small trickle falls into the brackish water. I take my water bottle from swim practice, swish out the blue energy drink at the bottom, and refill it with the water from the waterfall. I bring it to Kai and make her drink.

Nothing happens at first, but then it happens so fast I almost miss it. The swelling and redness disappears, along with the fissures of glass on her hands. Even her cheekbones are flushed, which is better than the sickly green thing she had going on.

Then the chirping dies down. The frogs jump back into the pond. Grass rustles in the breeze. The dryness of the ground is encroaching, sucking the lush green from the blades and leaving wilted hay.

"Tristan, look," Kai says.

A bright light fills the trunk of the tree. The waterfall dies, and a creature emerges from within. First, a golden head. I cannot see her face but I'm too stunned to care. She grips the sides of the trunk and pushes herself out. It's like she's been dipped in golden paint, down to her nails, down to the softness of her forelegs kicking out in the water with gold hooves, until lastly her hind legs are out. Her tail swishes at the water playfully, coming out of the stream and onto the bank across from where the three of us stand.

"What is she?" My mouth is open.

I'm expecting her to neigh, but her mouth is a bird's beak. Her black eyes are a stark contrast against the gold contours of her face. She is like the pure light of the sun, and I can't stop looking at her.

"She's a centaur," Kai says. Then leaves a pause for the obvious: *but she's got a beak.*

The centaur gallops in a circle, then stops to bow in my direction. She spreads her arms wide, then up to the sky. The water at the base of the tree is rippling, the light as bright as the stars, swirling into a funnel. And I can see it. The golden head of the trident. A thin spark of lightning shoots from the prongs and up into the velvet blue sky. The sparks rain back down in a drizzle of lights. Insects buzz, vibrating their song into the breeze. I head straight for the trident like my feet are possessed.

Then the oracle cries out, sharp like a falcon. A shadow springs from behind the great tree, jumping on the centaur's back. His massive arms wrap around her throat. She can't cry out. His weight makes her legs tremble and give out.

"I knew you'd make it, brother," Archer says.

He's got her arms pinned down, a muscular thigh across her body. She kicks out and pecks at him until he lets go. He hits her hard and she falls down.

"The trident," Kai yells behind me.

The head of the trident spins inches over a tiny whirlpool.

I push off the ground as hard as I can, but so does Archer.

The air around us is a vacuum, sucking the trident back into the dark water. Archer splashes in first. I kick and pull myself out of the spring. I roll over onto the dry grass and shout at the oracle. "Where did you send it?"

Archer lunges at me. Birds cry and flutter away. The tree sheds a torrent of leaves. He's got one hand on my throat and one on my wrist, pinning me to the ground. I'm holding my scepter with all my strength, using my other arm to grip his neck, but it's like trying to squeeze a baseball bat.

I bring up my knee, but even though I hit him where it hurts, all he does is grunt the pain away.

He lets go of my throat and grabs my scepter. The effect is

instant. His skin burns, blackening where flesh curls into itself. His scream is terrible, and as he drops it, I smile. It's a stupid thing to do because that's what he wants. Every part of my hatred and anger feeds him.

Archer rights himself, panting. He holds his palm up. The black blood dries on his palms, healing instantly.

Gwen and Kai form a barricade in front of the oracle, but Archer smacks them away. Even Gwen's outstretched fingers sizzle, powerless.

"Where did you send it?" Archer is a wild thing, grabbing the oracle around her middle and bringing her down. I run behind him and use my scepter as a bat. No, no, no. He can't hurt her. He can't.

He turns to me and hits me right in the gut.

I fall to my knees. Need. Breath.

He holds his arms over his head, the crooked curves of his dagger facing down.

I step forward.

"Death sets fire to the eternal well, brother." A slick wet sound fills the air.

"I am not your brother!" When my hand closes around my scepter, a great bolt of light shoots out into the sky. Then the sky spits it back in tiny balls of fire that singe the dry earth.

The oracle is slumped behind Archer. Her blood is red fire, dripping over her and into the ground. The flames sizzle, consuming and spreading all around.

I pull out my dagger and drive it through Archer's chest. He groans at first, but then he returns it with a right hook. "Mother wishes to see you, so I can't hurt your face too badly."

He cocks his head to the side, predatory and seductive. Then he looks to Gwen and Kai and seems torn. Like he can't decide which one he's going to attack. "We will all be a family soon."

Then he plunges into the black pool beneath the tree.

Smoke fills the sky, which feels too low and the land too small. Dry earth breaks off in chunks and sinks into the encroaching blackness. Eternity.

Frogs and even birds dive right into the mouth of the pond beneath the tree.

Something is quivering inside the trunk.

"*Kai*," I say, in warning. Everything, the earth around us, is consumed by a black void, breaking off into space.

"We have to go." Gwen sinks one foot into the spring. "Now."

"We don't know where that leads," I say.

"The only other options are getting sucked out into a *nothingness* or burning up," Kai shouts.

Birds and butterflies fall right from the sky, dead all around us. The leaves of the tree have caught fire. One lands right on Kai's shoulder. It leaves an angry red blotch.

"Come on!" Gwen pounds the ground. It cracks beneath her fist, spreading under Kai. She slips and I scramble to my feet and yank her onto what's left of solid ground.

The gnarly old tree stretches up again, and this time the branches pierce the sky. A branch reaches up and touches a star. The flame ignites and courses down the dry bark.

Gwen jumps into the pool.

I hold Kai's hand and we run in together, sinking like stones down a black tunnel. But I keep my eyes open, skyward.

Even the sky is on fire.

chapter THIRTY-SEVEN

The spring leads us back to the sprawl of shipwrecks and geysers. The same fish. The same light. As if nothing has changed since we left.

But that isn't right. Everything is changing.

I sift through patches of grass and try to find the door again but it's gone. In its place is turned-over grass. I use my scepter to blast at the ground, showering us in slow-settling clouds of rock and sand.

Over by the biggest ship, in front of a sea garden of colorful plants, Kai kneels. She presses her forehead to the sea floor. Fish swim around her like a kindness of ravens around a graveyard.

"What should we do?" Gwen swims beside me.

"I think someone should go back to Toliss. Tell my grandfather everything that's happened."

"He won't like that we've been to the spring. Or that it's—gone."

I groan, which sounds like gurgling. "It doesn't matter. He needs to get the island prepared in case of an attack."

Kai swims in circles around us as if she senses something in the water. "The fish, Tristan. They're gone."

I see him from the corner of my eye. The merrow has a long red face, eyes like ink smudges, and tiny rows of black teeth. Long red thorns protrude from his arm. In one sling, they shoot out at us. Kai swims to the right, but a thorn tacks her tail to the wood of the ship. She pulls, ripping the flesh bloody. In seconds, it mends again.

The merrow is about to blow on the golden conch hanging from his chest, when he goes into a frenzy at the scent of her blood. He swims after her and Gwen holds out her hands. A bright light bursts from her palms, throwing him backward. He spins and dives back for them. I throw a rock at his head to get his attention. The power of the scepter surges through me. Anger, that's the trigger. Right now, my anger is all consuming. The quartz lights up, and as quick as lightning, I hit the red merrow in his chest. He explodes in black chunks of meat and red scaly flesh. They float everywhere, contaminating the water around us.

Kai picks up the conch with her delicate fingers. She brushes off the black sludge and slings it around her shoulder.

I make a face and she says, "These are really useful."

"We have to go back." Gwen stares at the fleshy pieces descending to the sea floor and grimaces. She swims ahead, her melancholy song leading the way back.

When we near the New York coast, Kai turns away and heads for Toliss. For a moment, I contemplate stopping there myself. I've only been there once, but find myself drawn to the clear lake of the court, the merfolk drinking and dancing and soaking up the sun. I want to stand before my grandfather and show him the scepter. I want to yell at him for leaving me in the dark my whole life. I would demand answers. I would say, "Are you happy now?"

Instead, I keep swimming, Gwen trailing quietly behind me until we reach Coney Island. We surface a bit away from shore to make sure we aren't seen. The moon casts a silvery light on the beach. The rides are still shut off.

I half-shift onto the sand and let myself fall into the surf. I'll regret it later when I'm trying to wash sand out of my crevices, but right now it feels so good. When I was little, I'd paddle around right at the edge and pretend I was Robinson Crusoe and I'd just washed up on shore.

I flip over and stare at the bruised plum of the twilight sky. There's a sound in the distance, like a siren. My insides feel smooshed together, as if someone is stepping on my lungs. I bang my fists into the wet, soft sand.

"Don't do that, Tristan." Gwen sits beside me. The surf blankets our feet. "You haven't lost yet."

My laugh is bitter. "She keeps coming out of my blind spot because I stop expecting her."

"The rules have changed. Nieve has always been there. Perhaps you should start seeing her as a new champion."

"Yeah, one with an army."

She laughs. How can she be funny at a time like this?

"Adaro has an army," she says. "So do Brendan and Dylan. Even Kurtomathetis commands his own battalion of the guard."

"That leaves me." I sit up, bending my face to my knees.

"I can't believe the kings have kept the springs from us for so long." She stares ahead. "Then again, kings have many secrets."

"How do you know?"

She doesn't answer. Her white blond hair blows all over her face. She self-consciously covers the thin pear-colored slits where her gills would be. Right over that are long layers of scars that trace from the opening of her ear down to her clavicle.

"Stop staring," she whispers, tracing the scar along her throat. "It isn't polite."

I know I shouldn't ask but I want to know. "How did he do it?"

Her hand remains on her scars.

"You never talk about it, Gwen."

Her face is hard. "There's nothing to talk about."

"He *hurt* you. The man you were supposed to marry actually hurt you." She gets up and walks down the shore away from me. I hate how casual she is about it. "Wasn't there anyone you could go to?"

"He's dead. Twice over. Don't bring it up again." She stops and faces me. "Why do you care?"

"You're my friend." I grab her by the shoulders and smile. "Even if you don't want to admit it."

Her face is smooth and she's looking at me like she wants more from me than I can give her. Her eyes are like little moons and she sets them on me. She rests her hands on my chest. The breeze is cold where my shoulders have just begun to dry off. A drop trickles down my spine. In this light, at the base of the pier, her scars are iridescent. Her lips are pink and swollen. With her index finger, she traces my jawline, tucks my hair behind my ear.

She leans up to kiss me.

I turn my face away. "I can't."

"Right." The little moons turn into little storms. She backs away. "You've already got someone."

"It's not that I don't think you're beautiful." I can't call her hot. She is, but she's more than that. She's this burst of lightning and the calm right after it all in one. She's just not for me.

"Can't blame a mermaid for trying."

My laughter is nervous. "You're the one who said I never had a chance with you."

"That's before I really knew you." She brushes her hair away from her face. "When I heard they were presenting you at court, I thought you'd be a stupid skin sack."

"Why do you even call humans that? Merpeople have skin too."

"And you make me laugh. I saw how insanely brave and stupid you can be for your friends. Elias never cared for me that way. It made me long for that. Maybe I just liked the way you held that scepter."

Gwen turns over her shoulder with that mischievous smile. She closes the space between us and brushes away the scales at my hips to reveal the skin beneath. "Is her hold over you so strong?"

And I don't hesitate, holding her by her shoulders at a distance. "There is nothing I wouldn't do for her."

Layla. The name hangs between us like a pendulum ready to snap.

"You can do better than me." I rummage for clothes in my backpack. They're all wet, but it's better than walking home in glittery underwear.

"I'm not used to having an actual choice in this. Before, Elias was *it*."

I hug her. Her hands hang at her sides at first. I can feel her breath hitch.

"That's the great thing about now," I tell her. "Now, you get a real choice."

chapter THIRTY-EIGHT

My feet feel foreign.

They're numb. Awkward. Possessed.

They're leading me past my own street.

No, I can't go home yet. I can't stand in my kitchen and cross off the end of another day.

I pick up the pay phone and dial her number. On the second ring, she picks up.

"Did I wake you?" I can hear her rub her eyes and kick the covers off.

"Tristan?"

"Only if you want it to be."

"Shut up. Where are you?"

"Down the block at the bodega."

"My dad is *this* far away from putting remote control bars on all the doors and windows because of you."

"That's never stopped you before," I taunt.

"Is everything okay?"

I inhale loudly. Nothing comes out. "I'll be on your porch." I hang up and turn the corner.

Her mom's garden is overgrowing, leaves wild and swaying in the cool night. I used to pluck a flower and give it to Mrs. Santos. She never complained that I took it from her own garden.

"You look like crap," Layla says.

"Exactly what I wanted to hear after swimming in torpedo-fast underwater currents for over ten hours."

She comes around from the back entrance. She's wearing her black Guardian Knight T-shirt and denim shorts. I wonder if she sleeps in her underwear. As if she knows what I'm thinking, she smacks me on the back of the head. "I'm familiar with that grin on your face."

She sits beside me, and I get a hot flash. Damn, I thought these things only happened to women. She burrows herself into my shoulder and says, "Tell me."

I run my hand along the top of her hair. Why is it that girls have this effect? Things like long hair and long eyelashes and the smell of flowers just throw me. I squeeze the bridge of my nose.

"Tristan, you're shaking."

She rubs the cold away from my arms. The iridescent sheen of where my scales were rubs off on her palms. For a moment, she smiles down at her hands, then at my face. Then dusts it away and says, "Gross."

It calms me, and I tell her about Violet (she laughs) and Kai (she laughs some more). Then the sea dragon. (No, I didn't hurt it, thanks.) Kai's father. Eternity burning.

"The oracle was a centaur?"

I nod. "I was expecting a mermaid or something with tentacles."

"Actually that makes sense, because Poseidon did create a horse as a gift to Artemis."

I take her head in my hands and kiss it. "Smart chicks are so hot."

She bats me away. "I just read, you dumb jock."

We laugh together and it's the best I've felt all week. Except for yesterday in the locker room, but this is an inside kind of good. I remember Kai singing underwater for her father, the way it made me long for something more. That's why I couldn't kiss Gwen. That's why I can't kiss anyone but Layla.

"That's horrible about Kai's dad."

"They're weird about death. It's like they take a moment to see it happen and then they move on. It doesn't feel natural. And he literally turned into coral." I sit up. "I wonder what will happen when I die, since I'm half and half?"

"Don't," she whispers. "Don't say that."

"There's a chance," I admit. "I was so close to that trident. But I hesitated because I wanted to help the oracle. In the end, she died anyway. Nieve is stronger every day and she's coming for me."

"Then you just have to be stronger than her." Layla makes it sound so easy.

I hold her tighter. "When I'm with you, I feel like I can do anything. I don't want to mess this up."

"Us? Or the championship?"

This sounds like one of those girl trick questions that I shouldn't answer. I'm too quiet. Every part of me hurts. I should drink some of the spring water but I want to save it for something more important, not just wimpy pains I can get at the gym.

"It doesn't matter," she says. "There can't be an *us* anyway."

"Shut up, dude," I scoff. "You're so totally my girlfriend. You've been dying to be my girlfriend since we were in the sandbox. Marked your territory by peeing on me and everything. I'm just going to tell everyone that you're my girl, and then you'll make me look like a loser when you try to deny it. Can you really do that to me?"

She punches me in the ribs and I *kind* of exaggerate the pain so she'll rub it. "Seriously, Tristan. This is fun, admittedly. But we shouldn't do that to each other. Not now, at least."

"Why? One," I count my fingers in front of her face, "you like me. You know how I can tell? You keep feeling up on me all over the place. Don't act like it's my *mer thing* because you like my mer thing just fine."

I brace for the next jab in the ribs, harder than the first.

"I knew Angelo shouldn't have taught you to fight."

"Are you done?" She sits back. "Was that the one reason?"

I pop my lips. "Yep."

"My turn," she says. "One, I've known 80 percent of the girls you've '*dated*.'"

"Don't. Come on. Don't use air quotes."

"Two, you're a *merman*."

"I can't control that. That's like your hair when it gets frizzy in the summer or the crooked little toe on your right foot." I realize that won't help my case.

"Three, I can't breathe underwater, Tristan. I've thought about this since it first happened and I-I trust you with my whole life. But this—where does it leave me when you're king and I'm stranded on the Coney Island beach wondering which ocean you're in?"

"Layla, I will *never* leave you."

"You aren't listening to what I'm saying." She grabs chunks of her hair and then smooths them down. "We've waited sixteen years to be together. I think we can wait another week and see what happens."

I take her hands in mine. But I don't want to wait another week. So I'm like, "I don't want to wait another week."

That's the thing about girls. Sometimes they say one thing and they mean another. She traces the outline of my lips and gives me a quick kiss.

"See?" I say, to prove my point.

"Hey, what happened to Gwen and Kai?"

"Kai went to alert my grandfather, just in case." At the mention, I think of Gwen trying to kiss me. Should I tell Layla? Unbidden, Angelo's voice pops into my head and he says, *"She didn't ask so don't tell her."*

I say, "Gwen went wherever she goes."

"Do you hear that?"

"Sirens," I say. "A lot of them the last couple of days."

Sunrise creeps over the houses across the street. The siren horn dies down, and Layla and I are sitting on her front porch. I remember what Gwen said about thinking of Nieve like I would another champion. I've been to three oracles. How many of the other champions can say that?

"New battle plan." I slap my knees and stand up. All of my joints pop and ache. My mind is dizzy with exhaustion. "It seems everyone's got themselves an army."

Layla's eyes peel back to me with this new realization. "So what you need is—"

"An army of my own."

chapter THIRTY-NINE

After I leave Layla, I head home.

My temples pulse. A whisper fills my head. I don't know how I quite make it to my bed. Exhaustion blankets me like fog. When I close my eyes, I'm in water.

It's a cave made of smooth, bright-white stone. Skinny red and black plants sprout from thin cracks in the sparkling walls like bloody membranes.

When I see her, I jump back and hit the wall, hear the crunch of my skull.

Nieve, pale as snow and as skinny as when I saw her the first time, is resting on a bench carved into the wall. Her silver scales gleam, and her cold blue mouth is slightly open, tiny bubbles coming in and out.

Around me, the water turns pink with my blood. It trails across the cave to where the silver mermaid is sleeping. She sniffs at the air and rouses. A thin blanket-like thing falls off her shoulders and onto the floor. Her eyes flutter open. She smiles when she sees me; the sight of her shark mouth pulls at my gut. I can't move.

She tucks her hair back. The motion is slow, pained. She's weak, skinnier than ever. But still with the face of a goddess—the refined cheekbones, the sharp slope of her nose, the silver eyes fringed with long blue lashes. Her mouth is a blue pout. Then she opens her mouth at the cloud of blood. She tastes it. Swallows it.

"You're so gross," I say before I can stop myself.

"You came."

"I wasn't trying to."

Nieve moves forward off her bench. She starts to sink to the floor and has to kick extra hard. It's too much for her, and she falls on her knees right in front of me. She undoes the button of my shorts. They're the same ones I went to sleep in. Yep. I'm dreaming. I don't remember sleepwalking. I was asleep somewhere in my house. Probably beside Kurt.

She moves her hands over my chest and makes a parting motion. My T-shirt rips away. The cloth floats to the ground.

I have this terrible image of her biting into my ribs and tearing me apart so I say, "That was my favorite shirt."

"I'm not going to hurt you." She cocks her head. "Unless you ask."

"I'm pretty sure I won't ask." I'm convinced this is a dream. A gross, twisted dream. I need to wake up right now.

"Why don't you shift, Tristan? I hate seeing you in these human clothes." Before she can get a little too close to my goods, I do as she says. There go my shorts.

"Are you going to let go of me now?"

When she doesn't bare her teeth, she's incredibly beautiful. Hard to believe she's a monster. She does that thing with her hands again and the invisible force holding me goes away. She swims back, away from me and onto her bench.

"How did I get here? Where is this place?" I reach at my side and come away empty. What I wouldn't do for my dagger.

"This place is very dear to me. It is where I go when I'm weak. This very moment, my son is bringing me something special. Something to make me strong. The way I was before my brother put me away. You do look like him, in your own way."

"You made Archer kill the oracle."

She shakes her head softly. "The oracles killed themselves, wicked, tricky devils that they are."

I hate the pressure of her on me. It's worse than struggling against the currents. "You won't win, you know."

"I already have." She doesn't smile. "My brother has broken the seas. He started this many years ago. I intend to make it right. We will put the seas back together."

"How generous of you. It'll make up for all the people you've killed."

"I didn't kill you." She undulates like an eel until her face is right over mine. "Don't you remember the wave, Tristan?"

I wish she'd stop saying my name. "How could I forget?" I thought I'd gone insane, floating underwater until I saw her in her silver splendor. She cut me with her fingernails. Then the shark attacked her and carried me away.

"I wanted to see your heart. So I lured you. And you came

after me so willingly, not even stopping to think that it might not be real.

"The first time I held you was the first time since your birth that you shifted into your true self. I knew who you were just as I knew they were searching for you, my brother's heir. I wanted to kill you."

I remember the trace of her nails, the jagged edges cutting across my chest.

"Then I tasted your blood. Blood can tell you so much about a being. It is life. It is your past and future. In it, I could see exactly how invaluable you were to me. I've lived so long, and my future is linked to a boy. Funny, aren't they?"

"Who?"

"The fates."

I swallow hard. "And how exactly am I invaluable to you?"

"Because we could be great together."

"You're a killer." I hate the way I sound, like a scared, dumb kid.

"You will be one too. Just because you killed a merrow, my child, does that make you better?" She *tsk-tsk-tsks* at me. "What will you do when you have to drive your sword through one of our kind to keep the peace of your new broken kingdom?"

"Shut up."

"Do you know what happens when you're alone for ages?" She squeezes my face with her hands, forcing me to look straight at her. The white of her eyes. The blue of her eyelids. "Do you? The pitch-blackness of the Caves of Tartarus. The creatures that live there, caged like beasts when far worse lies in my brother's own court. Whimsical, he is, sitting on a throne that should've been mine, entertaining half breeds and stripping our own to pacify beings far beneath us." She coughs, clutching herself as if there is not enough water or oxygen down here. "I don't mean you. You're special."

She flicks her hand at me again and I'm paralyzed once more. I pull against a force that weighs me down until it pulls me to the ground. Red plants sprout from the ground and weave all over me. Everywhere except my face. She swims slowly, cutting through the water with the elegance of a shark. She props her elbows on my chest, her tail right on top of mine.

"My sons will be here soon. I will drink from Eternity and I will be strong again." She puts a finger to my lips. My tongue is heavy and fat in my mouth. I can only grunt in protest. "You will see that the only way to keep your loved ones safe is to be with me."

I want to scream but my voice is gone.

My lips are numb.

She traces the length of my cheek and whispers, "Soon..."

She lowers herself with her mouth slightly open, coming down for a kiss.

chapter FORTY

The blast of a horn wakes me up.

Kurt is standing over me.

I roll over and realize I'm naked again. "Stop doing that, creep."

He's jittery and the energy crackling around him is frantic.

"Get dressed," he says. "Something's happened."

I throw on a pair of shorts off the floor and a T-shirt that smells vaguely clean, and we're out of the room and into the kitchen.

Layla's drawing a black X over Tuesday on the wall calendar. When she sees me, she smiles. I finger-comb my bed head before kissing her cheek. The tiles are cold under my feet.

"Where are my parents?"

"Doctor," Layla says. "Everything is fine with the baby, but it's her first time going. She's so scared."

I splash water over my face in the kitchen sink and use a paper towel to dry off. The last thing I remember is Nieve's blue lips coming down on me. Why does everyone try to kiss me? There should be rules against that.

"Kurt, spit it out. You guys are freaking me."

Layla opens the window, letting the cool air out and the warmth of the overcast day in. Curry, sea air, and smoke—the neighborhood smells waft in with something else. The horn blast.

"What is that?" A thin strand of lightning crackles on the horizon.

"Adaro," Kurt says. "He's here."

I whip around. "Like *here,* here? Coney Island here?"

"That's what the call is," Kurt says. "This place is too noisy. I didn't think it could be one of *our* calls. There are too many sirens in this place."

"But why is he here?"

"He's requesting an audience with you." Kurt takes his arm knife and checks the blade. "It seems he's acquired the center staff of the trident."

The front door cracks open and we jump, even Kurt.

"It's just me," Thalia says.

Kurt's voice is like thunder. "Where have you been?"

Thalia's face is hard, greener than usual. She ignores her brother and runs right up to me, pointing at my chest. "You're bleeding."

When I look down, beads of blood bloom through the white of my shirt. I take it off and rinse it in the sink, then clean the wound.

"I want to show you guys something."

I go into my backpack and bring out the water bottle.

"Gatorade has a new flavor?" Layla laughs unevenly.

I pour just a single drop on the cut. The skin grows back, stitching itself back together. "The effect doesn't last long. It's from the springs…which are now gone." I retell them about the Hall of Records, the channels, and the springs. Even though Layla only heard it hours ago, she still nods along enraptured until I get to the dream of Nieve when they all share a grimace.

Thalia takes the plastic bottle in her hand. "To think, eons are reduced to this container."

"I want you guys to drink it."

They stare.

"Why?" Kurt asks.

"Nieve." Even saying her name makes my tongue feel like lead. "She's more than just an angry mermaid with a grudge. She wants to be queen. When Archer brings her the spring water, she'll be strong. She can make more merrows." I think of Adaro waiting for me out on the beach. I punch the wall.

"Now she needs the trident and we're making it easy for her. Two of the pieces are right here. Me and Adaro. She can march up the shore with her mutant mermen and pick us off. To prevent that, we have to do a few things. Step one is you all have to drink this."

"What about you?" Layla asks.

"Don't worry about me."

"What the hell do you mean?" She follows me to the window and gets in my face. "I have this necklace. I—"

"What if it's not enough?"

"Tristan, all of us know the risks," Kurt says. "We're still here."

The conch horn blasts again.

"What the hell is up with this guy?" I ask. Come to think of it, that horn's been blasting since we got back on Monday. Sarabell knew he was here when she came up to me at Luna Park, when we were out on our date. I feel so used.

Thalia shrugs, setting the water bottle on the table. "If we were on his land near the Galapagos, he would have to return the favor."

"What, I go to him and make nice?" Then I think of the army I need to form. Having Adaro as a temporary ally wouldn't be the worst thing in the world. "The last time we heard of him, we had just missed him at the Vanishing Cove. Now he has the Staff of the Seas. Why hasn't he made himself known until now?"

Kurt buckles his sheath around his waist. "That's precisely what we are going to find out."

chapter FORTY-ONE

A few weeks ago, on a day like this, I would've been sitting on the lifeguard tower. I would be in my uniform—an orange Speedo with orange trunks over that, which is the least flattering color on anyone who isn't a lifeguard. The circumference of towels below would be full of girls baking in the sun, each asking stupid questions like, *Hey, Mr. Lifeguard, if I drown, will you give me CPR?*

I'd even be playing along.

Today I'm on a political mission with Kurt as my ambassador. Hell, before they explained it to me, I wasn't sure what an ambassador actually did. It helps having the girls along. Thalia said a champion shouldn't go anywhere without an entourage. I guess this is the closest I'll ever get to feeling like a rock star.

"Don't pout," Thalia whispers to me.

"I'm not pouting." But I know I am. This is the way I felt when I lost my first meet—helpless and angry and stupid because I hated the idea that someone could be better than me. I press my hands on the waterproof nylon of my backpack as a reassurance that I am the king's champion and I have the Scepter of the Earth. But then Adaro has the staff. We're equals, and I have to make him see that.

"Hey, Tristan," Layla says dryly. "I'll bet you twenty bucks you can't guess where on the beach Adaro is."

"That seems like a perfect waste of bucks," Kurt says.

"How come I didn't get a celebration tent?"

They laugh, stepping off the boardwalk and onto the sand. Amid the early beachgoers setting up camp with towels and blankets stained in the wash, Adaro's celebratory tent is glaring. All silks and shimmering threads, the canopy shields him and his entourage from the gray brightness of the day.

Kurt pulls me back, suddenly apprehensive. "Let me introduce you."

"I've already been introduced! Remember that big ceremony on Toliss with the introductions?"

He ignores me, stepping right in front of Adaro's makeshift court. He holds his hands at his back and bows his head with a smile. I don't want him to bow to anyone.

"Hello there!" Adaro says. "What a pleasant surprise."

"Hard to ignore all the conch-blowing action," I say, eliciting a nudge from Thalia.

"Adaro, son of Leomaris and champion of the Southern Seas," Kurt flourishes in my direction. "I present to you Tristan Hart, son of David Hart and champion of King Karanos."

Freaking Adaro with his shiny golden staff and wind-tossed black hair. The white of his teeth is blinding against his cinnamon skin. He's loud and maybe a little drunk. He's in full human mode, though right at his ankles are a leftover spattering of red and yellow scales. I realize they're there on purpose, letting him wave his family colors like a flag. So I let my blue scales surface on my wrists.

He sits up, sloshing white slushie down his chest and abs, and soaking the hem of his golden Speedo.

I start cough-laughing and Kurt gives me a few good smacks.

"I didn't peg you for a piña colada kind of guy," I say.

"It's a piña colada kind of day!"

"Here we go," Layla mutters behind me. Despite the tension in her body, she keeps her chin up.

"It's wonderful to see you!" Adaro opens his arms wide toward me. Does he expect me to hug him? He pulls me into a bear hug, lifting me way off the ground, then kissing me on each cheek. He looks Thalia and Layla up and down with drunk golden eyes and kisses the back of their hands. Then, looking down the beach, he does a double take. Gwen in a long, white dress, stark against the grayness of the beach.

"I didn't realize Princess Gwenivere was here," Adaro whispers, patting my back too long.

Her eyes twinkle the closer she gets, and she smiles, letting me take her hand for a kiss. I hope she's not still mad about this morning. She bows to Adaro, offering congratulations, before joining the others in the tent. Adaro drinks his piña colada faster. "Is it getting warm here?"

A mermaid close to him draws out a fan and starts batting it at him.

"Please, sit!" Adaro gestures to his makeshift court. "Make room for our welcome guests."

Every princess, except for Sarabell, does as she's asked. They trade wicked glances, like they hope any moment Adaro and I will just start going at it. Right, court politics. It's not like I haven't played this game before. Angelo calls them "faux bros." Guys from other swim teams that we hang out with even though they're our competition.

"I must tell you," Adaro says, taking a tiger-shell plate of oysters and passing them down my way. "I'm not much for cold seas, but this shore is rather charming. It's like a parade of foot-fins! Look, look at that one!"

A jogger passes by. He's muscular and has a lion tattooed over his chest. He lowers his sunglasses to get a better look at us but doesn't stop. I catch Sarabell gazing after him, and when she sees me staring, she scoots away from me as if my very presence offends her.

"I should be congratulating you." I try to match his enthusiasm, but it's hard to keep up with.

"And I you." His golden eyes are happy and wet. He combs his hair back coolly and opens his mouth, accepting the golden grape Princess Violet of the loveliest purple hair feeds him.

I lean over to Kurt and whisper, "She got over you really quickly."

I don't give him time to react. I lean forward to Adaro and ask, "So what's the story, man?"

"The story?"

"Yep, the story." I take the tray from Sarabell, despite the nagging looks from Kurt and Gwen as I do so, and suck down an oyster. The salt wakens up my taste buds, and the meat is tender so I take another. "Every adventure comes with a story."

Gwen leans back and says, "Everyone knows how Tristan found the quartz piece."

Sarabell eyes me. "Yes, the youngest sightless oracle deemed you worthy."

My eye twitches when she says that, but I keep my smile frozen.

"Tell it, Addie," Violet says. Her voice is like pressing the belly of a doll that sings back to you.

Addie, I mouth to the bronze merman, who doesn't like his girlfriend's nickname coming from me.

"Sit back, cousin. I will tell it," says Sarabell. She stands with her back to the water. Her skirts are the color of sunset, the material sheer and threaded with gold. It has the effect of a great flame. Her smile is wicked, marring the smooth, chiseled lines of her face. "Our family is descended from one of the original kings of the sea, Ellanos—he carried the staff. Wielded it to shape the caves beneath the sea, the hidden places where we would seek shelter. It seems fitting that it would fall into our family again."

Layla moves closer and leans against my chest. The look I get from Gwen brings a memory flash of her trying to kiss me. Even when her lips hovered, it didn't feel right. Cold. So cold compared to Layla. My heart is running laps, and Layla is looking up at me, pressing her hands right over it. She whispers, "Relax."

"Where was she?" Thalia asks. "The oracle."

This time it's Adaro's turn to shine. "She was in plain sight. In the tunnels beneath the Glass Castle."

Somewhere in my memory of the crash course Mer History 101, I remember them mentioning the Glass Castle.

"For the foot-fins, I'll clarify," Sarabell says to me. "It's the most wondrous of our homes. Our home beneath the sea. Far lovelier than Toliss. Our most prized kin live there—the keepers of our histories, our musicians who train for court, even our guard and the bigger armory.

"When the Glass Castle was destroyed in the first war with the fey thousands of years ago, its destruction was devastating. But we pulled through. We always do. Kurtomathetis and Thalia's parents helped rebuilt it the second time."

"Hold up," I say. "This thing was destroyed twice?"

The mermaids and merdudes nod sadly. Thalia says, "We were forced deeper and deeper by our enemies. The first time by the land fey. The second time during our *civil war*." She says "civil war" like it's made of glass itself. I wonder where Adaro's family stood in all of this.

"If you would," Sarabell says. "Now it stands stronger as a fortress instead, the Glass Castle, more beautiful than ever. Am I not correct, Kurtomathetis? You would come over to our wing and play. So little you were, always in a corner with your scrolls and tablets, the odd one of your bunch."

Kurt's jaw tightens. I don't like the way she says this. Some of the girls trade glares. What did I miss? Might as well be at the school cafeteria.

"Maybe one day, you'll visit." Adaro tells me. As much as I'm trying to not like him, to put him on my shit list for being a natural rival, I can't. He's kind of a cool guy. He's kind of like me.

"How did you find her?" I ask.

He looks up to the drifting clouds playing hide-and-seek with the sun. "She came to me in a dream…I couldn't see her face but she whispered my name. It echoed in the halls of the castle. My father told me I was mad. He swears on augurs, but they led us nowhere, and after the third night of the same dream, I knew to trust myself. I swam beneath the castle, where the last circle of dragons is said to be kept. Only, it was empty. The dragons were gone, replaced by a ring of blue combat fire. As if the oracle wanted me—"

"Dragons," I repeat. "The sea dragons were gone?"

"It is what he said," Sarabell snips.

Behind her, Gwen shakes her head from side to side. She presses the top of her finger to her coral lips.

"Sorry," I go, "bad ear."

"The fire was a mirage. So I swam through the tunnel, so deep I thought my insides would burst. That's when they came. They were shadows at first, slithering around my arms and my tail until they were solid black vines. We use those for prisoners."

Thinking of the black vines that bind Arion to the ship, I say, "I know."

"The vines pulled me in different directions. It was the most painful moment of my life. All I could think of was my limbs ripping right off clean."

"How did you fight it?" Kurt asks for me. He can tell I don't want to sound eager. In a way, I don't want to know. Could I have done it? Could I have found that oracle without my friends? The only one who comes to me in my dreams is Nieve. No oracles, and I can't help but wonder.

"I didn't. It released me. I could barely stay afloat. There was a deep grumble and the ground moved. It took all my strength to swim into the tunnel. The ground kept moving. Not until the wall closed behind me did I realize I was inside a giant eel. I was too big and it was choking on me. With the little strength I had left, I picked up my sword and cut myself out.

"There she was before me, the oracle. What happened then, I will not say." He holds the Staff of Eternity in a powerful fist. The symbols etched all along the shaft are the same ones along the hilt of my scepter. "This is what matters now."

"And now you're here."

"I know it's too soon for celebrations," Adaro says. "The trident head is—"

"*Adaro!*" Sarabell yells between gritted teeth.

He holds his hand up to her and she's instantly quiet. "If I am to be on Tristan's land—"

"Technically," Layla says, "some of it belongs to the State of New York."

Adaro offers her a tray of pink wiggly stuff. "I like you. I wish the rest of court were as funny as you!"

She reaches for the cube of jellyfish brain and knocks over a drink onto one of the princesses beside her. I pick up the glass and use my own T-shirt to dab at the princess's dress by way of apology. Besides, it's too hot to wear a T-shirt. The makeshift court shoots Layla dirty looks, like if I weren't here, they'd drag her into the surf and drown her. I sit up a little straighter, wrapping my arm around over her shoulder, because no one looks at Layla like that.

Then Adaro gets stone faced, eyes shifting from side to side. I see a spark of fear, and I know his journey has been just as rocky as mine.

"Come," I say, taking him by the arm, away from Sarabell's prying eyes.

"Cousin," she says, reaching out for his hand, and he pulls out, but Gwen makes her sit back down.

"Oh, leave them to their champion talk," Gwen says. "Tell me, has anyone heard of the others?"

Note: Thank Gwen later.

Adaro and I walk down to the shoreline. This late in June, the water is still cold. It wraps around our ankles in frothy white bubbles, washing away the smallest trace of scales on our ankles.

"Is it true?" He squints and blocks the sun from his eyes. I'm trying to picture him as the sort of guy who'd set fire to Greg's home, but I just can't.

"You have to be a tiny bit more specific."

"There have been whispers that the silver witch has escaped her prison." He leans in closer, voice hushed. "That she's alive?"

I bend down to scoop up some water and splash it on my face. The mention of Nieve makes my entire body hot. "Yes, Nieve is out there."

It's a physical reaction for him too. He's shaking out his legs like he's cramping up. "My father always said King Karanos should've killed her when he had the chance. Sarabell says this shore was attacked by full-grown merrows. That's partly why I came."

"What's the other part?"

He looks back to the laughing girls. Gwen is telling some story and they're all enraptured by her—the way her face shifts from emotions, the fluid movements of her delicate hands. Even Layla joins in. There's something twitchy and nervous about Adaro. It's not the booze and it's not his fear of Nieve and merrows. He twirls the staff with expert fingers.

"I think we're better in numbers," he says. "We're competitors, you and I, not enemies. Elias hasn't surfaced since you two—and Dylan is way up north."

"Brendan is south. Our ships passed each other, but he's safe."

"Good, good. My men are on my ship, ready if another such attack happens."

"Adaro," I say slowly, testing the waters of our camaraderie. "Have you been attacked by those creatures?"

He bites his lip. Then, as if his body is a balloon losing air, he holds on to my shoulder and presses his fist to his mouth. Really, I can't stand someone else puking on me.

"I'm okay," he says. "But I lost over a dozen of my guard. They were great mermen, all of them."

Despite the strength of his body, when his amber eyes look at me, I find the fear, the helplessness. And I know, even though we're fighting for the same throne, right now we need each other. I have to make him see that he needs me too.

"I think I can help," I say. "Is there somewhere more private we can talk?"

chapter FORTY-TWO

Adaro's ship is so elaborate that it makes Arion's look like a cardboard box with sheets attached.

A giant eel, similar to the makara but with the head of an ancient lion, is etched into the mast. It has red jewels the size of my head for eyes, and the body is washed in gold, just like the mast. A red flag waves. There's a golden octopus right at the center to match the medallion around Adaro's neck.

When we reach the ship, I turn back and there it is: Coney Island. Adaro's men hoist us up. Layla lets go of my shoulder and I let her go up first.

The deck is a flurry. Dozens and dozens of men swab the deck, tend to sails and ropes. A group of girls fuss over Adaro, dressing him in traditional merman armor—a chain-link skirt and an elaborate breastplate to befit his station. He purses his lips and I suspect it's because he misses the golden Speedo.

He motions for us to follow him into his captain's quarters, and then he takes a jar of a familiar fizzy green liquid and drinks deep. My crew—Kurt, Thalia, Gwen, and Layla—wander around, admiring everything from the massive candelabra with its long taper candles to the sailing trinkets strewn about his table.

Adaro only lets Sarabell remain.

The door bursts open and a tiny old man runs in. He surveys the room, stopping only to bow to me and Adaro.

"Sire, your father would not approve. This is the king's champion."

I smile. "Thanks."

Adaro rolls his eyes as well as any teenage girl I've ever known. "I know very well who he is. See the quartz scepter tucked in the harness between his shoulder blades?"

"But—"

Adaro looks at his nails as though examining his cuticles. "You are dismissed."

The man thunders back out, unceremoniously slamming the door.

"I think he's right," Sarabell says.

"Then you, Cousin, are welcome to leave."

But she doesn't. She makes sure the windows are all shut and there's no one at the door. A slight burning smell is coming from a tiny hearth. The soot and cinders are slightly red with embers.

"It seems," Adaro says, "that we have a mutual enemy."

"Nieve," I say, as he shudders at the name.

"Are you sure you've seen her?"

"A few times, actually."

Adaro's thick black eyebrow arcs suspiciously. "Then why are you still alive?"

"She thinks I'm cute," I say, annoyed. Then I answer as honestly as I can. "She's playing with me. It's what she does, isn't it?"

"How?" Sarabell asks.

"Gee, I don't know, let me give her a conch call and see if she answers. The point is, she's going to kill us for our trident pieces."

Adaro and I pace the room, leaving our respective entourages dizzy. Adaro bites his cuticle and I tell them of the centaur oracle, leaving out some important details like the water of Eternity and the prophecy.

"The merrow who speaks *killed* an oracle?" Adaro sits down on his golden chair. He looks to Sarabell as if for guidance, and I realize this is his life. His father telling him what to do. These men reporting back to him. His family hovering around like vultures awaiting their return to power.

"The oracle in my dream," he says. "She told me I would find what I was looking for here."

"Adaro!" Sarabell hisses.

He squares his jaw and takes on the most commanding tone I've seen of him today. "If you are going to question my decisions, you are free to leave, as I already said. Don't make me repeat myself."

She sits back and crosses her arms.

It makes sense. The secrecy from Sarabell. Adaro's shiftiness.

"You mean an oracle," I say. "Here."

"Another?" Kurt is incredulous.

"The other reason you're here," I point out.

Adaro laughs nervously, trying to maintain our friendship. "I think we're stronger in numbers, don't you?"

Yes, I do. That's why I wanted to talk to him. But with this new information, it's hard not to walk away and scour the city for the next oracle. The trident head. The centaur must have sent it to her sisters, which is why Adaro hasn't found anything.

"This presents a new problem," I say. "You and me, here. We each have our own winnings. This makes us targets. And now we're on the same shore. The third trident piece means Nieve will come for us, faster and stronger."

"What do you propose?" Adaro asks.

"Numbers, just like you suggested. Nieve has numbers. You have numbers."

"It seems you're the only one who doesn't," Sarabell says. "Have numbers, that is."

I shake my head, keeping my face as even as that of Frederik, the High Vampire of New York. "I have people on this shore. The Thorne Hill Alliance is loyal to me. I just have to pick up a cell phone and they'll help."

It's a lot to bluff. But like poker night with Shelly, I have to bet it all.

"Vampires? Werewolves?" Sarabell is about to scream. "The very fey who pushed us deeper into the earth? You would side with them?"

Thalia stands forward. "Don't forget the landlocked."

"The *banished* folk?" Adaro says, more thrilled than repulsed. "I've never met one, but if they're willing to listen and die for my—our—lives, why ever not?"

Kurt interjects. "I doubt it'd be that simple."

"You may be surprised, Brother." Thalia says. "Perhaps you should speak to them before casting them aside.

"Let's hear what they have to say," I suggest. "Thalia, you know the way."

chapter FORTY-THREE

We trek down the dark and foggy Brooklyn streets until we reach the kind of alley that gives this city a bad rep. Sarabell turns her nose up at the moldy couch where a family of rats is taking a nap. Adaro is fascinated by the graffiti. He sounds out all the letters and has a good laugh, followed by, "How charming."

When Thalia finds the manhole she's been looking for, I say, "It's like déjà vu all over again."

I volunteer to go down first and no one stops me. I regret wearing flip-flops the moment my feet hit the ground. The water is thick and slippery like chicken soup, which I now think I can never eat again. "Is it okay if I throw up on you?"

"This is nothing," Kurt says. I can see the faint outline of his smile. "You've never swum near Biscay Bay."

"Follow me," Thalia says. Her yellow-green eyes glow like headlights down the sewer tunnels. Layla keeps her fingers hooked on the loops of my cargo shorts, and I keep my hand close to my dagger. I lose track of the turns, right and left, and another left, and straight on 'til morning. The rattle of the subway accompanies us the whole way until we reach an open door.

I blink hard against the fluorescent brightness of the room. When my eyes adjust, I realize there's only one flickering fluorescent tube. The rest of the ceiling is covered with fat fireflies. A couple of them break away from their feeding frenzy and waddle through the air around us.

"They brush honey on the ceiling," Thalia points out. "Otherwise they'd be flying all over the place."

"So this is where you've been spending your time." Kurt snatches a lightning bug from his ear and crushes it in his hand. He smears the green slime on his cargo shorts. She avoids Kurt's stare and turns to me.

"Is this a bunker?" I ask.

The walls are lined with all kinds of books. There's a small stage centered against the back with uneven rows of chairs facing it. Open cabinets are stuffed with boxes and cans of food. A dartboard and a pool table that look like they've had their last games take up a corner, beside a couch coming apart at the seams.

I feel a set of arms wrap around my leg.

"Tristan!" the little boy squeaks. It's Timmy. I bend over and pick him up, patting the hard shell of his back.

"What's up, little man?"

He shrugs in that exaggerated little kid way that makes all the girls smile, except for Sarabell, who looks like she'll catch the plague from touching anything.

Penny isn't far behind, hand in hand with her boyfriend, who I've only seen from afar. Little suction cups pop out at her wrists as if coming up for air. They're both still wearing their aprons like they ran out in a hurry. She's surprised to see me, but when she sees Adaro and Sarabell, she doesn't seem happy.

I shake both of their hands and Penny asks, "What are you doing here?"

"We come to enlist your services," Adaro says matter-of-factly.

I hold out my hands and say, "Actually, we want to talk."

As the landlocked file in, some realize who we are and sneer in our direction. It reminds me of the time Gaston Guerrero threw the soccer game and everyone walked past him with looks of disgust. I feel like freaking Gaston Guerrero.

"Maybe this wasn't such a good idea," I whisper.

Layla and Thalia flank me.

"No, Tristan," Thalia says, "this is perfect. They need to know what you have to say."

Some are kinder than others. I recognize the man I gave my food to on the boardwalk and he gives me a smile. A few bored college-aged girls lift their sunglasses with blue webbed hands. One winks a big blue eye at me. Her friends elbow her and they break into giggles. Their lives seem pretty good to me.

There's a man with a sallow face lit up by the lantern protruding from his head. It casts ghoulish shadows all over his features. There's a man who takes up three seats that sink beneath his weight. He clears an entire section, running his hand over his face, trailing green mucus.

There's even a guy in a suit who tosses his long, blond hair back every couple of seconds. He hesitates before sitting down and then gets the brilliant idea to place his newspaper on the seat.

These are the landlocked. I wonder what they've all done to get banished from the Sea Court. I can't imagine any of them being all that powerful. Our presence has them all unnerved.

"Is that the son of the king?" someone whispers.

Another replies with, "That's the grandson. The king only has daughters."

The last person to walk in doesn't even look around the room. He walks slowly, straight toward me, like he knew I was here even before he started weaving through the tunnels. His face, arms, and legs are all wire thin. His shoulder-length hair is bleached blond. The roots are black and greasy. He uses the cuff of his sleeve to wipe at his raw, red nose.

He holds his arms out, and at first I think he's going to hug me. Adaro takes it as a threat and draws his sword. Instead, the bleached blond pulls a dart from the board and uses it to pick his teeth. When he's done, he twirls the silver dart between his fingers.

The landlocked fidget and whisper among themselves.

I grit my teeth and say, "Adaro, put that away."

When the bleached blond smiles, it takes up his whole face. "So the Sons of the Sea have come slumming."

"I'm—"

"I know who you are."

I hate the way he cuts me off. And from the way his body tenses and his face grimaces in my direction, he doesn't think much of me, either.

"And who are you?" I say, minutes away from losing my patience.

"This is Jesse," Thalia says.

Jesse lingers where we stand, like he's sizing up his opponents or avoiding dog shit. He proceeds to take center stage, a preacher welcoming us to his church, extending arms wide. "Welcome to our weekly community meeting."

His arms go slack and he groans. "Yes, Ben, what is it?"

The guy in the suit has his hand raised. He's got scars all across his knuckles. When he tucks his hair back, I notice his ears are shaped like fins. "I'd just like to say that I'm confused. I thought we were going to *vote* on when we brought the champion in. I mean, we are still a *voting* group, right? I'm just saying."

Jesse's smile is tight, annoyed. Even though he's a skinny, oily, grungy little punk, he leads them. "Don't worry, Ben. No one is changing any rules. I knew the champion of the sea would come to us eventually. Didn't I say that? What I didn't expect was *two* of them."

Adaro crosses his arms over his chest, his dagger gleaming in one hand. The air is getting denser. Everyone sweating. Nerves sizzling like crossed wires.

"Thalia, it is good to see you again," Jesse says, cocking his head and squinting way too hard at Kurt. "I look forward to the day we can count you in our ranks. Now. Let the champion come forward. Come, come. I'm sure you're brimming with kind words for us."

I move from the back of the room to closer to the raised stage. Sweat runs down my back and my mouth is dry.

"Do you know what we are, Tristan?" Jesse asks me.

"You're Sea People," I say.

"Were. We *were* Sea People." Jesse smiles with his red, raw mouth. "Now, we are the landlocked. Excommunicated. Discarded. Unwanted. Untouchables."

Jesse paces, weaving that silver dart between his fingers. The flickering bulb gives his hair an orange glow and deepens the shadows of his face. His lips look swollen, but they might just be big. His teeth are too prominent. I kind of hate him.

"For some of us," Jesse says, "it wasn't our choice to be here. Unlike your mother, not all of us fancy being on two legs. Clumsy, ugly, nasty things. Foot-fins, you call us."

He hops off the stage and passes through the crowd, and they follow his wiry body, snake-like in the way he turns his neck. I wonder if his tongue is forked. I make a note to punch him the next time he talks about my mother.

"You broke the law," Kurt says. "That's why you don't have your fins anymore."

Every eye turns to him. The volume in the meeting hall shoots up. Their voices are a mixture of curses and explanations of how they were wronged. But mostly curses. Jesse uses his hands and shushes them like children.

"Don't mind the young soldier," Jesse says. "He was raised to lead the Sea Guard. He could never understand us."

Kurt's head looks like it might pop right off his head with how angry he is. "What is there to understand?"

"That we were once sea creatures, like all of you. Some, like Penny and her little turtle boy, were born on land. Her mother was a cephalo-maid. Her father human. Her mother, ripped of her ability to shift, was left on land to raise a child she could never explain. She died when Penny was only twelve, and Penny's father left her in an orphanage. It wasn't until she found some of us that she could truly know what she was, who she came from.

"Ben, over there. His parents were part of the first rebellion. And now he's banished from court. As his children will be. And their grandchildren and so on, until the blood of the sea is no longer in their veins."

Ben crosses his arms. His muscles strain against the fine tailored suit. "I've got too much invested in my firm to have kids, anyway."

Jesse murmurs a curse under his breath. "Really? I'm trying to prove a point here."

He swipes at his watery nose with the back of his hand. Despite my really casual pose, I force myself not to recoil as he walks up to me, twirling that dart. He smiles with his horse teeth. "Do you know how your grandfather punished me? He took his trident and stuck it right in my spine. The pain was ghastly. I could barely swim to shore. I was lucky. Some of the others got eaten up by the shark guard who, by the way, weren't fed for a week just for that purpose.

"They never had a chance. Sitting here, underground, we still don't have a chance. Up there, we're deformed, forever bartering with tricksy court fairies for their glamours because we have no protection of our own."

"You have protection," Kurt says.

"The tithes? Giving what little we have for safety from each other?" Jesse laughs. The sound is brittle, broken, like taking a hammer to glass. "Do you suppose all of us can survive as humans? Ben, he can hide his ears with that mop of his. Penny can shift back and forth from her tentacles. What about the rest? Jim and the flashlight on his forehead? Alice and her crocodile eyes?

"It's time for a change. I've watched us dig our way deeper and deeper under this city, and the tunnels are giving out. How much farther can we burrow?"

"What is it you want?" It's my turn.

"We want what the Sea Court has." He walks back to the center of the stage. "We want a fair chance."

The wood sinks under our weight. When I'm this close to him, I can see the eternity in his eyes. They're black as oil slicks. "Don't forget my mother was just like the rest of you."

"Princess Maia knows nothing of our suffering. The Sea King made the change easy for her. He gave her gold. She had her beauty. Her human lover. She had you. We didn't have the *luxury* you've been given, and yet you're technically still one of us." He puts an arm around me and I suppress a shiver. His skin is clammy and cold, but there's a spark at his fingertips. "How do you suppose you'll rule at court and not know the Rites of Summer? The way to control the island? The names of every merman and maid that breaks themselves to build your castles, your thrones, your weapons. How will you know?"

My heart is racing. His voice has swallowed all our breaths as he inhales steadily, calming. I look out at the motley crew of the landlocked. There's hatred in their eyes and I know it comes from Jesse. This is what he's good at—filling people with hate.

"I have no way of knowing what your lives are like," I say, "and Jesse's right. In many ways, you have been forgotten." In the back, Adaro and Sarabell don't like that I've said that. "But in a couple of days, there might not be a Sea Court to go back to."

Jesse's eyes light up.

"This right here," I say, "is the city you've called your home. Imagine it all gone. Swallowed up by an army of merrows that won't hesitate to destroy you. Because this *is* your home, just as much as it's mine. That's why I'm here. That's why I ask you to stand behind us."

They talk among themselves. Some call me crazy. Others call me worse things.

"We want to be part of the sea again," Jesse says. He doesn't consult them. He doesn't let them speak. "We offer our support in exchange for yours. Our wish is simple."

I hold my hands up. I can't let him corner me. "Easy, isn't it? Standing up here and telling them what they want to hear. Promises are easy. My dad, who is very much human, taught me a few things. Other than how to tie my shoes, that is." Penny and the girls around her laugh, which is a comfort in the tension of the room. "He taught me that I'll never get anywhere by making false promises." Granted, I'm pretty sure he was talking about girls, but it stuck with me.

"Your lives have pretty much reached a level of suck that I will never know. Jesse's right. I've lived my whole life with everything handed to me.

"But when my grandfather handed me this championship, I could've backed out. I could've gone right back to high school. I'd probably be with the girl I care about instead of wasting time with princesses who want to bite my head off."

Ben pumps his fist in the air and shakes his head. "Been there, bro."

"I've seen the kinds of things—punishments—that I would never want to see done to anyone. Especially people like me, because you guys *are* like me. Right now, the only promise I can give you is that your voices will be heard."

"Hear my voice right now, land prince." Jesse studies my face. "Will you restore me once you are king?"

Adaro steps forward. "This isn't about kingships. This is about protection."

But Jesse is thrilled. He turns to Adaro and says, "And what of you, champion of the Southern Seas? What will you give us?"

Adaro backpedals and Sarabell stands in front of him—like *she's* his body armor—and I realize this is why she's the only person he trusts. "Our family doesn't negotiate with the banished. You can either acknowledge that you will need our guard to protect this shore, or not."

The landlocked are up in arms despite my attempts at quieting them down. Jesse does that best. "Here we have it, two champions who will offer us nothing."

He lets the words sink in and we don't deny them. Adaro won't and I can't.

Jesse takes the dart in his hand and throws it at Adaro.

Adaro recoils and Sarabell stands in front of him. Everyone jumps out of their seats, scrambling for an exit, but Jesse claps his hands and laughs. The arrow has turned into a slick blue bird. It flies around the room in a swift circle and lands on Jesse's open palm where, in a flutter of wings, it vanishes. There's a regular old dart in his hand again.

"How did you do that?" I demand, resting my hand on the hilt of my sword.

"It was a gift from a very old friend." Jesse shrugs, all, *Who, me?* "Nieve, the first daughter of King Erebos and true queen of the seas."

The landlocked do everything from shouting and whispering to demanding explanations to storming out. The sisters with webbed hands are texting.

"She has come back for us," Jesse says. "This time around, her power will be so great that she will cast a shadow over the sun."

The landlocked watch us with anxious eyes. There are those who scurry out of the room. There are those who get up quietly and form a cluster behind Jesse. "What have you for us now?"

I unsheathe my dagger and point it steadily at him. "This doesn't turn into a butterfly when I throw it."

Jesse smiles with delight. "I think I can see why she likes you after all."

Ben cocks his eyebrow. He shakes his head and rolls up his newspaper. "Screw you, Jesse. What about some glamour for the rest of us, huh?" He pushes his hair away and cups his hand behind his ear so he can make sure we get a good look at it. It's iridescent and wiggles with him excited like this.

"In time, my friend."

"I am not your friend, Jesse." Ben picks up his briefcase and turns to the door. "You seem nice, Tristan. One piece of advice? Let the Sea People destroy themselves. It's what they're good at. In a few years, I'll be in Acapulco with Miss Universe on my lap and enough money that she won't even care about my little ear problem. Toliss will be under the sea where it belongs, and the rest of them?" He throws his newspaper in the air, and it comes apart in a mess in Jesse's furious face. "*Poof*, just like that."

Poof, just like that, the landlocked resume their shouting with each other. Old rivalries surface. A water bottle flies over my head and spills everywhere. They crowd the room, reaching for Adaro, who pushes them away and makes a run for it with Sarabell. I grab Penny and say, "Take Timmy and go."

"We won't follow Jesse," she reassures me. She's the only one.

"Right now," I say, "just think about your family."

She nods, letting go of my hand. With her boyfriend pushing people out of the way, they leave.

"Let's go," Kurt says. He takes Thalia by her arm and shoves one or two guys on the way out.

"You have nothing to offer." Jesse stands beside me, watching the discord he's created. Feeding off it. "Make the smart decision for yourself. Together we can help these people."

"From where I'm standing," I spit, "all you want to do is help yourself. Turning darts into birds isn't going to help you."

"I could show you the full extent of my gifts." He turns his greasy face to me. "But that would ruin tomorrow night's fun."

Thalia and Layla grab at my hands before I can punch him. I shout, "You don't know what Nieve is capable of."

And then his voice is in my head as I walk away from the pandemonium of the meeting hall. It's an echo, forcing its way into my thoughts. Jesse, speaking to me. "I do know, Land Prince. I know *exactly* what she's capable of."

chapter FORTY-FOUR

"How could you?"

Kurt's voice thunders through the tunnels. Thalia walks with her head hanging low, a rag doll with nowhere to go. "How could you do this to me? To us? Don't forget *we* are your family. I thought he was going to kill us. And you—my own sister—right beside them all."

I've never seen Kurt so freaked out. His heavy breathing is the only sound as we make our way through unfamiliar dark tunnels. Thalia leads the way. The rattle of subway trains is faint but close. We take so many turns that I don't think I'd remember the way back even if I wanted to. I don't breathe easy until we go through a door that exits into the subway. We walk through the crowds like it's no big deal, ignoring the "Do Not Enter" sign at the end of the platform.

Outside in the sort-of-fresh Brooklyn air, we cross the empty street even though the red hand is telling us not to. I've never had a brother or a sister, but if fighting one is anything like fighting with your friends, it's not going to get fixed overnight. Behind me, Layla and Gwen quietly keep pace.

At the corner of my street, the light above us flickers.

"Where did Adaro go?" Layla asks.

Gwen shrugs. "Probably ran back to his ship."

"Guys, did no one else hear what Jesse said?" I tap Kurt on the shoulder to steal his attention from Thalia to me. "He said he'll show me what he's capable of tomorrow night. They're coming for us *tomorrow night*."

Gwen shakes her head. "He could be lying. Why would he give you a chance to prepare?"

"Because Jesse's boastful," Thalia says. "He'd want Tristan to be afraid because he knows Adaro won't join with Tristan now. When they attack, it will fall to us."

"Were you ever going to tell us?" Kurt asks. His hands shake in fists at his side. "They could've killed you. They hate the court. They hate *us.*"

Because I know Kurt isn't going to stop, I take her hand reassuringly. "Thalia, why did you keep this from us?"

Her hands are all over her hair in that frantic way girls have when they want to hide behind it. "I can't say."

"You can't turn to me, your own flesh and blood, but you can turn to those creatures? To Jesse?"

"That is exactly why I could never tell you, Brother." Thalia's finger flies to his face like a gun. "*Those creatures* are just like you and me. They love the sea. They love being part of it. Without it, they're—"

"Fish out of water?" I offer, taking a chance to lighten the mood.

Thalia tries not to laugh. "You haven't been there," she says to her brother. "I've found something that makes me feel worthy."

"Is our family not enough?"

"What family? While you're off seeking revenge for the death of our parents? While you're off with your paramours? You are not the only one who feels alone." She throws her fists and punches him. "You *left* me. You left me at court with princesses who treated me like a barnacle they needed to scrub off their heels. I finally found someone who loved me, who needed me. Now he's gone. Don't you *dare* scold me like a child."

Thalia puts her hands to her eyes. It doesn't stop her crying. I know Kurt should be the one to do this. I know he wants to be the one to hug her. I also know that no matter how bad he feels, Kurt isn't going to give her the comfort she needs. So I do it. I bring her in and wrap my arms around her, because I want to make all her pain go away.

"Like it or not," Kurt says, "you are a *mermaid.* You are ancient, eternal, part of a lineage that extends beyond the beings crawling on this earth without a purpose, without *meaning.*"

"Things can change, Kurt."

He stops and turns to his sister. Then he looks at me. I look at my dirty toes. If there were ever a way that I would've wanted Kurt to find out that I promised Thalia to make her human, this was not it.

Then he sticks his finger in my chest. "I thought you weren't giving out promises."

"It wasn't exactly—" But he doesn't let me finish.

Kurt turns to Thalia with his hand pressed over his heart. "You want to be one of them. You want to stay here?"

We both move to speak but he turns away from us.

"Kurt!"

"Come back!"

But he crosses the street. I can't lose Kurt, not this way.

"You guys go home," I say. "I'll bring him back."

If I could come up with Kurt's signature fragrance, I'd say it'd be Parfum de Uptight.

Having been with him with so long, I can follow the scent of his rage and confusion and loneliness. I keep a slow pace behind him, mirroring his posture, hands tucked in pockets, head down but eyes up. He's nearly at the boardwalk when he turns around and faces me.

"I'll return when I'm ready," he says.

I close the space between us, taking a step up so that we're at eye level. "Have your sibling fight on your own time. You're no good to me this way."

He scoffs. "You don't want me around. You just want my sword."

I punch him. "I'm going to take that as meaning your actual weapon and not your—"

"Stop making jokes, Tristan." He shoves me back and

keeps going up the ramp. The boardwalk is deserted. Not even the usual hobos lie about in the shadows. "Can't you take this seriously?"

"Fine," I say. "Let's take this seriously. Starting with you can't treat Thalia this way."

He digs his finger into my chest. "You should have said something to me."

"Why? It's her decision." I shrug. "You're not her decision-maker."

"I'm her brother!" He starts walking away, then turns back. "You'll understand soon."

"You're being a dick."

"I'm being a dick? My sister turns to *you* for help."

If he's going to get all puffy-chested, then so will I. He's got an inch, maybe two with the height of his hair. For the first time, I notice a triangle of freckles on his shoulder and the fat vein on his throat when he's pissed off, because Captain Cool-and-Collected never gets pissed off this way.

"Look," I lower my voice. "You and Thalia have a lot more to talk about than her decision to become human. Don't you see? All she wants is a family, and she's not going to have any of it—nothing—if we let Nieve win."

He doesn't argue. We walk side by side until we reach the boardwalk gazebo. I make a right into it and face the horizon. The storm is still out there, building slowly. I can feel the change in the wind, cold and hard for a summer night.

When Kurt grabs me, I think he's going to punch me.

Instead, he pulls me down on the floor and presses his finger to his mouth. He whispers, "It's Adaro."

The footsteps clamor onto the boardwalk. Sarabell's and Adaro's voices intermingle in their bickering.

"We should leave this shore at once," Sarabell says.

"I gave Tristan my word," Adaro says. "I told him he could count on my guard to help protect his shores."

"No, no, no." She takes his face in her hands. "Don't you see? You already have the center staff. All we have to do is return to Toliss and let the sea witch destroy him."

He pulls out of her grasp. "What then?" He leans on the railing. If he took three steps to the left, he'd see us. "Then she'll just come after me."

"You heard him tonight." Sarabell gets in his face. "He would allow those vile creatures back into our court. He believes he's already king!"

"There's still an oracle here, Sarabell. The oracle told me in my dreams that I would find what I'm looking for on this shore. I won't listen to you. Not after you led us to a dead end with that elder."

"Whatever the old man told Tristan led him to an oracle. For all the good it did them—they let the trident get away." She smacks his shoulder and jabs an accusing finger in his face. "Don't blame me, when you brought the combat fire to threaten him."

Greg. *They* killed Greg. I twitch to stand up but Kurt puts a firm hand on my shoulder.

"It was an accident," Adaro shouts. "He wouldn't come out of his house, and I dropped the vial."

"Perhaps—" Sarabell paces around her cousin. Her dress is a wild thing around his body, like a wraith encircling him. "Perhaps this is what the oracle meant."

She doesn't elaborate, making Adaro give her his undivided attention. "What do you mean?"

"There *is* a piece of the trident on this shore. She didn't say you'd find an *oracle*. She said you'd find what you're *looking for*. And you're looking for a piece of the trident. The scepter."

Kurt and I look at each other. Sarabell takes a step back and leans against the gazebo. All she has to do is turn around, and there we are. Would they screw the championship rules and try to kill me now?

"That doesn't sound right."

"Don't be white-bellied, Adaro." She flicks her hair to the side. "When you both make it to Toliss, you'll have to kill each other. That's how the championship ends. You're letting your feelings for the mutt cloud your vision. He isn't your friend. If he had the chance, he'd do the same to you."

Would I? I was just starting to like Adaro. If we survive Nieve. If we go to Toliss. One of us has to die.

"You won't even have to kill him," Sarabell says.

"I won't?"

She shakes her head. "The silver witch will take care of that. You heard that barnacle Jesse. Pledge your allegiance to her."

"Sara—!"

"Not truly, of course. Once you've got the quartz piece, you can destroy her. Then there will be one trident piece left and you will be king."

She has it all worked out.

Note: The key to success is a crazy cousin.

"I don't think the silver witch works that way," Adaro says darkly.

"Come." She holds out her hands to him, a mother calling to her child. "You need rest. Tomorrow will be a very long day. You heard Jesse. The silver witch will be here by nightfall."

They jump the railing and land on the sand. Adaro holds out his arm and she takes it. When they reach the water, I sit up.

"What a sea bitch," I say.

"They killed Greg."

"They're going to kill me." I stand and dust sand off my shorts. "Well, there's a very long line. They'll just have to get in it."

We leave the boardwalk and head back home. Before we get back in the elevator, Kurt says, "You have to be ready."

"For what?" I press number 14. "There are so many things to be ready for. My premature death. The sea witch and her merrows. Jesse and his new magic tricks, the zombie apocalypse—"

"No, Tristan. You have to be ready to kill Adaro before he can kill you."

And I say, "Yes. I know."

chapter FORTY-FIVE

My sleep is black. The first true sleep I've had in weeks.

Then the nightmares are back. All screams and melting faces. I wake up choking, like there are hands around my throat, and a shock runs through me, telling me to wake up.

I lie in my bed with my arms spread out. The ceiling fan spins. My bedside clock glows red numbers. My room smells like sweat and salt water, and there are clothes everywhere. Thursday morning.

Behind my closed door, I can hear voices in that loud whispering everyone thinks is so secretive, but it's the same as yelling. I get dressed and go to kitchen Command Central to see what the hell they're all doing.

My heart jumps to my throat as they shout, "Surprise!"

"Jesus, you guys."

My parents, Kurt, Thalia, and Layla are huddled around a very blue birthday cake. The sugar hits my nose first. It's better than a caffeine rush. I look at the calendar and realize it's June 24.

Thursday. Someone's already crossed off last night, and I want to take the marker and fill the whole square in black.

"Are you seriously telling me you forgot it's your birthday?" Layla comes around and kisses me right on the mouth. In front of everyone.

"I seriously did." I stick a finger in the icing and let the sugar coat my tongue. My whole mouth explodes from the sensitivity of not having eaten anything yesterday.

"Your mother wanted to have a huge party—" Dad starts.

"But with everything that's going on," Mom says, "we figure something smaller would do."

"Cake for breakfast," I say, hugging my mother for as long as I can, "is the best birthday present ever."

Mom lights seventeen candles. I'm seventeen, and I've aged a thousand years in the last two weeks. Call me Rip Mer Winkle.

Kurt eyes the frosting with a mixture of amusement and temptation. I can tell that all of last night's information is prominent in his thoughts, but we decided to keep it between the two of us. "We don't celebrate birthdays on Toliss."

"Sure we do," Mom says. "At least, I did after seeing humans on a beach. I tried to get my father to make me a cake once. But the cooks came up with kelp pancakes and king crab claws as decorations."

"That is so messed up," Layla says.

"Blow out the candles," Mom says, "or the wax is going to drip."

I bend closer to the seventeen little flames. I haven't made a birthday wish since elementary school. I was never the kind of kid who made wishes on stars or cakes. Swimming came too naturally and I have dozens of trophies to prove it. Girls came naturally, and I also have the trail of angry ex-girlfriends to prove it.

Since I started shifting, I don't know what to believe in anymore. I know more things are possible. I've been to Eternity and back. I had an oracle give me a powerful weapon. I met my grandfather. I kissed the girl I love. But most importantly, she kissed me back.

Layla squeezes my hand, and I know that I'm not going to wish. I'm going to pray, something I haven't done in equally as long. When I saw Kai doing it near the shipwreck, I wanted to get down with her, but I didn't.

Maybe it's the same as a wish, the same as a promise. A totally intangible mass of hope that everything will work out the way it's supposed to be. I take a deep breath and blow.

On the news, there's a storm warning. The beach has been evacuated. A murder victim on the boardwalk. Ben's face pops up on the screen. The details are vague, other than that his hands, feet, and ears were cut off. No suspects yet.

While everyone eats cake in the living room, I volunteer to get them drinks. I take the bottle of Eternity water and pour it into their drinks. I pour the rest into an empty bottle of eyedrops and pocket it. I picture my centaur maid's fiery blood flowing, the head of the trident sucking back into the murky black depths. Just what every guy wants on his seventeenth birthday.

"You don't have to do that," she says.

I jump, and when I turn around, my mom is standing there. I wonder how long she's been watching me, but I realize it's long enough.

"Yes, I do."

"I thought they agreed not to drink it unless you did." She comes to me and lifts my chin with her finger. "You can't save everyone."

"I'm sorry," I say. "For everything I said to you. I didn't mean it."

"Yes, you did." She cups her hand on my face. "You were right. For a long time, I thought I could keep my old life away. The past creeps up like the tide. I wish it hadn't pulled you in."

"Literally," I say, laughing.

She kisses my forehead. "Happy birthday, my darling."

We take the glasses to everyone and drink.

We load my dad's car with weapons. Swords and bats and more arrows than I can count.

"I can't believe your dad lent you his car," Layla says. "He loves his car."

I pat the trunk of the trusty Mustang. Kurt and Thalia are scoping out the length of the boardwalk. There's only one way Nieve and her merrows will come onto the shore, and that's through the sea.

"Has anyone ever seen Nieve on feet?" Layla asks.

"I don't think she likes being on legs," I say. I think of how she forced me to shift into my tail. "She'll be out in the water."

"Is it too simple to say, 'Don't go in the water'?"

"I don't want them to break the boardwalk. If they go into the city—"

A sharp whistle blows behind me. A police officer comes our way. "This is a no-parking zone."

Layla points angrily at the sign above us. "No it's not. Read right there!"

The cop holds on to his belt. There's something funny about him. I can't pick it out. "I can't read. Why don't you read it for me?"

His mouth twitches. I take a step closer to him and breathe deeply. "Cut it out, Marty."

The shape-shifter doubles over laughing. He looks both ways before shifting back into his familiar cheesy smile. "You should've seen your faces."

"Hey, when I'm on Toliss, I'll hire you as my court jester."

"No thanks, bro," Marty says. "I'd rather be queen, but I hear that job's already taken." He winks at Layla and she returns it with an eye roll.

"Tell Frederik I finally went to see the landlocked like he suggested and it didn't go well."

"Tell him yourself," Marty says. "He's waiting for you."

I look up at the white disk behind the gray sky. "I'm guessing he can't come out right now."

"I'll stay with Layla," Marty says. "He wants to speak to you alone."

Frederik lives on the boardwalk.

I feel let down in his vampire skills. This whole time, I thought of him as living in some cool hotel with all of his crime-fighting friends or even a mansion, but we're short of mansions in Brooklyn.

The face of the building has three arcs, all boarded up. There's an old mosaic of waves that's chipped away to reveal the plaster beneath. The metal gate has been pulled halfway up. A slow rain starts falling. I breathe in the dampness of the air. I'm waiting for the stink of merrow, but it doesn't come, and I remind myself that they'll come in the shadows.

I push the gate the rest of the way up, and once I'm in, I close it again.

I trust Frederik, I do. At least, I think I do.

But the way I feel, like I have to inch my way through the dimly lit hall in case he comes zooming down at vampire speed to take a chunk out of my neck? That's just instinct, and no matter how cool I think he is, I know I'll never get rid of that.

The inside of the building has been hollowed out. It used to be a restaurant and then a roller rink and now it's empty. The ceilings remind me of scenes from the '20s. My dad says that's the last time we built beautiful things. After that, it was all straight lines and plaster. I pick up a funny-looking gold vase that doesn't look like it can hold much of anything. I feel the chill break through the cracks of the building.

"Frederik?"

He's standing beside me. I jolt and drop the vase. It shatters.

"That was an antique, Sea Prince."

"Yeah? Well, put it on my tab."

He starts walking farther down the hall and I follow. He opens another door and I hesitate. "You're not still mad that I beat you at poker?"

When he smiles, a yellow fang peeks from a corner of his mouth. "I had the beginnings of a very promising flush."

"So you folded on purpose?" I step inside the room. "Why?"

That terrible tingling feeling comes over me, like a thousand spiders are walking over my spine.

"Because I want the sea folk off this land." He flicks the lights on. "And helping you is the only way I can accomplish this without breaking any rules of the Thorne Hill Alliance."

The large room is split in half. To the right is a floor-to-ceiling library. I lose count of the numbers of shelves and the age of the spines. There's a rickety ladder that moves from one end of the wall to the other.

"Read any good books lately?" I ask.

Frederik glances over his shoulder. I realize that, for the first time since I've met him, he's wearing all black. It brings out the death in his complexion. His eyes are blacker, and for a vamp, the dark circles under his eyes look more like bruises.

To the left is a different kind of library full of plants. There are test tubes, microscopes, and a large machine giving off steam. That side of the room is carefully arranged in shadow, and when I step farther into the room, I can see why. The colors of one plant radiate in the dark, while others are regular green.

"You're a gardener?"

Frederik grumbles.

"You're being extra cryptic. And coming from you—"

"I don't like the rain," he says. He picks up a book, the old kind that's bound and has letters pressed in gold on the cover. I can smell the moldy paper swelling under the humidity. "When I was human, the streets of Copenhagen were filthy in the rain. I would stay in the castle libraries."

"I see you've always been a people person."

To my surprise, he laughs. "Years later, I still hate it. Even worse is the rain in the night. Like never-ending darkness. As people of the sea, you will never know what it is like to never see the sun. Though as I learn more of your histories, I might prove myself wrong."

"What are you getting at?"

"I heard you finally went to see the landlocked." He thumbs through the book, then clamps it shut.

"Then you heard it didn't go well."

"Maybe your approach was wrong." He leans against the table, shoulders slightly hunched and tense in a way that looks more pained than predatory. I slip out of my backpack straps and set the pack on the ground.

"I knew the sea witch would come for me. And for the other

champion that's here, Adaro." I lean against the wall of books. "I went to the landlocked. I asked them to fight for this shore."

He's nodding methodically to my words. "What did you offer them?"

I'm quiet.

"Nothing?" He stands and walks to the dark part of the room where his greenhouse is. I remember the vial full of a little flower that he played during poker. He takes a jar filled a third of the way with water. At the center is a slender purple flower. The delicate stem moves around in a dance, and every time it does so, a faint light pulses from within. "You always have to offer something, Tristan. Otherwise, why will they fight for you?"

"Isn't that worse? To lie to them and have them die anyway, thinking they're getting rewarded when they aren't?"

"That's how battles are fought, Sea Prince." He sets the flower jar on the table between us. "Without a reason to live, you'll have a field of dead soldiers. I will help you see that."

It takes me a moment to realize what he's said. "You're going to help me?"

He nods once, holding his hands behind his back, calm as a shark out for a stroll.

"In exchange for—?" Killing you the next time I see you? Restoring traitors to the court?

"Lover's Breath."

"In exchange for backing me up you want my…breath?"

The familiar exasperated glare is back. "It's a pearl that grows inside two clams at once. The Venus pearl. I was hoping you hadn't already given it to one of your paramours."

"Paramour, singular. And no, I wasn't planning on it since I already gave it to one girl. It just feels wrong. Especially since they know each other. What do you need it for?"

"My plants. I'm developing a new species, like the saltwater orchid I gave to your grandfather." He taps his finger on the sides of the jar. "Like this."

"And you'll bring an army of vampires?"

"Not just vampires. The demigods here. Werewolves, though they don't like to get wet. The solitary fey are always up for a rumble. The battle may not just be on the sea but on this shore. What happens on this shore concerns the Thorne Hill Alliance, and what concerns the alliance concerns me. You're from here, and you know how devastating something like this could be."

"It's just for your plants?" It's the smallest thing he could ask for. He could ask for a nip of my blood. He could ask for a year's worth of laundry service.

"Don't worry, Sea Prince. I'm not an enemy of the world."

"That's what an enemy of the world would say."

"It only took a couple of hundred years to realize I like being here." He returns the jar to its shelf. "Don't let it be the same for you."

When he returns, I hold my hand out and wonder if this time he'll shake it.

He takes it.

His hand is cold, like gripping metal left out in snow, and suddenly I'm glad he doesn't shake my hand more often. He lets go first and I breathe a little easier. Frederik and the Thorne Hill Alliance will help me protect the shore. Outside, the rain seems to have stopped, and the familiar blast of Adaro's horn whispers its way through the walls.

Frederik clears his throat.

"Oh yeah." I unzip the pocket of my cargo shorts where I keep the pearl.

The pocket is empty.

I unzip the front pocket of my backpack, and after removing empty candy wrappers, it's still not there.

Frederik starts pacing with his arms crossed, stopping periodically to flick his unnerving black eyes.

I dig into my cargo pockets again, and in one of them is a tiny piece of paper folded a dozen times. When I open it, I see it's a drawing. Frederik comes and looks over my shoulder. At the slim shoulders and the slender neck and the face that's tilted slightly down, like she's thinking, sighing, lamenting. She's incredibly familiar, like a dream that I've had.

Only it wasn't a dream; it was a memory. This is the woman I saw when I was going down the well.

"Call Marty," I say. "Tell him to bring Kurt over here now."

Kurt, Thalia, and Layla follow a happy-stepping Marty McKay.

They proceed carefully into the vampire's lair. Frederik grumbles. Marty whispers that they're not used to company and the only things to eat are stallion blood and jalapeño chips.

When Kurt sees the drawing on the table, he snatches it back. "Where did you get this?"

"My pocket!" I point to him. "You're wearing my shorts."

Kurt folds the paper until it fits in the closed palm of his fist. "What have you done, Tristan?"

"I'm getting what Adaro and Jesse won't give us. *Numbers*. Now empty your—my—pockets."

Kurt does as I ask. A few crumpled bills, a stick of gum in its wrapper, a handful of coins, and finally, the Venus pearl.

I can hear the sigh of relief in Frederik's unbreathing body. I wonder what kind of species of flower the pearl will bring. I hold it by the chain over his cold, open palm. It spins in a circle, once, twice, and then it's in the hands of a new owner.

"Brother?" Thalia places her hand on Kurt's arm. "What is it?"

Kurt has a coin in his hand. He's turning it over, examining all of the ridges. He looks up at me. "Where did you get this?"

"The bank? Actually my dad. Money for food, that sort of thing."

"I guess merpeople don't really have allowances," Marty says when he looks at the coin in Kurt's hand. It's dull gold with the Roman numeral II stamped on it. Marty seems confused. "You've met Comit?"

"He said he had a collection of bizarre creatures." I explain about the sea dragon and Comit's rescue. "Why?"

Kurt can't seem to put words together, saying only, "You should've mentioned this."

Marty shakes his head. "That place is bad news. I've seen people go down there and never come back out."

Layla takes the coin from Kurt, who snatches it back.

"Madame Mercury isn't that bad," Frederik says. "Why would they invite you?"

I cross my hands in a T formation. "Time-out. Who the hell is Madame Mercury? Why are you getting so pissed at me, Kurt? And what's wrong with me that they wouldn't invite me somewhere?"

Kurt holds out the coin to me. "I've found her."

He says it with so much reverence that I don't understand what he means until he flips the coin, revealing the engraving of a split-tailed mermaid. The engraving is so precise that she even has minuscule scales along her hips. I think of Kurt making the drawing of the same mermaid that's taped to our Command Central wall.

"That's the oracle," I say. "Adaro was right. There is another oracle here." *Idiot*, I tell myself. An oracle, right under my nose. "I just threw the coins in my pocket and wrote Comit off as another Coney Island crazy."

"You guys." Layla holds her hands out. "It could be coincidence. Maybe this place just has a mermaid as its mascot."

Frederik speeds out of the room and then returns with the same coin. It has the number II stamp, but when he flips it over, the picture is not of a mermaid but a sliver of the moon. "This is what the coin normally looks like. Those are a message for you."

I snatch the other coin from the table and say, "We have to go to her before Adaro figures it out."

I suit up in my sternum harness.

"What about tonight?" Thalia says. "What about when the merrows come?"

"Sunset isn't for a few hours," Frederik reminds her. "This gives us time to prepare the shore while Tristan finds his oracle. We should reconvene at the aquarium. It is our emergency stronghold."

And then Kurt and I are back out in the gray summer storm. The wind is forceful, like hands pushing us, until we break into a run.

chapter FORTY-SIX

The door Comit showed me is simple and black with a II above it. The psychic stand is lit neon pink and purple beside it, red velvet curtains drawn to reveal the session going on. The psychic is my English teacher, Ms. Pippen, and she's holding an eager young woman's hand. When she sees me, she gives me the dirtiest stare, meant to make me feel guilty for nearly kidnapping her last week.

The door isn't locked and Kurt is the first one to push it open. The entrance is pitch-black. I've closed my eyes to adjust to this new lighting when a hand emerges from the dark and braces against my chest. Two torches light either side of the entrance. The man steps forward, dressed in a black suit and black tie. His hair is buzzed close to his scalp with a design etched on either side of his head.

"Comit sent us," I say.

He holds his hand out. "Entrance."

We each give him a coin. He motions to the wall in front of us. It opens in half to reveal a winding stairwell.

Beside me, Kurt has a possessed glimmer in his eyes. He takes the steps two at a time, which is something he just wouldn't do. He's usually all calm and collected in the face of danger. Who knows what this oracle will ask for? Another promise? Maybe this one will ask for a body part or a year's subscription to *Vogue*.

"Slow down, Kurt. We don't know what this actually leads to." I know something is wrong when *I'm* the voice of reason.

The stairwell coils around a dozen more times. When we hit the last step, Comit is waiting for us. "Hope you aren't too dizzy. It's a long way down."

"No worse than tumbling away from a sea dragon," I say.

Comit introduces himself to Kurt. They lock eyes, and instead of shaking hands, they dip in tiny bows. Comit's getup makes me feel underdressed. His suit is pin-striped black and blue with a neat golden handkerchief in his pocket. His bow tie is also gold, which matches the chain trailing into his pocket where he pulls out a watch. His fingernails are incredibly neat and painted black, gripping the head of his walking stick.

"I thought you'd have found your way sooner." He sharpens his mustache into a finer point.

I stuff my hands in my pockets. "Took me a little while to figure it out. It was Kurt who noticed the mermaid on the other side of the coin."

"Must always look both ways." Comit seems pleased with himself, tapping his cane on the floor with a happy *click*. "Ah, Madame Mercury, these are the gentlemen we were expecting."

At the top of the double grand stairs is a lady dressed from another decade. She's saying good-bye to a man and a girl in a long white gown. When the girl in white walks away, I notice the wings at rest. As that couple walks slowly up the steps, another man comes down. He's also wearing a suit. His hair is disheveled and there are fresh bites on either side of his neck. He nods only at Madame Mercury and disappears the way we came in.

Madame Mercury turns to us. I think of Frederik saying, "Madame Mercury's not so bad," and I can see what he means. Her corset is crimson satin, pulled so tight at the center I could circle her waist with my hands. Her skin is pale, except for the scarlet blush of her cheeks. Her skirt is a long black trail that looks like rippling water. Her movement is delicate, from the way she traces the air around my face to the way she turns her black eyes and bats extremely long eyelashes at Kurt.

"What is this place?" I ask.

"This is the Second Circle." Madame Mercury looks at me from head to toe. "A place where the heart's deepest desires can come true."

"Uh-huh. So who are you?"

She circles me, the diamond baubles on her ears dangling in her scarlet hair. "Surely you've already guessed *what* I am. As to who I am, Comit has already introduced us. Then there's what I do, which is collect, as Comit collects his creatures."

"I don't get it."

"Follow me. I will show you."

She turns gracefully on the polished dark wood floors and walks down the hall to massive double doors carved intricately, patiently until every detail was perfect. Even the brass handles are twisted and etched just so. I wonder how much people pay to be down here. It's not just dripping with golden frames, lavish drapes, and tapestries that would put the Metropolitan Museum of Art to shame. It's the secrecy that comes with being somewhere like this.

"Here we are." Madame Mercury presses her hand on the door. From inside, the locks turn, undoing themselves. She gives the door a little push but doesn't go in. "*Shout*…if you need me."

Surely, I hope there will be no shouting.

I'm the first one in. Nothing has prepared me for this. Not the creatures of Toliss, not the oracles I've already found. The tiles are wet. I notice too late and fall on my ass.

A little chuckle echoes against the high ceiling.

Like the rest of this place, the mosaic is artfully done. I follow the patterns down along the walls to the center of the room where she rests in a great pool. It's her. Copper hair, milky white skin, and eyes like warm green water. Her mouth is a dream, moist and red. There's nothing girlish about her. Not the arc of her eyebrow when she looks at me, or the pleased smirk when she finds Kurt, who is walking toward her. He takes baby steps. After we hauled ass to get here.

One. Two.

He sighs. Reaches out.

Three.

She swims to the edge of her pool. I wonder how she can float like that. Her tails are magnificent, green like pine.

Four. Five. Six.

He falls to his knees, all the while staring at her face. For a moment, she looks sad, holding his face with her slender wet hands. The breath between them makes the room shudder until it's too much to bear.

They kiss.

I try to look at the opulent black tile of the room, the plush bench set off to the side, surely for decoration only. I don't see the two-tailed mermaid having tea on it. I feel pervy standing around staring at them. He stands, bringing her up with him, pressing her against his body, until the water reaches her hips at the start of her scales. One of her hands disappears and I think I've had enough.

"Should I—wait outside?"

Kurt lets go first.

"Stay, Prince Tristan." She lets go of Kurt's hand and traces the red flush of her mouth. "Come, let me look at you."

Just when I was getting tired of these people twirling me around like I'm Cinderella in a new dress. Does she want me to tap dance while I'm at it?

"You're stronger than I'd thought you'd be," she says.

"Thanks?" Something about her sets my entire body on edge. "You're less creepy than I thought you'd be."

"*Tristan.*"

"No, let him. This is what I like about him. He says what he means. Even if I should clip his tongue with his own dagger."

My hand goes to my sheath. My dagger is gone. It hovers in the air above us.

"Lucine, don't."

"Don't be cross with me, my love. Everything I've done has been for you. No one knows you like I do. No one ever will."

I grab Kurt's arm. "What is she doing?"

"Lucine, you know why we're here. Do you have the fork of the trident? If you don't have it, then there is still one out there. The sea witch, Nieve, is getting stronger. They killed one of your sisters. Tristan needs—"

"Tristan *needs* to learn his place in the world." Lucine laughs. It's a terrible sound that crawls over my skin. "Though he has done admirably, especially for a half breed." She grips the golden edge of her pool and a fury comes over her features. "How *dare* the king defy me even after I showed him what would happen? How long have I lived alone in these shallow pools with people taking and *taking*. That's all they do—take, take, take from the future but never learn."

She waves her hand. Makes a mirror appear on the wall, like iridescent oil on water.

"Do you know what happens to a person who stares right at their future, Tristan?"

I shrug. "I don't know but I'm sure you're going to tell me."

"They forget to live it. My sisters and I live in between the worlds. They with their laria and hordes of petulant pixies. Yet I, *I* must always be alone."

"You weren't alone." Kurt reaches for her. "You had me."

She takes his hand. "I waited a thousand years for you. And

when I had you, it was too, too, too much. You'd lie in my arms and in sleep, your thoughts turned to chaos. Then I sent you away."

"So you see the future?" I remember when I met the first oracle, Shelly, the youngest. She could only read corny shells. She said she was born with the smallest bit of magics. If Lucine is the strongest, that means she is the eldest.

"I see what the fates bid me to see. Sometimes it's everything all at once. Tiny voices and faces hurting, loving, dying. Flocks of ravens tearing at each other's wings. Worms digging deep into the dirt. They're all in *here*." She places one hand over her temple and one over her heart.

"I'm sorry this happened to you," I say, "but there's a really nasty mermaid who wants to take over the throne and I need that trident. She's even left you guys unprotected by sending away your sea dragons."

"The day Nieve, daughter of the sea, commands any of my dragons is the day I breathe my last breath, and that day is not yet upon us."

"Your dragons?" If only I had my dagger. "*You* sent the dragon?"

"How else could Adaro, witless as he is, reach the staff? How could I get you to trust Comit to guide you here without them?"

I feel like I've been set on fire. "But you *told* Adaro he'd find what he was looking for on this shore."

"And he will." Her smile is cruel. "Don't think for a moment that we don't know what we're doing. The king was the foolish one to go against our wishes. I *told* him what needed to be done and he defied us." She swims to the center of her pool and pulls it out of the water. The trident. It's brighter somehow. The gold etchings glisten. Sparks fly between the prongs. If she points that thing at me, I will fry.

"This," she says, "is the true power."

I step closer to her. Kurt and I are side by side. I can feel the scepter between my shoulder blades reacting to it, glowing with the same light.

"What is it you want?" I ask her finally.

"I want one thing." She lowers the trident. "To give the power to the true heir of the king—"

I hold out my hands. But I can see it in her eyes. I want to run. I want to fight. I want to grab it from her and shove it into her heart. Anything to make this moment untrue.

"*The last son of kings*, Kurtomathetis."

Part III

Yet echoes in my heart a voice,

As far, as near, as these—

The wind that weeps,

The solemn surge

Of strange and lonely seas.

—WALTER DE LA MARE, FROM "ECHOES"

chapter FORTY-SEVEN

Here in the Second Circle, beneath the saloon of belly-dancing girls and Madame Mercury's collection of monstrous beauties, is Lucine, the oracle who can see the future. She holds the trident for Kurt to take.

Kurt, who appeared in the form of a fish in my bathtub the first time I shifted. Kurt, who led me to Toliss Island, who fought by my side, who taught me how to hold a sword properly. My friend Kurt. I work out the family tree in my head. If he's the last son of kings, then Kurt is my uncle.

"Did you know?" There's a twinge in my spine. And what if he did know? What if he spent all this time letting me feel special and chosen when he knew he was the true son of the king? Then I say it louder. "Did you *know*?"

Kurt shakes his head. He can't look at me. He can't look at her. He bows his head and looks at his hands, the deep grooves and callouses, the thin fissures of scars.

"When did you begin to suspect the truth, Kurtomathetis?"

Lucine asks. She's manic and giddy, and I want to skewer her with my scepter. *My* scepter.

"I was sharpening the weapons," Kurt whispers. "On Arion's ship. When we went down to the cove. I was sharpening our weapons and I realized what I was holding. Triton's dagger. It—it didn't burn me. After we saw the oracle, and it wasn't you, I was furious. She trapped me in a memory chamber, and I could see my mother with a shadowed figure who wasn't my father."

"I couldn't tell you directly," Lucine says. "I knew you had learn it on your own. I knew you had to see it. I asked my sister to show you, both of you, the memory of the king."

And I remember our trip down the well. The memory of Kurt's mother holding him. Then the woman beneath the man. I want to reach out to Kurt, to let him know I'm here for him. But the walls he's putting up are strong. He wants to be alone. He wants to put his fist through something. It's in his eyes, the tremble of his arms.

Kurt shakes his head. "No, my father is dead."

Lucine laughs again. "When the next king is called, your father's powers will ebb completely, and only when the next king arises will he die. I told him to crown his true son. Nieve, her perversion of our kind, and the coming war are all of *his* making. By denying you, he gave her opportunity. So you see, my darling, your father lives until you piece together the trident and take the throne."

"The king dies when the next king is called?" My words are a shadow in the brightness of their conversation.

Lucine nods methodically. "That is our way. The father will die, and the last son of kings will take the throne."

"Stop saying that." Kurt yells. He points a finger in her face. He turns around like he's going to walk out that door. "Give it to Tristan. I don't want this."

"She's crazy, Kurt," I say. I look at the trident fork in her hands, the look in her eye. If I move the wrong way, she's going to hit me with it. "But just take it! You were the one who found her, not me. At least if it's with you—we'll figure something out." *Yeah, we'll figure out a way to not kill each other.*

Lucine lets out a terrible wail. She rises taller than the pair of us. The water of her pool splashes in a whirlpool of its own. I'm afraid the candelabra chandelier is going to fall right over us when the doors burst open. Two bouncers come in and grab at us. I put my foot on the edge of Lucine's pool, jump, and pull my dagger from its invisible hold. Behind me, I hear Kurt wrestling with one of them. I swing with the pointy end and miss.

He's fast and smells faintly of wet dog. His fist, decked out with fat gold rings, hits my face. I fall to my knees and throw a weak punch. He punches me again. The room feels like a carousel. They squeeze my arms 'til I think my veins will pop right out. We're out the door, up some steps, then I'm on the ground. My cheek is swelling by the second, and blood pools on my tongue from a cut on my lip. I spit on the ground.

"Kurt?"

The sky rumbles like the heavens are putting their foot on the gas pedal of the coming storm. It starts to drizzle.

"Kurt?"

I roll over and let the rain wash over me. Holy shit, it hurts. Just when I'm about to fall asleep to the soft patter of rain, the steady pulse of the bruise on my face and rib cage, a cold hand smacks me on my cheek.

"Wake up," she says.

"Layla?"

"You wish." Madame Mercury holds a black umbrella over my face. She holds out a hand. It's cold and surprisingly strong. "I'm sorry for my men, but once one of my girls sounds the alarm, we have to protect her."

I take the umbrella from her and hold it over us. The street is desolate, full of leftover food that didn't make it into the garbage cans. "Where's Kurt?"

"Still with her."

"Of course he is." The drizzle turns into rain.

"Come with me." She turns back to the black door. When I don't follow, she peers over her shoulder. "Well?"

I realize I'm staring. I take one last look at the street. Other than a scavenger digging through the trash can, it's empty. Next door, the pink psychic shop is still glowing, but the session is over. Madame Mercury presses the door open. I close the umbrella, tuck it under my arm, and follow her back into the Second Circle.

chapter FORTY-EIGHT

"Why are you helping me?"

We skip the winding steps and go through a service hallway. Quiet girls and guys fold and steam blankets, polish silver, and filter a white liquid by pressing flowers.

I find myself tripping and bumping into everything. It's like the time I was supposed to be a stagehand during *The Wiz* to pass drama class. I single-handedly demolished the Emerald City from backstage.

"You didn't answer me."

Vampires aren't supposed to breathe, but Madame Mercury sighs. "I owe a very handsome vampire a favor. Seems you got on his good side."

"I knew Frederik would take a liking to me eventually."

"He doesn't like anyone, darling. Except for Marty."

We stop in the middle of a hall lined with six-inch-square circuit breakers. Mercury opens a little door, revealing two unmarked switches beside a window. When I look inside, it shows Lucine's room.

I jump back.

"Calm down," she says. "They can't see you."

"Do all these things look into a room?"

"Of course. Cameras are too detectable. Instead, we keep two-way mirrors just to make sure the body count stays down. This switch is for sound and this one to set off the sprinklers. We don't want another fire like the Hellgate incident." She runs her hand through my hair, admiring my face. "That was before your time. Don't you worry."

"I thought Lucine made that mirror appear."

Madame Mercury scoffs. "She likes that trick. Makes her look fancy. Now, I'll tell my staff that this service corridor is off limits. But you won't have much time. If someone walks by, look busy."

"How am I supposed to do that?"

She presses her red lips on my cheek, then hands me a broom. "Good luck, Sea Prince."

"Thanks, Lady."

She turns on her heel and sashays back down the corridor. The blackness swallows up her dress first, then the red of her corset, but not the white of her back.

I lean the broom on the wall beside me, take a look around the empty corridor, and peek into the window.

I can't remember which switch is which.

Through the window, Kurt is banging on the doors. There are

no doorknobs. Lucine moves around in her pool. The water is calm now that I'm gone. She dips down to her shoulders and tilts her head back and floats around with her tailfins twisting in the air.

Kurt stops fighting with the door. He doesn't look mad anymore. I understand the feeling. I could never be mad at Layla for too long. He steps carefully on the wet floor. There's a splatter of my nose blood on the tiles. He stops and grimaces. He doesn't even ask if I'm okay.

Instead, he keeps his eyes on Lucine. He takes his shirt off. When he gets to his shorts, he stops. Lucine is saying something but I'm afraid to flip the wrong switch. You know what? If the sprinklers hit, I'll just dip out. They're merpeople; they can handle a little bit of rain.

The switch snaps like a BB gun. I grab the broom in case someone walks down the hall. Their voices come through like a whisper.

"Hush now," Lucine says. She undoes his button and he steps out of the shorts. It's like a car crash I can't look away from. He steps into Lucine's golden pool and sits so they're face to face. "Don't forget I can see your thoughts. Even as you have me now, alone, you think of Tristan?"

"I'm thinking of many things, Lucine. One of which is why you aren't letting me go. You've done it before. Thrown me out of your chambers just like you did Tristan. At least he was fully clothed, unlike the way I was the last time."

She pouts. It's a pretty pout. As a guy, I don't know if I can fault him for staying. As his friend, I want to beat him with this broom.

As his nephew…well, that's gross and I don't want to think about it too much.

"You aren't still cross with me, are you?"

He answers her by grabbing her waist. The water glows as he shifts. He picks her up and sits her on top of him. She leans forward on his chest. Their noses touch. Her tails wrap around him. I let go of the broomstick and decide I shouldn't be looking at this.

"I've missed you." I've never heard Kurt sound this way. Sweet and longing. He presses his mouth on hers.

"Too hard, bro," I say to myself, remembering how Angelo was the one who gave me pointers on kissing. Our sworn secret.

She pulls back and touches the bite on her bottom lip. Now, she's no longer an oracle. She's Kurt's. Her green eyes are bright, unworried, unburdened. He bends forward and she gasps. Water floods over the brim of the pool.

My throat is dry and I swallow. I flip the sound switch off. I shut the door and randomly peek to check if they're finished. This is the girl he was talking about on the field? I open the door again and the pool is still.

Lucine settles her weight on him. She kisses his chest, right over his heart. Then she swims to the opposite edge for her golden comb. It has pearls along the handle and a ruby dangling on the end. I flip the sound back on.

"You always surprise me, Kurtomathetis."

Oh, give me a break.

Kurt blushes. "And you me, Lucine."

"Tell me, now that your mind is calm, have you accepted my challenge?"

He splashes out of the pool, grabs a towel from the bench. He dries off as best as he can before putting his clothes back on and finding that they're wet. Duh, Kurt, everything in the room is wet. "Do you expect me to forget my true father in seconds? I've always been loyal to the throne. To take the trident would be to go against everything I stand for. It would make me a traitor to the—"

"Don't you see?" She grabs at the air with her fist as if she could manifest her truths just by pulling them out of space. "You are the throne. For anyone to rule that isn't you is already treason."

Kurt's silence is crushing. He starts to speak and stops, like he doesn't want to say the words, but he must. "If the king had wanted to be my father, he would've announced it long ago. He's had over a century."

Lucine shakes her head and looks up to the ceiling. There's so much wonder in her eyes that it's like she's looking at the moving sky of Eternity. Then she focuses back on this plane, on Kurt.

"My love," she says, and he walks right back to her and takes her hands. "It was never the king's wish to deny you. It was your mother's. The affair would've broken her husband's heart. One day soon, you will ask the king yourself. Until then, I will show you what will happen if you do not claim your birthright."

She takes his face and turns it to the mirror on the wall. My heart jumps when their eyes fall on me. But they can't see me. I wave at them and then they vanish, replaced by a watery image. It starts off like an oil slick, then becomes clear as day. The sky bleeds with lightning. It pours over Toliss Island. The trees are on fire. The waves threaten to swallow it whole.

The image shifts to the Glass Castle. Merrows and mermen alike tear at the structure and it shatters. Mermaids and tadpoles float, dead, then dissipate into surf. Even the elders vanish painfully into nothing. Then it's me, lying on the beach. I choke. The crown falls off my head, washes away in the tide.

"Stop it!" The image disappears when Kurt pulls out of her hold. "You're making that up."

While he's turned away, Lucine still stares at the mirror, right at me. She can see me. She wanted me to see.

Turning back to Kurt, she says, "You know very well that I can't make it up. Really, love, I fear you've been around humans far too long. The fortnight is nearly over. The trident has been found. You must take it back to your father."

He hesitates. Suddenly it makes sense, the way the nautilus maid greeted both of us as champions. The same curious eyes Sarabell gave Kurt when she called him the "odd one out" in his bunch. The reason why my grandfather singled him out as the best warrior.

"The sea witch approaches." Lucine takes the fork of the trident from her pool. It hovers just over her palms. An offering. "You will need this to stop her."

He stares at it the way I stare at the scepter, like it's calling to me. The trident is calling to him.

It's an electric hum, a whisper.

I can hear it too.

Kurt, son of the king, steps forward and takes the trident.

And when he does, I flip both switches and make it rain.

chapter FORTY-NINE

When I trigger the alarm, I make a run for it.

I trip over a devil girl carrying a tray full of champagne flutes, then the dessert cart rolling down the hall. The floor trembles as heavy boots run behind me. When I look over my shoulder, the same friendly werewolves that lovingly chucked me out the first time are coming for me.

They growl and snap at the air, teeth crunching like the grind of a bear trap. Yellow eyes and snouts elongating from their faces. I pull my scepter from between my shoulder blades. The light of the quartz fills the dark and doorless hallway. Their howl turns into a laugh, and I wonder if I'm heading out the right direction. I have a vision of two gnarly wolves tearing me to pieces, and I point the quartz over my head.

The charge comes quickly, from my chest, up my arms. The blast hits the ceiling, illuminating the falling debris. The bouncers howl and curse at me. A small fire builds quickly in the narrow hall. Smoke fills my lungs and the sprinklers rain down. I can see the red exit sign, and I push harder and harder until I'm out on the street.

I don't know how big the Second Circle is, but I'm not where I started.

It takes me a second to orient myself.

Despite the familiar buildings, the area doesn't look right without the usual crowds. I stand in the middle of the street. The lights change from green to yellow to red. There are no cars. No sirens. No passersby.

Instead, there are dozens and dozens of birds all along the fence that marks the New York Aquarium.

Ravens and golden eagles and even bats are beating their wings against the drizzle. Their cries form a united melody, a warning in song. I head straight for the aquarium, but I ram against an invisible barrier. I press my hands on the barrier, and every time I hit it, a tiny shock of electricity jolts me.

One of the ravens turns into a girl no taller than my chest. Her arms are wings and her hair is as black as her feathers. "Announce yourself."

"You're kidding me."

The steely black look in her eyes tells me she isn't.

"I'm Tristan Hart," I say. I hold the scepter in my hand. The crystal emits a soft glow.

The raven girl dips into a short bow and opens her wing to the side. The force field opens. I can't see it, but I can feel the temperature difference, like a line of heat separating the aquarium from the outside world.

When I take a single step forward, someone screams my name. Gwen is running down the street, soaked through and through.

I take her by her shoulders, concerned about the fear in her eyes. Gwen is never scared. "Are you okay?"

She nods and attempts to smile. There is no way she would ever admit to being nervous, so I take her hand and try to step through the doorway. But the raven girl closes it again and a sharp caw flies from her throat. "Frederik says only the Sea Prince is to enter."

"She's with me," I growl.

The girl becomes a raven again and pecks at my hair before lining up with the others on the fence. But she does not stop us. We cross through the gate, where the cold, wet night doesn't follow.

"Where were you?" I ask.

We sprint across the parking lot, cutting across to the entrance to the aquarium.

"The princesses," she says. "They've all gone."

The guard at the door doesn't stop us. I don't know what he is—human, android, ghost—and I don't care. He nods at me once and opens the door.

This leads to the reef portion of the aquarium. Tanks are backlit with white and blue light. The ceilings are so low to the ground that I feel like I'm swimming through a tunnel. I look into the glass of the contained ecosystem. My breath fogs. The giant turtle swims directly at me. He presses his nose to the glass. There's something in his eyes that is old and so eternal. A creature of the past. How do you survive, I wonder. How are you still here?

I snap around to see Gwen. It makes me laugh. She's twisting her fingers with her own hands. She refuses to look at me. She's staring at the tank of jellyfish. They bloom and glow like shimmering ghosts across the water.

"I'm glad you're here," I tell her.

"Tristan." She touches my face. Her hands are so cold. I'm not ready to talk about what I've just seen, and whatever is on her mind, she isn't going to tell me. We stand in the quiet blue darkness of the aquatic house. "I—"

I take a step back to give her some space. I can't have her trying to kiss me again. Not now. Not here. Not ever. I need her strong and I need her present. "What is it?"

"We should find your friends."

I lead us through the tiny maze of giant tanks. The fish follow us with their open mouths pressed against the glass until I push on the double doors out onto the main road that divides the aquarium houses. True to Frederik's word, the Thorne Hill Alliance is here. I feel like I'm at the Vanishing Cove all over again. In the middle of the plaza, weapons are being exchanged.

I scan the crowds but don't see the faces I'm looking for.

"Tristan!" Thalia shouts from above. She's on the observation deck, waving us over.

We race up the flight of steps, under the canopy. Layla stands beside Thalia. They're sweating and out of breath, holding swords in each hand. I'm filled with a need to drop everything and pick her up in my arms. But the thunder and rain break against the barrier, and all I can do is squeeze her hand.

Frederik and Marty are conferring with Rachel. She's got a bigger crossbow. They're pointing at the gray line of the horizon. A thick fog is settling over the shore.

When they see me, they stop. Rachel's bow vanishes to smoke.

With my scepter in hand, I stand before my friends. They're staring and searching. They can see that I don't have the trident and I don't have Kurt.

"It's almost sunset," I say.

"What happened, man?" Marty takes off his cap and scratches his head. "Where's your new pitchfork?"

"Where's my brother?" Thalia asks.

My mouth is full of saliva. I turn to the side and spit.

"Frederik," I say, "fill me in."

Frederik hesitates, taking stock of the tension I'm giving off in waves. "I have a group of valkyries who will stay behind, led by Rachel. The first line is on the beach right now—vampires and werewolves. They won't go in the water so we know they'll make sure nothing gets past."

"Good." I'm nodding too hard. "Good."

"What about other mermen?" Frederik asks. "The other champion?"

I level my turquoise eyes to his black ones. "Adaro isn't fighting with us."

"I see."

"When it comes to merrows, you have to cut off their heads or stab their hearts. Otherwise, they won't die."

"I'm familiar with the method." Frederik flashes a yellow smile, then turns to whisper something to Rachel. She smiles at me, and the action is so bizarre that, in that moment, I realize she thinks I'm a dead man.

"In case of a retreat—" Frederik begins.

"Way to put a damper on such a sunny day, Freddy," Marty says.

"It is my duty to be prepared," Frederik responds coolly. "If we must retreat, we return here. The reef house has a floor latch that leads down to our tunnels and back out onto the boardwalk."

"Good." I'm still nodding too hard. "Good."

"*Tristan*," Thalia says forcefully. "Where is my brother?"

"He's still down there," I say, turning away from her and readjusting the harness across my chest. "In the Second Circle."

Marty mutters darkly. "I told you guys."

"Did something happen?" Layla asks.

"Did the oracle not have the trident?" Gwen asks.

"Tristan," Frederik says. "The others are dividing weapons if you'd like to further arm yourself."

"I've got weapons," I say.

But Frederik grabs my arm and gives me a push in the direction of the steps. "Just in case."

I realize he's giving me a way out and I take it. I can't be the one to break the news to Thalia. How will she take it? Surely, nothing's changed between them. They're still siblings. They still grew up together. It shouldn't matter.

I head toward the weapons and immediately recognize a face.

"Penny," I say, surprised. "What are you doing here?"

She's holding a sword in her hand.

"Do you know how to use that?"

"I'm not just a waitress," she says, pointing it at my heart.

"What about Jesse?" I say. "And the others?"

"The landlocked are free to make their own choices." She motions to a small group of people I saw at the meeting. There isn't anything threatening about them. Their skin is slightly green and blue. One hacks at the air, grasping a steel club with webbed hands. "That is the one thing that binds us. I want to show my son that he has the freedom to do anything he wants."

"Where is Timmy?"

She holds the blade to her eyes so she can see her own reflection. "With his father."

"What happened?" Layla runs up to us. "Where's Kurt? How did you and Gwen get here?"

My thoughts are racing, trampling over each other. I place my hands on her shoulders and look right into her eyes. "Kurt is still with the oracle."

I pause for effect.

Her eyes widen. "You mean *with* her?"

I nod. "I'm sure he'll find us."

"And she didn't have the trident?"

"She did."

"Then where is it?"

I can't breathe. Something is happening to me, weaving its way through my thoughts. Kurt is my uncle. Kurt is the son of the king. Kurt has the Trident of the Seas. Wind and rain whip against our invisible force field. The giant birds' song is a terrible wail pounding against my temples.

I try to shut it out, but I realize it's not the birds. Someone is screaming.

"It's starting," I say.

The guard I passed at the entrance marches up to me. "It's a girl. She came alone."

"We'll go check it out," I say. "The rest of you stay here."

I follow the guard back through the reef house.

Marty marches alongside me. "I was getting claustrophobic in there."

Under the arc of the aquarium where the boardwalk meets cement, Sarabell pounds wet fists against our shield.

"Let me in," she cries.

"So you can kill me?" I point my dagger at her.

"*No, Lord Sea.*" She shakes her head wildly. Her black curls are matted to her face. "No, Lord Sea. I wouldn't—Adaro—Adaro—" Her cries are hysterical. She tries to stand but falls back down.

I turn around but her scream rips through me. I fight against my own reason. But with the encroaching darkness, can I really leave her out there alone?

"Adaro is what, Sarabell?"

Her eyes are red, tears mixing with rain. "Adaro is dead."

chapter FIFTY

A fire explodes in the distance where Adaro's ship was hidden. Hundreds of voices scream in the darkness. The shadow of our first line of defense is a wall cutting across the sand. They're standing, waiting.

Sarabell presses her hand on the invisible wall. "Please, she's going to kill me too."

I keep my dagger level to her face. "Tell me what happened."

She cries and looks back at the dark horizon. "Please..."

"Let her pass," Marty says. The avians rustle their feathers, and a breeze blows in as the invisible fortress opens.

I pick Sarabell up off the ground. Her legs give out. I kneel to be at eye level with her.

"Look at me. Sarabell, look at me. What happened to Adaro?"

A torrent of rain beats against the barrier. A fat drop falls onto my shoulder.

"The avians were supposed to be weatherproof," Marty says, shielding his eyes from the drizzle.

Then the ravens caw, flapping foot-long black wings. The avians leave their posts and take off into the sky where they blow up like lightbulbs, shattering sparks down on us. Their high-pitched screams become a chorus as feathers scatter and fall like helicopter leaves.

The barrier is gone and the rain beats down.

Frederik jumps from the observation deck down to where we stand. He grabs one of the guards by his shirt and seethes into his face. "What. Happened?"

Confusion spreads through our army. No one answers. The guard shakes his head, uselessly attempting to cover his eyes from Frederik's black glare. "I-I don't know, Fred. They were fine a second ago."

"Get back to the plaza," Frederik says. "*Now.*"

I grab Sarabell by her arm and lead her back in with the others. I sit her down on the bench. "Thalia, stay with Sarabell. Don't let her out of your sight."

"What happened to the birds?" Layla asks.

Up on the observation deck, the valkyries line up with their crossbows. Down here in the plaza, we ready our weapons. I push Layla behind me, smelling the stupidly brave smoke she's giving off. I search for Gwen in the crowd, but there are so many of us.

"We've been breached." Frederik's face is calm but I pick up the tension in his voice. "The barrier is external. Only someone inside can break it. I want *everyone* to form ranks at the entrance!"

I grab Sarabell by the arm. "Did you do this?"

She shakes her head, crying. I scream at her. I shake her. She's a wet doll in my hands. Someone screams my name, over and over again, but my ears are popped, like I'm in a channel leagues and leagues beneath the sea.

There's something else weaving in the air, beneath Sarabell's frantic sobs and the pouring rain. My dagger hums. My scepter glows. I can feel it. Energy. Crackling static. It pulses like a ring around the reef house. Stronger and stronger.

"Get down!"

I say it too late.

The reef house erupts. Sends us flying backward. My ears ring. A warm trickle snakes from my forehead to my chin. The observation deck is now a hole. The animals in the tanks gasp for breath on the floor. Rachel and her troupe reappear as smoke around us.

"Don't look so happy to see me," she says.

I get up from the ground. "Is everyone okay?"

Layla wipes my face with shaking hands. "You're bleeding."

"You too." There's a cut on her cheek. The skin mends instantly.

"It's a good thing I'm already dead." Frederik pulls a long piece of glass from his collarbone.

Marty groans, "Do you know how hard it is to get blood off corduroy?"

"It's black." Layla rolls her eyes. She winces when she arcs to crack her back. "You can't even see it."

Thalia picks up Sarabell and sits her between two rows of bushes. Everyone raises their weapons toward the crumbled reef house. At first we only see shadows breaking through the settling dust.

Jesse emerges from what's left of the building, trailed by more than a dozen of his faithful landlocked. His clothes are shredded. Under the rain, a thin layer of crushed sheetrock and brick clumps on his skin. He peels back his raw, red mouth around buck-sharp teeth. Rachel shoots, but Jesse holds his hand up and the arrow turns into sand.

I step forward. Jesse picked the wrong day. He smiles with his fat, raw lips.

"All this time on land," I tell him. "And you never thought to get braces?"

We charge each other at the same time. Arrows whiz by. The wet slick of swords piercing flesh fills my ears.

I can't see anyone but Jesse. I punch him across the face, but his head snaps right back. His nails bite into me as we tumble across the debris. His scaly knuckles tear at the thin skin of my temple. I jab a fist once, twice in his gut and a knee to his groin. Jesse chokes, and in the moment it takes for him to cradle himself, I take my dagger, hot in my hands, and drive it straight through his chest.

I take pleasure in watching his black eyes roll into his skull. Lips twitch. Body convulses. I hate myself for it. I wonder if he'll break apart the way the merrows do. I wonder if he'll turn to coral the way Kai's father did. I'm hoping for the coral. That way I can crush it with my bare hands.

Instead, Jesse's eyes come back into focus. He shows me his palms; the red dots spreading like a stain around his wrist.

Where he touches the blade in his chest, his hands give off smoke. He screams against the burn, elated as he pushes Triton's dagger away and out of his chest. He throws it at my feet. The gash in his chest singes but heals just as quickly.

"She's here," he says.

I pick up my dagger and charge at him again. If the pointy end won't make a difference, then there's always the other end. I crack his skull. He stumbles backward, laughing.

"You can't hurt me! Can't you see? Her most loyal subjects have been rewarded. She is here, land prince. And she is waiting for you." A growl rumbles from deep inside him, like a giant after waking from a hundred-year nap.

My friends have formed a semi-circle behind me, swords, fangs, and—where did Marty find a baseball bat? I point at the dead bodies around him.

"You brought your friends to die," I say. A voice inside my head whispers, *He wanted them to die.*

"They understood their purpose," he says. Jesse's face is distorted. "As you will understand yours."

Then there's another crack of lightning, this time so close that I can feel the jolt in my bones. It cuts through the air and goes straight for Jesse, grabbing him like arms ten feet above the ground. The ribbons of electricity don't come from above. They come from the parting crowd, where Kurt stands in a half shift, wielding the Trident of the Skies.

With one final gust, the three prongs crackle, taking hold of Jesse once more. The lightning rockets him miles into the air, until he's nothing more than a shadow in the night sky.

chapter FIFTY-ONE

"What is this?" Thalia asks her brother.

There's a definite and distinct look of awe in every set of eyes that turns to Kurt. I know there is nothing like this kind of jealousy that's creeping through me. It's ten times worse than when he formed the instant bond with my mother. One hundred times worse than when I saw Lucine hand him the head of the trident, her manic green eyes looking at me through the two-way mirror. She wanted me to feel this way.

Everything is falling away with the rain, cleaning the ground for the future she saw come to pass. Kai's words have never rung so true or so loudly: *Nothing matters to them but their secrets.* Their need to be listened to and needed in a world that's forgotten them.

The question still hangs in the glances traded like notes between class periods. He got into her pool. He stepped up and took the trident from her. And yet, he still can't say the words. So I do.

"Kurt is the last son of the Sea King," I say. There's a slithering black thing in my heart. It's jealousy and it has taken form. He flinches when our eyes meet. "Adaro is dead."

Pulled out of his spell, Kurt notices Sarabell. Dirty from Jesse's blast and red in the face from crying. "Nieve?"

"Which means," I say, "she's taken his staff."

Frederik steps forward like a shadow at my side. He shouts, "Form ranks!"

Kurt turns to Sarabell. He lowers the crackling prongs of the trident to her face. She stares at the lightning, then at his face. "If you lie to me, witch—"

"I'm not lying!" Sarabell cried furiously. "Adaro wouldn't listen to me. He wanted to come to your aid, and then came the silver witch. Adaro threw me off the ship and the others fought. I could hear them. They said they would wait until your barrier was down."

"All of our avian shields were destroyed," Frederik says aloud. "After you entered. Aren't you one of the sea folk rarely gifted?"

"Aye. But as Lord Sea knows…" Her smile is slow. She trembles in the cold. "I am not the only one."

Gwen doesn't flinch. Rain washes away the dirt from her, head to toes.

Sarabell raises her hands slowly. I can feel the spark of her magic pulling from the air around us, directed right at me. I raise my scepter at the same time Kurt does his trident.

Neither of us are as fast as Rachel, holding her crossbow. The crowd stands back. The spring is released and it flies past my ear.

Sarabell's open mouth gapes at the air, unable to scream as her body breaks down into foam under the rain.

My heart is a hammer in my eardrums. I look to Rachel and all I can say is "You?"

"I owed you," she says.

There is no time for thank-yous. Frederik freezes, listening to the air as if there are voices only he can hear.

"They're coming ashore," he says.

We race through the archway and onto the boardwalk.

Dozens of them. Rot and death cutting through the fog. I hold my scepter by the hilt over my head, casting a light over our first line. The vampires are fast and strong, but the merrows come in massive numbers. Archer leads the way, curved swords in each hand, and hacks at anything in his way. The blue fire of Adaro's ship is coming closer, threatening to crash against the pier.

"Call them back," I tell Frederik.

"What?"

I break into a sprint, jumping over the railing and onto the sand. "Just do it!"

Archer doesn't see me. He's confused as the Thorne Hill Alliance retreats so willingly.

Tap, tap…my fingers to my forehead, my utterly silent Morse-code prayer.

I flip the scepter. Point the quartz down. Earth-shaker, Kai called it. I slam it into the ground, and like a ripple, the earth shudders and opens beneath our feet.

chapter FIFTY-TWO

The crack in the ground spreads like broken glass.

Water fills the hole quickly, pushing the merrows into the opening. It disrupts the path of the sea and a wave crashes over us. I feel hands all over my skin and I blindly lash out with my scepter. The light pulses, suspended underwater. Their open mouths swim at me from all sides. The tide pulls us back and I push my arms harder and harder to get back to shore. I stab the ground once again. The tremble shakes all the way to the boardwalk, rippling the wood as I close the wound, devouring the merrows, trapping them in the earth.

Another wave crashes, and the next line of Archer's army slithers onto the sand.

I hold up the scepter as a light beam.

And then they're running onto the sand. The merrows fall away in a mudslide of melting flesh as the Alliance crashes over them in a fury of fangs, claws, and swords.

Kurt's encircled by a breeze. In his hands, the trident is a torch of lightning, pushing the creatures of the deep back into the shallows.

I unsheathe my dagger, cutting cleanly across the neck of a merrow. He breaks apart at my feet and I move on to the next one. This time the merrows are faster. Stronger. Every time I kill one, more and more spring right out of the sea.

I go to the aid of a vampire; a merrow with the head of a swordfish is ramming needle-like fingers into the vampire's heart. I come from behind and stab the merrow through the back of his head.

"Good thing it isn't wood," I say.

He growls but manages a wry grin. "Still hurts."

"Take the wounded to the Wreck," Frederik says, suddenly a flash beside me. He wipes his mouth with the back of his hand. He spits over and over but is dissatisfied. "That is the most wretched thing I've tasted in my life."

Something hits me from behind and I fall on top of him. The wave crashes behind us and we start retreating farther up the beach. They're like hydras—we cut off their heads and more keep coming out of the sea.

I flip the scepter back to the ground but Marty screams at me. He's covered from head to toe in oozy, black merrow blood.

"Don't! Not unless you want to decimate the boardwalk. That thing's barely holding on as it is." He swings a sword and grimaces as another merrow breaks away at his feet.

"I'm sorry," I scream, back to back with him. A ring of the gnarliest mermen I've ever seen, scarred in patches like Archer, forms around us. "I know when you woke up, killing sea creatures wasn't the first thing on your mind."

"I did." Marty breathes like a bull. "I had lox on my breakfast bagel."

My laughter confuses my opponent and I jab him in the jaw. He doesn't move but keeps charging. I freeze as tentacles wrap around his face, slithering through his nose. His body convulses as a small gray thing slides out from his nostril. The whites of his eyes are spiderwebbed with black veins until he bursts. As he washes away, the tentacles turn into hands. Penny's face is surprised and ecstatic.

Marty pulls his blade from another pile of merrow mush and grimaces at Penny. "You are one sick mother—"

Marty tenses. A long red needle pierces through his chest. My body follows his to the ground. I press my hand on the wound. The blood pools all around his neck. Behind me, Frederik is paler than ever. Marty's trying to speak, trying to joke.

"Don't talk, Marty." Frederik pushes my hand away and replaces it with his own. Marty tries to laugh but he spits out blood. I scramble for my pockets until I find the tiny bottle. I twist off the cap.

Frederik asks, "What is that?"

"It's all that's left," I say, dropping half the contents on the wound and tipping the rest into Marty's mouth.

"Of what?"

"Their secrets," I say. "Take him."

Frederik looks torn. Marty's slack in his arms. "You need me."

"He needs you more."

I turn around, hoping that my last drops of spring water can save Marty. I run around the dead bodies on the sand. The merrows are frantic at the smell of blood. They stop fighting and devour, leaving them defenseless against our swords.

Even Archer can't get their attention, but he's busy on his own. Kurt blasts him with crashing electricity that would reduce a man to ashes. But Archer lies on the wet sand with eyes wide open, like he's drawing life from the water. He gets right back up and barrels into Kurt. Kurt presses his feet on Archer's stomach and flips him over. Kurt swings the trident across Archer's face.

He doesn't need my help, so I run to Thalia. She's got a nasty slash running down her arm. She glances at it like it's no big deal and helps one of the Alliance—a wire-thin guy about my age with glowing yellow eyes. Our numbers are falling faster and faster. More merrows are coming in with the waves. We reform our line, even closer to the boardwalk. Kurt steps in beside me.

"We can't let them get into the city," I say to Kurt.

"There are so many of them," he replies.

Frederik returns. If his heart were beating, I know it would be thundering out of his chest. I want to ask if Marty is okay. But the vampire growls like a lion.

The next wave of merrows is marching up to us. Kurt and I move forward, he with the head of the trident and me with the scepter, like Kleos and Ellanos, the old kings of the sea.

Then a bright light rises from the waves, behind the line of merrows.

A conch blasts through the air.

Riding on the back of a great sea horse is Princess Kai. Behind her surfaces a small army of mermen, their breastplates shimmering in the dark.

"That's my guard." Kurt takes a step forward. "What are they doing here?"

"Who cares?" Frederik says. "As long as they're here to fight."

Kai blows on the conch once again, waving her golden sword in the air.

And we race against the merrows, a clash of sand and sea.

chapter FIFTY-THREE

If my boys had asked me how I was going to spend my summer, never would I ever have said this:

Screaming at the top of my lungs until I don't recognize my own voice. Running, running, running against the wave of merrows, accompanied by an alliance of supernatural creatures and members of the Sea Guard.

If I'd once thought Kurt was threatening in his stoic poise, I know now that's nothing compared to the way the Sea Guard moves. They're a unit, as if they read each other's minds. The night is full of final screams before the opposing fighters fall away into the coming waves. The tide pulls away the bodies, those that don't break away the way we do.

In the onslaught, Archer wades toward me. He's weaponless.

"This is your chance, Archer." I hold my scepter between us, the light dragging shadows across his chiseled face. "Go back to Nieve and tell her she'll never have me and she'll never have Kurt."

He bares his canine smile at me. His eyes flicker to the right where Adaro's ship is floating precariously. Layla's scream fills the night—over the warrior yells, over the pulse of my heart in my ears. I can't see her, but I know she's there.

"She already has you, brother."

My feet pound the sand, racing through the battle, toward the fire, as Archer shouts, "And when she has you, she will never let go."

Though I can hear someone call my name, I don't stop. A horde of merrows step in my way and I drive my scepter downward, ripping into the sand. A wave pushes the merrows into the rift, and when I pull my scepter free, the ground closes.

I keep going toward the blue flames on Adaro's ship.

I climb up the side, past the painful moans of merfolk floating below. I think of what my mother said to me earlier: "You can't save them all."

It's childish and stupid to want to ask why? Why can't I? But here I am, hoisting over the side of a ship gone up in flames. The sails have been reduced to cinder and the mast breaks. I jump to the side as it falls against the pier. I shout her name. *Layla, Layla, Layla!*

It isn't her voice that answers but Adaro's. Under the shadows of his fiery ship, Adaro lies alone on the deck. His eyes are barely open, but he grabs the sword in his chest. Like with Kai's father, it's just short of a killing blow. I kneel beside him. I'm afraid to touch him. He might fall apart like the others. I wonder, how many times will I have to hold on to the dead?

Adaro grunts. There's nothing for me to do here but try to give him the smallest bit of comfort. There are tiny thorns on his chest, red where the poison has trickled into his veins, black and pronounced under thinning flesh.

"Do you want me to save him?" Nieve asks. When I turn around, she's not there.

I inch step by step along the deck.

Her voice carries over the ship.

She's nestled in water. It wraps around her and raises her level to the deck. Her fingers grip the Staff of Eternity.

She's playing me. Nothing can save him. I know it deep in my heart. "Where is she?"

Nieve has regenerated. Her skin breathes with new life. Her white hair shines under the nearly full moon, just visible against the black sky breaking through storm clouds. The blue is gone from her lips, replaced by a full scarlet mouth. "I can do it, you know. Save him."

"In exchange for this?" I hold my scepter sideways, so hard that my knuckles are white.

"How did you know?" Her voice is dry, amused, and full of venom.

"Everything has a price."

"So true," she says. "But I am no oracle. I do not require anything but your devotion. Your love."

"Look at what you've done!" I spit over the ship at her. "How could anyone love you?"

"I didn't start this, Tristan." She's serene in her confidence. "My children know the things I did to make them well when no one else would take them. All our creatures are precious. I do this for our kind. I do this for us."

"That's why you sent Jesse to die for you?"

"That's why I sent Jesse to distract you." She turns the staff in her hands. "You're as impulsive as my brother, never stopping to look. You see only what's directly in front of you. Only what you want in the moment."

"You're a crazy bitch, you know that?"

"Don't you dare..." Behind me, Adaro's voice comes in an angry whisper. "Don't you dare give in to her."

That's the tricky part, isn't it? If I let him die, it'll be my fault. Like Ryan, like Marty. No, Marty's fine. I saved Marty, like I couldn't save the others. Everything that's happening here is my fault. In the dark of the night, the silver witch waits for me to devote myself to her.

Deep in my heart, I know what my grandfather would do. He locked her away for a reason, but she found her way out. Everything she does is calculated, studying us like prey before she swoops in and swallows us whole. She's one step ahead of me, knowing that I won't let her kill Adaro. If I were my grandfather, I would have done things differently. Then again, I'm not him. I'm me.

"I thought you'd hesitate." She squeezes her hand, and when I turn around, Adaro screams like he's burning from the inside. It's cut off abruptly as, little by little, he erupts into bubbles, trickling away on the deck until he's nothing but a pile of sand. Everything he ever was. Everything he would ever be is blowing away in the wind. *Poof,* just like that.

On the deck of the ship, I point the quartz scepter at her.

"I'd be careful if I were you, Tristan." She lifts herself in the wave again. The wind is drying her hair, giving her the effect of flying.

I ready myself on the ledge. "Get off your wave, and we'll settle this once and for all."

"You can't kill me. You must know that."

"Because Archer brought you the spring water."

She nods. "And the more I drink it, the stronger my magic and the more I can help our kind."

"I can still hurt you," I say, hoping it's true. Hoping Layla is safe.

"This is all wrong, Tristan. Don't you see? I don't want you dead. I want you with me." The rains start up again. She lifts the staff over her head and pulls at the sky until the lightning returns. "And the scepter, of course. If Adaro's life wasn't enough, then perhaps this one will make you feel differently."

She casts light over the pier.

Gwen stands at the edge, a small silver knife in her hand, the blade pressed against Layla's neck.

chapter FIFTY-FOUR

"Gwen!"

She won't look me in the eye. Like inside the reef house. Like before and after she tried kissing me on the beach. "Gwen, look at me."

She doesn't.

But Layla does. Her lips are trembling. I can smell it on her, anger like kerosene, like the blue fire eating away at the ship now that the rain is settling.

I ready myself to jump off.

"You stay put." Nieve wags her finger at me, and my body feels like it's wading against the current. I grip my scepter tighter, fighting against the force of her magic.

"Don't look surprised, Tristan," Gwen says, finally meeting my eyes for a second before looking back down at Layla.

That's the thing. "I am. How can you do this?"

"I don't understand," Nieve says, "how you can pass over my Gwenivere for this creature. When Gwenivere told me her advances were futile against your human, I pictured something a little more—lush."

"You fought alongside me—"

"No." Gwen's eyes, the gray eyes that stared right into mine as she helped me find Shelly, are shadowed. "I fought against you. You were just too blind to see it."

Everything crashes over me. The way Archer tried to save her when the merrows attacked us in Florida. The way she helped me find Eternity. One step closer to finding it for Nieve. Nieve, always one step ahead. "It wasn't Sarabell who killed the avians. It was you."

"Oh no, that was Sarabell," Nieve says. "I told her I'd spare her dear cousin if she did as I asked. Foolish girl."

"Then you let in Jesse," I say. "*Look* at me, Gwen."

Finally, she does. One, two, three seconds go by and she turns away again. "You mean nothing to me, Tristan."

But she's wrong. I know the way she looked at me, sitting on the beach, laughing. She wasn't faking our friendship.

"Why?" I ask her. Even in the dark I can see the sad grimace on her face. "Because your husband sliced you up so now you hate the world?"

Her laugh makes me shiver. "Elias didn't give me any scars. In fact, he was afraid of me. He wanted to marry me thinking I'd serve him, be his private witch. Instead, I made him hide in the dark. I made his nightmares come to life."

"But you said—"

"No, *you* said Elias did this to me. I let you believe it. Every scar I have I wear proudly because it reminds me of what I am and where I come from."

"And where do you come from?"

This time, Nieve answers. "From me."

I think of every time I'd see Gwen in the corner of my eyes. The white of her hair. They don't have the same faces, but the haughtiness is there. With them side by side, I can see it now.

"My brother made me throw her away. The king, my brother, made me leave her. She was deformed in their eyes. Merrows, we call them. We leave them to die in bottomless holes in the sea. Then he locked me away and I healed her. I loved her and I fixed everything so that she could return to court where she belonged. And I did it for all my children. Never as good as Gwenivere, but Archer is the beginning of something new. Together we will make a better kingdom. Without fear of living on the outside. And you will give me what I want, Tristan Hart, or you will watch your human die."

I hold the Scepter of the Earth in my hands. The quartz glows so brightly that I fear I've lost control. Layla tries to shake her head, even with a knife at her neck. She doesn't want me to do it. But I'll find another way to fix it, to make this right.

I hold the scepter by its base.

The quartz faces the silver witch.

Her eager hands rise from the wave, ready to snatch it.

chapter FIFTY-FIVE

The blast comes from the pier, behind Gwen.

"*No.*"

Nieve loses her balance and falls into the water with a splash.

I hop over the deck onto the mast, which forms a bridge between the ship and the pier. My eyes are locked on Layla, who struggles against Gwen's grip. Gwen throws the knife to the ground and puts a hand over Layla's nose and mouth. "No!"

They dive.

On the pier, Kurt shoots another bolt of lightning to where Nieve floats. It blasts hard and hits the ship. The mast spins beneath my feet and I fall, hitting the back of my head on the wood before crashing in the water.

I swim, screaming in the sea with every bit of breath I have. She's gone.

They're gone.

The night is black and the storm is gone too.

Water dries against the heat of my skin. I think I'm burning from the inside out. I run back onto the pier, holding onto my scepter like a baseball bat, and swing with all my strength.

Kurt with his big, stupid violet eyes. How did I not see it? He's got an inch on me, maybe two, but the similarity is there. His face, familiar in the way my own is. Right now, I want to bash it into the back of his skull.

He moves side to side, avoiding my swings, but he doesn't swing back. "I had to!"

"No, you didn't!"

"Would you have given your power away to the sea witch? Would you have let her be the end of us? All for—"

"Say it!" I shove him with all of my weight. "For a human? In case you hadn't noticed, that's the way I was raised!"

"Are you finished?"

I laugh, bitter and ugly and hateful. "I'm not even close to finished."

He raises his trident at the same time I raise my scepter. The metals clash, sparking at every turn. I bet he didn't think I paid attention during our lessons. But I did. I mirror his every move. Side shuffle, three o'clock, turn, and six o'clock.

It pisses him off, Mr. Predictable. He sucks in the air around us and blasts me with his trident. My quartz absorbs the blow, taking the force deep into the crystal. I have to hold the scepter hard so it doesn't shake out of my hands.

From the corner of my eye, I see that the battle is coming toward us. The Sea Guard clusters on the beach and kneels in Kurt's direction. They hold their swords up. One of them says, "Sire—"

"This is between us." Kurt holds his hand up to stop them. And I want to laugh, because I know I had the same look on my face the first time Kurt called *me* "sire."

Then there are the others, Frederik leading his Alliance, Penny, and Kai. In the back of my head, I can hear Shelly saying, "And in darkness we will remain."

"I don't want to hurt you," Kurt says.

I hold out my arms. "It's too late for that."

We both extend our weapons and fire again. The light of my quartz and the lightning sparks of his tridents are white-hot beams clashing at the center. This whole time, he's underestimated me. As a man. As a friend. As an opponent.

"Stop!" The scream comes from the left. Thalia is going to walk right in the middle of our fire. "Stop it!"

I pull away first and a spark of the trident hits my chest. I fly back and hit the balcony of the pier, cleaving the wood in half.

"Tristan was going to trade his scepter for Layla," Kurt shouts. "I had to do it."

"Where is she?"

I gesture at the black water. "Gwen and Nieve took her."

"We will figure this out," he says.

"In case he forgot," I get up and thunder back to him, "Layla can't breathe underwater. She might already be—"

"Nieve wouldn't," Thalia says, pleading back and forth to both of us. "Not knowing what she means to you."

"You never even wanted to be here, Kurt," I say. "Why don't you go back to your cougar girlfriend and have her read you some more bedtime stories about your new father."

Kurt's fist slams into my cheekbone. Thalia's shaking, putting her arms between us. I can feel it. The one thing that held us together is dissolving. Kurt is no longer my guardian. He's my opponent.

"Oh, of course you'd never get mad at Tristan." Kurt turns away from Thalia. "Forgive me! Why would you have any sympathy for your *bastard* brother when Lord Tristan is going to make you human? That's what you want, isn't it?"

"I have never been ashamed of you." She points her finger in his face like a dagger. "Not now, not ever. But I see now that you will never love me if I do what makes me happy."

She turns away, running off the pier and into the shadows of the boardwalk.

"Way to go," I say.

"Oh, shut up," he says, and I know he's wanted to say that to me for a long, long time.

"I don't want to see you again."

"Neither do I." Without looking back, Kurt runs off the pier. He shifts in the air. The violet of his scales catches the moonlight, and in the swiftness of a dive, he's gone.

chapter FIFTY-SIX

The Sea Guard is gone.

The Thorne Hill Alliance has brought all of their wounded into the Wreck. They turn the dinner tables into emergency stations. I'm lying across the bar top with my dagger on my chest and my scepter in hand. I make it turn on and off like a light switch.

Rachel walks past. "You fought well."

"I think I'm dead and I've gone to hell," I say. "Because you're being nice to me."

She nods at Marty and keeps going to tend to the others.

"You saved my life," Marty tells me. "I thought I was dead. I saw a big light at the end of the rainbow, and it was Santa Claus holding a ball of light. He doesn't really wear red. He wears brown leather, because when the reindeers get old, he uses them to make clothes."

Kai comes around and takes the bottle from Marty's hands. They shake and she has to pry away his fingers. I think I hear her whisper, "It's okay." But there are so many whispers I can't be sure.

I can hear alcohol poured over wounds and the howl of pain that comes after.

When I close my eyes, I feel like I'm lying on the beach. The sun is shining. The tide is coming to get me. Rising and falling. My mouth is numb. I can't feel my legs.

"I can't go home," I say.

"That's what they say," Marty says.

"My parents are having a new baby."

Frederik passes by. I grab his hand. "I trusted her."

"Sleep, Sea Prince."

"I can't."

"You will." He holds a dropper over my lips. The liquid is neon and blue like the flowers in his library. I want to ask what it is. But I don't. It coats my tongue like honey. My eyelids are heavy, and when I close my eyes, the scream is caught in my throat. I can only see her face.

There are hands touching me.

Shaking me.

I open my eyes.

My head is pulsing. I say, "I know you. Bro."

"Thanks, Cousin," he says. "I know you too. Easy does it."

My cousin Brendan lifts me up. *That's* what family is for. Unlike Kurt. He's the worst family ever.

Part of me wants to complain and say this is totally emasculating. The other part of me, the part that can't even move, is totally fine with being carried. I can hear voices. Frederik and Brendan. I can hear hands clasping and lots of *yes-I-understands* and *I-can't-believe-its*.

Soft hands push my hair back.

"Where are we going?" I don't like the way I sound. Like I'm five and we're taking a long trip and we aren't even there yet.

"Just leave that up to me," says my cousin Brendan.

There's more movement. Some lifting. Another set of arms grabs hold of me. Someone smacks my face with an open palm. "Drink this."

I shut my lips to it. It smells like my underwear.

"Drink, Master Tristan," Blue says.

I'm like, "Did you just smack me?"

No one answers.

I drink. The liquid warms my insides. It banishes the sleep. I can feel my legs again. That's the problem. I can feel everything again. All of it. I choke on my own whimper. Real mermen don't whimper. It's the alcohol. It's the smelly tea.

"Rest, Master Tristan," Arion says.

"Where did you guys come from?"

I'm lying on the deck of Arion's ship. Brendan is modeling a very black and blue eye.

"We arrived too late, it seems." Arion hovers over me. The morning sun hits his scales and their reflection blinds me. "Princess

Kai conch-called me. She's below deck. I'm told we have a new rebellion on our hands."

"Everything is gone," I say. I tell them about Kurt's oracle. Gwen's betrayal. Archer and Frederik. I don't spare any of it, because I've been holding it all back and I can't take it anymore.

After they let me vent, I don't want to talk about me. So I ask, "I thought you were off chasing adventure's ass?"

"It sort of bit me." Brendan points to his black and blue eye. "That's a different story, though. I felt terrible for abandoning you while I was needed. I haven't got many cousins, so I swam back to make it up to you."

"Oh yeah, and how's that?"

He stands, and the wind blows his red curls all over the place. I know that smile. I've worn that smile. That smile gets guys like us in trouble.

"If you want your girl back and the sea witch gone, we have to get you real power, the oldest known in all the seas." He leans back and rests his hands behind his head, admiring the blood-red sun.

"I thought that happens when we piece the trident back together."

"There is another way." Brendan shakes his head conspiratorially and says, "We're going to awaken the sleeping giants."

ACKNOWLEDGMENTS

It takes a village to raise a debut novelist. Among the residents of this village whom I'd like to thank are:

Adrienne Rosado, my agent, once again for many things. You deserve a prize (my first born?) (no really, I insist) for all that you've done for me. For listening to all my doubts and complaints without judgment. For always offering words of encouragement. But most importantly, for sharing my love of bourbon and fried foods. Cheers, my friend.

Miss Kelly Skillen, for letting me borrow you as the vampire Madame of the Second Circle. Though it scares you, you are my hero.

To all of my wonderful Sourcebooks family, especially Aubrey Poole and Leah Hultenschmidt. You've transformed this book, draft to draft. Tristan and the gang are better for it. Derry Wilkens, the best publicist a girl could ask for. Jillian Bergsma and the amazing production and art teams for creating the sexiest merman books ever. Tony Sahara, once again, for the *epic* covers, and my publisher, Dominique Raccah.

Dharampaul Gopal, my oldest friend and partner in crime. (This is not a confession if the FBI is reading.) Thank you for teaching Tristan to play poker.

#1 Steven DeSiena. I pulled some of the epigraphs in this series from the mermaid book you gave me!

My Ecuadorian tribe: the Medinas, the Guerreros, the Sterns, the Córdovas, the Vescusos, the Laucellas, and the Ruscittos.

All of my old friends, new friends, and family who attended my book events and supported me in this endeavor. I can't thank you enough.

To the fans who read these books. Tristan is a very happy merman because of you.

The YA community of writers and bloggers I've met on the publishing road. Especially the Apocalypsies for making this journey less scary.

To the end of the world, and beyond.

ABOUT THE AUTHOR

Zoraida Córdova was born in Guayaquil, Ecuador, and grew up in Hollis, Queens. Her favorite things are merdudes, Montana, and the New York City skyline. Visit her at www.zoraidacordova.com.